Previously published as *Mörderischer Morgen*, by Calonego Media Inc. in Canada in 2019. Translated from German by Peter and Rosa Stenberg.

Published by Calonego Media, Inc., Gibsons, B.C., Canada

bernadettecalonego.com

Paperback ISBN: 978-1-9992302-4-1

Ebook ISBN: 978-1-9992302-5-8

Cover design by Vila Design: viladesign.net (Photos Depositphotos, fransz, imaginechina-Tuchong)

Interior design by Heike Fröhling: writerontour.de

Editing by Lindsey Alexander of Reading List Editorial: readinglisteditorial.com

Editing of the German original: Gisa Marehn

MURDEROUS MORNING

Bernadette Calonego

MURDEROUS MORNING

Translated by

PETER AND ROSA STENBERG

 darkKanada

For Stephanie and David

PROLOGUE

The bear smells its prey from a long way off. She stands on her hind legs and takes in its scent.

It is not far away.

She runs toward it.

She has had nothing to eat in the last few days, nothing that would really fill her stomach, only roots, grass, mushrooms, leaves, a mouse.

The chickens near the house have disappeared. The bear has been killing and devouring them for weeks. That is child's play for a grizzly. A couple of swats from her giant paws and the fences came down. She emptied out the chicken coop.

The bear is hunting in the woods. She knows that when it comes to this prey she must not make much noise, must not break through the bushes or step on rotten wood.

The smell is nearby. Only a few meters away. All of her senses are on high alert.

The doe is standing there quietly. It looks around. Its ears are pricked up; it cannot see the danger ahead.

The bear gets ready to attack.

The doe flees, but the bear is quicker, and with a few leaps she has reached her prey. A deep bite in the neck and the battle is over.

She dives into her dinner. Her great sharp teeth rip through the hide, into the warm meat. She licks the blood from her muzzle and chews. Then suddenly she raises her large head.

Voices. Much too close.

The voices come from the house, the house with the chickens.

She has to find out whether the voices are a threat to her dinner.

She must defend her prey. Nothing can get in the way. Furiously she pushes her head through the bushes toward where the voices come from. High-pitched voices and deep voices. She smells man.

The people see her and get louder and more agitated; some run away. One person stays there for a time and then gradually moves away, never taking his eyes off the bear.

Then there is a shot. The bear is frightened and pulls back. She knows the sound of a shot. It is better for her to run away from there. She must take her prey to a safe place.

She drags the doe deeper into the woods. Then she waits and listens. No more voices, no more shots. She fills her stomach and buries the rest of the cadaver.

When she lies down she once again hears a shot, but it is much farther away. She is still on alert, but after that it gets quiet.

It is now warmer in the woods. It's better to wait until it is dark.

In the night she goes out hunting again.

She smells something very strange. She runs in the direction of the house.

At night she is safe there. She smells blood, and something is lying in the grass. Out in the clearing.

She gets close, sniffs out the dead body from top to bottom.

It's something she's never eaten before.

She gives herself plenty of time to sniff the dead person.

Nobody disturbs her. No sounds from the house. Just this smell from the blood.

Then she continues her rounds. Leaves the dead body lying.

She's full.

For the time being.

1

The appointment with her client was nearly over. Tessa Griffins was glad about that because the worried-looking face of her assistant had already appeared twice behind the thick glass wall that separated the conference room from the other offices. As the client gathered her documents together, Tessa slipped her feet into the black-and-white pumps she had bought two days before.

She felt a lot more comfortable in her running shoes, but she should have thought of that before she took a job as a lawyer with Boyd Shenkar. She had met Boyd two years earlier when she turned thirty-three and was made partner at the law firm, now called Shenkar & Griffins. Boyd was the best colleague she could imagine, but he had no tolerance for dressing down, not even on Casual Friday. Many firms in Vancouver allowed their employees to wear jeans and T-shirts on Fridays. Tessa loved the idea, but it would have shocked conservative Boyd, who was ten years older than Tessa.

In the meantime, it had become second nature to her to dress in fashionable and expensive clothes. Tessa had gained a reputation as an energetic and hard-nosed family rights lawyer in Vancouver. She did not want to be seen as the girl from the outback, which she once had been. She came from the small, isolated mining town of Whatou Lake in northern British Columbia. The town was still only reachable by plane, unless you were willing to slug your way for days across mountains, through swamps and virgin forests, and across rushing rivers. Or risk a dangerous boat trip along the wild Pacific coastline. There were a few dirt roads in and around Whatou Lake, which forestry and mining companies had put in, but instead of leading to civilization, they ran ever deeper into the wilderness.

There will always be people crazy enough to want to find their precarious freedom out in Nowheresville. When Tessa's father, as a young doctor, began to get job offers from the big hospitals in Vancouver and Toronto, his relatives and friends thought he was out of his mind when he accepted a position in Whatou Lake instead. Kenneth Griffins hated the hierarchy and bureaucracy of large institutions. He loved untamed nature. At heart, Tessa liked to believe, her father thought of himself as a pioneer. For the people of Whatou Lake, he was a minor king, and the wilderness all around him was his kingdom. Much as it was for the grizzlies who crisscrossed the land.

Tessa felt an unpleasant fluttering in her stomach. That always happened when she thought about bears.

She accompanied the client to the door and hurried back. The assistant's round Asian face looked very worried. "You must call your father right away."

Tessa's throat tightened. "Has something happened to my mother?"

Martha Griffins had recently discovered a new lump in her breast that fortunately proved to be benign, but the experience brought up the possibility that her parents might soon die, although both of them were only in their early sixties. She hadn't visited for two years already, because she really didn't want to face the daunting prospect of a trip back to Whatou Lake. Her parents had flown down to Vancouver a couple of times. "That's a nice little vacation," her mother had said. "It's no problem for us to fly down there." Tessa believed her. Surely there were occasions when her mother also liked to get away from Whatou Lake.

"No," the assistant said, looking at a note with only one name on it. "It's about Fran."

"My half sister," Tessa said. That wasn't quite true. Fran wasn't her half sister, but one of the many foster children Martha Griffins had taken into her house. Fran quickly won a place in Tessa's heart. Maybe because they were so different. Tessa was very ambitious and spunky, and Fran was shy and quiet. At least in the beginning. Under the wing of her foster mother, she blossomed and gradually got over the first traumatic years of her life, as much as a girl can.

Just like Tessa, the adult Fran had put some distance between herself and Whatou Lake. But she hadn't sought protection in a big city twelve hundred kilometers away.

She'd settled in a large clearing in the wilderness. She'd married a man named Hank Miller, a lumberjack, and built a log cabin with him, with power from a generator and water from a well. She raised three children with him.

What had happened? The last time Tessa had talked to her on the satellite telephone, she thought that Fran seemed stressed out and a bit lethargic and withdrawn. That was about three weeks ago. In the background she had heard children's voices: Breena, Clyde, and Kayley. The oldest child was eight, the middle one was six, and the youngest was four. Fran homeschooled them. Tessa thought that all sounded very intense. But Fran had chosen this life and didn't want anything else. Tessa couldn't help noticing that Fran was very much tied to the house while Hank was often away. Initially he worked as a logger, then he found work at Watershed Lodge, a rustic tourist destination on an remote bay surrounded by virgin forest.

Tessa helped him get the job. As a bear guide, Hank took tourists grizzly watching. The lodge belonged to the Sitklat'l First Nation, with whom Tessa had a very good relationship, since she had helped them to defend their land claims in the courts against the British Columbia provincial government. The Sitklat'l had claimed the land they had used before the white settlers took it from them. Tessa and her team had compelled the government to right this wrong. That was before she had broken up with Tsaytis Chelin, the son of the Sitklat'l band chief.

She avoided thinking about Tsaytis, since his name brought back too many painful memories. All of her thoughts were now focused on Fran. She told her assistant that she would deal with this immediately and went into her office.

Kenneth Griffins picked up the phone on the third ring.

"Tessa." That was all he could say.

"Dad, what's wrong? What's happened to Fran?"

"You've got to come right away. We need you."

The voice didn't sound like her dad's. It was the voice of a stranger. Tessa felt an ice-cold breath blow into the room.

"Dad, tell me what's going on. What's happened?" She heard a deep sigh on the other end of the line.

"Hank is dead and so are all the kids. Fran . . . we don't know where she is. They still haven't . . . found her."

Tessa froze. The bank building, where pigeons and gulls rested on the protruding ledges, began to blur in front of her eyes.

"What are you saying? Dead? What happened? I don't understand."

"You just have to come here immediately," her father repeated. His voice was shaky. He held back a groan. Never before had she known him to sound so distraught. Kenneth Griffins was always in control; he always knew what had to be done. Dr. Griffins was a father figure not only for her family but also for the people of Whatou Lake and the Sitklat'l reserve. He was always ready to help anybody. Now he seemed to be completely helpless.

She let the lawyer in her speak, a reflex she had relied on a thousand times. She blocked everything out and reached for her pen. Maybe it was all just a misunderstanding, an awful dream.

"Dad, I'll get there as fast as I can. But first I need some information. Who is dead?" Her matter-of-fact tone seemed to help Dr. Griffins to regain control.

"Hank and the kids—all four of them are dead."

Oh, my God. Tessa gripped the pen so tightly her fingers hurt. "What did they die of?"

Her father didn't seem to hear her. "Fran, where is Fran? We've got to get a search party out." He sounded desperate.

"Dad, where did they find Hank and the kids?"

"Hank in front of the house and the children inside. Tsaytis Chelin called the police."

Tessa's heart skipped a beat.

"What was Tsaytis doing out there?"

Hank and Fran's farm was so far from everything that nobody just showed up there by chance. Especially not Tsaytis Chelin.

"I don't know. I could only talk to him very briefly. Everything . . . just happened."

Tsaytis found the bodies. How strange. "What else did Tsaytis tell you?"

"He saw a lot of blood." Her father's voice broke off.

Tessa held her breath.

Don't let it be true. Please, don't let it be true.

Her father's voice staggered on. "I talked briefly with the people at Watershed Lodge. Hank didn't show up for work the last two days. You know Hank and Fran. They would have let the lodge know if Hank was sick."

There was only a satellite phone in Fran's house. All the scattered settlers in the area could listen in, but it was indispensable for emergencies.

"When was Tsaytis at Fran's house?" Tessa asked.

"Um . . . three or four hours ago. I don't know exactly. The police are there now."

Tessa noted everything on her pad. As if her father was a client.

"Do you know what Tsaytis first noticed when he arrived at the house?"

"The dogs were barking like crazy, but they were locked in the storeroom. That's what first drew his attention. No one came out of the house. The children were always so . . . you know . . ."

Tessa clung to her catalog of systematic and chronological questions.

"What did he see there?"

"He found Hank dead out in the clearing in front of the house."

"Did he see any wounds?"

"Yes, bullet wounds." Once again her father's tortured voice fell silent.

Tessa took a deep breath. Bullet wounds!

"Then he went into the house?"

"First he found Breena in the children's room." Her father was on the verge of crying, Tessa could hear that.

"Was Breena dressed, or was she under the covers?"

"On the bed, not under the covers. Dressed. Tsaytis said she was shot . . . all of them were shot dead."

Shot dead.

Tessa closed her eyes for a moment. As if that could make the horror go away.

"And Kayley and Clyde?" All three of them slept in the same room in Fran and Hank's log cabin. There wasn't much room; it was easier to heat a small place.

"You've got to come as fast as possible, Tessa. As fast as possible." Her father was in no state to say anything more. But there was one more thing Tessa had to know.

"What about Fran?"

"She's not there. She's disappeared."

"What do you mean, disappeared?"

"Nobody knows where she is. Nobody can find her."

Tessa heard her mother's voice in the background.

"Yes, she's coming, she's coming," her father answered. And then he said to Tessa, "When will you fly up?"

She looked at her watch. Almost five o'clock.

"I will try for today but at the very latest tomorrow morning."

"I'll pick you up at the airport."

"Dad, you can always reach me on my cell."

"The police . . ."

"Tell the police that I'm on my way to Whatou Lake, and give them my cell phone number, please."

"Good, good, I'll do that. Will you call again when . . . ?"

"As soon as I can book a flight. And take care of Mom. She needs you."

Kenneth Griffins whispered: "Savannah is with her. Otherwise I'm afraid she would have a nervous breakdown."

There was a silence that neither interrupted.

Fran had been very close to Martha Griffins as a small child, maybe even closer than Tessa, Martha's biological daughter. But Tessa had moved to Vancouver and Fran into the wilderness. Only Savannah, who like Fran had been a foster child, remained in the area.

Savannah, of all people, whom Tessa had never really trusted. Still didn't.

"Keep an eye on the two of them," she said to her father before saying good-bye.

2

"Fran has disappeared? What do the police think?"

Boyd Shenkar had been listening to her describe the events in Whatou Lake with great concentration, without interrupting. Tessa made every effort to keep in control, although her heart felt as soft as a sponge. Boyd did not waste time expressing his sympathy. No "Oh, that's terrible" or "You must feel horrible." No worried look and no meaningless words of compassion.

He seemed to be sitting calmly in his office chair, his relaxed hands in his lap.

But Tessa knew him well enough to know that he was taking her information very seriously. Boyd was often mistaken for a well-known dark-skinned Canadian news anchor, whose parents, just like his, had been from Trinidad. It was easy to underestimate him. At first glance he seemed to be a hedonist, with his Ermenegildo Zegna suits and his flair for other Italian designers.

Tessa knew he was a tough defender of justice, dressed in a dandy's clothes. Time and again people judged him by his appearance, his weakness for expensive shoes, or the diamond in his right earlobe. Later on, in court, after he had won his case, the same people regretted their misjudgment. Boyd was almost fanatically devoted to his role as a defense attorney. In this moment, it was Fran that interested him most.

But Tessa couldn't give him any answers. "I don't know what it means that she's disappeared."

Too uneasy to sit, she leaned against the sideboard by the wall.

"Did someone phone Fran's cell? Go through her laptop?"

She shook her head. "Fran doesn't have a computer. There is no Internet in the backcountry. And no cell phone reception."

Boyd wrinkled his forehead. "You've got to get there as fast as you can, Tessa. In a little place like Whatou Lake, they certainly won't be prepared for such a big case."

A big case.

That's what she would have said, too, if there had been different victims. "I've got to find out if Fran is a suspect. Or if she's also been killed and the police have not yet found her body."

She pressed her middle fingers to her eyes to stop the tears.

Good god, it's Fran I'm talking about!

Boyd stretched out his arms on his desk. "Or if she's been abducted."

She hadn't dared to raise this possibility, but it was obvious. She pushed herself away from the sideboard like a swimmer from the starting blocks.

"How long can I stay away?"

"Just go and we'll see about that later. Conny can take care of your cases. There aren't any court cases coming up. And you can use your overtime hours. I'm sure you have plenty of them."

She nodded. Sometimes her calendar had to be altered dramatically. That was nothing new. Regular routine in an office. But this was different. A family affair.

Boyd folded his arms. "You do understand that we cannot take this brief on. That's clear, I hope?"

She did understand. That was against the rules they had agreed to before they became law partners.

"I will only advise my parents," she said, in order to make it perfectly clear. "I just can't leave them in the lurch."

Boyd bent over the tabletop. "I have no worries about that." He looked at her seriously. "You've made enemies there, and they could easily get some dumb ideas."

"Do you think . . . ?"

He interrupted her. "I want to have you back here hale and hearty." He pushed his chair back and got up. "Send me an email or give me a call whenever you can. And as far as the press is concerned, your trip is entirely private."

Of course. The media. She had to warn her father. The journalists would dig everything up sooner or later. Her family had to be protected from it.

Tessa couldn't get a flight for that evening. She informed her father that she would reach Whatou Lake the next morning. At the same time, she warned him not to talk to reporters or to deal with nosy phone calls.

Already in her office, she had found the first accounts online. They were only brief police reports: *Four bodies have been found at a remote farm about one hundred kilometers from Whatou Lake. The cause of death was currently under investigation, said a police spokesperson in Whatou Lake. The identity of the victims will only be made public after all relatives have been informed. The RCMP spokesperson did not confirm rumors that the victims had been shot, and that one more person was being sought. The police will inform the public as soon as possible when new information becomes available.*

On her way home, squashed in the packed SkyTrain, Tessa looked at her iPhone for any new reports. One news flash caught her eye: *A team from the Special Division 76-A has been flown into Whatou Lake.* Tessa knew about this elite group; they were responsible for investigating complicated homicides. She gasped so abruptly that the guy next to her in the train looked up questioningly.

In her apartment in the former Olympic Village, Tessa took

off her shoes and settled into the soft chair that sat at the door to her balcony. The horror of it now flowed uninterrupted into her body. Her throat tightened up. Breena, Kayley, and Clyde dead. Shot. Hank, too. And Fran gone.

Her thoughts became unbearable.

She jumped up and went to the balcony door. A number of dragon boats shot across the still waters of False Creek. Arms and paddles rose and fell to the beat of a drummer in the bow of the boat. The kids and Hank would never see this race. Fran might not, either. Tessa began to tremble; she had to talk to somebody or she'd go crazy.

Her fingers numb, she dialed Dana Eckert's number. Dana had been a social worker in Whatou Lake before she retired. Tessa had become a friend of hers after finishing her university studies in Vancouver and returning to her hometown. She could talk about many things with Dana that had to do with her work as a lawyer. And they'd kept in touch after Tessa had left Whatou Lake.

Dana answered immediately. "I thought it might be you," she said. Her quiet, warm voice almost made Tessa cry.

"Dad called me. Tell me what you know. I can't believe it. I just can't believe it."

"Me neither, Tessa. The only thing I know is that the kids and Hank have been found dead and that the police are searching for Fran."

"What are they saying in Whatou Lake? Has Fran been abducted? Or . . ."

She couldn't bring herself to finish the sentence. It seemed that an evil spirit from the past had come back. Dana had stopped working five years ago, the same month Tessa left Whatou Lake. Back then Tessa just couldn't get away fast enough from her hometown.

In her job, Dana had seen just about everything that apparently normal people were capable of doing: domestic violence, people in the throes of psychosis, rape, sexual assault and incest, animal torture, the terrors caused by drunken parents, drug abuse, fatal arson, and even children who had starved to death in their own homes.

Dana didn't beat around the bush.

"Nobody thinks that Fran . . . would be capable of killing her family. But you and I know that the police will have to clear that up. I pray that they find her quickly. But I don't know if it's right to hope . . . ?" Dana fell silent.

Tessa suspected there was something she could not say aloud.

"What about Hank?" she asked instead.

Dana sighed. "I don't know him very well. But Fran . . . she never said anything bad about him. Did she say anything to you?"

"No . . . she was often alone with the children."

Tessa remembered a satellite phone conversation from several months ago. Fran and Tessa had switched to French off and on to stop others from listening in on them. They had used snippets of French as teenagers when they had secrets to tell each other.

Tessa remembered that Fran was happy about Hank's well-paid job at Watershed Lodge despite everything. It meant that they didn't have any financial worries anymore. But Fran feared the lonely days ahead of her without him. "Come visit us in the summer and we can read books aloud to each other, and you can take photographs and go swimming in Beaver Lake with the kids." Tessa could still hear the pleading in her voice. It was not how Fran had imagined life in the bush was going to be. She hadn't imagined a life there without Hank.

"I assume that you'll be coming here." Dana simply stated it. She knew that Tessa had had good reasons for fleeing Whatou Lake, but she also knew that the daughter of Kenneth and Martha Griffins would not leave her family in the lurch when it really mattered.

Tessa's mouth got dry. "It'll kill my mom, Dana."

"You've got to stay strong, girl. If you need a shoulder to cry on, come to me."

Just then Tessa would have liked to leave it all behind. She said quickly, "I'll call you when I'm there."

For a few seconds there was static on the end of the phone line. Tessa heard only one thing more.

"Don't wait until it's too late."

3

After two hours of marching through the dark rainforest, they emerged into the light. Tessa had to squint. Her parents didn't know where she was or who she was with. They would give her a talking-to. Or worse. After all, she was only fifteen.

But that didn't bother Tessa at all. She was happy to be alone with Tsaytis Chelin at this place. The beach stretched in front of them in a white semicircle, like a descending moon.

Whitesand Bay.

Waves came rolling in on the flat, sandy beach, their white caps glittering in the sunlight. On the right side, sharp cliffs rose like terraces in the North Pacific. Tessa discovered three seals lying on the sun-drenched stones. Her eyes wandered over to the other side, where a brook flowed into the sea. She knew from her father that this was where grizzlies showed up, when the salmon spawned in the pools of water under hanging branches. But the bears fished in September, not June. She convinced herself that she had nothing to worry about.

She went slowly over to the sandy beach, trying not to scare off the sun-bathing seals. Tsaytis followed her silently. Not far away were the sacred final resting places of the Sitklat'l ancestors.

The spirits of the dead, Tsaytis had told her, still resided there near the old graves.

They sat down on the warm sand, drank ginger ale, and bit into the sandwiches she had brought along.

"It's good fishing here," said Tsaytis. "A protected bay. Good for boats." His black hair gleamed in the sun. Tsaytis was exactly the same age as she was. She liked a great deal about him. For instance, his faint accent when speaking in English, a reflection of his mother tongue, a noticeable lingering over consonants. She liked the way he moved, limber as a mountain lion, and even the fact that he hardly ever smiled but let his eyes do the talking. She loved his eyes, which shone like amber, the clearly defined lips, and the contours of his dark face. His shoulder-length black hair fell over his forehead. She particularly liked the fact that a little bit of him belonged to her.

Her parents had taken in Tsaytis for half a year. The school on the Sitklat'l reserve on Telt-shaa Island had burned down and had to be replaced. The older kids were sent to Whatou Lake because they had to take entrance exams in order to continue on to college. Tsaytis's father, Chief Doug Chelin, knew Tessa's father well. And so it was that the chief's son moved into the Griffins household. Tsaytis went to the same classes as Tessa, and pretty soon they were hanging out together. Tessa didn't care that other students teased her. What really got on her nerves was the fact that Jenny Dole was also interested in Tsaytis.

Jenny was the best-looking girl in the class, a fashion trendsetter, the princess in the annual Whatou Lake parade. She was also the star of the local cheerleading team. Her hair glittered white-blond, her blue eyes had long lashes, she was the first in their class to use mascara. In addition, she had long, thin legs like hockey sticks. She wasn't much focused on school, but she liked sports and dancing.

And she liked competing against Tessa.

4

The Twin Otter droned like a prehistoric bulldozer.

Tessa had almost forgotten how noisy these machines were and regretted that she didn't have her earplugs in her hand luggage. A miner who had been visiting relatives in Salmon Arm was snoring next to her. He had gotten up even earlier than she had.

The morning fog began to lift over the mountain range beneath her, a massive pile of stone along the coast where rain clouds often let loose like overripe pustules. The Twin Otter flew over fjords and small islands. Dark and steely, the water in the North Pacific shimmered. The small plane was gradually descending. Through the window Tessa could recognize the layout of the coast. A stony beach came into view, gradually turning to light-colored sand. Behind it there was a bright green strip of vegetation providing a stunning contrast to the dark pine forest. Whitesand Bay. The view of it took Tessa's breath away. All these years she had tried to forget this unhappy place. But now it was there again.

The screams. The horrifying sounds that come with the fear of death.

Then awful silence.

She had never returned to Whitesand Bay since that afternoon. She hoped that she would never see that goddamned place again. Now she couldn't turn her eyes away from it.

Something bright was shining in the morning light. A tall white cross.

On it, in dark letters, was a name forever burned into her memory.

Jenny Dole.

The young man next to her stirred. He rubbed his eyes. "Are we there already?"

"Too late for anything else," Tessa answered.

Her father stood with crossed arms on the edge of the landing field, to which mere mortals were forbidden access. Kenneth Griffins could allow himself many privileges because he had been the highly respected and only doctor in Whatou Lake for a long time.

He spread out his arms when she ran to him. She let herself fall into them and didn't understand at this moment why she always put off coming for a visit.

"I'm so happy that you're here," her father said. Tessa looked in his face and instinctively realized that it would be up to her to embrace and comfort him. He looked like a broken man. She felt a sharp pain in her chest. This was only the beginning. Holding back her tears, she adopted a serious tone.

"Come on. Let's go get my stuff and drive home as fast as possible."

In the small arrivals room, people were already looking curiously at her. The news of her return will spread like wildfire. She steered her way through the room without making eye contact with anyone. Outside, her father's ruby-colored Nissan Pathfinder waited.

"Do you want me to drive?" she suggested, and to her amazement he agreed. The approximately three hundred houses of Whatou Lake were clustered around a flat piece of land a glacier had carved out of the mountain many thousands of years ago. The valley was two kilometers wide and stretched out into the interior, where it became even narrower. Kenneth Griffins preferred to live on the edge of town. Unlike most of the inhabitants of Whatou Lake, who chose a life near to neighbors, as if they were looking for protection from the mountains, which dominated everything.

Tessa drove the Pathfinder across a bridge to the other side of the river, which snaked its way for many kilometers through the valley before emptying itself into the Pacific. When she turned onto the main street of Whatou Lake, her father mumbled to her: "Sometime today I have to identify them."

"You mean . . ." She avoided a banged-up pickup that had turned without signaling.

"The bodies," said her father. "They are now in the hospital."

"Who did . . . ?"

"They handed it to Dr. Fletcher." Her father fumbled with the seat belt. "No doubt it'll be too much for him."

"Dad, that's not fair. Dr. Fletcher . . ."

"They're flying in a medical expert today from Vancouver. And some RCMP people. A sergeant will be in charge."

"That's normal, Dad. This isn't a case for regular police."

A big case.

"Fran has nothing to do with the . . . she has nothing to do with it. The rumors are already circling, like vultures . . ."

Tessa had to slam on the brakes. A red light. Two years ago, there were no traffic lights. Other than that, Whatou Lake hadn't changed much, as she could see from inside the car. Two churches, a bank, a laundromat, a Tim Hortons, a pub, a supermarket, a lumberyard, a gas station that doubled as a post office, a clinic, and a funeral parlor. Some of the stores along the main street had colorful new aluminum facades. Color had reached Whatou Lake. Tessa discovered a new store, a florist's. Just what they didn't need.

And now a violent, brutal crime had happened.

"Are they looking for Fran?" Tessa asked.

"Yes, it was even on TV. A public appeal. We had to supply the police with a photo."

They drove by the police station, which seemed to be strangely empty.

There was not even a police car standing in front of the building. She withstood the temptation to stop and storm into the building.

"Martha is trying to talk me out of it."

She glanced over at the passenger seat. "Talk you out of what?"

"Identifying the bodies myself."

"Do you want me to identify them instead?"

He shook his head decidedly. "I want to see the wounds myself. I want to see what they did to them, and I can't have someone else do that."

Her father's condition frightened her; she had never seen him so broken up. As a doctor, he never lost control. She wanted to tell him that she was happy about an expert forensic doctor coming in from outside. She saw that as a sign that the whole thing was being taken seriously. Whatou Lake didn't have the right personnel for such a crime.

She would have liked to ask her father many questions: What happened? Who could have done such a thing? What had happened over the last couple of weeks? Why Hank? Why the children? And where could Fran be? But she was afraid that if she asked, she would no longer be able to concentrate on the driving.

They left the last houses of Whatou Lake behind them. The valley where the town lay was nothing more than a broad cut through a sea of trees, which climbed far up the sides of the mountains. Hundreds of kilometers of virgin forest in every direction. The border of this green sea crept slowly up to the cleared fields of the plateau, as if it wanted to swallow them right back up again.

Whatou Lake was known for having the third-highest waterfall in Canada and for the many grizzly bears in the area.

The people in this valley often wondered whether the forest protected them or if it was a tremendous enemy against which they had to defend the small cleared piece of earth on which they lived. The Sitklat'l, on the other hand, saw the coastal forest as a universe whose inner life was unknown to the white settlers. Spirits with life-giving powers lived there.

After three kilometers Tessa turned off the highway onto an unpaved road that led to her parents' house. Patches of snow were still lying around on the grassy fields, although it was already June. In Vancouver people were already swimming in the Pacific. Three weeks earlier, Tessa had also dived into the ocean. She was a strong swimmer who, as a teenager, had already qualified for the provincials. Her mother had lovingly named her "My wild one," but with a nervous undertone. She had always complained about not knowing what her lively daughter might do next.

An imposing log house appeared not far from the edge of the forest. Kenneth Griffins had bought it three decades earlier from a local businessman whose wife no longer liked the rustic style of the house.

"Welcome home," he said.

Tessa tensed up inside. She hadn't been here for two years, and nothing had changed. Mother's painted wooden sculptures still decorated the terrace on the south side near the massive stone chimney, which dominated the facade. There were covered stairs on the right-hand side of the house, which led to the main door. Stuck in the grass was a carved lacquered sign with the image of a moose and the name of the owners: *The Griffins Family.*

Tessa turned off the car and got out. A small wiry woman hurried out of the house, and a surge of affection swept over Tessa. Without saying a word, she embraced her mother and didn't want to let her go. The lump in her throat got bigger.

Somebody called out: "Can I help you with the luggage?" Tessa recognized the voice immediately. Her mother freed herself from the embrace. Her face was wet with tears. "Savannah is here."

Tessa didn't say anything, but her mother knew that she was less than delighted. "She's cooking and also doing the shopping for us," she whispered.

"That's good," Tessa answered.

Like Fran, Savannah was a foster child who had been taken in by the family. Of all the dozen foster children for whom her mother had served as a substitute parent, Tessa liked her the least. Savannah had been a possessive child, clinging to Martha Griffins and constantly telling on the others. This was especially true of Tessa, who had never forgiven her. She held grudges and didn't try to conceal them.

Savannah came up to her. "Hi, Tessa," she said.

"Hi, Savannah," Tessa answered as politely as she could.

"You look so . . . different." Savannah made a face.

Tessa knew right away what she meant. Her slightly asymmetrical new hairdo with the reddish tint. Daring and modern. She also now had pierced ears and wore tiny diamond studs. She outlined her hazelnut-brown eyes with black eyeliner.

Savannah, two years younger than Tessa and one year younger than Fran, had started wearing tons of makeup as a young teenager, as well as scandalous tank tops and miniskirts. As far as Tessa could remember, her mother had always turned a blind eye when it came to Savannah.

"Let's go in." Kenneth Griffins interrupted before Savannah could make any potentially damaging remarks. He carried Tessa's suitcase upstairs to the main entrance and left it in the hall.

Tessa went into the bright kitchen with the long wooden table that could seat sixteen. A glass door separated the kitchen from the rustic living room with its enormous vaulted ceiling. Though there were oversize windows that opened onto a spectacular view of the forest and the coastal mountains, the Griffins seldom sat in the comfortable sofas and armchairs in front of the large stone fireplace. They almost always gathered in the kitchen at the long table. When Tessa compared this to her small apartment in Vancouver, it all seemed gigantic. The house was built for a large family and many guests.

A smell of goulash came from a pot on the stove and swept through the kitchen. She had to admit that Savannah had always been a good cook. But how could anyone think about cooking on a day like this? Savannah leaned on the kitchen buffet. Tessa sat down at the table.

Her mother gave her a cup of coffee. "You couldn't have slept much last night," she said and sat down next to her. "I didn't sleep a wink."

Tessa grasped her mother's hand. Her face seemed to be worn out; maybe it was because of tears. She still dyed her curly hair brown like she used to and was wearing a checkered flannel shirt over her blue jeans. She looked at Tessa with red eyes. "I hope you don't have any problems because you had to leave your office so suddenly." She spoke slowly and seemed to be out of it. Dad must have given her a sleeping pill or tranquilizer.

"That's the least of our problems," Tessa reassured her. "I'm just here to help."

She hardly touched the coffee. She had been avoiding caffeine for many years. In Vancouver she had just begun meditating. It helped her to get through the stressful times. But she didn't tell her parents this, as they swore by strong coffee and garden work. And took pills when it was really bad.

Mom pressed her hand under the table. "I'm worried about your dad," she whispered. "He's acting like he's on the verge of a nervous breakdown." They could hear his voice on the upper floor. He seemed to be talking on the telephone with someone.

Tessa didn't want to waste any time. "I asked Dad whether the police or anybody else was looking for Fran, but I didn't get a clear answer."

Her mother sighed. "Fran's house and the area around it are off-limits because the police are there. Nobody can go in there."

"But they have to go searching as quickly as possible . . ."

"Lionel wants to organize a search party with volunteers,"

Savannah broke into the conversation, mentioning Hank's brother. She had a smartphone in her hand. "But the police want him to wait before he does that."

Tessa shook her head. "I don't understand. The first twenty-four hours are crucial. You can't waste time."

"Where should they search?" asked Martha Griffins. "In the bush? You get lost in the bush. Nobody should go in there without a gun."

"A photo of Fran on TV is not enough . . . you've got to also go to Facebook and Twitter and set up a website." Tessa felt her blood pressure rising. She looked around impatiently; she wanted to do something.

Where was her father? His voice couldn't be heard anymore.

Tessa got up and mumbled: "I'll be right back."

She hurried up the stairs to the upper floor. Her father was sitting at his desk with his head in his hands.

Tessa remained standing in the doorway. "Dad?"

He turned around. "Close the door, but quietly," he whispered. Tessa did what he asked. He ran his hands through his thick white hair. "The police want to question us. All of us. I can't allow that."

"But Dad, you don't have any choice. You can have a lawyer with you . . ."

"We can't put Martha through that. She won't be able to take it."

Tessa leaned over to him and put a hand on his shoulder. She said as calmly as she could: "It has to do with Fran, Dad. The police have to do everything to find her. And the murderer."

He paid no attention to what she said. "I'll see that a doctor declares Martha not capable of being questioned."

Tessa sat down on a chair next to the desk and leaned forward. "First ask Mom what she wants to do. Maybe she'd like to help the police."

Her father turned his head. "You don't understand, Tessa. You've been away too long."

"What does that have to do with Fran?" She spoke intensely. "Dad, somebody has killed Clyde, Kayley, and Breena. And Hank is also dead. We have to do everything to find Fran. She is certainly still . . ."

"Everyone thinks that she was the one who did it. That Fran murdered her own family. And do you know why? Because they don't want Hank to be a murder suspect."

So that's what was up. Tessa felt herself becoming annoyed. So it was not about the police. It was about Hank's father. About Harrison Miller, the mayor of Whatou Lake. Kenneth Griffins' enemy number one.

She tried to stay calm. "They're sending police reinforcements here from Vancouver. You told me that yourself. The police aren't in bed with Harrison Miller."

Old fights were once again flaring up. Harrison Miller and his wife had tried to stop the marriage of their oldest son, Hank, to Fran. Fran wasn't good enough for them. Hank's mother was furious that this couple wanted to settle down on a farm out in the bush. How would they ever get to see their grandchildren, she had complained loudly. And the nastiness flared up again when Fran announced that she would homeschool her children.

"I think," Tessa said, but then her cell phone began buzzing. She looked at the display. A Vancouver number. She answered.

"Sergeant Ron Halprin of the RCMP. Am I talking with Tessa Griffins?"

"Yes, it's me."

"Where are you right now?"

"At my parents' house in Whatou Lake."

"Very good. Can you come to the police station at Whatou Lake? I would like to talk to you."

"Yes, of course. When?"

"Would one o'clock be all right?"

"Yes."

"Good. So we'll meet here."

When she looked up, she saw her father staring at her. "That was the police, right?"

She nodded.

He played with bits of paper. "People from the RCMP already called earlier. I said to them that we don't want to talk to them and that you would tell them why."

She put her hand on his arm. "In principle, I think that it's better if we work with the police. We don't want them to think that we have anything to hide."

Her father stood up so abruptly that it shocked her.

"Hide? There's nothing to hide! We're the victims of a crime. Fran was like a daughter to us."

Was like a daughter to us? Why was her father speaking in the past tense? Tessa slipped her cell phone into her jacket pocket. She had been prepared for lots of things but not for a stubborn father. Maybe she was misjudging him. Her parents were in profound shock. As was she.

She hugged him. From below, she heard people calling.

She opened the door.

Savannah stood on the landing. "There's a helicopter in the air. They must be looking for Fran."

Tessa felt a trace of relief. At least something was happening.

But as she went down the stairs and saw her mother sitting at the table, a thought came to her, apparently out of nowhere: Fran might easily be in a location where no helicopter could find her.

5

TWENTY YEARS EARLIER

Jenny would have been the undisputed queen of the high school class if Tessa hadn't had a trump card to play. As the daughter of the respected town doctor, she had a status that nobody really dared to challenge. Nobody wanted to play games with the man who saved lives. Or with his daughter. Besides, Tessa always won the girls' races on sport day at the school, which impressed the young guys.

But there was one thing that Jenny could take away from her rival: the son of the Sitklat'l chief.

Over my dead body, Tessa thought, and she felt sure of herself on this.

Especially on a day like this one.

She looked out across the water. "Why do the Sitklat'l live on an island rather than here on the coast?" she asked Tsaytis.

He dug the heels of his sneakers into the sand. "Maybe it was too dangerous. Earlier, long, long ago, the Sahintas would come down the coast in their canoes and war against the people who lived there. They took many of our men and women as prisoners and made them slaves."

"Slaves?" In their history class, they had just started studying the slaves from Africa who had been forcibly taken to America.

"Yeah, exactly like that." Tsaytis chewed his sandwich and explained, his mouth full, "My father says that all around Telt-shaa Island the fishing has always been fantastic. Probably they thought it'd be easier to settle down right there."

"Cool. How do you know all that? Your people never wrote down anything about the past."

"Our ancestors told the stories. We are very good at remembering stories, and we don't forget anything." Tsaytis's voice sounded very proud.

Tessa got excited. "Maybe your ancestors lived on this bay before they settled on Telt-shaa Island, and maybe we'll find something they left behind."

For half an hour they looked for things on the beach and in the bushes on the edge of the forest but didn't find anything.

Suddenly Tessa saw a dark shadow out of the corner of her eye. She turned quickly around.

A grizzly.

Tsaytis grabbed her arm.

The bear came closer.

"Quick, we'll climb a tree!" Tsaytis exclaimed. He ran into the woods; she was right behind. Tessa climbed up on a cedar as high as she could. Tsaytis hesitated and stayed below. "Climb, keep climbing!"

Tessa couldn't understand what he was waiting for.

She saw to her horror that the grizzly was heading in his direction. Now Tsaytis climbed nimbly up a neighboring tree.

This position gave them a deceptive feeling of security. Grizzlies are great climbers, as Tessa well knew.

The bear hung around only briefly, maybe a few minutes, but to her it seemed like an eternity. Then it wandered off.

Tessa hung on to her branch so powerfully that her grip hurt. Fear paralyzed her.

She heard nothing at all from Tsaytis. She couldn't have said how much time went by until she heard his voice.

She peeked down. He was standing there. His face looked like that of a wild creature under attack.

"Come down," he said. "We've got to get out of here as fast as possible."

"Where is the bear?" she asked with a hoarse voice.

He pointed to the other side of the cove. "It disappeared over there. This is our chance." She glided down from the cedar, and they searched for a path through the bush that led back to Whatou Lake.

Just as she entered the woods, she heard something that froze her blood.

Terrible, shrill howling. The sound of an animal in its death throes.

The noise of breaking bones—so clearly.

So close.

They didn't need to say anything. No seal screamed like that. No deer, either.

They stopped for a few seconds, looking at each other. The screams seemed to go on forever. Only gradually they faded away into horrible, long gasps.

The silence that followed was unbearable.

Panic drove them forward. They ran the whole way back to Whatou Lake.

It was only the next day that they heard who had been the victim of the grizzly attack.

Jenny Dole.

First they found the old ATV Jenny had driven to Whitesand Bay.

Several hours later, some men found her shredded, partly buried body.

6

"I want to see the children." Martha Griffins threw this sentence out into the stillness of the kitchen. Tessa sat beside her eating a bowl of wheat flakes, into which she had grated some apple. She was determined to make it through the next couple of days. She put her spoon down.

"But Mom, that's not how you'll want to remember them."

"No, Tessa and I are going." Kenneth Griffins spoke from the doorway, where he had stopped. "Don't do this to yourself . . ." He stood there blocking the exit as if stopping a flight attempt.

Her mother didn't look over at him; she was only looking at Tessa. "I never wanted her to live alone in the wilderness. Hank was almost always away. I often said if something should happen, what are you going to do then? That's not good for the children." She breathed heavily, as if she had a cold. "We practically never saw her over the winter. They were here for the last time in April, and Fran left the children with me when she had to go to the dentist." She sobbed as she spoke. "Breena was wearing her bright new rubber boots that I had given her as her birthday present. Kayley always wanted to hold my hand. She's still so small and sweet. I would have liked for her to stay with me. Clyde is growing like a weed. He looks more and more like his grandfather." Tears were falling down her cheeks. She spoke about the children as if they were still alive. Tessa also choked up, and before she could really react, Savannah embraced Martha Griffins.

In addition to her sorrow about Breena, Clyde, and Kayley, Tessa felt a different sadness, one she thought had been put to rest long ago: the feeling that her parents were never going to be hers alone. She could have been the only child of Martha and Kenneth Griffins. But that would never have been enough for her mother. Martha opened her arms and her heart to the other children they'd taken in to the big log house on the edge of the forest.

"It's high time you left, Tessa. Savannah can drive you into town. I'll pick you up there, and we will go together to the hospital."

Tessa pushed away the unfinished bowl of cereal.

"Couldn't I take your car and come back here with it to pick you up?"

Her father would not hear of it. He needed the Pathfinder.

Savannah put on a worn-out jeans jacket over a much-too-tight pink top, which was covered in sequins.

Tessa kissed her mother's wet face. "I will tell the children how much you love them," she whispered into her ear.

Martha Griffins threw her arms around her. "I hope Fran didn't do anything bad," she whispered back.

Tessa froze. She freed herself from her mother's embrace and looked her in the eye. What she saw there was desperation. And fear. Tessa cursed the fact that she couldn't speak to her mother right away, alone. "I'll be back in a couple of hours, Mom. I'm not going anywhere."

Martha Griffins nodded and wiped away the tears.

Again she avoided looking at her husband.

"You really look very different, more like a city slicker," Savannah remarked as she drove down the unpaved driveway.

Tessa tried not to roll her eyes. She couldn't help noticing that Savannah's large breasts were flattened by the seat belt. "Thanks for the compliment. I've never seen you as a bleached blonde, either."

Savannah didn't get the ironic undertone. "I think I look a lot better as a blonde. But I also like your red highlights."

Tessa noticed the black roots of Savannah's hair and the smell of her perfume. In her law firm, perfume was not allowed due to her clients' potential allergies. Company rules. But that sort of custom had not yet reached Whatou Lake.

She looked out the side window. The dull sky spread a gray veil over the mountains and valleys. A bald eagle took off from a tree branch and disappeared out of sight. Wherever she looked, she saw a green carpet of trees. She had never been more aware of the fact that it would be very easy for a person to disappear into this labyrinth.

Everything was so unreal. She couldn't believe she was talking to Savannah about hair color on their way to the morgue, but she had to attempt to be friendly. She needed Savannah on her side.

"Where do you work again?" she asked.

"In the new day care on Elmo Drive. Three days a week." Savannah glanced at her. "Do you still have the same boyfriend you used to have, the tennis player?"

"No. And he's not a tennis player. He's a squash pro." Mom must've told Savannah about him.

"I've given Abe the boot, too. He spent all his money on a new snowmobile. He'll never manage to buy a house that way."

They reached the highway. Tessa suddenly saw a new building down below in the valley. Whatou Lake hadn't yet reached this end of the plain because a large part of the land belonged to the government of British Columbia. Moose and deer could often be seen in these grassy areas.

She stretched out her arm. "Who owns that house down there?"

"That? You' re not going to believe this. Harrison Miller built it."

Tessa couldn't hide her amazement. Right here, virtually within sight of the Griffins' house, was where Hank's parents had chosen to settle down? No wonder her father always felt like the mayor was provoking him.

"You know that at the end of April Fran was here in Whatou Lake?" Savannah said.

"Yes, Mom told me that." Tessa noticed that her voice sounded somewhat irritated.

Savannah didn't seem to have heard it. "Officially she was at the dentist's; he comes here every four weeks. And maybe she was. But I saw her at other places, too." She paused dramatically before she went on: "She was at Pleeke's."

Pleeke's was the funeral home in Whatou Lake.

Tessa snorted. "What? You want me to believe that? You must be kidding."

"Whether you believe me or not, I saw her going in there."

It was trademark Savannah, the chief tattletale. Tessa, at the last moment, refrained from making the caustic remark on the tip of her tongue. She had to get every morsel of information about Fran.

"What do you make of that?" she asked.

"No idea. Maybe you'll find out something more."

"Does Mom know about it?"

"Certainly not from me."

"Savannah, don't try to tell me that you didn't tell Mom about this right away."

"But I didn't. Fran worries Mom enough as it is. But she knows anyway."

"What are you trying to say? Did somebody else tell her?"

Savannah tilted her head and looked at her. "It's quite possible that somebody else also saw her at Pleeke's."

Once again Tessa wished she could talk to her mother. Without Savannah.

They drove toward Whatou Lake. On the right-hand side junked RVs cluttered the landscape. They had been temporary housing for miners who had no place to sleep because building could not keep pace with the mining boom. And now the poor guys couldn't buy houses because the bottom had fallen out of the zinc and copper markets. And they didn't know how long they might still have jobs.

"Do you still live on Willow Road?"

Savannah stepped on the gas. "Yes, but I often sleep over at Mom and Dad's. You have to be at the police station in half an hour, right? We can do that easily." It took a few seconds for her to pick up the thread again. "Mom wants to have me around all the time."

"*Your* mother?" Tessa knew that Savannah's biological mother lived in Edmonton. She had left Savannah behind in the care of the Griffins and had done practically nothing for her.

"No. I mean Martha. She says that the house is much too big and seems so empty."

Tessa remained quiet. A feeling of guilt had been gnawing away at her since she had left Whatou Lake five years before. Nobody talked about it, but everybody thought Tessa Griffins had left her parents in the lurch.

A sign came into view: *Whatou Lake is taking part in a contest to be "Canada's Cleanest Small Town." Help us by cleaning up our town.*

Tessa felt the pressure inside her already building up and up. And she had only arrived a couple of hours ago. Savannah continued to blabber on. "Are you sure you want to go with Dad to the hospital? You don't have to, Tessa. It was bad enough back then for you, that stuff about Jenny Dole."

"Stop it. Right now!" Tessa yelled at her so loudly that Savannah briefly lost control of the car.

"For goodness' sake, I'm just trying to help you. In the end we're all in this together. We're all at the end of our tether, not just you. I'm going to let you out here. It isn't far to the police station. I don't want to run into any police cars since they gave me a ticket just yesterday."

Tessa got out and shut the door behind her without saying a word. She threw her purse over her shoulder and zipped her jacket up high. When she looked around, she saw Tsaytis Chelin on the other side of the street. Something that looked like a bunch of keys dangled from his hand. She hadn't expected to see him in Whatou Lake. She hadn't met him for five and a half years. Now she was painfully reminded of her last confrontation with him. A few months after that, she had fled to Vancouver.

She could not take her eyes off him. He would always stand out in every crowd, with his shiny black hair, chiseled features, and fire in his dark eyes. Her fascination with him went back years, and it had been mutual. The son of the Sitklat'l chief had fallen for the daughter of the highly respected town doctor when he was still a teenager. Then two things happened that changed all that.

Together they had witnessed the death of Jenny Dole, mauled by a grizzly. This had traumatized both of them, it followed them into their dreams. And later the self-confident young man didn't want to be seen by the members of his tribe as an intimate friend of the whites. He found himself a Sitklat'l girlfriend.

Tsaytis Chelin got into a black pickup. *Tsaytis*, she wanted to cry out. *Wait*. Too late. The pickup turned down the street and drove off. She shut her eyes in frustration. She had missed the chance to talk with him about Hank and the children.

In her anger about herself she had almost gone past the police station. Somebody nearby honked the car horn. It was Savannah, pointing at the entrance to the building. Had she been following Tessa? Or was she spying on Tessa the way she had once spied on Fran? In any case, she must have long ago figured out what Fran had been doing in Pleeke's Funeral Home.

7

The young woman at the desk looked at Tessa with obvious curiosity, as she was trying to reach Ron Halprin, the sergeant of the RCMP, on the phone. Then she led Tessa up the stairs to the first floor and left her in front of an open door.

Two men in plain clothes were standing inside, talking. One of them turned to her when she came into the room.

"Tessa Griffins," she said, introducing herself. "Sergeant Halprin?"

"Yes, that's me," he confirmed. He introduced her to the second man, a constable.

Halprin pointed to a chair. "Please take a seat."

The constable took up his position outside the open door. He seemed to be texting on his cell phone.

Halprin sat down behind the desk and leaned back with his right arm on the armrest, his left elbow on the table.

Tessa thought that, for an investigator from Vancouver, he seemed to act pretty down-to-earth. He could just as easily be a well-to-do farmer from the Canadian prairies. His brown hair was not completely under control, despite a neat cut and a splash of gel. His rolled-up sleeves revealed sturdy forearms; his upper body seemed to be more compact than athletic. No one in Whatou

Lake would think of calling the RCMP man from Vancouver a city slicker.

"I want to express my condolences for your loss," Halprin began, fixing his gaze on her. His piercing blue eyes strongly suggested Scandinavian ancestors. "Our people can certainly understand what a tragedy this must be for you and your family."

The sergeant had the face of someone who was permanently short of sleep but young enough that it didn't affect his looks. On the contrary. Tessa put him in his early forties.

"Thank you," she replied and tried not to think about the children. Not the children. She had to stay strong and professional. "The worst thing about it is the uncertainty that weighs on my family. We have only basic information about what actually happened. More than anything, we're in a panic because of Fran. Are you searching for her, and if so, where have you looked?"

"You know that I can only give you a certain amount of information, since the investigation has just started. With regard to Fran Miller, we have sent out a missing person alert to the media. We're watching the streets, the harbor, and the airport. We are going house to house. A helicopter is in the air. We're doing what we can." He leaned forward. His eyes darkened. "We need your help. The more we know about Fran and Hank Miller, the better."

Tessa nodded. "I'll help you as much as I can. I know from my mother that a friend of the family called all the acquaintances and relatives. Hank's brother, Lionel, and his wife, Cindy, are also checking with everyone. But apparently nobody knows anything. It's a small world here. News, especially bad news, spreads like wildfire. In general the people here are very willing to help."

He didn't comment on her exposition, instead asking the first question immediately: "When and where did you hear about these terrible events?"

"Yesterday afternoon. My father called me up. For the last five years I've lived in Vancouver. I went to university there, too, before. Is this an official questioning?"

Halprin's left hand opened as if stopping an onslaught. "No, I'm not recording this. I just want to get some clues so we can move forward. At the moment we have nothing to go on. Okay?"

"Is Fran a suspect?"

He took a pen and pointed it up like a lance. She didn't mistrust him, at least not at first glance. She needed to create a good relationship with him so that he didn't look at her as an adversary.

"At the beginning we can't exclude anything; I am sure I don't have to explain that to you. When did you last talk to Fran Miller?"

"Three weeks ago, by telephone."

"What about?"

"It was her birthday. I wanted to wish her a good one. She told me about her everyday life with the children—little things. She was disappointed that Hank couldn't get the day off because he had to work at Watershed Lodge, even on her birthday."

"Did you often have contact with Fran?"

"Maybe every two or three months. She doesn't have Internet at the house. Only a satellite telephone. That's not really private. Other people in the area could theoretically listen to the conversations."

He made a note. Then he looked at her and waited.

He suspects something, she thought, a real bloodhound. He's going to want to find out if someone listened in on her phone calls.

She disclosed some more: "We had some differences of opinion, but we basically liked each other."

"Differences of opinion?"

She crossed her arms. Something she had often noticed in her work was now happening to her. A crime like this forced everybody involved to reveal themselves. Intimate details, family secrets, private confidences—everything was dragged into the cruel light of the public sphere. A murderer not only killed his victim, but also robbed innocent people on all sides of dignity and privacy.

"I've always tried to convince Fran that she should send the children to school in Whatou Lake. I . . . I think that children need other children. They have to develop interpersonal skills. But Fran wanted to teach them at home." She concentrated on the pen in his hand. "In our last talk together, she admitted that she sometimes wondered whether she wasn't exposing the children to unnecessary danger."

Halprin sat up straight. "How exactly did she put that?"

"It was only one sentence. She still loved her life in the bush, but sometimes she thought about what I had said and wondered whether her decisions hadn't unwittingly put her children at risk."

"What decisions?"

"The house in the wilderness. The isolation, the loneliness. The distance from everything. The two-hour drive to Whatou Lake. In the winter, it's a long way on the snowmobile. Their homestead is really far away."

"I know. I was there this morning."

She took this in. Naturally he had to get to Fran's farm right away. The crime scene. Were the bodies still lying there when he arrived? Or had they been removed before nightfall? And what about the two dogs and the three cats?

Halprin broke into her thoughts. "We flew in with a helicopter, but nevertheless I got a feeling for the distance."

She changed position on the chair. "Don't misunderstand me: it was the life that Fran and Hank wanted. Away from everything. Being self-sufficient. It meant no access to electricity and only water from the spring. Hank had an accident when a big branch from a tree he was cutting down suddenly snapped and knocked him to the ground. He broke all kinds of bones. Logging had become too dangerous for him. So he took a job at Watershed Lodge. After that, Fran was often alone. In my opinion, too often."

48

"Did she know how to use a gun?" The sergeant threw this out nonchalantly.

She answered with a question: "So what I heard is true: Hank and the children were shot to death?"

He took his hands off the desk. His demeanor remained polite. "Unfortunately I cannot tell you this at the moment."

Frustrated, she looked over at the constable, who was still busy with his cell phone while standing by the door. "Yes, Hank taught her. Just in case. She could shoot pretty well."

She put her arms on the desk to give her next statement some weight. "So can I. When you grow up here in the bush, you learn things like that. You didn't ask me, but I'm telling you straight out, there is no way Fran would do anything bad to her children. She is the gentlest person I know. She's not psychotic or sick in any other way. I think it's more likely that she's been abducted. And it's driving me crazy to be sitting here while she's . . ."

She didn't want to articulate the thoughts that were really bothering her.

Halprin remained calm. He must have encountered many extreme situations like this. Just like she had.

"Who could have abducted her?" he asked.

"Some crazy person. A psychopath. What do I know? Wasn't there recently a guy on Highway 48 who faked car trouble, and then almost strangled a woman who stopped to help him?"

"That man is now in jail. He couldn't have done this. Can you tell me what Fran was doing when she came to Whatou Lake at the end of April?"

So he already knew. From whom?

Tessa pondered briefly whether she should tell Ron Halprin about Savannah's information. About Fran's visit to the undertaker. But then she decided she should do some more investigating first. Savannah had good reason to spread rumors about Fran. Fran was her competition for the favors of Martha Griffins. Always had been.

"Fran Miller was seen on Monday in Whatou Lake," the

sergeant said. "Do you know what she was doing here and who she was with?"

Tessa stared at him amazed. On Monday? A day before the murders? "That's the first I've heard of that. I . . . I have to ask my parents. But they didn't mention that, and I . . . ."

At that moment his cell phone vibrated. He excused himself with a gesture and went, cell phone in hand, out the door. She heard him talking in the corridor but couldn't understand anything.

A dizzying feeling of hope overwhelmed her. The hope that Halprin had received a call because they had found Fran. That she was alive and in good shape. Then she immediately dropped that thought. In good shape. Even if Fran had survived this crime, she would never again be in good shape. And neither would Tessa's parents. Or Hank's family. Or she herself, Tessa.

8

Halprin returned and sat down again. At no time did he take his eyes off her.

"You call Fran Miller your half sister?"

"Not in a legal sense, but . . . emotionally. My mother has always taken on foster children. Over the years, I think there were twelve or thirteen."

Halprin twirled his pen and made another note.

She took advantage of the opportunity to ask a question herself. "Is Tsaytis Chelin a suspect? I heard that he was the one who discovered the bodies."

Halprin looked at her searchingly before answering. "So far, there are no murder suspects, if that's what you mean."

Relief ran through her body. Only for a few seconds. Then she quickly realized that Halprin's words were not a guarantee that they didn't suspect Tsaytis.

"What exactly did he see at the crime scene?"

"We cannot give you any information about that for now. That's all part of the investigation."

Of course Halprin could not divulge any details that only the murderer would know.

She didn't give up: "Who saw Fran on Monday in Whatou Lake?"

He answered with another question. It was not her job to ask questions in this conversation. "Didn't Fran contact her parents? In order to let them know she was here?"

"I don't know anything about that. My parents certainly would have said something to me." Tessa felt like she was groping in the dark.

Halprin didn't show any sign of impatience. "I will talk to your parents. Every piece of information is important."

She recognized the message behind the words. The sergeant must have gotten an ambiguous impression of Kenneth Griffins, who had, up to now, avoided talking to him. She felt that she had to defend her parents. "You must understand . . . my father is the doctor. He's worried about my mother's condition. He's afraid that she would not make it through questioning. Fran Miller is like a daughter to her. And she idolizes her grandchildren."

Whom she would never again see alive. Tessa looked out the window at the facade of an automobile repair shop. She could never have imagined that her parents' world could break down in such an awful way. Four murders.

"I have to leave now," Halprin said and got up. "I'll be in touch with your family."

She also stood up. He was not taller than she was, maybe five foot five, but his body was like a fortress. *One that I'd like to break through.*

She asked herself what Whatou Lake would make of Halprin. He was in foreign territory, ripped out of his everyday life in Vancouver, maybe out of his family with children, his sports activities or whatever it was he did there. On the other hand, she was in familiar territory, but she now considered it hostile. They had one thing in common: like her, he was under great pressure to deliver answers about this tragedy as quickly as possible.

She stuck her hands in the pockets of her navy-blue tapered jacket. When she was at the door, she heard Halprin asking, "As soon as possible, could you please give me a list of all the foster children your parents took into the house and where they are now?"

She turned around. He was busy getting the papers on his desk in order.

"Yes," she said. "In one case, however, I don't know where the person is. Patricia Corte."

"We'll find out about that," said the sergeant somewhat absentmindedly. "Just write down the name."

"Patricia was an arsonist, a pyromaniac. My parents did everything they could for her, but nevertheless she went off on the wrong track."

This caught his attention and he made a note. "Are you or is anyone in your family in touch with her?"

"No, we haven't heard from her for many years."

"Did Fran and Patricia live with your family at the same time?"

"Only for a short time, maybe a couple of months. Fran was the absolute opposite of Patricia. Well-adjusted and obedient. "

"Inconspicuous," Halprin muttered, more to himself than to her.

She knew exactly what he meant. Inconspicuous people so often had dark depths to them.

"Sometimes Fran could also be stubborn," she went on. "After she graduated from school, she began a nursing program, but right in the middle of it she broke it off. She had almost finished two years, and she just stopped. My parents had a long talk with her at the time, but she wouldn't change her mind." She shrugged her shoulders regretfully. "She wanted to raise cattle with Hank, and that was also a flop. The price of meat tanked, and they had to sell the animals."

"How long ago was that?"

"Oh, a few years ago. By then she was already pregnant with Breena. But I don't want to hold you up." She nodded to the sergeant and hurried past the constable and down the stairs.

9

When she reached the street, she looked around to get the lay of the land. There was no sign of Tsaytis Chelin. She didn't see any face she knew.

Suddenly she felt exhausted, and her knees started shaking. Her stomach was almost empty. She hid behind her sunglasses and walked to Tim Hortons. As a student she had a summer job selling donuts and cheap coffee there.

She ordered some soup and a decaffeinated Americano. The young waitress said that she had to brew it up, since almost nobody here drank decaf. The lunch hour was over and the fast-food restaurant was almost empty. She sat down at a table with her back to the entrance. The place looked exactly as it had when she worked there. Clean and bare. She called her father on her cell and repeated the offer she had made before—that she would identify the bodies alone if he felt he should stay home with her mother. He once again declined. They agreed to meet in front of the hospital.

Without a real appetite, she ate the broccoli-cheese soup and in the meantime answered some emails from her clients. Fran had always made fun of her when Tessa, on one of her rare visits to the farm, began to get nervous and couldn't reach her Vancouver office by iPhone. If Fran had Internet or a cell phone connection, she would have left an electronic trail. And Tessa would now be looking at the display on the cell screen, hoping there would be a message for her. Time ran mercilessly forward, and there was still no sign of Fran. Tessa discovered a statement from the police on the Internet announcing a press conference in Whatou Lake the following Saturday. My God, that was three days from now!

Finally the coffee was ready. Still deeply immersed in her iPhone, she looked at her electronic appointment calendar and remembered that she had to send off the list with the foster children's names for Sergeant Halprin. Would all the people on the list be questioned and have their alibis checked? Savannah was the only one of them who still lived in Whatou Lake. All the others had spread out all over Canada. Philip was a successful businessman living with his wife and children in New Zealand of all places. Tessa had had only sporadic contact with some of the earlier foster children on Facebook or through Christmas cards. She always spoke with Philip on New Year's Eve on the telephone.

As far as Tessa was concerned, most of the foster children were simply intruders, competition that always created an imbalance in the family. Outsiders who took away her mother's attention. They caused problems and upheaval and were sometimes even threatening. Like Patricia, who had set fire to Tessa's hut in the forest. Dad had built the cabin for her as a refuge. He understood much better than Mom how much the constant expansion of the family weighed on her. Mother always expected her biological daughter to help with chores and babysitting. Tessa developed into a rebellious teenager, a disruptive daughter who would rather be losing herself in the wilderness or reading books in her small cabin in the woods.

Quite often Martha Griffins took in children with problems. In Tessa's eyes, Patricia was by far the worst. Even worse than Savannah. She stole, lied, and fought constantly with Tessa. It was only when Patricia set fire to the hut in the woods that her mother admitted she was at her wit's end. Patricia was put in a home for especially difficult children, where she terrorized other kids. Finally she was sent to juvenile detention after she seriously injured a girl by cutting her with scissors. After she was released, she joined a street gang and became a prostitute, and that was the last the Griffins heard about her.

These days Tessa understood such children better, the draw of the downward spiral in which Patricia landed. Children who didn't know love had no chance. For some, help from good people like Martha Griffins came too late.

"Who do we have here? Tessa Griffins! Why do such awful things always happen when you're around?" Tessa shuddered when she heard the sharp voice. Lola Dole. Jenny Dole's mother stood in front of her. A little bit older and larger now but with the same carefully styled hair. Tessa would never have expected to run into Jenny's mother in Tim Hortons. Lola Dole was not a woman who frequented fast-food restaurants. She would be much more likely to invite women from the United Church for coffee and cake at her very nice house.

"Many people would call that karma." Lola Dole took a step toward her. That opened up her view of the counter, where an older woman nosily looked in her direction. Tessa assumed that someone had phoned up Lola Dole and told her that Tessa was at Tim Hortons.

Lola's face collapsed into a bitter laugh. "God does not allow any evil deed to go unpunished, and if you don't believe that now, then even God cannot help you."

Tessa put down her spoon next to the soup bowl, gathered her things, and got up. She placed herself right in front of Lola. "You simply don't want to believe that Jenny lied to you back then. So now you make life miserable for other people who are not guilty of anything. You should read the Bible more carefully, Lola."

She turned on her heel and aimed for the door. There, Lola's curse reached her. "The Bible says, 'May my blood come over you.' Maybe Fran was eaten by a grizzly like my Jenny was."

Tessa hurried down Main Street in the direction of the hospital. Suddenly everything overwhelmed her. But what did she expect? There were plenty of reasons why she had left Whatou Lake. And Jenny had never really been buried.

Tessa tried to mobilize the strategies that had helped her as a lawyer so she could remain calm and functioning. Most important: Separate emotions and job. Second: Analyze the situation. Third: See what would help to solve the case. Fourth: What's a priority, and what can be dismissed for the time being? Fifth: What is the next step?

The bodies.

She saw the ruby-colored Pathfinder in the parking lot of the hospital, in the spot reserved for doctors. Her father was waiting in the car. She had hardly taken her seat on the passenger's side when she started to shiver. Kenneth Griffins put his arm around her to calm her down.

"Lola Dole," she spit out. "She wants . . . a grizzly to attack Fran."

Her father looked at her questioningly. It took a while before she was in a state to tell him about the run-in with Jenny's mother.

He sat there without speaking, hugged her strongly, and nodded several times before he slowly said, "Lola lost her daughter, Tessa. You don't get over a thing like that." She looked at him. His eyes were red and watery. "Let Lola be Lola, dear. We have to take care of other things."

His words were like a cold shower. Shocked, Tessa realized again why they were here. Her father held her hand so tightly it hurt.

"It will be hard for us, but I want to take a very careful look. I want to know how it happened. The police are not going to give us much information for a while. You know that better than I do. It's our best chance to find out more." He pulled his hand back. "We have to go now, Squirrel. Be strong." Squirrel. His nickname for her. How long had it been since she had last heard it?

When they entered the hospital, she was gripped by fear, as if she was going into a house of horrors. They hurried through the empty corridor of the basement. The building was astonishingly big for a small town like Whatou Lake because it was the clinic responsible for people and settlements in an area covering hundreds of square kilometers. For a long time, Tessa's father had been the only doctor around here. Now there were three doctors in town, and all the personnel they met in the corridor greeted Kenneth Griffins with deep respect. A slender woman with a childlike face stood in front of the door to the morgue. She introduced herself as the forensic expert from Vancouver.

Kenneth Griffins had insisted he wouldn't identify the bodies by photos, which was almost always how it was done these days. Apparently, because he was a doctor, they did not try to change his mind about this. After her father had exchanged some words with the forensic expert, Tessa repeated to herself the sentence that had become a mantra: *I have to do this for Fran. I have to do this for Fran.*

Somebody hurried down the hallway toward them. Ron Halprin. The chief investigator in person, wearing a dark suit with an official RCMP badge. He introduced himself to the two others present before giving Tessa a quick, slightly surprised look.

"Miss Griffins, are you ready?" the forensic expert asked.

Tessa nodded.

They went into the morgue where a young male nurse wearing a large apron was waiting with the corpses. The forensic expert gave him instructions that Tessa could only partly hear while she stared at the outlines under the sheets.

Halprin looked at the scene with a serious face.

First Hank's body was shown. The nurse pulled back the sheets over Hank's head. Tessa saw Hank's motionless face, the slightly opened mouth, the only half-closed eyes. It seemed to her that she was looking at a stranger. But it was Hank, no question about it. His head and his neck seemed untouched. The bullets must have hit him lower down.

"That's Hank Miller," her father confirmed.

They rolled away the cart bearing Hank's body. Tessa focused her eyes on a sign with instructions hanging on the wall, without reading the words. She only turned around again as her father whispered her name.

The first thing she noticed was the bare spot on Breena's head where the bullets had hit her. Her long, sandy-colored hair shaved away. Breena was so proud of her hair. Although she was only eight years old, she knew exactly what an impression it made. Tessa closed her eyes before forcing herself to look at Breena's face. It seemed to be less waxy than Hank's, much more alive, as if she were only sleeping. Tessa almost gave in to the temptation to stroke Breena's cheek, to kiss the snub nose. Her father had already told her on the phone that Breena had been lying in her bed, meaning that the murderer had stood right in front of her. Tessa glanced at her father. His features had turned into a mask. Would both of them get through this?

When she saw Clyde, she wanted to run out of the room. The bullet had gone into his right eye. She stared at the wound. Somebody had shot the six-year-old child in the eye. Her father grabbed her arm. Was he looking for support, or was it an attempt to support her?

She tried to read the expression in his eyes. *Dad, why did you force this on yourself? And on me?*

But Kenneth Griffins kept his face turned away from her. The forensic expert said something to them. It sounded like a warning, but Tessa wasn't listening. Didn't want to listen. She just wanted to drag her father away from this horror show. Four-year-old Kayley had been his favorite child, even as a baby, but his adulation became even stronger when she began to talk. Every time Kayley had come for a visit, he told Tessa about her mixed-up words, which always made him laugh. He missed her babbling and her sweet face after she returned to the farm with her parents and siblings.

The nurse pulled back the fourth sheet. Tessa looked at her

father as he neared the autopsy table. The pain distorted his face. Then he abruptly turned away and went to the exit without looking at anybody. She heard the door slam.

Tessa looked up and met Ron Halprin's gaze. He's registering my reaction, she thought. The forensic expert already wanted to pull the sheet back over Kayley's face. Tessa, with a wave of her hand, stopped her. She wanted to see the child. Slowly Tessa's feet started to move. As if she were in a trance, she walked around the autopsy table. She shuddered as she saw the little girl. Sweetness was completely gone from her small face. Her lips were skewed and her tiny teeth were visible, the eyes half-opened and turned upward so you could only see the whites of her eyes.

"What in God's name . . ." was the only thing she could say before her voice failed. The force of the bullet had shredded the girl's skull. As Tessa looked at the gaping wound, she felt coldness creeping up in her. She was so icy that she felt anesthetized. And the horror. Suddenly everything in her was quiet. As if her strength was loading up and ready to explode at the right moment. Her brain emptied itself of all ballast and set her free to take care of everything she had come to Whatou Lake for. She turned to Halprin, a silent presence, but she could only manage a nod. Without saying anything, he nodded back.

All the children had been shot in the head. The wounds she had seen said all she needed to know.

Shot right up close.

All three hit in the same way.

Executed.

10

His shoulders sagging, her father sat on one of the vinyl chairs in the hallway.

A dark-haired young woman was handing him coffee in a paper cup as Tessa came out of the morgue. Kenneth Griffins silently took the coffee. Tessa sat down next to him and put her hand on his arm. The young woman introduced herself as a reporter for the *Whatou Lake News*. She was new in town. Reporters didn't last long in this journalistic wasteland.

"I'm Tessa Griffins. Unfortunately, we can't say anything about this," Tessa explained and was surprised at the strength of her voice. So normal. As if nothing had happened. "We don't know much of anything at this point."

The reporter rocked on her fashionable ankle boots. "What do you think? Who killed Hank Miller and the children, and why has Fran Miller disappeared?"

Tessa kept her rising anger under control. The reporter was only doing what her boss had told her to do. And the media was important in the search for Fran. "Please help us find Fran Miller," she appealed to the young woman. "We have no idea where she might be. Please ask your readers to report to the police anything relevant they might have noticed. Every little observation might help us find Fran."

"We will certainly do that," said the reporter. "Maybe you could also be helpful . . . to us, then everybody would be helping each other."

So young and already so smart, Tessa thought. She couldn't really be mad at her because she recognized herself in the reporter's ambition. She spit out: "Fran was apparently seen on Monday in Whatou Lake." She saw how her father shuddered and spilled coffee on his pants.

The reporter's face lit up. "Where was she seen?"

"I have no idea. I didn't have time to really look into it. Maybe you could pursue the matter?"

Out of the corner of her eye, Tessa saw Ron Halprin exiting the morgue with the forensic doctor and the male nurse. "Maybe the chief investigator from Vancouver could also tell you something."

The reporter moved right over to Halprin. Tessa was sure she wasn't going to find out anything from the sergeant. She grabbed her father by the arm and pulled him toward the doorway.

When they got to the parking lot, he handed over his car keys to her. He only broke his silence when they had left Whatou Lake behind. "Why did you tell the reporter that? This is news to me."

"So Fran hadn't told you about Monday?"

"No, no. She . . . What did actually happen?" Exhausted, he collapsed on the passenger seat and groaned like a wounded animal.

She stopped the car, leaned over, and put her head on his chest. With her arms, she embraced his shoulders. "Poor Dad," she said over and over. "Poor Dad." And then she also began to cry, but they were tears of anger, anger at whoever did this. The perpetrator had brought so much unhappiness to their family. Actually, two families.

She waited until her father's body stopped shaking. He sobbed one more time into the Kleenex she gave him. Then she put the Pathfinder back into gear. It began to drizzle. Thin ribbons of clouds were drawn across the gray sky like furrows on a forehead.

"I am sorry, Dad. I didn't want to overwhelm you with this news. We have to find Fran. And for that, we need all the help we can get."

Her father didn't answer.

Discouraged, she went on: "Although I don't know if it really helps much. You know the people here better than anyone. They won't go to the police if they know something. They just don't want to get involved. They would rather gossip about it afterward. They don't stand up and tell the truth. They're afraid of retaliation."

When they reached the highway that ran through the valley, Tessa sped up. The road behind her was empty, which she was glad to see. Nobody was following her. The reporter from the *Whatou Lake News* was certainly just the beginning. It was only a matter of time before the national media got interested in this story. Suddenly she heard her father's voice, coarse but now under control.

"Tessa, my dear, we've got to pull ourselves together. We have to have a talk before we are home. We have to think about what we're going to say to your mom."

She let him keep talking. He had to decide how far he wanted to go. He started with the victims.

"They recognized the guy who did this," he said. "It was somebody they knew, otherwise they wouldn't have let this guy get so close to them."

She thought about it. "Or Hank didn't consider him to be a threat. Where was Hank found?"

"Tsaytis Chelin said that Hank's body was outside in the meadow in front of the house."

"And Breena was lying on the bed in her clothes?"

"Yes. Clyde was in the bathroom. Tsaytis didn't want to talk about Kayley. He . . . simply refused. The only thing he would say was: 'She was by the basket.' After that, I couldn't get anything more out of him."

She blinked over and over because the tears were starting to come again.

"Maybe he meant the laundry basket in the parents' bedroom." The two little ones often played there so that Breena could have some peace and quiet in the other room.

The conversation they were having sounded so surreal after everything they had just seen. Since yesterday, the rules of the normal world no longer applied.

She didn't take her eyes off the road. "This might have been how it played out: First this guy shot and killed Hank outside in the meadow. Without the children noticing. Hank often did shooting practice outside. The kids were used to hearing shots." She took a deep breath. "Then the perpetrator went into the house. The children didn't have any reason to be suspicious. Breena was next. Because she was in the children's bedroom. Clyde, who was in the parents' bedroom, must have heard the shots. Maybe he went to see what was going on and saw the murderer. He fled into the bathroom. Had somebody kicked in the door there?"

Kenneth Griffins shook his head in desperation. "I don't know. Tsaytis didn't say anything about it. And now he won't talk about it anymore. Not a word."

She wasn't surprised. Tsaytis certainly must have known that the family would see him not only as a witness but also as a potential murder suspect.

Kenneth Griffins broke into her thoughts. "Maybe he tried to hide Kayley."

"Who?"

"Clyde. He always wanted to be Kayley's protector. The last time he was at our place, he pulled Kayley away from me. 'It's my job to protect her,' he said."

Tessa wrinkled her face. "But surely not from you, Dad."

"I think he was a little jealous." Kenneth Griffins's voice

became soft. Then he abruptly changed the pitch of it: "The monster shot Clyde through the right eye."

She grabbed hold of his hand and held it, just as he used to do with her. She found it impossible to tell him that she had read about a similar wound; that child had been killed by her own mother as she came home drunk after a fight with her boyfriend. She shot her four children. One of the bullets had also gone through the right eye of one of the victims.

She stopped short, opened the door, and ran out to the embankment where she threw up with terrible cramps.

She heard a car stopping, but when she tried to turn around, she vomited again. She heard voices and footsteps, and then her father grabbed her by the sleeve. He passed a water bottle over to her and looked worried. She rinsed out her mouth.

"I'm okay, it's getting better," she said to him.

Then she saw a tall man standing next to a dark pickup. He was wearing a cowboy hat and a checkered flannel shirt but didn't have the usual jeans on; instead he wore clean cargo pants.

Kenneth Griffins waved to him. "Thanks for stopping by, Telford. I'll give her a lift back home now."

The man put his hand on his hip. He hesitated to get back into his pickup. "I . . . I'm so sorry . . . about what happened to your family. Can hardly believe it."

"Neither can we," Kenneth Griffins replied, getting into the driver's seat of the Pathfinder and starting it up.

"Who is that?" Tessa asked when the dark pickup passed them on the road.

"Telford Reed. Eric Reed's son."

Eric Reed was someone she knew about. An outfitter who brought clients from all over the world to the Whatou Lake area and guided them on hunting trips through the Watershed Valley and the coastal mountains. One day, the Sitklat'l made him an offer. They would pay him a lot of money each year if he agreed not to use the outfitter license he got from the provincial government. The Sitklat'l, who owned Watershed Lodge, didn't want trophy hunters killing grizzlies or other animals in the area, because that would scare away the tourists who came to the lodge for bear-watching adventures. Every year Eric Reed agreed to this arrangement. A couple of months ago, he'd died of a heart attack, and it was still unclear what would happen with his outfitter license.

Tessa drank some more water and wiped her mouth with a paper napkin.

"Eric has a son?" Tessa asked. "Did you know that?"

"Yes, some years ago I heard that there was a son living with his mother in Kelowna. After her divorce, she moved there."

"And what does the son do?"

"Well, he's the legal heir of Eric's outfitter license."

"But he doesn't want to go back to trophy hunting, does he?" Her voice was still hoarse despite the water.

"Nobody knows. The government . . ." He broke off.

They had turned onto the dirt road and driven up the hill. Tessa saw what had distracted her father. A dark-brown pickup in front of the house.

"That's Lionel's." Kenneth Griffins shut off the motor.

Lionel. Hank's brother. Tessa's stomach was in knots. Maybe he had some new information. Maybe they had found Fran.

Both of them jumped out of the Pathfinder and ran into the house.

They were met with voices—and barking.

Fran's dogs!

11

Tessa rushed into the kitchen ahead of her father. The husky mix jumped up on her. Martha Griffins held on to the collar of the German shepherd.

"Have you found Fran?" Tessa called, with an almost childlike hope.

At the same moment, she saw Lionel Miller sitting at the table, his face looking like a death mask. His wife, Cindy, sat next to him with the corners of her mouth twitching nervously.

Tessa knew the answer even before Savannah, who was standing at the window, said, "No."

She felt as if she had been hit in the face.

Her mother bent over the shepherd and buried her face in its coat.

Tessa sat down across from Lionel. "Do we have anything new?" she asked. Lionel looked at her silently. His eyelids sagged over his lifeless eyes.

Martha Griffins straightened her upper body. "How did they look?"

"As if they were sleeping." Kenneth Griffins stood behind Tessa's chair. "They didn't suffer. Everything must have happened very quickly."

Tessa stared at the tabletop and avoided looking at the others.

Lionel's hands turned into fists. "Why wouldn't they let us into the morgue, Ken? Was this in agreement with the hospital? Or with the RCMP?"

Cindy pressed her lips together. Her makeup was perfect, as always.

"Not now, Lionel." Savannah's voice sounded harsh. "This is not the right time for such things."

Tessa looked at her surprised. Earlier Savannah would never have spoken with such authority. Earlier she had always played the victim. Or the perpetrator. In extreme situations people acted differently than they usually did. As a lawyer, Tessa knew that all too well. Just as Lionel, under overwhelming pain, turned confrontational today. Otherwise she knew him as a sympathetic loyal friend.

He was not avid for revenge like his father Harrison Miller, the mayor. Lionel had always supported the marriage of Fran and Hank—just the opposite of his parents. He was the younger of the brothers, an electrician who had his own firm in Whatou Lake. Soon after he had established it, he was able to hire three people.

Tessa did not really get along well with Lionel's wife, Cindy. She came from Banff, and just because of that she felt superior to the people in Whatou Lake. Cindy owned a high-class women's clothing store she named Cindy's Boutique, but Tessa never shopped there. Sometimes she felt almost sorry for Cindy. Life in monotonous Whatou Lake could not have been easy for her. Even if she had married a very handsome man. Lionel had gotten his good looks from his father.

He had met Cindy at international sporting events. Both of them wanted to make the Olympics in rowing. Lionel had been kicked off the Olympic rowing team because supposedly he had used performance-enhancing drugs, something he vehemently denied even still. His sports career was destroyed by the doping accusations. Cindy's ambitions didn't materialize, either. She had never recovered from a bad shoulder injury. Tessa assumed that they both looked for comfort and understanding and found it with each other. In any case there was a time when Lionel had tried to leave Cindy, shortly before their wedding. She had become depressed and bitter. She simply couldn't deal with her failure. Cindy's pain reminded Lionel of his own crushed goals, which he loathed. Hank and Fran, who could see the problems coming for this marriage, did not openly take Lionel's side. But privately, they agreed with him. In the end Cindy gained the upper hand with the active support of Harrison Miller, who thought Cindy was a good catch for his son. Compared to Fran's problematic background, Cindy's family looked attractive.

Tessa shifted her eyes from Savannah to Lionel. "When are we going to start searching?"

He wrinkled his brow. For the first time, he looked more like a human than a mummy. "Didn't the police inform you? You were there today."

"Inform me about what?"

"Somebody found Fran's jacket."

Tessa's heart started beating wildly. "Found where?"

"In Whitesand Bay."

She felt all eyes on her. Even her mother looked at her briefly before lowering her gaze.

Whitesand Bay. A cursed place that still haunted Tessa. Nobody in Whatou Lake would associate the name anymore with a bright, beautiful sandy beach. Or with a pretty bay lying at the edge of the temperate rain forest where, on a hot summer day, you could find yourself sitting in the shade. For the last twenty years, they would think only of Jenny Dole and her tragic death. And after Jenny, they would think about Tessa Griffins and Tsaytis Chelin, who were there on the same day. After that dreadful tragedy, Tessa had never gone back to Whitesand Bay. What in God's name was Fran doing there?

"Why are you all looking at me like this?" Tessa's nerves were on edge. "You all seem to know more than I do."

Savannah blurted out: "Hogan Dole found the jacket. He went out there to see if Jenny's cross was still standing. That's where he found Fran's jacket thrown over the cross."

Hogan Dole. Jenny's father. After his daughter's terrible death, he had erected a white cross in Whitesand Bay. The cross Tessa had seen that morning from the plane. But there was no jacket on it then.

"How does he know it's Fran's jacket?" Her father said exactly what she thought.

Lionel jumped in ahead of Savannah this time.

"Hogan found an old library card with her name on it in an inside pocket."

"Anybody could have put that in there." Tessa shook her head angrily. "Surely that has been staged."

Fran would never have gone to Whitesand Bay, and especially not to Jenny's memorial cross. Tessa continued: "Or somebody dragged her out there against her will. Has anybody searched the place?"

"We're only allowed to go there once the police have secured it." Lionel hesitated, then he added: "Hogan is going around saying that he saw blood on the jacket."

Her father looked at her. "Tessa, tell us what Sergeant Halprin told you."

Once again all eyes turned on Tessa.

"Fran was seen in Whatou Lake on Monday. The day before the murders."

Lionel hammered on the tabletop with his fists. "What, and I'm just hearing about it now? How can I organize a search party when nobody bothers telling me things like this?"

Cindy tried to calm him down. "Darling, you shouldn't think that you have to take on all the responsibilities. Tessa is here now, and she will be a big help."

"In any case, the search has to be coordinated with the police," Tessa added.

"Whose blood was on the jacket?" Savannah chipped in.

"Enough of this." Kenneth Griffins cut off the conversation. "We'll discuss that in my office."

Martha Griffins suddenly raised her head. Her eyes looked glazed. "No, I want to know everything. That's the last thing I need, for you to keep some information secret from me."

Savannah pushed back her chair. "Maybe the RCMP should interrogate Hogan Dole. I mean, it's an amazing coincidence that he's the one who found Fran's jacket."

Tessa tried to ignore her. "Where's the jacket now?"

Lionel stood up. "At the police station, Hogan says."

Tessa looked up at him. He was a mountain of a man. Cindy also stood up, almost as tall as Lionel, but her soft voice seemed to belong to a smaller person.

"Tell them what you are planning to do next, dear."

Lionel put his arm around her shoulder.

"We'll begin searching at Whitesand Bay, as soon as Sergeant Halprin gives us permission. The police are already going door to door in Whatou Lake. We'll also check out the area around Whitesand Bay. For instance the path through the woods."

Tessa frowned. "And you won't be searching around Fran's house?"

Lionel patted one of the dogs that was rubbing his legs before he answered. "The RCMP have already started there. And I only want a few experienced people who know their way around in the bush. This is no place for Sunday hikers."

Tessa knew what he meant. In the wilderness it was very easy to get lost or break a leg.

"Hank was having problems with a grizzly before he . . ." Lionel cleared his throat. "The goddamn bear wanted to get at his chickens, and it wasn't even scared off by gunshots."

"That's what happens when you have hens in grizzly country." Savannah was standing behind Martha and put her hands on her shoulders.

Tessa felt provoked by this gesture just as much as she was by

Savannah's words. "That's because they needed the eggs. Is that so hard to grasp?"

Savannah changed the subject abruptly. "By the way I'm warming up some noodle gratin. And goulash. Cindy and Lionel, do you want to eat with us?"

Lionel shook his head and turned to Tessa. "I picked up the dogs from the police station. But the cats are still out at the farm locked inside the house, as far as I know. The RCMP people are feeding them, but . . ."

Her father answered for Tessa: "Could you take care of the cats, since we're taking the dogs?"

Cindy waved him off with both hands. "My little dog goes hunting for cats."

"We'll take the cats." Martha Griffins's voice cut through the room. "Those are the children's cats, and that's what Fran would expect of us."

Tessa couldn't see her father's face. He rarely showed any open opposition to his wife's wishes, preferring to manipulate her slyly to get his way. When Tessa was growing up, he never complained about the problems that originated from an ever-growing number of foster children. When he came home from a stressful day at the office, he was often met by chaos rather than peace and quiet. Maybe he would have liked to build a hut in the woods for himself where he could get away from the noise. Tessa often wondered what kind of dynamic existed in her parents' marriage.

She turned her head to see if she could get a feel for her father's mood. But Lionel was blocking her view. He was looking over at Martha Griffins. Tessa had the impression that he wanted to say something to her mother that he couldn't say out loud. As if he felt bad because he couldn't do anything to help her. Lionel was somebody who would quickly blame himself for problems, Tessa had realized over the years. His father, the mayor, expected a lot of his sons. Hank had gotten himself free of the pressure by settling in the wilderness. But Lionel, who had stayed in Whatou Lake, still regularly felt the sting of his father's expectations.

Tessa saw that her mother briefly raised her head and mumbled: "Thank you for coming, Lionel. And for your help. It is very important for us."

Lionel hesitated for a moment, as if he were looking for an answer, but Kenneth Griffins was already leading him and Cindy out the door. Tessa heard the three of them talking outside, but she couldn't understand any of the words because Savannah was feeding the dogs, and their whining had turned into loud slurping.

Martha Griffins got up heavily and opened a drawer. "Savannah has cooked up some noodles. You've got to eat something, Tessa."

"And what about you, Mom? Are you also going to eat something?"

Martha Griffins didn't answer. Tessa gently stroked her hair. She was a whole head taller than her mother. She took the plates out of the cupboard and set the table.

To her amazement her father came in, carrying a bottle of wine. "This will help us to get some sleep," he said.

Nobody protested, but Tessa filled her glass with water. She had to have a clear head. Somewhat worried, she took a long look at her mother. Was she taking Valium again? Alcohol and a powerful tranquilizer should not be mixed.

Everybody ate silently, but at least they were getting some nourishment. Tessa was about to say something when Savannah began to talk. "What actually happened out there at Whitesand Bay, Tessa?"

Immediately her mother jumped right in. "That is not something that we should be discussing here . . ."

Her father agreed. "Savannah, you know exactly what happened out there."

Previously Savannah would have had enough sense to keep her mouth shut. But now, unmoved, she pressed on: "Maybe it would help us find Fran. She had apparently been out there."

Tessa pushed her half-empty plate across the table and fixed her eyes on Savannah. "Is this about me, or is it about Fran?"

"I'm just asking myself . . . ," Savannah said, but Martha Griffins cut her off by waving her hands.

"Just let it drop, girl." There was such a profound sadness in her voice that it stopped everyone talking. The dogs were rubbing their noses on people's legs while trying to push their way between the chairs. "Somebody's got to take them out," Martha Griffins said.

With a series of sharp commands, her husband drove himself and the dogs out of the house.

Martha pulled on Tessa's sleeve. "Come on, I'll show you your room."

"I'll help quickly clean up the dishes," Tessa said.

Her mother increased the pressure of her hand. "No, you can do that afterward. Come with me now."

Tessa understood her message.

12

She followed her mother up the stairs into the upper floor. Her old bedroom was on the other end of the corridor, a long way from her father's office. Nothing in the room reminded her anymore of her youth. There was a new big bed standing in it, and her mother had replaced the yellow curtains with new ones that had teddy bears and lambs printed on them. This is where Clyde and Kayley slept when they were visiting Grandma and Grandpa. Breena had her own room. Tessa realized all of a sudden that the children would never again spend the night in this room.

Her mother sat down on the bed. Tessa closed the door. Finally she could talk to her alone. She sat down next to her and put her arms around her. Tears ran down their cheeks. But they were too exhausted to really have a good cry. And they didn't have much time.

"I don't take the pills your dad gives me anymore. They make my head feel it's underwater. And then I run around like a ghost."

"Maybe they would help you to get some sleep?"

"I don't want to sleep. Because I get these terrible nightmares." She grabbed Tessa's wrists with both hands. "Last night I dreamed that Fran was dead. She came to me and wanted to get me to join her."

Tessa could hear the panic in her mother's voice. She asked herself whether her father wasn't right to give her tranquilizers.

"You're working through all the horror in your dreams," she said helplessly, "and . . ."

"What happened to the children and Hank? What did you see in the hospital?" Mom looked at her desperately.

Tessa had dreaded this question. But she also knew that her mother would never find peace until she got an answer. "Dad already told you. They were shot to death. Hank, too. We didn't see much, only had a quick look. All we saw was the head, nothing else. Everything must've happened very quickly." If she repeated this version often enough, she'd end up believing it herself.

"They didn't deserve that, Tessa. Not Hank and certainly not the children."

Tessa pulled her mother closer. "I know, Mom. I know." Her voice gave out.

Her mother could hardly speak, either. "Fran would have defended her children. Why wasn't she there?"

That was a question Tessa also asked herself. Why had Fran been in Whatou Lake one day before the murders happened? She thought about this for a while before she answered. "We simply don't know how all of this played out, Mom. The police will certainly find out."

They heard the heavy front door slamming shut. There were footsteps and the sound of dogs' paws scratching on the wooden floor. The stairs creaked.

Tessa looked at her mother's ravaged face. This valuable time with her had run out.

"It's quite possible that Fran was in Whitesand Bay," Martha whispered.

"Why?" Tessa asked surprised.

Her mother looked toward the door. "She wanted to find proof."

"Proof of what?"

There was a knock. Martha Griffins gave a start.

"Just a moment, please," Tessa called. She softly turned to her mother and said quickly: "We'll talk again later." Martha Griffins nodded.

Her husband stood in the doorway. The husky mix ran into the room. Kenneth eyed his wife questioningly. "You might want to lie down for a while, dear," he said, holding out his hand.

"I'm going to take a shower," Tessa mumbled while her father pulled his wife along.

As she came out of the bathroom, she saw the husky rolled up on her fluffy bedside rug. He half opened his eyes. She patted him and listened. It had become quiet in the house. She slipped under the covers and opened her laptop. The murders were only worth a short article in the national media. But the *Whatou Lake News* reported that Fran had been to see Dr. Rhonda Kellermann on Monday. Neither the doctor nor the police wanted to explain why. Tessa was quoted with her plea to the general public to come forward with information about Fran. The reporter described her and her father as being relatives "who clearly were suffering from shock."

Tessa closed her eyes. Some hours later, a noise woke her up. It was dark outside. She noticed a shadow in front of the window: the dog was standing there growling. Still groggy from sleep, she sat up and listened. Rustling near the house, followed by renewed growling. She got up, went to the window, and opened it. Wet, cold air hit her in the face. She listened. Nothing.

But after a few moments, she heard a muffled stamping, as if somebody was running away on soft ground. The dog darted to the door. She closed the window and looked at the husky.

"You can't go out yet, my old pal. It's much too early." The dog wagged his tail.

She could hear a voice on the other side of the door.

"Tessa, are you awake?" Her father. She let him in.

"I heard something when I was in the bathroom," he whispered.

"Dad, I think somebody was sneaking around the house. It made the dog growl." Her father closed the door and sat down on the bed. He turned on the bedside lamp. In the light he looked pale like a ghost.

Tessa went back to the window. "Should we go out and look?"

Her father remained sitting. "Whoever or whatever that was out there, it's gone by now."

"Do you think we're in danger?"

He shrugged. She understood: She could no longer expect him to have all the answers. Now he depended on her, the lawyer. She sat down next to him so that she could whisper her words. "We have to be careful. Nosy people are going to show up here. The media. Wannabe detectives."

Her father nodded resignedly. "Martha has to be kept out of all this. She is sleeping deeply right now. The pills are working."

"You are giving her pills?"

"She won't take any voluntarily, so I mix them with her tea."

"Dad, you can't do that!" Tessa was incensed.

He looked at her sadly. "I don't want her to do anything to herself, Squirrel."

"Has she been talking about suicide?"

"No."

"Dad, I think Mom is perfectly capable of deciding for herself." Tessa felt her blood pressure rising.

Her father's voice sounded defensive. "I just want to help her. Go back to bed, Squirrel. Tomorrow will be a long day."

After her father had left, dark thoughts ran through her head. Why was Fran's blood-smeared jacket—if it really was hers—

found in Whitesand Bay of all places? Did her parents think, in their despair, that there was a connection between Jenny Dole's death and Fran's disappearance? Could it have any connection with the murders on the farm?

Before she went back to bed, she took the pistol out of her purse. It was a small gun that was easy to hold. A Sig Sauer P320 she had gotten a license for because she had received death threats after a trial. Back then she had realized what a dangerous life she was leading. She put the pistol, which she hid in the purse, on the nightstand.

But she stayed awake for a long time. She could not forget the terrible things she had seen in the morgue. She put her laptop in front of her and wrote down everything that came into her mind. It was only as dawn broke that she fell into an uneasy slumber, and in her dream she was being hunted down by Tsaytis Chelin.

13

A long-legged wolf spider climbed high up the wall. It was as big as a baby's outstretched hand.

"We don't usually see them this early," Dana Eckert remarked as she placed a glass over the spider, which ran around in its prison. "Please give me some paper from my scrap pile." She pointed at a wastebasket next to the chimney.

Tessa reached for an envelope that had a stamp of a blossoming Pacific dogwood tree in the corner. The handwriting on the envelope seemed familiar to her, but she had no time to think about it. Dana pushed the envelope carefully under the glass and walked with it to the balcony door. A quick swing with her hand catapulted the unwanted visitor into the garden. The envelope landed back in the wastebasket.

"I'll make some tea for you." She turned on the kettle in the open kitchen and fumbled around in the cabinets.

Tessa took a quick look at her cell phone. Boyd Shenkar's name appeared. She had asked him for information about Ron Halprin. Boyd had sent her a text message. *He is very good, but don't mention my name with Halprin. I successfully defended a client Halprin had investigated for years. The client received only two years' jail time. The crown council had asked for twelve. Halprin must have been really mad about that. But now you have him on your side. Make sure you keep him there.*

Dana turned to her. She had a short and stylish haircut. Even though she was fifty-nine and had had a very difficult job as a social worker, Tessa couldn't see many gray hairs on her head. A lot of people took her for a Sitklat'l, but her ancestors had actually come from southern Italy. Not only was her skin olive-colored, but she had also inherited a great love of cooking. Despite her substantial figure, Dana was quick on her feet.

She raised her expressive eyes to Tessa and asked: "How do you manage to stand up straight, my poor little child? I know you're going through hell right now."

Tessa rubbed her fingers together and sighed: "I've become a robot, Dana. No feelings, just cold blood."

"Why do you say that?"

"Last evening I went to sleep immediately. Something woke me up, I lay awake for a long time, but at some point I went back to sleep again. That's just not normal."

With her strong hands, Dana poured hot water into a teapot. She had brewed strong tea from medicinal herbs and grasses, a mixture Tessa had often drunk at Dana's.

"What do you mean by 'normal' here? You're trying to protect yourself, Tessa. You're shoving it into different drawers so that you can keep functioning. You want to keep functioning because you want to find Fran. And because you have to help your parents." She put two teacups on the table. "Sit down, my love. Otherwise you're going to fall like a sick bird from a tree."

Tessa followed her suggestion. With Dana she didn't have to play the role of a tough lawyer from Vancouver. They had known each other too long for that. But she didn't tell her friend what she had seen in the morgue. She didn't want to talk about it. Instead she said: "That's something Dad was able to do, too, cut himself off . . . But now, he seems to be falling apart. Last night when someone was sneaking around the house, he didn't even want to go outside to see what was going on."

"What actually happened last night?"

Tessa gave her the details as far as she could remember them. She didn't mention the pistol on the nightstand.

Dana opened the honey jar. "You're lucky to have the dogs. They're on guard when you're sleeping."

But they couldn't protect Hank and the children. Somebody had locked them up.

Lost in her thoughts, she stirred her tea. "I just hope that the police find Fran soon. Do you have any idea where she might be? Or why she was at the hospital on Monday?"

"Of course I heard about that. I talked to a few nurses. But they're sticking together because of the police investigation."

"When was the last time you talked to Fran? Have the police talked with you?"

"No, they haven't, but it's just a matter of time. Fran visited me in April when she was in Whatou Lake." Dana's colorful earrings jiggled as she spoke.

"The police already know that. Did she say anything unusual? Did you notice anything?"

"Drink the tea, sweetie. It'll help you." Dana touched her on the shoulder. "Fran and I, we talked about the dam on Grouse River. She wanted to convince me to support the complaint she was putting in against the government."

"I didn't even know she was protesting against the dam. She . . . that doesn't affect her at all. Grouse Valley is a long way from here."

"She actually wanted to move to Grouse Valley," Dana blurted out.

Tessa looked at her in disbelief. "Did she say that to you?"

Dana nodded. "She wanted to buy a farm there and get involved in agriculture."

Tessa had trouble digesting this information. "But Hank, he had his job at Watershed Lodge. He liked it there. Did he also want . . . ?"

"That I don't know. I didn't ask."

Tessa shook her head. "Buy another farm? They don't have the money to do that." She had often given fairly large sums to Fran in order to help her get by. But she didn't want to tell Dana about that. Fran wouldn't want her to.

Tessa took some big sips. The familiar tea aroma calmed her a little. Dana had offered to go with her out to Fran's farm to pick up the cats. She had driven Tessa to Whatou Lake in the morning, but when she had stopped in front of the Griffins' house to pick Tessa up, Dana had refused to leave the car. Tessa found that strange.

"Are you sure you want to come with me?" she asked, although she really needed Dana.

"Of course. We'll take my pickup. And my ATV is still on the back of the truck. That might be really useful, and I have cat cages, too."

Ten minutes later they left Whatou Lake. The early summer sun cast a pleasant shine on the wet grass. Drops of water glistened on the new blades. It must have rained in the night. It occurred to Tessa that they might be able to find some footprints around her parents' house. Traces of the nightly invader. She felt the impulse to turn around and check it out. Too late.

The air was clear and the wooded flanks of the mountains seemed very close. The coastal range rose on both sides of the valley. Their peaks were still snow-covered, their green rocky spurs looked like animal claws that wanted to grab the narrow plane. Every time Tessa came back after a long absence from Whatou Lake, she realized how wild and overwhelming the landscape was here. During her last visit she climbed with her father to the top of Whatou Falls, which roared down four hundred meters into a huge ravine. From the dizzyingly high plateau, she could see forest, forest, and still more forest. With her father, Tessa had sat down on the rocky outcropping of the cliff wall not far from the abyss and taken in the depth and width of the ravine and the intimidating beauty of nature. It took her breath away. Nevertheless she had left all this behind her.

Dana turned on the local radio station. They listened as the host played two pieces of music and then talked about the murders in the wilderness. Feeling uneasy, Tessa heard how the announcer summarized everything that was already known to the public. Fran's visit to Whatou Lake on Monday was mentioned, and also that she had previously lived as a foster child with the Griffins family.

Then the host started talking about the jacket at Whitesand Bay. The police were only going to give information about that in the afternoon, he announced. Tessa's stomach tightened. Jenny Dole's father was asked about it. Dana turned up the volume. "I found the jacket by the cross I put up for our poor daughter," Dole said. "Right away I had the feeling that it was Fran Miller's jacket. There were dark spots on it. I thought, that has to be her blood. I packed up the jacket and drove back. Now the police are examining it. That is a sad place, I can tell you. So many bad things have happened since Jenny lost her life. I don't know what Fran Miller might have been doing there, but I don't believe that she will be found alive. The way the jacket looked. Whitesand Bay has become a place of death. Maybe it's time somebody paid for Jenny's killing."

The announcer did not comment on Hogan's words and continued with other news of the day. Dana turned the volume down.

"He's really lost his mind," Tessa said. "This stinks to high heaven." Dana didn't say anything. Tessa kept talking. "First of all, he doesn't know if it's really Fran's jacket. Second, if it turns out to be an important piece of evidence and Hogan picks it up and brings it to the police, he has contaminated it. He should have left it there, untouched. If you ask me, I suspect he actually put it there, in order to once again remind everyone of Jenny's death." She was shaking with anger. "And he did it because he knows I'm in Whatou Lake; it gave him a good chance to take another whack at me." And especially at Tsaytis Chelin, she added in her thoughts.

They turned off the highway onto a gravel road full of potholes. A sign warned them: *Forestry Road. Use at your own risk.* They drove on deeper into the wilderness. The forest swallowed them up. It had become dark inside the car. Gigantic trees rose on both sides of the dirt road. Behind them, a jungle flourished. Ferns on the ground, decaying tree stumps, moss-covered cedars, low-lying salal, a straggling, humid, decomposing habitat with hardly any sunlight. The trip to Fran's house was long and difficult. It took at least two hours on the curvy gravel road that meandered uphill and downhill, with endless potholes everywhere. Tessa understood why Fran didn't often make the trip to Whatou Lake.

Dana agreed with Tessa on Hogan. "He'll certainly talk the RCMP's ears off with this baloney about who's responsible for Jenny's death. The police may very well ask you some questions about it. What are you going to say to them?"

"I'll tell them the same thing I told the police before." Tessa pushed back the car seat and stretched her legs. "We heard screams, but we didn't see anything. We didn't know if they came from a human or an animal. We had no idea Jenny had driven out to Whitesand Bay on that day. There was nothing we could have done."

Dana tried to locate the truckers' channel on the radio to find out if any trucks were headed their way on the forestry road. Nobody wanted to encounter one of those beasts by surprise. From time to time, cars were involved in horrible accidents with them. Dana was an experienced driver, but on the bumpy road, the pickup jostled. She continued to look at the rearview mirror to make sure the ropes keeping the ATV in place were still holding. They progressed slowly.

Suddenly she jammed on the brakes, and her truck slid to a halt. "What the hell?" she exclaimed.

A dark pickup had shot out of the woods and just missed them by a hair. Without slowing down, the driver fled in the direction of Whatou Lake.

"What an idiot," Dana screamed. "He could've killed us!"

She looked at Tessa, who was shocked at the thought of what could have happened.

"Did you recognize the driver?"

"No, how could I while I . . ."

Dana opened the door. "Where did it come from? There's no side road going in there." She got out. Tessa hesitated for a second before following her.

They saw a path in the underbrush. Tire tracks in the wet earth. They had only walked about thirty steps when they discovered wet patches on the ground.

Dana whispered: "Where did all this blood come from?"

14

Tessa suddenly felt cold. Her pistol was in her rucksack in Dana's pickup.

"Look over here!" Dana pointed at a bundle of hair on the ground. She kneeled down to get a better look at it. "An animal. Looks like a bear."

"A poacher?" Tessa moved back a bit. "I really can't see any identifying track marks."

Dana got up and crossed her arms. "Dark pickup trucks are a dime a dozen around here. It's too bad we didn't see the license plate."

"We have to remember this spot," Tessa said. She followed Dana back to the pickup.

"No problem. I have GPS in the car. And a satellite phone."

Tessa frowned. "If we call the police now, they will no doubt want us to wait for them to come. That will hold us up."

Dana nodded.

"It could also be a moose and not a grizzly," Tessa said as she climbed into the pickup.

Dana made the decision. "It's still an hour to Fran's house. When we get there, we can tell them what happened."

"Poachers. That won't not sit well with the Watershed Lodge

people," Tessa remarked as Dana put the pickup in gear. "Not to mention Telford Reed."

Dana turned down the radio channel. "Who?"

Tessa told her about her unexpected encounter with the son of the deceased outfitter Eric Reed.

Dana put the vehicle into all-wheel drive. The next six kilometers would be the worst part of the logging road. After that, it became flatter again. "Why should Telford Reed worry about poachers?" she asked. "He couldn't care less. All he does is take the money from Watershed Lodge so that no other outfitter can organize groups of trophy hunters on his lands. He's not responsible if somebody poaches there."

"No, he's not responsible, but if there's poaching, people would wonder if he's giving someone the green light to illegally hunt here. "

"Or whether he himself poaches bears?" Dana shot back.

Suddenly Tessa felt like a drone floating above the unreal scene that was playing out below. There was the almost detached way she was talking to Dana about everything. And the distance she was putting between herself and the fear she felt for Fran, and the horror after the murders. She tried to suppress the images of the dead bodies with all her might. She knew she had to put everything in the back of her mind in order to keep herself upright.

After half an hour, grassy fields began to appear on their left side, dotted with boggy ponds.

"Stop here!" Tessa called out.

"Here?"

"I want to go over to Beaver Lake, to Fran and Hank's cabin."

Dana looked puzzled. "Don't we want to drive on to the farm first?"

Tessa was opening the door. "I just want to check it out."

"How will you get there?" Dana asked, who already must have guessed what the answer would be.

"With the ATV. Do you want to come along?"

"No. I'll wait here. You'll be right back, won't you?"

Tessa nodded. She pulled on her hiking jacket. If Savannah could see her now, in her old hiking boots, worn jeans, and sweatshirt, she would have a hard time calling her a city slicker.

They went to the back of the pickup and used the wooden planks Dana always had with her to build a ramp. Then Dana drove the ATV down the ramp.

Tessa took along the rucksack with the pistol in it and straddled the ATV. "About half an hour, okay?"

Dana nodded in agreement, although Tessa could see that her friend wasn't very happy. But she didn't have any time to waste. She steered toward the clearing in the woods, which led to Beaver Lake. She stuck to the periphery of the forest, where the ground was stable, mowing down the low underbrush on the way. The ATV climbed up a steep ridge. From there she could see the cut she had to follow. She stepped on the gas and drove toward it. At first she was relieved to see that she was on the right track. But then she noticed tire marks in the ground. Police? Had they already searched the cabin? Or had somebody else been up at the lake?

She tried to keep calm. Maybe it had been somebody who came up here to do some fishing. After another fifteen minutes, she could see the roof of the cabin Hank had built a couple of years earlier. It stood close to the lake, which had also become visible. There were whitecaps on the water. Reeds on the shore were swaying back and forth in the wind. Hank had used his chainsaw to clear a flat place for the cabin, a tiny, insignificant spot, easy to overlook in the midst of the great forest that encircled the lake like a tight green collar. Tessa turned away from the seductive scenery and quickly covered the final meters to the cabin. Its door was wide open. She jumped off the ATV and listened intently. When she didn't hear anything, she walked over to the entrance. From the open door, she peered inside. What she saw there was complete destruction. The kitchen table had been overturned along with the chairs. On the floor, cans, tools, fishing equipment, boots, and broken dishes lay strewn about. Some kind of white fluffy material flowed out of the sleeping bags, reminding her of sliced-open animals.

Tessa looked at this mess, bewildered. Who could have been so furious at Fran's family that he didn't even leave a remote cabin in peace? She felt her way over to a corner where Fran had installed a secure hiding place beneath a plank. She found the spot and once again was stopped in her tracks. The plank had been hammered shut with nails.

Suddenly she heard a noise outside. She climbed to the door and looked out.

15

He stood ten meters away, looking at her.

"Tessa," Tsaytis Chelin said.

She felt as though her inner self were being pulverized. Her hands were moist.

Goddammit, why does he still have such an effect on me?

She was on her way to becoming one of the best family lawyers in Vancouver. She had the reputation of being tough. A wolf in sheep's clothing, as one of the prosecuting attorneys had called her.

And here she stood with her knees shaking. Ever since she had moved to Vancouver, she had lived under the illusion that this would never again happen to her. But today she realized that she could no longer pretend not to care about him. It was still all there: his dark eyes, that penetrating gaze, the face that showed strength, pride, and perseverance. And there was no overlooking the powerful body and the coal-black hair that reached down to his brow, just as it used to do. She loved his mouth above the distinctive chin. Always relaxed and always still when he wasn't talking, rarely smiling. How often Tessa had stared at these lips, when she was waiting for a response from this man.

Just like the last time they'd met, five and a half years ago, before they had split acrimoniously. What he had said back then had opened up a deep chasm between them.

She pulled herself together. Today there was something completely different to talk about.

Before Tsaytis could take even a step in her direction, she said: "Stay where you are!"

He was carrying a hunting rifle over his shoulder.

"Throw your rifle down," she bellowed at him.

Tsaytis stopped for a moment and then threw his rifle on the ground.

"Get over there," she ordered, pointing at a tree stump a bit farther away.

"I'm not going to do anything to you," he said, visibly annoyed. But he followed her directions.

She ran over to the rifle and picked it up. She opened the ammunition case, took out the bullets, and put them in her pocket.

He looked at her without emotion, his hands placed easily on his hips.

"Maybe you also have a gun on you," he said.

"You can bet on it." She showed him the pistol, and then put it in her vest pocket. "What are you doing here?"

His eyes bored right through her, but he remained silent. Her throat was dry. She held her distance at ten steps away from him.

"Who broke into the cabin?"

He raised his eyebrows. Still didn't say anything. He seemed to be completely absorbed in relishing the sight of her. As if he were looking at a beautiful painting.

She didn't let him off the hook. "How come you suddenly show up here at Fran's cabin?"

He turned his head around and stared in the direction of the lake. "You still haven't found Fran, right?"

Tessa shook her head. "What are you doing here with a rifle?"

He sat down on the tree stump and casually put his hands in his lap. Hands she had held back then when they were friends.

He was still gazing at her with his penetrating eyes. "Somebody has to be looking for Fran who actually knows the area here."

"Are you looking for Fran?" Her voice didn't sound as harsh anymore.

"Me and a couple of other people from the tribe."

"How come it happened that you of all people found the bodies?"

Tsaytis understood immediately what she meant by that. He was used to reading her thoughts. "I was not alone. I have a witness."

Surprised, she looked at him. Tsaytis had a witness who could give him an alibi.

"Who was with you?"

"Ask the police."

She automatically took a few steps toward him. "Why aren't you helping me? Isn't everything already hard enough?"

His face remained completely calm. "Sergeant Halprin doesn't want me to talk about this. I wouldn't do anything that might hinder the investigation."

His cool answer ticked her off. "And then I run into you here at Fran's cabin, and you're carrying a gun. Tsaytis Chelin in the role of the chief inspector."

Ignoring her reaction, he slid down from the tree stump. She instinctively moved back as he got up onto the ramp that led to the cabin door.

"Come on," he said. "I'll show you something." He knew her too well. Knew that she couldn't resist this invitation. With one hand she held tightly on to the pistol that was in her vest pocket. When they entered the cabin, he ignored the mess on the floor and pointed at the wall. At eye level, Tessa saw a lengthy row of vertical notches in the wood.

"And here." Tsaytis pointed to the corner. The same notches. She didn't have to guess.

"A bear," she said.

He went over to the door.

"And here. What can you see here?"

"Where?"

"Take a good look at the door."

She examined the surface, first outside, then inside.

Just a few scratches.

If the bear had found the door locked, the animal would have demolished it with its claws. But the door was almost untouched. The bear must have just pushed it in with its weight.

"The door wasn't locked when the bear came," she said without looking at Tsaytis. He didn't move from his spot, didn't let her pass.

"The door was normally secured with a chain," Tessa continued. "Fran and Hank would not have left the entrance to the cabin unchained. Not with fishing gear inside."

"Locked with this chain here?" Tsaytis walked down from the ramp. There it was, lying on the ground in front of his hiking boots.

Tessa looked at the chain. Had Fran hidden herself in the cabin and then fled in panic? Did somebody rummage through the cabin? And then left the door unlocked?

The sun that now stood high in the sky blinded her. She stepped into the shade of the cabin. "Do you know anything that might be able to help us? Did Hank have enemies?" She realized she was asking for help from a man she had once seriously insulted. And then banned from her life.

She needed help. Fran needed help.

He looked at her with some compassion this time. "I . . . I want to help, but the fact is that I simply have no answers at this point. I'm as lost as you are."

She looked out over the sparkling lake, the dark-green edge of the forest around it. Hank and the children would never fish here again. Fran would never again find comfort in this cabin, where she had spent time drawing. Every hour that passed made it less likely that they would find Fran alive. She recalled her run-in with Lola Dole in Tim Hortons.

Maybe Fran was eaten by a grizzly just like my Jenny.

When it happened, Lola circulated her own version of the event. She never mentioned the possibility that her daughter had secretly taken her father's ATV and traveled alone to Whitesand Bay. Two things that were expressly forbidden, even more so if her goal was to see what Tessa and Tsaytis were up to out there. That's what she had told her girlfriend, who then told her mother and then the police. The whole town knew that Jenny had lied to her parents; she'd told them she would be spending the afternoon with her girlfriend.

Two wildlife officers located the grizzly the next evening, when the bear returned to the buried victim. They shot the animal, that defended its prey with all its might. An autopsy concluded that the bear was missing many teeth. Its jaw had a wound, which had become infected and which left the bear in constant pain.

Almost everybody in Whatou Lake believed that Tessa and Tsaytis didn't know anything about Jenny's trip to Whitesand Bay. Despite that, the Doles' despair was aimed completely and in all of its bitterness at Tessa, who was lucky to escape with her life the day their daughter died. In Tsaytis they saw a goddamned Sitklat'l who had made such an impression on Jenny that she had taken her father's ATV and betrayed her parents' trust in order to follow him out to a forsaken place.

Tessa felt Tsaytis's eyes focusing on her and heard him talking. "I've been waiting for you, Tessa. So that we could speak in peace and quiet."

"Were you at our house last night? "

He didn't deny it.

She made a dismissive gesture, as if she had to wipe away a spider's web.

"You learned how to remove me from your life. Did you think I didn't notice that? You didn't want to have anything more to do with a white person. That had already started at the university." She couldn't look him in the eye as she went on. "You thought you'd lose your identity if we stayed friends. You got radicalized, and I even understood that. I understand anger and resistance really well." She adopted a sarcastic undertone to her voice. "What I don't understand is why that blinded you to everything else."

"Tessa." He put his hand on her shoulder. His touch went through her like an electric shock. "You're making it too easy on yourself with your interpretation of events . . ."

She waited for an explanation. But Tsaytis remained silent as if he had changed his mind. As if he didn't want to start a new battle on an old front.

He went to where he had put down his gun. When he picked it up, she didn't protest. The threat didn't come from this rifle. But she couldn't have said where the danger was coming from.

"I've got to go back," she said and reached for the bullets in her pocket. "Dana is waiting for me."

Now he was paying attention. "Dana Eckert?"

"Yes." She pointed to the rifle. "You'll need that. Poachers are on the prowl."

"Where? Have you seen anybody?"

"I will tell you if you tell me what you saw at the farm . . . ."

His face turned back into a mask. "That's not up for discussion."

She threw the bullets on the ground and walked over to the ATV. Over her shoulder, she shouted: "So we're not going to help each other?"

She saw a boat that had been pulled halfway up onto the shore. He must have come from the south, across the lake.

Tsaytis stood motionless, his gaze averted, his powerful figure upright, anchored to the ground. He kept his emotions under control. *She* was the one who, during their last meeting five and a half years ago, had gotten out of control. Tsaytis had never lost his cool.

"How can you let that happen?" she had repeated over and over. "How can you just let that happen?"

"Our culture is not your culture," he had answered, unmoved. "Our laws are not your laws, and our sorrows are not your sorrows."

"Baloney! All people suffer the same way."

At that, Tsaytis uttered a sentence she never forgot: "Don't start preaching to me, Tessa. Those days are over."

Those days are over.

She shouldered her backpack when she heard Tsaytis's voice behind her.

"Hank had taken two days off when it happened. When the murders happened. Normally he worked for three weeks straight at the lodge and then had five days off. But he asked for time off those two days. I don't know what the reason was."

She gave him a sharp look. Tsaytis always knew what was going on at Watershed Lodge. The lodge belonged to the Sitklat'l, and Tsaytis's wife, Noreen, was the manager.

"He had to look after the kids," she explained, "because Fran had to go to the doctor in Whatou Lake."

No reaction.

She cleared her throat. "Just before kilometer forty-nine, there's a cut on the left side of the road. It's visible if you pay attention. When we were heading out here today, a dark pickup suddenly showed up and turned onto the road. It almost hit us. And then drove off like a bat out of hell in the other direction. We stopped and searched around. Found blood and grizzly hair. Or moose. More likely it was a grizzly."

"Did you recognize the driver?"

"No. It all happened too quickly. We were too shocked."

He seemed to be thinking over this information. Two vertical frowns appeared on his forehead.

"Now it's your turn. What did you see? Who is your witness?"

Once again he looked withdrawn. "Ask the sergeant from

Vancouver," he said. In a few leaps he reached his boat and untied it. She heard the motor as she got on her ATV. A wave of emotion rolled over her as she drove over roots and stones. Anger, pain, frustration, exhaustion, disappointment. She dashed mercilessly over all the rough spots on the trail. What a mess. A missed chance at reconciliation. A missed chance to learn more about the murderer, who might still be active in the area.

When Tessa reached the gravel road, Dana's pickup was gone.

16

Tessa couldn't believe her eyes.

In some places she found deep tire marks. She could not say which vehicle they might have come from. Maybe Dana had simply been tired of waiting. Tessa had promised to be back in half an hour. But it took her almost twice as long. Her friend had certainly not driven back to Whatou Lake. Fran's house wasn't very far away now.

Tessa decided to continue on the ATV. She passed the fork in the road where the logging trucks could turn to take their logs to the south. After ten minutes she reached the driveway to the Millers' place and then she saw the pickup truck and Dana talking to a policeman. She recognized the constable she had met the previous day.

She jumped off the ATV and let her frustrations fly. "Why did you drive away without me? I had no idea where you might be."

Dana remained calm. "A logging truck came through, and I had to make way for it. I had no choice." She looked at the policeman, who was watching the scene and then looked at her. "I've already told the constable why we're out here."

Tessa didn't want to change the topic. She hadn't encountered

any logging truck herself. She was still mad. "I don't understand
. . ."

Dana cut her off. "The constable told me that we can't just simply go on the property."

The officer nodded. "This is a crime scene, which we have not yet opened. Only the police can go in there now."

"But they told us we should go in and pick up the cats," Dana answered.

"Who told you that?"

"Sergeant Halprin," Tessa spit out without thinking.

"Wait here," the police officer said promptly. "I'll ask the sergeant."

That was a mistake, Tessa thought, as she looked accusingly at Dana. The policeman turned his back on them, and then told another policeman to go and get Sergeant Halprin.

Dana raised her eyebrow.

Two minutes later Ron Halprin showed up. She didn't think he seemed angry, but more surprised, which put her at ease. His calm voice didn't show any impatience when he said: "Miss Griffins. You're here? I thought you would be with your family in Whatou Lake."

She kept herself from saying out loud: "I thought you would be in Whatou Lake, too."

Instead she answered: "Lionel Miller brought back the two dogs. He said—at least as I understood it—you wanted me to come pick up the cats. They were getting in the way of the investigation."

"Oh yes, the cats." He kept looking at her. Tessa got him off track by introducing Dana. "Miss Eckert used to be a social worker in Whatou Lake," she explained.

Halprin let her repeat Dana's name. She was sure he was putting it on a mental list of people he should remember.

"How many cats are there?" he asked.

"Three. We have three cat cages with us."

Halprin scratched his chin. He looked down at her dirty hiking boots. His thoughts were obviously elsewhere.

"I think we have two cats locked up in the storage room, but the third seems to have escaped from us." He addressed one of the constables: "I'll take Miss Griffins with me. Please wait here with Miss Eckert."

"I'll look around the house for the third cat," Dana suggested.

Halprin shook his head. "The whole area around here is a cordoned-off crime scene only the police can enter. We don't want to have any clues become contaminated." His voice sounded forbearing.

Tessa saw a tinge of disappointment on Dana's face. "Keep your eyes wide open when you're inside," she whispered to Tessa, as she took two cat cages down from the pickup. Tessa muttered her agreement, but she didn't expect to be allowed into the house.

Halprin led her up the dirt road to the side of the farmhouse. Hank had added a room to the house, which was used as storage.

"The cats are in there," the sergeant explained.

"Can I go in?"

"Yes, but you'll have to put on these plastic overshoes. Did Hank sometimes lock the dogs in here?"

"Not normally. Only if somebody was visiting and the dogs went crazy. Not that they were aggressive, but they were big and could get very excited about visitors, and sometimes they were just too much for them. They might be locked in for an hour or two. That never bothered me; they calmed down quickly." Suddenly something occurred to her. "When the dogs were locked in there, it must have been because of someone who didn't like dogs. Or who was afraid of them. Otherwise Hank wouldn't have—"

He interrupted her with another question. "What time of day did Fran teach the children in the house?"

"Always in the morning."

Halprin noted down this information and then started looking for something in his jacket pocket. Tessa couldn't stop thinking about his question. Why were the children in the house when their father was outside? On Hank's rare days off at home, the children always spent every minute with him. It hadn't been raining. Did Hank send them into the house because he suspected that something dangerous was going to happen?

Halprin gave her some latex gloves and put some on himself. There was something else she wanted to know.

"Sergeant . . ."

"Ron. Can I call you Tessa?"

"Yes, of course. Ron, can you tell me who was with Tsaytis Chelin when he discovered the bodies?"

He narrowed his eyes. "Who told you that Tsaytis Chelin wasn't alone?"

"He did. I was just about to tell you that I was briefly in Fran's cabin. You certainly must already know about the cabin on Beaver Lake. I took the ATV and ran into Tsaytis there. It was completely unexpected. He had crossed the lake by boat. I . . . the inside of the cabin was a complete mess. A bear had forced his way in. We found claw marks."

He pressed his lips together. "It would have been better if you had informed me before you went over there, Tessa. We have specialists who see to it that clues don't get contaminated."

"Ron, you're right. I didn't touch anything and neither did Tsaytis. It was a spontaneous decision on my part because I happened to be in the area. A sudden hope that Fran might be there and because every minute counts."

She knew Halprin wouldn't be happy about what she had done. As a lawyer she could under no conditions talk her way out of this by claiming she had no idea.

"We know very well that every minute counts. That also means that the earlier we get a piece of information, the better."

She nodded. "I assumed that the Miller family or somebody else already told you about the cabin. But maybe it would interest you to know that there is a hiding place underneath the wooden floor in the corner by window on the west side. Under a loose wooden plank. Fran showed it to me once when I was visiting. She told me that she wanted to put a gun in there. She would feel safer if she were alone at the lake. Whether she did that or not, I don't know. When I was in the cabin earlier today, I saw that the plank was nailed shut. I thought that was strange."

"What kind of weapon was Fran talking about?"

"No idea. Certainly there were also rifles here on the farm. Hank actually has a hunting license. I remember that."

The sergeant looked over at the edge of the forest and then back at her. A quiet meowing could be heard from behind the door to the storeroom.

"Our people already made a brief visit to the cabin to check if Fran was there. Everything at that point was still intact. The bear must have showed up later. I'll send somebody else up there. Thanks for the tip." He curled his fingers under the latex like claws before he asked: "So you didn't want to be at the press conference today?"

"I thought it was on Saturday."

"Yes, there will be a second one then. The one today will be very short."

"Can you tell me who was here at the farm with Tsaytis?"

"No," Ron answered drily. They were still in front of the door, which for some reason he hadn't yet opened. He stood so close to her that she could clearly see the lines in his forehead.

His stoic behavior somehow provoked her and made her say: "That's the reason you're here and not at the press conference in Whatou Lake. Because you'd rather not say anything at all."

"As a lawyer, that can't be new to you," he said in a friendly way. "But we always try to keep some key information confidential." He wants to stay a few steps ahead of the perpetrator, she thought.

"And Fran? Do you know anything more? What about the jacket in Whitesand Bay?"

If he had begun to feel interrogated, he didn't show any sign of it.

"The jacket is Fran's, and the blood is also hers."

"How did that jacket get out there?"

"Oh, I can't tell you that." Halprin put his hand on the doorknob. "Tessa, we're doing the best we can, but this is a murder investigation and we don't want to make any mistakes. There are people out there who are looking for Fran. We're getting the word out over many radio stations and TV channels and in many places."

She remembered Boyd's text: *He is very good . . . Now you have him on your side. Make sure you keep him there.*

She looked up and could read compassion in his eyes. It moved her. Despite the demands of his profession, he was still a decent person.

"Thanks," she replied as softly as she could. "Please tell me if there's anything I can do to help."

He nodded. "The cats."

"So there are only two in here?"

"Yes, we only found two."

They slipped into the room and quickly closed the door behind them.

Tessa flipped the light switch. The first cat was easy to catch. She came meowing up to them. The second made a fuss and kept hiding underneath the shelves. The overstuffed storage space looked to Tessa like a junk room. Cross-country skis, a tricycle, old toys, all sizes of shoes, and furniture that Fran was planning to paint.

"Please turn the cat cage so the opening is on top," she said to Halprin after she finally had the second cat in her arms." She pushed the animal behind first into the cage and quickly closed the door.

At that moment Halprin asked: "Did Fran have a diary?"

She immediately assumed he hadn't found any.

She brushed away the cat hairs from her jacket. "It was more like a sketchbook. Fran was a visual kind of person. She drew."

"Where did she keep this sketchbook?"

"I don't know. Somewhere in the house, I assume. She also drew on loose sheets of paper she sometimes showed me. They're probably lying around somewhere."

They went outside with the cat cages. Both of the animals protested loudly about their imprisonment.

"We'll keep looking for the third cat," Halprin promised.

"Thanks. When will I be able to go into the house?"

"In a couple of days. After we have completed the investigation. We take that very seriously."

Tessa noticed even in her overtaxed emotional state how important it was to Halprin that she continue to trust the police. *Trust him.*

Because she was a lawyer? Because she could cause him problems? Whatever happened now, she still wanted him on her side. "When you're done, will you please tell me right away? I don't want people to go into the house illegally."

He gave her a close look. She couldn't remember having seen another man with such bright eyes. Maybe it was just the sunlight. "I'll see what I can do," he mumbled as he took off his latex gloves.

"I've got to tell you one more thing," she said. "Somebody told me that when Fran was in Whatou Lake at the end of April, she saw Fran coming out of the funeral home. I . . . I don't know how reliable this information is. It comes from Savannah. She was one of my Mom's foster children and now lives in Whatou Lake."

"She saw Fran coming out of the funeral home?"

Tessa nodded. The whole thing now seemed absurd to her. "I have no idea what Fran could have been doing there. Savannah is a bit of a . . . gossip and has a tendency to stretch the truth sometimes. Maybe there's nothing to it. That's why at first I didn't want to say anything."

He opened his mouth as if something was on the tip of his tongue. But then he closed it again and picked up the cat cage.

"This thing is pretty heavy."

Did he have pets? Children? How had he felt when he looked at the bodies of Breena, Clyde, and Kayley?

They had almost reached the pickup. Dana leaned on the fender and looked over at her in anticipation.

Suddenly something occurred to Tessa. "The sketches of the children used to be in the chest of drawers in the living room. Maybe Fran's drawings are also there."

He nodded but was noticeably distracted. In his thoughts, he once again seemed to be elsewhere. Trying to keep ahead of the murderer. Maybe they had already searched the chest of drawers. He put down the cat cage and wished them a safe journey home. Her eyes followed him as he walked to the house, where a person wearing a white protective suit was waiting.

"What was that about the children's sketches?" Dana asked when they were already sitting in the pickup.

"Apparently they can't find Fran's sketchbook. It was like a diary for her."

"You didn't find it when you went through the cabin down at the lake?"

"A bear had broken in and destroyed almost everything."

"You find anything important despite that?"

Tessa tried to come up with a convincing reply. It took her too long.

Dana could see right through her. "You're really a collector of secrets, my friend."

Tessa allowed this remark to go unanswered.

17

The cats outdid each other with their pitiful meowing. There was no escaping it. Dana found a radio program that filled the car with country music. They could still hear the cats complaining over the music. The pickup hopped down the rough road. Dana's driving was too wild for Tessa's taste. "What are you going to do if we meet a logging truck coming at us?"

"They're done for the day."

"I hope they're not doing overtime," Tessa murmured.

Suddenly the pickup went off the side of the road. Tessa and Dana were both caught by the seatbelts, and the cat cages slipped forward. For a couple of seconds the pitiful meowing stopped. Then it became even louder.

"For God's sake," Dana complained. "This road gets worse and worse. The trucks are wrecking it."

Tessa put the cat cages back and talked quietly to the animals to calm them down.

The eerie atmosphere on Fran's farm stuck to her bones. Normally the place was alive with children laughing and dogs barking when she arrived. But today there was a paralyzing silence. What had actually happened there that Tuesday? Not knowing everything had driven her almost crazy since visiting the morgue. On the radio the Bee Gees were singing "Staying Alive." She had recently read that three of the four Gibb brothers were now dead.

She felt like she had a concrete block in her stomach. The cats' unease reinforced her feeling of helplessness. Suddenly the music stopped, and a familiar voice could be heard inside the pickup. Her mother's voice.

"Fran, maybe you hear me wherever you are. Come home right away. We are there for you."

Then a male voice: "With these words, Martha Griffins is appealing to Fran Miller, who has been missing since Tuesday. Fran is a former foster child of Martha and Kenneth Griffins. She . . ."

Tessa's upper body shot forward. "What the hell?"

"Shh," said Dana. The cats continued to protest.

"Breena, Clyde, and Kayley were found shot dead in their house two hours away from Whatou Lake. Their father, Hank Miller, was lying on the lawn in front of the house. He had also been shot dead. The police explained today at a press conference that they have eliminated the possibility that Hank Miller shot the children and, after that, himself. Fran Miller, the children's mother, who is married to Hank Miller, is still missing. Two dozen members of the RCMP are out looking for her on the ground and from the air. Bloodhounds are also in operation. The police are being supported by volunteers from the area. Corporal Kate Jennings said today at the press conference in Whatou Lake . . ."

A female voice jumped in: "At this time, we are going on the assumption that Fran Miller is still alive. We know that a jacket belonging to her was found in Whitesand Bay. We can now confirm that the blood on it is hers. We're asking the local people to pass on any information they think could help us in our investigation of these terrible crimes. We are doing everything possible to find the missing person and the killer or killers."

Then the radio announcer spoke again. He repeated the

information from the police that there was no immediate danger to the public. If anyone wanted to help in the search for Fran Miller, they should contact the police, and not go off on their own. "This wilderness is a dangerous place where you could lose your life. Keep an eye on your children and don't let them wander off. Don't linger in dark and isolated places."

Dana and Tessa looked at each other.

A short conversation with Harrison Miller, Hank's father, followed.

"This is a tragedy . . . not only for my family but also for the whole community. Four innocent people were brutally murdered, and we don't know where the mother of my grandchildren is. We . . ." His voice broke down briefly before he collected himself. "We cannot understand that this sort of thing could happen in the Whatou Lake area. I am warning everybody who had anything to do with this, this heinous act will not go unpunished. My son and my grandchildren . . . sorry . . ." Harrison Miller could no longer go on.

The announcer said they would make sure to update listeners and that they would be taking tips. Then he went on to talk about the upcoming election in British Columbia.

Dana turned the volume way down. "No immediate danger to the public," she burst out. "How could they know that? They can't exclude anything."

Tessa was bothered by something else. "At the same time they say that you should keep an eye on your children and not let them wander off alone, especially not in the dark. That doesn't fit."

"What a lot of crap. They must be out of their mind."

Tessa pushed her hair back in a forceful gesture. "They say they don't think it was a murder-suicide. Well, I would hope so! And then Harrison says we don't know where the mother of the children is. That can only mean one thing."

"That they think Fran is the killer."

One of the cats meowed really loudly behind them. Tessa

loosened her seat belt, reached back, and put the cat cage on her lap. "It won't be long now," she said to the animal, that looked at her with wide-open eyes. It had a sparkling collar around its neck. "We'll be there soon. Soon, soon." She opened the cage, reached in, and stroked the cat's soft fur. She felt a raspy tongue on her fingers. She became calmer, her thoughts clearer. Ron Halprin and his colleagues must have a strong suspicion, that was her impression. Maybe not Fran. But maybe they had enough information to suspect a certain person. A person who was already under observation. Probably there were undercover investigators working on the case. Maybe in little Whatou Lake they would be taken for non-local engineers at the copper mine, or other contract workers. She shared her thoughts with Dana, who was driving more carefully down the logging road. Her friend nodded.

She didn't say anything for such a long time that Tessa couldn't stand it any longer and told her about her encounter with Tsaytis Chelin. When she was done, Dana only said: "You and Tsaytis."

"What do you mean by that?" There was nothing more to be gotten from Dana. She just turned up the music. Tessa turned it back down again. She patted the cat and asked: "Why did Dad allow that to happen?"

Dana looked over at her. "What do you mean?"

"He let Mom get behind a microphone. Why didn't *he* do that?"

"Maybe she just really wanted to."

"Mom? I can't imagine that."

"Your mother has changed, Tessa. She's doing what she wants now. I think she wants more autonomy."

"I didn't realize that. Maybe I don't know everything about her." It was something she didn't gladly admit.

"I don't think your father realized it, either," Dana replied drily.

The tone of their discussion made Tessa uncomfortable. She

didn't dare ask Dana questions about her mother. Does one ask other people to talk about one's own parents? Martha Griffins seemed to be more open with Fran, Savannah, and maybe even Dana than she was with her own daughter who had moved away to Vancouver.

That was certainly her own fault. Because of her work, she had spent too little time talking to her mother. She preferred to keep a distance between herself and Whatou Lake.

What had made her mother change? Hearing her on the radio —and maybe she had even been in front of cameras—shocked Tessa. Hopefully she would be able to talk more with her soon.

But as they drove up to the Griffins' home, Tessa realized it would be a while before that could happen.

A police car stood in front of the house.

18

Tessa put the cat cage down on the car seat and hurried into the house without waiting for Dana. She was expecting something bad. On her way in she passed Savannah and found her mother at the kitchen table, sitting across from a policewoman. Both had a cup of coffee in front of them.

Tessa greeted the police officer with a nod before she kissed her mother on the cheek. "Mom, what's happened? Has Fran been found?"

Martha Griffins seemed astonishingly composed. "Corporal Jennings drove me back home, Tessa." She directed her words to the police officer: "This my daughter Tessa. She's a lawyer in Vancouver."

The officer stood up and introduced herself. "I'm a member of the homicide division, and I'm responsible for contacts with the public. I come from Vancouver, too."

Tessa's tension gauge went into high gear and then up a notch. *Whoa. Calm down, Tessa, get your blood pressure back to normal.* She sat down across from the police officer. "Thank you for driving my mother home, corporal. I haven't heard the latest news. Fran's still missing, right?" She did her best to sound as if she was all business.

"Yes," the police officer said, who looked like she might be of East Indian origin and, like Tessa, had an asymmetrical hairstyle. "I work with Sergeant Halprin."

They were distracted by noise and voices in front of the house, before Jennings continued speaking. "Your mother gave me a list of her former foster children."

The list Tessa was supposed to have delivered. She had promised it to Ron Halprin.

The main door opened and then closed again. Pitiful meowing filled the kitchen. Savannah briefly stuck her head in the door. "Tessa, I'll bring the poor creatures into the guestroom for now. This morning I bought pet food and cat litter. Luckily, the dogs aren't around."

She disappeared before Tessa could react.

Outside the sound of an engine that quickly disappeared. Dana had not come in. Tessa would phone her later and apologize for the awkward good-bye.

"Those are Fran's cats that Tessa has picked up," her mother explained to the officer. "Fran loved her children and her pets. She never would have left them behind."

It occurred to Tessa that she hadn't mentioned Hank.

"They were at the farm?" the mountie asked.

Tessa nodded. She didn't feel like answering any questions as long as her mother was listening, and this time she was glad that Savannah showed up again.

"Both of them are hiding under the bed," she announced.

"But there are three," Martha Griffins called out.

"We haven't found one of them," Tessa explained.

"She has to be in the shed. Did you look there?"

"Mom, we'll find it, I promise."

Why are we talking about a cat when Fran is still missing? Tessa thought. She found the conversation unpleasant.

Savannah made the situation even more difficult. She talked about dinner. As if anybody could be in the mood for it. "Should we wait until Dad gets back?"

The police officer was the first to respond. "I have to go now, but I'll contact you again. And you can, of course, contact us at any time."

Tessa thanked her and led her to the door. The officer turned to her once again and said: "We depend upon the cooperation of everybody involved. I hope you help us."

"Of course," Tessa answered, noting the reminder. "Is there anything new?"

"You'll have to ask Sergeant Halprin about that." The officer left and rushed to her car.

Tessa quickly closed the door and went back into the kitchen. Her mother sat at the same spot with an absent look on her face.

"Where is Dad?"

"At the funeral home," Savannah answered, bent over the dishwasher.

Tessa stopped short. "Why? Have the bodies been released?"

"No, but Robert Pleeke called him up. He owns the funeral home." She gave Tessa a knowing look.

The phone rang.

Martha Griffins shot out of the chair and grabbed the receiver.

"Hello, Dana," she answered and slowly wandered out of the kitchen. "Yes, I will tell her. No problem. She definitely doesn't hold that against you. Everything is chaotic here and . . ."

Her voice drifted away to the back part of the house. Tessa was irritated. Dana's phone call was definitely meant for her. Savannah began to bang around with the silverware. Her strong, tattooed arms were moving constantly.

She set the table and looked at Tessa as if they were conspiring.

"You have to tell Mom that she should be more careful around the police. That every word that she lets slip counts."

Tessa heard the criticism in Savannah's words, but she controlled her annoyance. She very much wanted to hear what Savannah had learned.

"What did Mom actually tell the police?"

"That Fran, in the last couple of months, was behaving strangely. That she sometimes came to Whatou Lake without the children. She found that very strange. Fran didn't tell her what she was doing in Whatou Lake and who she was doing it with."

Tessa could hear her mother's muffled voice. What private matters were she and Dana talking about? Tessa put out the knives and forks while Savannah noisily put the glasses on the table.

"Don't you also find that strange? Before, Fran always brought the children to Mom when she went shopping on her own or to the dentist." Savannah bent down over the table and lowered her voice even more. "Fran and Mom had an argument. Maybe Mom should talk to you about it first before she talks to the police about it."

Tessa stood with the knives in her hand. "What were they arguing about?"

"I don't know. One time I came into the house and heard loud voices. Dad was in town. I only heard Mom say: 'You wouldn't dare. I'll make sure of that.' And Fran said very quietly: 'I have to know the truth. You've got to understand that.'" Savannah lowered her head, trying to hear Martha's call.

Tessa was getting impatient. "Was that everything?"

"The wind blew the open door shut as I came in, and they stopped talking. Fran came out to see who was there. She said a quick hello and left the house."

"When was that?"

"In February. She came without the children. And without Hank."

"And Mom?"

"What's that about me?" Martha Griffins appeared in the doorway.

Savannah immediately got her act together. "Are you having wine or . . . ?" Just then a car pulled up in front of the house and stopped.

'That's Ken," Martha said. "Wine for me, please."

Tessa seized the moment and quickly went outside.

Her father sat in the Pathfinder as if he couldn't force himself to get out and face the situation in the house. Tessa opened the passenger door and sat down next to him. A happy whining greeted her in the interior of the car and a moist nose snuggled on her cheek. She noticed dark shadows under her father's eyes. His voice sounded exhausted. "Fran was in the funeral home in February and was looking at coffins. Robert Pleeke told me that. Not that they have many coffins there, only about half a dozen. He said she stood there for a long time looking at them."

Tessa grabbed her father's hand, which felt cold.

"Fran told Rob that even as a child she had been curious about how a funeral home looked, but that she had never dared to go inside one. After that, he said she hardly said anything more, and just looked."

Tessa couldn't make sense of any of this.

"Maybe it's just a coincidence," she offered. "Maybe it was really like she said."

Her father's gaze seemed to travel into the distance. "Robert said if the police questioned him, he would have no choice but to tell them about this. Nevertheless he first wanted to tell me."

"Dad, did Fran have mental problems? Had she been acting strangely lately?"

He let go of her hand and ran it over his distraught face. "I don't know. She hardly came by to see us. And when she did come, I wasn't home."

She told him about the argument between her mother and Fran in February. Was there some connection between these things? *Fran had a dispute with Mom and then went to visit the funeral home?*

Her father looked at her suspiciously. "Martha never mentioned any of this. She would have been very upset by something like that."

"Maybe she just didn't want to let it weigh you down."

He remained silent.

Tessa recalled Dana's remarks about her mother: *She's doing what she wants now. I think she wants more autonomy.*

Maybe that was also the case with Fran. Fran didn't want to tell her parents about her plans. She didn't want to admit to them that she wanted to move far, far away from them to Grouse Valley, which would make it even more difficult for the parents to visit their grandchildren.

Fran wanted to get away.

Did it have to do with Hank, with the fact that he wasn't home often? Or was there another woman? At Watershed Lodge, Hank came into contact with many female guests and coworkers. Tessa suppressed her wild speculations. In order to learn more, she would have to fly up to the lodge as soon as possible. Even if Tsaytis Chelin was there.

Her father's voice broke into her thoughts. "What was going on in Fran's house? Who did you meet there? What did you see?"

Before she could answer, Martha appeared in the open main door. She beckoned them in.

"Actually I didn't see anything except the storeroom. I'll tell you later," Tessa said quickly. She had already opened the car door when she felt her father's hand on her knee.

"Harrison wants the dogs. Legally he probably has a right to have them. But I can't bring myself to take them to him."

Tessa looked at him in surprise. "Harrison? But surely Mom wants to keep the dogs . . ."

"She already has Fran's cats. Didn't you bring them with you?"

"Yeah, yeah. I just thought . . ."

"I can't tell Harrison he can't have them. He's Hank's father. He called me up and said that, for him, the dogs were a connection to Hank."

She hesitated and looked back. The dogs had lain down when they noticed that the people weren't getting out.

"Does Lionel know that his father wants the dogs? There's a reason he brought them to us."

Kenneth Griffins opened the car door. "Harrison probably doesn't tell Lionel everything. But that's not our problem."

When they reached the main door with the dogs, Martha Griffins met them with a suspicious look. "What have you been talking about so long out there? Dinner's ready. Savannah went to a lot of trouble."

They sat down at the table and ladled soup into their bowls. Tessa noticed it was more of a reflex, a routine that they were holding on to.

"We're waiting for news," her mother complained.

Tessa apologized. "There's nothing much to report. All I did was to get the cats—two of them were locked in the storeroom. We are still looking for the third one. I wasn't allowed to enter the house. The whole place is still a crime scene."

"I want to know everything." Martha Griffins would not let up. "It's worse not to know anything than to have some version of what might have happened. I'm imagining the most awful scenes."

"I know, Mom. I hope very much that we'll know more soon."

"Savannah has put up a Facebook page for Fran. People can write on it if they know something."

"But nothing useful has come in yet," Savannah jumped in.

"People would be better off contacting the police if they know something," Kenneth Griffins remarked and looked at his wife. "Please eat a little, dear."

Martha played with her spoon. She looked worn out. "What did you hear in town?"

"Not much. You know how people are. They don't want to get involved or expose themselves. They don't want to get mixed up in any murder investigation. And nobody tells me what kind of gossip is running around."

"People can give the police anonymous tips," Tessa suggested.

Her father nodded. "Lionel, by the way, has organized a search party for tomorrow. He's included you two."

Tessa took notice without saying anything. She hadn't eaten much the whole day and was relieved to get something warm in her stomach.

"I need Savannah here with me," Martha Griffins protested.

Kenneth didn't change his position.

"*I* will be here, dear. Every person counts in a search."

"They'll be searching with helicopters and dogs." Martha poured herself another glass of wine.

Kenneth ignored her remark. "Lionel sent you a message, Tessa. So that you know where to meet."

Tessa felt guilty. She hadn't even had time to check her iPhone.

Martha Griffins suddenly changed the topic. "Dana and Tessa saw poachers."

Tessa stared at her mother. What else had Dana told her about their trip to Fran's house? Then she calmed down. She knew Dana. She would have let some pieces of information come out in order to satisfy Martha Griffins's nosiness. But she wouldn't say anything more than that. Nevertheless, Tessa felt uneasy.

Her mother was going over the event as Dana had described it.

"Unbelievable," exclaimed Savannah with her mouth full. "The area is full of cops, and these guys are out to hunt bears."

"We don't really know that they were out to hunt bears," Tessa argued.

Savannah shook her head. "I've heard rumors that two of the grizzlies near Watershed Lodge have disappeared. Why don't you ask Tsaytis Chelin, if you don't believe me?"

Tessa glanced at her mother to see whether she knew about Tsaytis at the cabin at Beaver Lake, but Martha Griffins was concentrating on her salad and didn't react. Dana evidently hadn't said anything.

The disappearance of the two grizzlies must have made the

people at Watershed Lodge nervous. The lodge relied on bear watching, which drew tourists from all over the world. Fran, too, would have been very upset about the killing of the bears. She loved and respected bears. She had also defended the grizzlies who, in Lionel's words, hung around her farm.

Had the poachers gotten wind of this bear? Had Fran gotten in their way? And had they gotten rid of Fran and the whole family? The uncertainty was enough to drive anyone crazy.

Martha Griffins pushed away her half-eaten dinner. Tessa did the same and helped to clean up.

The dogs, that Savannah had already fed, were antsy.

"Can you take the dogs out, Tessa?" her father asked. "I'll take care of the dishes." He turned to his wife. "Dear, do you want to go and lie down?"

"I'll lie down in the guestroom so the cats will have some company," said Martha, who had thrown back two glasses of red wine during dinner.

Tessa took both dogs out on their leashes. She really didn't have any desire for another car trip, but she needed some space. She drove down the hill to the turnoff, where she stopped as a dark pickup approached from the left. She saw how it stopped just after the fork in the road. A tall guy got out and waved.

She recognized him right away.

19

She got out, too. Telford Reed came over to her. "I was hoping I'd run into you somewhere. Your family and you must really be having a hard time."

He was wearing a Stetson hat again, which very few men around this region still did. Most had switched over to baseball caps. Maybe Telford Reed thought that it would make him look less like a city slicker.

"We still haven't found Fran. Have you heard anything that might be helpful to us?"

To her astonishment, he answered: "Maybe. Can I talk to you for a few minutes?"

"Here? I have two dogs in the car that I have to let out."

He rubbed his chin. "Do you think we could take a quick ride over to Tennigan Park? We could take a little walk there to talk something over."

She blinked and tried to assess the situation. It would be light out here until ten o'clock in the evening. She could risk that. She would send a quick text message to Dana to tell her where she would be. And she would put her pistol in her pocket for the worst-case scenario.

"Good," she said. "I'll follow you."

They reached the turnoff to the park after ten minutes. A dirt road that was bordered by trees and bushes led them to the park entrance. The barrier was up, the tourist season had officially begun, but in June there were very few campers out here in the wilderness. Tessa parked the Pathfinder near Telford's pickup. She opened the trunk door and the dogs jumped out, wagging their tails. Telford, without being asked, grabbed one of the dogs' leashes. The husky mix happily greeted him. She hoped that Telford wouldn't notice the outline of the pistol in her coat pocket. A forest trail led past the unoccupied campsites.

Telford looked at her from the side. "Harrison Miller wants the dogs, right?"

She stumbled in surprise. "Who told you that?"

"I'm coming from Harrison. We had some business to discuss. He's looking forward to having the dogs. Because they are Hank's dogs. He wants to hang on to everything he can. He's a destroyed man."

Tessa made an effort to keep her rising emotions under control.

"Yes, that's what happens with murder. The perpetrator not only kills his victims but also destroys everything around them." She let herself be pulled along by the German shepherd. "Sometimes that can go on for generations."

"You're right. Look, I know that you're a lawyer in Vancouver. I may be able to use your services, if that's an option for you."

She frowned. "Mr. Reed . . ."

"Just call me Telford."

"Telford, I'm here because of my parents, not because I'm looking for new clients."

"I know that I'm really surprising you with this, but let me explain."

She was too curious to try and stop him. And didn't he say he had information about Fran?

Telford pulled the husky away from a pile of moose droppings. A light wind spread an unpleasant smell around.

"Harrison wants to buy my outfitter license. He came to me a couple of weeks ago with an offer. He wanted . . . it for Hank."

Despite her amazement, she let Telford keep talking.

"I get the impression that Harrison is dreaming about a second lodge, one like Watershed Lodge. I personally think the Sitklat'l should get my license. I'm ready to sell it to them for a decent price. But some of the elders don't want to pay for the license. Many band members say that it's their land. I know that this question has been settled in the land claims treaty with the Sitklat'l. Your legal team, Tessa, negotiated an agreement with the provincial government that favored the Sitklat'l."

She confirmed what Telford said, still uncertain what it was that he wanted from her.

"I can't just give away a license without some kind of compensation," he continued. "I need the money. I have a firm for alternate energy in Alberta that's expanding, and I have over fifty workers. Which brings me to my point: Do you think it would be possible that the provincial government might be willing to help out with the financing of the outfitter license? Watershed Lodge is a successful business. Shouldn't the provincial government be interested in backing an indigenous project that has the potential to be a financial winner for generations? Do you think there's any room for negotiations?"

Tessa, in a trance, shook her head. She struggled to say something. "Telford, I . . . This is not the time or the place for such . . . consideration . . . I . . ."

Under other circumstances, she would immediately have told him that the government had had an open-door policy in regard to the hunters' lobbyists for years. The female head of the government liked to have herself photographed with them, and they did nothing to protect grizzly bears. These politicians didn't seem to comprehend that the tourist industry around bear-watching was worth much more money than trophy hunting. But today she was too tired for a discussion. Reed understood quickly that he had gone too far.

"Please excuse me for being so insensitive about this. How could I be so unprofessional? I wouldn't mention any of this at the moment if it weren't for the fact that it also has something to do with Fran."

The dogs were impatient; Tessa was almost running to keep up with them. Telford hesitated to go on, but she called out: "Just keep talking!"

"Fran contacted me and asked to speak to me as soon as possible. She wanted to meet at a place where nobody would see us. That was four weeks ago. We met right here in front of the gate to the park. She had heard about Harrison's plans and . . . she said that Hank didn't want the license, and she didn't want it because Harrison's money came from dirty sources. From illegal deals with mining companies. She also told me that she and Hank would soon be moving away from here."

Now I know at least *one* other person met secretly with Fran, she thought. Just as she was about to answer Telford, she noticed something. The dogs were very interested in another pile of droppings. It looked very fresh; it had certainly come from a bear.

Tessa turned around. "We'd better get back to the vehicles. A bear can't be far away." Telford agreed. She tugged the German shepherd's leash. "Let's continue talking so that the bear hears us and we don't surprise him," she said. "What else did Fran say to you?"

"She admitted to me openly that Hank didn't know anything about her meeting with me. She was not going to tell him anything because she didn't want to be accused of causing trouble between him and his father."

"Did you tell the police about this?"

"Yes. I think that was my duty. How can we get to the bottom of this awful crime if we hold back information from them?"

Tessa looked over to the bushes. Something dark was lying between the branches. She could only see the outline. Instinctively her hand gripped Telford's arm. Now he also saw it.

The extremely agitated dogs smelled blood. Tessa smelled both death and decay.

Telford handed her the leash and went over to the carcass. He came back with a very dark look. "Half a moose," he said.

"Did a bear kill it?"

He shook his head and took one leash out of her hand.

"Hunters shot it. Poachers."

She tried to keep up with his fast pace. "We've already found three other moose carcasses," he explained. "Always near a place where tourists like to stop. I think somebody puts out the meat as bait."

"Who is *we*?" Tessa asked. As an answer, she heard a loud growl. But it didn't come from the dogs.

They both spun around. The dogs began to bark wildly.

A midsize grizzly had stepped out of the bushes about thirty meters behind them.

"Holy shit," she heard Telford whispering.

The grizzly took some steps toward them and shook his big head back and forth, ready to attack. Tessa breathed faster. "Let's go slowly backward. Always facing the bear," she said as quietly as possible. "Bear, we're not going to do anything to you, we're not going to take away your dinner. We're just going to get out of here."

They moved back step by step and tried to keep the dogs under control. The bear hesitated for a few seconds and then kept moving forward.

"Hold the leash!" Tessa pushed it into Telford's hand.

"What are you going to do?"

She took the pistol out of her pocket.

Telford took a quick look at it. "That's not a—"

"Hold the leashes really tightly; I'm going to shoot in the air." She fired a shot. The bear looked confused, but didn't retreat. The dogs strained at their leashes. Tessa knew that they were used to the sound of shooting. She set off one more shot. "Go away, bear, go away," she yelled as loudly as she could. Another shot ripped through the forest. The grizzly stopped and then disappeared into the bush as quickly as it had appeared.

"Let's get out of here," Tessa said. They slipped silently through the empty campsites, and then the outhouses came into view. It wasn't far to the parking spot, although it seemed like an eternity to Tessa. Telford ran steadily a couple of steps ahead of her. The husky pulled powerfully on its leash while the German shepherd trotted at her side. It was only after they reached the two vehicles and the dogs were secured inside the Pathfinder that they dared to look each other in the face.

Telford started talking first: "I really hope that we catch this guy."

Tessa took a deep breath. "The bear was just defending its food."

"I'm not talking about the grizzly. Somebody laid that bait out there. Always where people come together. These idiots want the bears to become dangerous. Then they can shoot them." Telford took off his Stetson. She could see how furious he was.

Her forehead was sweaty. "Who discovered the bait you mentioned?"

"They found some near the viewing platform at Seven Point. Lionel Miller discovered the second spot near the picnic table at Killnair Park. And the forest ranger just got a call from a miner who came from the V4 forestry road."

"I think we saw poachers on that road," Tessa exclaimed. She still was on the lookout for suspicious activity in the bushes. The bear might turn up again. She gave Telford a brief description of what she had seen that morning.

"It was a dark pickup, but we couldn't read the license plate." She was listening for a cracking noise in the bush, but aside from the birds chirping and the wind there wasn't anything.

"I'll inform the ranger." Telford put the Stetson back on and took the car keys out of his pocket.

At that moment Tessa began to shiver. She tried to stop it but couldn't.

Telford Reed looked at her nervously. "Are you cold?"

She crossed her arms but continued to shiver.

"I don't know, what . . ." She even had trouble speaking.

Telford got closer to her and with some hesitation put his arms tightly around her shaking body.

"That will soon go away," he mumbled. "That's the reaction to the stress."

She nodded weakly, shocked that her body had a life of its own. Telford talked to her softly. After a while the shivering ebbed away, and he let go of her.

"Are you okay?" He looked at her with some skepticism.

"Yes, yes, thanks, many thanks." She tried to play down her embarrassment. "I think I should go home now."

"I'll follow you in my car. I don't want anything to happen to you."

She felt too confused to protest. The familiarity of the instruments in the car helped calm her. In the rearview mirror, she saw Telford's pickup. Who was this man? Four days ago she didn't even know him, and now she had gone through two disturbing events with him.

When she parked her car next to Savannah's in front of the house, Reed's pickup had disappeared. He must have turned around discreetly. Savannah stepped out in front of the main door. She was in a short-sleeved shirt, despite the cold, clear evening air.

"Mom is already sleeping," she said, as Tessa walked toward the house. "Just go on in. I'll bring the dogs in and then I'll drive home."

That was music to Tessa's ears. Some breathing room from Savannah's suffocating constant presence. She entered the house and her father came down from upstairs.

"Anything new about Fran?" she asked hopefully.

He shook his head. "I just called the police station. All they would say is that they had some tips they were following up on, but couldn't say anything about it yet."

Savannah silently let the dogs into the house and closed the door behind her. Her father stood on the steps and looked at Tessa questioningly.

She shrugged. "I'll take the dogs with me tomorrow when we go out on the search for Fran. Maybe they'll put us on the right track." She realized that she was desperately grasping at straws.

Her father wrinkled his brow. "Those dogs are not bloodhounds. They will just get in your way."

She followed him into the kitchen with wobbly knees. "I've got to have something to eat. That soup I had for supper didn't do the trick."

As she warmed up some leftovers and sat down, she told her father in a muted voice about her encounter with Telford Reed and the grizzly. Suddenly a thought popped into her brain. She reached into the pocket of the jacket she hadn't taken off because she was still cold.

She didn't hear her father's reply, because her head had begun to play tricks on her.

The pistol wasn't there.

20

"I'll be right back. I have to get something from the car," Tessa said hastily and ran outside.

She searched the Pathfinder, using her flashlight to look into every corner, but she couldn't find the pistol. Only reluctantly, she gave up her search. She really didn't have the energy to go back to the park in the dark.

"Lionel just called," her father told her when she came into the house. "Tomorrow at eight o'clock in the morning, he'll be here. Before the search begins, he wants to talk with you."

She nodded, exhausted. "It's better if I just go to sleep now." She kissed him on the cheek. "You should also get some sleep, Dad."

He held tightly to the banister. "I feel like if I sleep I'm betraying Fran. How can I sleep when she's in danger? " His eyes teared up.

"Oh, Dad." She put her arms around him. "I get it." She struggled for words, for something to give them some strength. She couldn't think of anything. Silently they climbed the stairs, the dogs behind them. When Tessa went into her room, the cats jumped anxiously off the bed, where they had made themselves comfortable. She talked to them gently. Later, half-asleep, her hand felt soft fur on the bed cover.

Although she had taken a sleeping pill, Tessa woke up early after a fitful sleep. At dawn she left the dogs, that were happily wagging their tails, in the quiet house, and drove to Tennigan Park. She stopped the Pathfinder at the same spot where she and Telford had stood the previous evening, and searched the ground around it carefully. Nothing. She kept glancing around so she wouldn't miss any movement in the bush. The bear couldn't be far from the bait.

With all her strength, she tried to concentrate. She couldn't have lost the pistol on the trail because she had kept her hand on the weapon in her pocket the whole time, afraid that the bear would show up again. She remembered that clearly. The only time she had used both her hands was when she got the dogs back into the car.

She took a deep breath.

What about when Telford Reed held her tightly? When she was shivering so much. Could the pistol have fallen out? She had to ask him. Somehow she had to get his telephone number.

Savannah! She had let the dogs out of the Pathfinder the night before. But if Savannah had found the pistol in the car, she would have certainly been dramatic about it. She was a gossip, not someone who could keep a secret.

Tessa walked again around the parking area. A couple of surprised birds flew over her. She looked at her watch. Time to go back. Almost as soon as she left Tennigan Park, she ran into the park ranger's pickup. Telford Reed must have told the ranger what had happened with the bear. In the rearview mirror, she saw him turn into the park. She should inform him about the lost pistol. If he found it, he would of course inform the police. It was her responsibility to do that before he did. She slowed down in order to turn the car around. But then she changed her mind. If she told the police about the lost pistol, she would have to fill out a bunch of forms. She already could imagine herself at the police station, waiting in a long line. The police could even take away her license because she had been careless with the weapon. She would miss the search for Fran—something she absolutely didn't want.

So far nobody knew she had lost her pistol. Maybe that was good thing: later she could claim that she hadn't yet noticed the weapon was missing. She had to hurry: Lionel Miller was certainly waiting for her. Her parents had no idea where she was. She stepped on the gas. As she drove up the hill to her parents' home, she saw a bunch of cars in front of the house, also a police car. She found the whole crowd in the kitchen: her parents, Savannah, Lionel Miller, and the policewoman Tessa recognized from her previous visit. The two dogs kept them company. There was a map of the area lying on the table.

"It's good that you're here," Lionel called out. "We're just talking about how we're going to organize the groups for the search."

Tessa took a look at the map on which somebody had drawn circles. Nobody asked where she had been.

"Are you also going to take part?" the policewoman asked.

"Yes, indeed." Tessa studied the map. All of the circles were in the area around Whatou Lake. None were near Fran's house. "What were your criteria when you made these circles, corporal?" she asked.

"Those are the areas of special interest for us," the officer answered.

Tessa wrinkled her nose. "You think Fran is somewhere around Whatou Lake?"

"We're not eliminating any options." The police officer looked directly at Tessa. "We think that in the circled areas, searching will be very useful."

"More than a hundred people will be on this search," her

mother called out from the other end of the table. "People really want to help us."

"That's fine, Mom. I'm just asking myself whether all of them know how to act in the bush."

Her objection was directed at the RCMP officer, but Lionel immediately had something to say. "We have a dozen people in every group. At least two per group are carrying a weapon for emergencies. Every group has a leader who knows his way around in the bush. Or her way."

Tessa looked at her father. So far he hadn't said a thing. Savannah, too, had been suspiciously quiet. In order to protect her mother, Tessa didn't ask the question she had on the tip of her tongue: *What are we really looking for? A corpse? Or a missing person? Is there anything in particular we should be looking for?*

The RCMP officer got up. "Mayor Miller is organizing the local volunteers at town hall. All of them should be there by nine o'clock. I'm taking off right now." She patted the husky's back and pushed him away from her pants.

Suddenly Kenneth Griffins spoke up. "I hope that Harrison Miller knows who he can send off with a weapon and who he can't. We have no idea who the murderer is, and my grandchildren and their father were shot dead. It could well be that the murderer is among us."

It was quiet for several seconds. Then Savannah said: "Or the *murderers*."

"Now you have all gone crazy!" Martha Griffins shook her head. "You really don't want to call off the search now. You can't look at everybody as a suspect."

Savannah, who sat next to her, calmly stroked her hand. "It wasn't meant that way, Mom."

Kenneth Griffins crossed his arms and fell silent.

Tessa knew that it was time for her to step in and try to defuse the situation. But she didn't want to oppose her father's statement. He wasn't wrong.

Lionel stepped in. "This is no time to dredge up your

differences with my father, Ken. We all have to pull together now. We want to find Fran as fast as we can. That must be our priority."

The police officer piped up again. "Our people are working around the clock, and we are very pleased to get your help. We know that we can count on you, right?"

"On me for sure," Savannah called out.

Tessa looked the police officer straight in the eye. "Absolutely, corporal," she replied.

As soon as the policewoman had left the house, Martha Griffins began to protest: "Savannah, you can't leave me alone today. I need you here. They have enough people, so it doesn't matter if—"

"We've already discussed that, dear," Kenneth Griffins interrupted. "It's important that Savannah goes on the search. Otherwise she would be very uneasy."

"But I . . ."

Lionel noisily pulled his chair back and got up. "Martha, Ken is right: every person counts. This is our chance. Time is of the essence."

"I'm just going to take the dogs out quickly," Savannah muttered, apparently wanting to get out of the discussion.

Tessa stretched out her arm to her mother; she had gotten up and tried to push her way past her. "Mom, you'll be well taken care of here, and we'll be back this evening."

Her mother touched her hand only briefly and left the kitchen.

"Just let it go. I'll talk to her," her father said reassuringly, and then followed his wife.

Tessa looked at Lionel. "My poor parents. It's tearing them up." She quickly added: "You must be having a tough time, too."

What she said must have broken down his protective wall, since a tortured look appeared on his face. As if he was about to break out into tears. Then, just as quickly, he put up the wall again. Neither of them could afford to lose it.

He turned around and folded up the map.

"Wait," she said, and he spread out the map again. She looked at the circles. Suddenly she started sweating. One of the circles included Tennigan Park.

"Why do you want to search the campground at Tennigan Park?"

"Why not?" Lionel started folding up the map again, until she managed to stop him.

"I've heard that an aggressive bear has been seen at Tennigan Park."

"In any case, that's not where we're going to be searching for the time being," he answered without looking up, as he put his cell phone and the map away. "So we'll be seeing you in an hour?"

He was obviously in a hurry, but she wanted to make use of the minutes alone with him. "What do you think happened to Fran? Who and what is behind these murders? Do you have a suspicion?"

He hesitated. For a moment he looked out into space. Then he let out a deep sigh. "Hank told me a couple of weeks ago that there were active poachers around. He said that grizzlies they could usually count on to appear for the tourists were no longer being spotted around the lodge. I said: Man, does the ranger know about this? And the police? He said he couldn't tell them about it. I couldn't understand why. And he didn't want to tell me under any condition."

Tessa was tempted to alert him to Telford Reed's report, but she knew she didn't have enough time.

"Do you think Hank and the kids were killed by poachers? And Fran? What did they do with Fran?"

"Goddammit, I don't know, Tessa. It's crazy. Absolutely crazy. How do *you* think we should proceed in order to make some progress on this?" She could hear the same desperation in his voice that she could feel within herself.

She looked out the open kitchen door. From upstairs she

heard mumbling. Lowering her voice, she said: "Fran wanted to move away. With everyone—her, Hank, and the children. She wanted to move to a farm in Grouse Valley."

Lionel looked at her in amazement. "Who . . . who told you that load of crap?"

"Two different people who are very credible told me that."

"Who?"

"Maybe they just wanted to flee," Tessa whispered quickly, because she heard noises from the open door.

Lionel kept staring at her when the dogs came running into the kitchen, followed by Savannah.

"If I didn't look after the dogs, nobody would." She shot a taunting look at Tessa. "Why didn't you let them out this morning?"

Tessa was annoyed, even though she had to admit to herself that Savannah had a point. "Dad says Harrison wants to have the dogs," she blurted out. "Has he told you that, Lionel?"

He had just gone out into the hall and turned around again. "He should really forget that," he growled. "This is out of the question." Without saying good-bye, he turned on his heel and slammed the door.

Tessa looked at Savannah and shrugged.

Savannah started the coffee machine. "We don't have much time anymore. We have to be at the meeting place soon."

"Which meeting place? And who is *we*?"

"Didn't Lionel tell you anything?"

Tessa gave her an annoyed look. Savannah filled up a jug with hot milk and put it on the table. "You, me, Lionel, and Cliff Bight make up group nine."

"That can't be; each group consists of a dozen people. Lionel just said that."

"Yes, eight groups of twelve. And we're the extras. Don't ask me why." She slammed the lid of the coffee machine down. "Lionel explained that this morning. I think he had something special in mind for us and wanted to keep the group small. But you weren't here yet. Where did you go off to?"

Tessa ignored the question. "So where are we going to meet?"

"At the trailhead."

"Which trail?"

"The one to Whitesand Bay."

21

An hour later, Tessa found herself with Savannah, Lionel, and Cliff Bight at the edge of the forest outside of Whatou Lake. They hadn't run into the other groups Harrison Miller had assembled at town hall. Tessa had protested against the fact that she of all people had been sent out to search around Whitesand Bay. Lionel convinced her to stop her complaining, when he declared, "Don't make it look as if you had something to hide." Tessa felt she was a victim of a conspiracy. But in light of the murders and their fears about Fran, it would have seemed really coldhearted if she had refused to go.

Both Lionel and Cliff were carrying hunting rifles. Savannah threw a meaningful look over at Tessa. Probably she remembered their conversation on the car ride. Tessa had admitted to Savannah that she had lost her pistol.

"Did you see it in the car?" Tessa had asked.

"What, you were running around with a loaded pistol?" Savannah had yelled. "Maybe I should get a hold of one, too!"

When they passed by Whatou Lake, Tessa sent an SMS to Ron Halprin and reported to him the loss of her pistol and the circumstances that led to it. She gave him all the necessary information he needed to identify the weapon. She informed

Boyd Shenkar as well, because her business partner had to know about such things.

Lionel stood next to his wife, Cindy, whose eyes were hidden behind large black sunglasses. Her elegant clothes signaled that she wanted to be fashionable even if she lived in a hole like Whatou Lake. Tessa knew she was being unfair to Lionel's wife, since Cindy owned a high-end clothing boutique and had to dress well all the time. But Tessa never forgot that Cindy was a close friend of Lola Dole, Jenny's mother. Would Cindy tell Lola that, of all people, Tessa would be searching the area where Jenny Dole was supposedly left behind to be torn apart by a grizzly's deadly fangs?

There was no doubt that Cindy didn't want to take part in the search for Fran: she was wearing high-heeled shoes. To Tessa's surprise, Cindy came over, hugged her and whispered into her ear: "I really hope that we find Fran soon." Tessa could smell her sweet perfume.

"Me, too," she answered. In order to cover her unease, she added: "How's Glenda doing?"

Glenda Miller, Hank's mother and Breena, Kayley, and Clyde's grandmother, had been against the marriage of her favorite son, Hank, to the former foster child Fran, even more than her husband. She was, on the other hand, happy to have Cindy, with her upper-middle-class parents, as a daughter-in-law. Fate took its revenge when Fran had one child after another, while Cindy and Lionel had none. But Glenda did not get to see the grandchildren very much because Fran preferred to bring them to Martha Griffins. She did this for some years, until Fran, during the last couple of months, didn't show up at Martha's, either. What had happened between her and Fran?

The expression on Cindy's face turned sad. "Glenda doesn't come out of her bedroom anymore. I do my best to help her. But Lionel also needs me, everything is on his shoulders."

With these last words, she turned to her husband, who looked distraught as she hugged him.

Maybe it *is* love, Tessa thought, even if she didn't want to admit it. Cindy could have left Lionel and Whatou Lake behind. *She'd rather be a big fish in a small pond than a little fish in a big pond,* Dana had once remarked sarcastically.

"She didn't hug *me*," Savannah complained to Tessa when Cindy drove away in her chic Mazda Miata. "As if Fran wasn't my sister, too."

I would never have called your relationship to Fran sisterly, Tessa thought.

Lionel and Cliff Bight were wearing hunting clothes and carrying backpacks. Cliff was one of Lionel's workers, a young, sluggish guy with a large, almost bald head. Lionel stepped into his role as the leader of the group. "Tessa, you and Cliff will search the right side of the trail, and Savannah and I will take the left side."

"Are we looking for something specific?" Savannah asked.

Lionel remained vague. "Whatever you find, take it with you. Or raise the alarm with the whistle. But don't forget to put on rubber gloves before photographing or touching anything."

He had equipped them with gloves, plastic bags, and whistles.

Tessa didn't find his leadership convincing, but she held her tongue. Should they really remove evidence from the site that might help the investigators? She knew that the police had already searched the path with dogs, after Fran's bloody jacket showed up in Whitesand Bay. What did the investigators, with the help of volunteer searchers, hope to find that hadn't been found the first time they looked?

It's quite possible that Fran was in Whitesand Bay. She wanted to find proof.

Tessa regretted not asking her mother what she meant by her remark. Proof of what?

"Hey, let's go," Lionel called out. "And don't forget to talk loudly; we don't want any problems with bears."

He didn't have to tell Savannah that twice. She cackled and followed Lionel into the rain forest.

Cliff Bight, on the other hand, remained quiet as they searched the area next to the trail. Roots, bushes, giant ferns, broken rocks, and turned-over tree stumps got in their way. They had to push low moss-covered branches out of their faces and watch out for deep holes in the ground. But even now, she couldn't resist the magic of the rain forest. She loved the aroma of wet cedars and natural decay, the mix of living and dying vegetation. New tree trunks that grew on top of the old ones and drew nourishment from their wood. The gigantic ripped-out roots of fallen cedars or pines knocked down by storms. Their roots seemed to be as big as the paddlewheels of steamboats. But the chaos also took away Tessa's confidence. How could they find anything in this enormous tangled wilderness? *Give me a sign, Fran. Please give me a sign.*

Cliff dragged his massive body with the help of a hiking stick through thorny bushes and heaved it with difficulty over dead trees lying in his way. He still hadn't said a word, probably because he was too shy or afraid that he would say the wrong thing. She wanted to break the ice and shouted over to him: "I'm really impressed that you're helping us out here, Cliff. Our family appreciates the support."

"Oh, there's no need to thank me." Cliff brushed the comment off and came closer. "Everybody is totally shocked. We really can't believe that something like this could happen in Whatou Lake."

"What are people saying in Whatou Lake?"

"Not much. Other than . . ." He seemed to be a bit out of breath. "I think a lot of people find it dangerous to live so far out in the bush. I mean . . . you don't have any neighbors or nothing."

Tessa was tempted to point out to him that there were many more murders in Vancouver, although people lived right next to each other and almost all people had neighbors. But she didn't want to make Cliff feel uncertain.

"So that's what people in Whatou Lake found remarkable?"

she repeated, using the same questioning technique she often used as a lawyer. "Don't a lot of people out here have a hut in the wilderness in order to get out of town and away from other people?"

"Unfortunately, I don't have one," Cliff admitted.

"But, for instance, Lionel and Cindy do."

"Yes, they're renovating it right now, and I'm helping them with it."

Tessa had heard about it. Lionel had been out there in his hut on the day of the murders, along with Cindy and Cliff. Lionel tortured himself with the thought that on that day he had been in the wilderness and couldn't be reached by anyone. He tearfully admitted to Martha Griffins that it was possible that Hank or maybe Fran had tried in vain to reach him. Tessa sensed that this guilty feeling would follow him as long as he lived. Although most likely it didn't make any difference where he had been at the time.

She and Cliff stopped and let their eyes wander over the surrounding area. Lionel and Savannah had progressed more quickly, their voices reaching them from some distance off. Tessa picked up the thread again. "Have people found anything else remarkable?"

Cliff cleared his throat. His face was red due to his exhausting efforts.

"Fran was . . . I mean, it's just that I've heard such things . . . She was against almost everything—against the mine, against the oil pipelines and all that stuff."

They climbed over a crumbling tree trunk that had become as soft as a sponge because of the endless high humidity. Tessa slid down and landed on her bum. She got up and rubbed away the dirt from her North Face pants. "That certainly wouldn't have impressed many people," she said carefully.

Cliff nodded. "The people here have to make their living somehow. It's already hard enough the way it is. You never know how long you'll have a job."

"But you don't really have any reason to worry about that. I assume that you're a really good electrician if Lionel hired you."

Cliff smiled, but it wasn't really a strong smile. "If there is no work anymore, even the best have to go."

"As long as the mines are running, business must certainly be good," Tessa said while scouring the ground.

"The big companies bring in their own electricians," he explained between loud panting. "They don't want us."

"Is there enough work for you in Whatou Lake?"

Cliff didn't want to answer that. It seemed to Tessa that it was a good idea to let it go. He had maybe already told her more than he wanted to. They worked their way through the woods slowly but steadily. All they could hear from Lionel and Savannah was a quiet murmuring from far off. After a while Tessa reached for her water bottle. Cliff had a Coke in his hands.

Up till now they hadn't found anything at all, not even a beer can or a chocolate bar wrapper. Very few people used this trail; most townspeople traveled on the dirt road with their ATVs and pickups to Whitesand Bay. There was also no real reason to disappear into the bush, not even to take a dump. It was easier to take care of that right next to the trail. But Lionel wanted to search the dirt road only after they had returned from the bush.

Suddenly Cliff spoke up. "Melanie Pleeke is an odd character. She wanted to bring along a soothsayer."

"Melanie who?" Tessa wiped off her face with a handkerchief.

"Melanie Pleeke."

"I don't know her."

"Rob Pleeke's wife."

"Aha."

She remembered: the director of the funeral home, where Fran had looked at coffins.

Cliff leaned over and supported himself on his hiking stick. "Melanie believes in spirits and séances and communicating with the afterworld. That's her specialty."

"She thinks she's a medium?"

At that moment they heard loud shouting through the bush. Tessa couldn't understand any words. Then she heard a whistle. Cliff stood straight up and braced himself with his pole.

"What the hell . . ."

A shot rang out through the forest.

22

Silence. Then bloodcurdling howling. Tessa sprinted off immediately in the direction of the noise. It was only after she reached the trail that she realized she had to wait for Cliff. She didn't have a gun. Cliff came from behind, panting after trying to keep up with her.

"Lionel! Lionel! Where are you?" she yelled.

"Here!" It was Savannah's voice. "We're over here!"

They couldn't be far away.

The trail snaked its way past giant cedar trees, and suddenly a group of several people appeared in front of them: Lionel, squatting grimly on the ground, Savannah, crouching over his leg, and two young men with war paint on their faces, who stared at them. Two young Sitklat'l. Tessa saw right away that they were not the ones who had fired the shot, since they didn't have any weapons with them.

"What's going on here?" she called out even before she reached the group.

Savannah looked up and said, "Lionel shot himself in the foot."

"What?" Tessa dropped immediately to her knees and looked over his wound, which was bleeding profusely. She grabbed the first aid kit, which lay on the ground, took out a sterile bandage, and started to clean the wound. "Looks like the shot grazed you," she said. "We'll put some pressure on it."

Savannah helped her dress the foot. They worked fluidly, since each was already familiar with the way it was done. After all, they had grown up together in a doctor's household. Lionel complained bitterly. Tessa gave him a strong painkiller.

"Watch out when you're fooling around with these shitty guns, man." The warning came from one of the young Sitklat'l and was aimed at Cliff Bight. "Otherwise another accident like that is going to happen."

"Man, how's that possible?" Cliff asked.

"Whiteys don't know how to use guns."

Tessa could hear the disdain in the young Sitklat'l's voice.

Lionel reacted immediately to the provocation. "It's not my weapon, goddammit. It's my father's."

Tessa looked over at Savannah to see how she was reacting to all this, and saw her looking concerned while shaking her head. "He heard something in the bush and quickly released the safety latch on the gun. Then these two guys broke through the undergrowth," she added with an almost invisible nod of her head in the direction of where the two young men stood, "and Lionel stumbled, and that's when the shot went off."

Tessa looked on, disgruntled. "That's just what we didn't need."

Savannah finished with the bandaging. "You can say that again."

Tessa got up and looked over at the two young men. "I'm Tessa. Kenneth Griffins, the local doctor, is my father. These people here are Savannah Cutter, Lionel Miller, and Cliff Bight. Who are you guys?"

The two gave their names in the Sitklat'l language. The only word she understood was Xhah, meaning *eagle*, a word Tsaytis Chelin had taught her.

"And what are your English names?"

"That's none of your business," one of them said.

"Maybe it is. What are you doing here?" She had a good idea what the answer was. A group of rebellious young Sitklat'l had been patrolling the area for some time, in order to enhance their land claims on the territory of their ancestors.

The two Sitklat'l looked at her provocatively. "What are you whiteys doing here?"

"We're searching for Fran Miller, who has been missing for three days," Tessa quietly replied. "Her three children and her husband, Hank Miller, were shot dead on their farm on Tuesday morning. You must have heard about this. Have you seen anything suspicious?"

"Yes, too many cops around Whitesand Bay, near sacred gravesites of our people. Nobody should be searching there."

"I know about the sacred gravesites of your ancestors. But somebody found Fran's bloodstained jacket at Jenny Dole's memorial cross. That's why the police are there. And that's why we're here. So you haven't found anything?"

They avoided looking her in the eye. She had the impression that they were beginning to understand the gravity of the situation.

Lionel tried to get up with Savannah's help, but sank down again with a pitiful groan. "I can't walk."

"We'll support you," Cliff said.

Lionel shook his head. "I can't put any weight on my foot."

"Shit," Savannah said, and Tessa could have said exactly the same thing. "We're at least an hour away from the car."

For a few seconds, they all just stood there, and nobody said anything.

Finally one of the Sitklat'l spoke up: "We're going to build a stretcher. We'll carry you back."

"Lionel's heavy," Savannah protested.

The young men grinned. "We're not weaklings like the whiteys."

It took them only twenty minutes to make a stretcher of

branches and lianas with their bush knives. Then, with Cliff's and Savannah's help, they laid Lionel on the stretcher.

"Tessa, you run ahead to see if you can get some help," Lionel ordered. "You're the fastest of us."

Before she could answer, Savannah insisted: "I'm going with you."

Tessa shook her head. "In an emergency, it's always better to stick together and not separate."

Lionel was insistent. "Not in our situation."

"We don't have a gun."

"You can have mine," Lionel replied. "I guarantee that it's working fine."

Nobody dared to laugh.

Lionel passed the rifle to Savannah and gave her some instructions on how it worked.

She nodded. "I understand. Let's go." Tessa stopped resisting and let Savannah take the lead. She wanted to keep an eye on the gun. Savannah set a remarkable pace for a nonathletic person, but that didn't stop her from talking. At first Tessa had trouble understanding her from behind, and it took a while for her to realize that she was talking about Lionel.

"If you ask me, Lionel shouldn't be carrying a gun." Savannah snorted audibly. "He's at the end of his rope. He's seeing the dead children and Hank, who has a bullet in his body, and he's ready to explode. He's close to a nervous breakdown."

"Lionel has not seen the children or Hank's bodies, as far as I know."

"Man, I only mean he sees it in his . . . imagination. It's doing him in."

"It's doing us all in. Maybe not you, though?"

Savannah stopped and looked at her in a strange way, as if Tessa had taken her by surprise.

Then she went on: "We can go home and howl, and he can't do that. Cindy wouldn't stand for it." She started walking fast again, but this time Tessa stayed at her side so that she could hear her better. Savannah's dramatic speech provoked her.

"You don't say. Do you really know Cindy that well? Do you have some kind of secret access to Lionel's married life?"

"For God's sake, Tessa. Stop playing the role of a big-city big shot. You weren't born with the silver spoon of wisdom on your plate."

"I'm really happy that *you* were born with it. Please explain to me what has escaped my brain because of my ignorance."

"Open your bloody eyes, woman. You just don't see what's happening."

At that moment Savannah tripped over a root, and Tessa caught her in time to stop her from falling. If the situation had been different, they could have laughed at this. They looked at each other, and Tessa asked, shaking her head: "You do have the gun locked, right?"

Savannah rolled her eyes. "Of course. How dumb do you think I am?" She turned around and marched ahead again.

Tessa decided not to reply, but Savannah's words went through her head for quite a while. She felt sorry for Lionel. He really couldn't cry in front of his parents, now that he was the only son. Tessa had to admit that she at least had Savannah's help, since she was taking care of her mother and father. And the cats and dogs.

But she had noticed something. She found it strange that Savannah didn't seem particularly disturbed or shattered by the murders and Fran's disappearance. This thought suddenly took hold of her like a virus. She stared at Savannah's back and her colorful leggings. An ancient feeling of anger crept up in her and opened its jaws. Tessa couldn't keep it under control.

"Are you really sorry about all that's happened? Or are you happy Fran is no longer in the running?"

Savannah stopped so suddenly that Tessa almost bumped into her. "What? What did you just say?" She stood there with her mouth wide open, as her red lips formed an angry circle. Like a fish out of water and struggling for air. When Tessa didn't say anything, she yelled: "You must be crazy! You don't know what you're saying." She took a step backward. "You have no idea. Fran didn't want to have anything to do with Mom and Dad anymore. That's the way it was. You should talk with Mom about it. But your time is too valuable for that, right? You'd rather be the great lawyer and talk to your equals. We're just not highbred enough." She took a deep breath, and her face got even redder. "Fran isn't dead; maybe *you* would like to see her dead. She took away handsome Hank; you probably still haven't digested that with an ego like yours."

Now it was Tessa's turn to silently glower at her foster sister. Then she raised her hand, gave her a slap in the face, and ran off. She hopped across the uneven forest floor as if it were a minefield. She concentrated only on keeping her feet on the trail ahead of her. She wasn't afraid of bears or wolves. She was completely fueled by anger.

After she had run a ways, she came back to her senses. She was ashamed. How could she let herself be so provoked by Savannah? How could she let such stuff play any kind of role when she was faced with the unimaginable tragedy threatening to tear apart her family? Could the murderer have also done what he did out of an uncontrollable impulse, like the one that led her to strike Savannah? Had the murderer gotten so mad for some reason that he started shooting? She thought about the children and abandoned the idea. Whoever shot the children did it with a plan. The killer ambushed them in the house, one after the other.

She pushed her way forward. *Tessa, don't give up. This is not the time to give up.*

It couldn't be much farther to the trailhead where they had started out more than an hour earlier. She stopped and checked to see whether she had cell phone reception. Nothing.

She couldn't just let Savannah carry on alone. So she turned around and started back. She called out Savannah's name over and over. When she heard her voice, she stopped.

All of a sudden, she saw something on the ground. A colorful stripe. Pink and glittery. She bent down and picked the thing up. She couldn't believe what she held in her hand.

Right then, Savannah popped up.

"Look what I just found," Tessa called out.

Savannah stopped in front of her. "You don't have the latex gloves on."

"What?" Tessa emerged from a dreamlike state.

"The latex gloves. Because of the fingerprints."

Shit.

Under other circumstances, she might have gotten mad that Savannah had recognized something she had missed. But now, with her discovery right in front of her eyes, she could only reply: "You're right."

Tessa took the gloves and a plastic bag out of her fanny pack and dropped the pink band into the bag.

"A cat collar."

Savannah wrinkled her brow. "So?"

"It belongs to one of Fran's cats," Tessa exclaimed. "You've seen the collars of the other cats? One is bright green, the other is yellow. And this one is pink. Don't you see? Here!" She turned the plastic bag over. On the back side of the collar, dark stains could be seen. And a name written in ink: *ROSIE.*

"Rosie wasn't in the storeroom of Fran's house. We couldn't find her anywhere when we were there. And now this shows up out here!"

"Holy mackerel. How the hell did it get out here?"

"I have no idea. First Fran's jacket and now this," Tessa said. "The dark stains. I'm sure that's blood . . ."

"For God's sake, Tessa. Fran would never have taken a cat way out here."

Tessa didn't say anything. She had asked Fran for a sign. And then she found this collar. She didn't know what to think. Maybe Fran had had the collar with her by chance and let it fall, as a clue for people searching for her? Was Fran somewhere nearby? Tessa put the plastic bag with the collar in her fanny pack and closed the zipper. "We've got to get back to the car as fast as possible."

Finally, her cell phoned signaled reception, and she called an ambulance. She also called Ron Halprin and told him about Lionel's injury and the arrival of the two Sitklat'l. Then she informed him about her remarkable find.

A short pause followed after she had finished her report. "We've also found something," she heard Halprin say, after what seemed an eternity, and the tone of his voice made her think that it wasn't good news. "Your pistol."

23

There was one thing about Savannah that Tessa had to admit. She did not hold grudges. Or maybe she found it best to not play games with Tessa. "I'll drive you to the police station," she offered right away, when Tessa told her the pistol had been found. On the way to Whatou Lake, a red Mazda Miata passed them from the other direction.

"Wow, you're back already," Cindy noted as she stopped and Savannah also rolled down her window. "Where are the others?" she asked. "Where's Lionel?"

Tessa and Savannah exchanged glances. Cindy obviously didn't know anything. They had forgotten to call Lionel's wife and tell her what had happened. Savannah cleared it all up and ended with: "We ran ahead and called the ambulance. And the police."

"Why didn't anybody call *me*?"

"Well, we forgot. We're in a big hurry, Cindy. The police want to speak with Tessa as soon as possible."

Tessa would have preferred for Savannah to skip that part, since Cindy dug right in.

"Why do the police want to talk with Tessa? Is there news?"

"No idea. They're talking with a lot of people. Weren't they also at your place?"

Cindy ignored Savannah's question. "When will the group with Lionel arrive?"

"It'll take a little while. Maybe an hour. So long." Savannah waved and stepped on the gas. "She doesn't exactly look very unhappy," she remarked after they had put some kilometers behind them.

Tessa looked over at her in surprise.

"I don't understand you. Cindy didn't look pleased at all."

"Lionel can't take part in the search for Fran anymore. She'll certainly be happy about that."

"Why do you say that?"

"Cindy keeps him on a short leash. She always wants to know what he's up to."

Tessa turned off the music Savannah always had on.

"I'm surprised that Cindy didn't pack her bags and get out of here a long time ago."

"Why should she? She's got everything she needs here. Her own shop, a nice house, and girlfriends like Lola Dole. And she might just go into politics."

"What? Cindy? You can't be serious?"

Savannah gave her a sideways glance. "Aren't you in favor of women getting involved in politics?"

Tessa didn't answer. She'd had enough of Savannah's annoying quips. Deep down she was still furious at her about the Hank comment. It was Savannah who had spread the rumors about a fling between Hank and Tessa, after he had begun popping up with increasing frequency at the Griffins' home. In reality, he wasn't at all interested in Tessa, but Fran was a different matter. The two of them were perfectly happy to have people believe that Tessa was the object of Hank's desire, as this meant they didn't have to put up with Hank's parents, who would have certainly forbidden him to visit the Griffins if they had gotten wind of

Hank's real love interest, Fran. This also had positive implications for Tessa: nobody cared about her growing attraction to Tsaytis Chelin.

At some point, Savannah must have figured out that Hank and Fran were a couple. She began to spread the story that Fran had stolen Hank from Tessa. For Fran, that made it even more difficult to be accepted as Hank's girlfriend. Kenneth and Martha Griffins were the only ones who showed full support for the two of them, when the relationship was no longer a secret.

Later on Tessa often asked herself how her parents would have reacted if their only biological daughter had shown up one day hand-in-hand with Tsaytis Chelin. Martha and Kenneth were very interested in the Sitklat'l culture. But would they have advised her against such a relationship? Would they have warned her about the social and cultural barriers? Tessa didn't have to deal with that, because suddenly Tsaytis didn't want to have anything more to do with the world of the whiteys. He had found himself a First Nations girlfriend. Neither he nor Tessa could have imagined that the bond of friendship between them would nevertheless survive. Until it came to the big fight.

"Tessa, are you listening to me?" Savannah's voice sounded irritated. "Should I wait for you here? Or should I pick you up somewhere later?"

They were at the police station. "No, no, I will . . . find someone who'll give me a lift," Tessa replied.

Once again she regretted not having made a reservation for a rental car at the airport. But the events of the last days had simply overwhelmed her. This was already her third day at Whatou Lake.

Tessa opened the car door and got out. "Thanks," she said, as she hurried up the stairs to the police station. It was only when she reached Halprin's office that she realized how dirty her pants were. When she saw the sergeant leaning on his desk with a big mug of coffee, her dark thoughts flew away. An unexpected feeling of warmth overpowered her. His shirt was rumpled and his pants were covered with dirt, just like hers. The poor guy had probably been up all night working. She could tell from looking at his light-blue eyes though that he didn't miss a thing. His gaze velcroed onto her.

He pointed at the chair as he sat down across from her and measured her carefully.

"Let's begin. What did you find?"

She pulled out the plastic bag with the cat collar from her fanny pack and put it down in front of him. "This belonged to the cat we haven't been able to find. Rosie. Look here. Her name is written on it."

"Where did you find it?"

"On the trail to Whitesand Bay, maybe ten minutes from the trailhead. I think there are bloodstains on it."

He turned the bag around in his hand and then looked again directly at her. "Who was there when you found it?"

"Nobody. I . . . Later Savannah came. Savannah Cutter. I was running ahead to alert the ambulance."

He turned the bag over, checking it out. Then looked at her again. "So there were no witnesses?"

She shook her head. When he looked at her like that, she became uneasy, which irritated and confused her at the same time. "Remarkable, isn't it, to find this cat collar in the woods?"

"Yes, I can't make heads or tails of this. Unless someone wants to lead us on a wild goose chase. The cat could not have gotten there on her own." He said it thoughtfully.

She frowned. Halprin was, of course, right. It was just the way how he worded it that made her nervous. "Do you think somebody let it drop on purpose right where I found it, to put us on the wrong track?"

"It's a possibility. How do *you* explain it?"

She hesitated, then took the offensive. "Do you think it's a possibility that *I* might have done it?"

"Wouldn't you think it possible, if you were in my place?" he answered.

"Theoretically not. But after thinking about it thoroughly, yes."

What kind of discussion had she gotten into? He didn't take notes about what she had said and there was no video camera running. Colleagues came in and out of the room, but none of them sat down.

"We are thorough; you don't have to worry about *that*." He took a piece of paper in his hand and put on a pair of glasses. Suddenly she found him changed. Even more attractive.

"I'm not at all worried about myself, sergeant . . . Ron. I'm worried about Fran. Can you tell me anything new?"

He took off the glasses again. "Why were you carrying a pistol when you met Telford Reed in Tennigan Park?"

She pushed her hair out of her face. It felt damp. The police had already questioned Reed. "I got a pistol two years ago because after one of my trials, which had led to a guilty verdict, I received death threats. I have a valid gun license."

Halprin supported his arm against the armrest, resting his chin in his left hand. "That doesn't really answer my question."

"Is that so unusual? Here in Whatou Lake there are plenty of people who run around with a gun. Many of them have a rifle in their pickup."

"But this is not hunting season."

She sank down into her chair. "I feel more secure when I have one with me, after everything that has happened around here."

"You're afraid of Telford Reed?"

"I hardly know Mr. Reed, and we were meeting in an isolated place."

"Did you make use of the gun?"

She would have liked to know what Reed had told the police. "Yes, a grizzly was threatening us, and I fired shots into the air to drive him off. You must know the rest from Mr. Reed."

"The rest?"

"That we discovered a moose carcass."

"Did that surprise you?"

She nodded. "Yes, of course. Especially here. And as you correctly pointed out, this is not hunting season."

"Was Telford Reed surprised?"

She tried to figure out why he asked this question. Was it all about Reed or about her?

"I had the impression that he was surprised. He told me that they had found such cadavers in other places, where people were often present. Tourists."

"When did you realize that your pistol was missing?"

"Last night. I was already home and I noticed it then. I thought I had it in my jacket pocket, but it wasn't there. I searched through my car and didn't find it there, either."

"Did anybody else have access to your car?"

"Savannah took the dogs out of it. I asked her later, but she hadn't seen anything. At least that's what she told me. This morning I drove out to Tennigan Park again because I suspected that the pistol could have fallen out of my pocket at the parking area. But you must know that already from the ranger."

"From the ranger?" An almost unnoticeable change in the tone of his voice told her that she had just told Halprin something new.

"The ranger's pickup came toward me on the main road. Early in the morning, before eight o'clock. I assumed that Telford Reed had called him about the bear."

Ron Halprin didn't say anything, but he squinted.

"Whatever," she continued. "Before Telford and I reached the parking spot last night, after we ran into the grizzly, I still had the pistol in my pocket, I'm sure of that. This morning I couldn't see it in the park. Can you tell me where you found it?"

"First one more piece of information: We need your fingerprints."

"How come?"

"Purely routine."

Her stomach tensed. This schemozzle she had brought upon herself. "Who found the pistol, Ron, and where?"

"We seized it from someone who had taken it illegally. That's all that I can tell you at the moment." He shoved his writing pad closer. "I would like to know why you met with Telford Reed in the park."

After briefly hesitating, she gave him the information he wanted: "Mr. Reed told me about his meeting with Fran. And that he had informed the police about it. It would be nice if I got that kind of information from you. Didn't you promise me transparency?"

The sergeant leaned forward and put his hands together. "We promised to support each other, you may remember. Part of that means that you don't keep any information from me that might be important. Just what is important, I decide—not you."

"For example?"

He could have angrily replied to this question, but he didn't let himself be provoked. His calmness impressed her.

"Did Fran have health problems?" he asked.

Naturally he already knew the answer, she suspected. "Sometimes she seemed depressed. Sometimes she went to the cabin on Beaver Lake all by herself. Hank built the cabin for her."

"Who looked after the kids, then?" She figured he also knew the answer to that.

"Dana Eckert, as far as I know."

He lifted his eyebrows. She wondered what he made of her answers.

She went on: "A couple of months ago, she apparently withdrew somewhat from my parents. Before that, she had had a very close relationship with them, especially with my mother. But recently it seems that there had been a nasty argument between the two of them. I haven't been able to find out yet what it was about."

Halprin moved his hand along the edge of the table and said smoothly: "Now, about that cabin on Beaver Lake. Our people were there first. The bear showed up before they could lock up the cabin with a chain. They had to escape from the grizzly. A mistake on our side."

"Did you search for the weapon?"

"We searched the cabin thoroughly. We knocked on the floor planks and found a weapon."

"Was it the murder weapon?"

"No."

She closed her eyes for a couple of seconds.

Once again she heard his voice: "So you think that Fran Miller could be the killer?"

She quickly responded: "No, just like *you* don't."

"What gives you that idea?"

"Because if you did, you'd warn the public about her."

He didn't take the bait. She didn't let up. "You've been watching one or more suspects, right?" She hoped that was the case.

He didn't say anything. His fingers were playing with the corner of the writing pad. It occurred to her that she might be one of those being watched.

Halprin looked up. "Did Fran Miller ever meet anyone at the cabin?"

"I doubt it. It was her private retreat. Only in the summer the family would meet together there sometimes."

"And she was ever in the cabin with you?"

"Only once. That was just after it had been built and she wanted to show it to me. We didn't stay there long."

"But she could have met someone there and nobody else would have known?"

"Why do you ask that, Ron?"

"Did Fran have an affair with another man?"

"No, no." Tessa shook her head. "What gives you that idea?"

"We follow up on all the gossip. So you've never had any such suspicion?"

"No, never." Gossip. She was upset. Did Hank's parents spread these kinds of rumors around?

Halprin didn't spend much time on the topic. Suddenly he was more interested in the events during the search near Whitesand Bay.

"Exactly what happened?"

He listened carefully to her description. Occasionally he took down some notes and drank some coffee.

"Were Savannah and Lionel alone when the shot went off? Or did the young Sitklat'l men see what happened?"

"As far as I know, nobody else saw it." She felt she was being squeezed like a lemon of all her energy and would have given a lot for a mug of coffee, like the one Halprin had for himself.

He didn't look as if he was planning on ending his interrogation very soon.

"Is there anything else you know that you think might be helpful to us?"

She made every effort to dig around in her recollections and shifted her eyes in various directions, as if she might come up with something somewhere.

Of course there was still something. She could no longer hide it. She had to stop protecting her parents. There was only one person who had to have protection now: Fran.

"My mother . . . She made a comment to me. She said it didn't surprise her that Fran's jacket was found at Whitesand Bay. Fran was looking for proof there, Mom said. Somebody interrupted us just then, and I haven't had the chance to talk to her again."

He scribbled on his writing pad. When he looked at her, something had changed in his face. She couldn't have said what it was. The brief moment dissolved. Halprin tapped on the table with his pencil. "Is that everything?"

"I would like to know when the autopsy report will be made public."

"The forensic team is still working on it. They will certainly announce it when the report is made public."

"And the police still won't say who was with Tsaytis Chelin when the bodies were discovered?"

"No."

Disappointed, Tessa remained silent.

Ron Halprin leaned back, with his hands on the arms of the chair. "Good, then let's take care of the fingerprinting."

Suddenly she recoiled: She had handled the cat collar without gloves.

24

"What should I do? What would you recommend?"

Tessa sat on a bench in the little green space that lay right in front of the monument for the World War II veterans from Whatou Lake. After the conversation with Ron Halprin, she had come here where she could talk quietly on the phone with her business partner, Boyd Shenkar.

"For the moment there's nothing that you have to do here," Boyd said. "You informed him about the missing pistol. You told him that you had touched the cat collar by mistake. Halprin is no dummy. But just who is this Telford Reed?"

"He holds the outfitter license for the Watershed area. He wants me to help the Sitklat'l by convincing the British Columbia government to give them some financial support to buy the license." She suppressed the memory of Telford's calming embrace after the run-in with the aggressive bear.

"What was your answer?"

"That I didn't feel I was in a position to discuss this option with him."

A lady with two small children approached the bench and kept looking at Tessa. The insatiable nosiness of bored residents in small towns. Tessa got up and tried to find some protection behind the veterans' memorial, which was engraved with the names of the fallen soldiers. A dozen names—that was a lot for the tiny village of Whatou Lake back then.

"Still no sign of Fran . . . or the murderer?"

She told Boyd about the bloodstained jacket.

"That's odd. Both the jacket and the cat collar. Odd finds in odd places. Has Ron Halprin told you anything?"

"No, he keeps things pretty close to the vest."

"It could also be a good sign, Tessa. Maybe they are hot on the heels of somebody and don't want to give out any information that only the murderer could know."

"That's the positive interpretation. I'm not so sure about that. Maybe they are as much in the dark as I am. Halprin asked me if Fran was having an affair. Apparently that was a rumor in town."

"Aha," Boyd commented.

"You find that interesting. It's the worst kind of cliché."

"Not when it comes from Halprin."

"I was disappointed when I heard him come up with this."

"He has plenty of experience to know that such things happen."

"What do you mean by that?"

"Please keep it to yourself, but I heard that Halprin went through a nasty divorce a couple of years ago. Apparently his wife was having an affair."

"Not every wife is like that. In Fran's case, I can't begin to imagine that she would do that." She was overcome with hopelessness. "I really wish that none of this had happened and that I was back in the office in Vancouver with you." She was well aware that this sounded childish and resigned.

But Boyd reacted with complete understanding. "It must be just terrible for you, Tessa. Call me up anytime if you need help."

She thanked him and put the cell phone away. As she headed to Dana's house, she had great difficulty holding back the tears that were trying to well up. She turned into the wind to let it cool her feverish face. She hadn't met anyone on the street and was glad about it. The lady with the two kids had disappeared. People were probably all sitting down for lunch. She still had a sandwich in her jacket pocket. Dana's modest house appeared in front of her. A person was just closing the door to the house. Tessa immediately recognized him by the way he walked.

"Dad!"

He turned around in her direction. She could see that he was as surprised as she was.

"I didn't think that I'd meet you here," she said.

"I . . . Savannah came back home without you. I thought that maybe you needed . . . maybe you were at Dana's. Should I drive you home?"

She hugged him. "Thanks, Dad, but I'd like to visit Dana first. Do you want to come in?" Actually that had not been her intention; she wanted to talk to Dana alone.

He waved her off. "I've got to go . . . to the church. Talk to the minister. Should we meet again later?"

The door opened behind them. "I'll bring her back to you, Ken," Dana said. "So we don't have to keep checking our watches."

Kenneth Griffins nodded in agreement and went back to his Pathfinder.

"Dad has always had this complicated relationship with his cell phone," Tessa remarked as she sat down on Dana's sofa. "He could have phoned me. Or you."

Dana found something to do in the kitchen. "In any case, he has to meet the minister," she answered. "Are you hungry?"

"I still have a sandwich."

"My pea soup would be perfect with that."

"I completely forgot to ask Dad about news. Did he say anything to you?"

"I'm sure that he expected news from *you*. What actually happened today?"

"Savannah's already told him, you can count on that." Tessa summarized what had happened when Lionel shot himself in his foot, as well as the meeting with the two young Sitklat'l. She also mentioned the cat collar.

Dana listened with deep concentration while she filled a bowl with soup and put it down on the table. "Come on, eat. You also stopped by the police station?"

"You already know that?"

"Why are you surprised? Your father was just here."

Tessa turned the soup spoon over in her hand. "Have the police already talked to you?"

Dana broke off a small piece of bannock bread, which she prepared every couple of days in the traditional Sitklat'l way. "Yes, Ron Halprin and another man came by this morning."

"Halprin asked me today about the cabin at Beaver Lake."

They ate silently for a while. Tessa felt like she was in an earthquake: crevasses were opening up all over the place.

She looked down at her soup and suddenly felt tremendously hungry. *In the face of death, my body wants to live, live, live.*

She put down the spoon and looked at Dana.

"Tell me the truth: Was there an affair going on?"

Dana paused for a time. A few heartbeats long. Then she put a piece of bannock in her mouth as if nothing was more important than this. The whole time she looked down.

Tessa tried to hold back her curiosity. "I know that it's a cliché and . . . I hate this nasty rumor, but the police seem to believe that there might be something to it. Do you know anything?"

Dana looked up; she seemed to be confused. "Who are you talking about?"

"Fran, of course. Did she have an affair?"

"Fran? That . . . I cannot imagine. She was devoted to Hank."

"But she was often lonely. And sometimes she was at the cabin on the lake and you took care of the children."

Dana looked at her as if she were nuts. "Are you trying to tell me that I covered for Fran so somebody could meet up with her there?"

"She wouldn't have to say anything to you. You wouldn't have even noticed it." Tessa now slid into the role of the advocatus diaboli.

"You don't believe that yourself, Tessa."

"I'm not asking you this for laughs, Dana. If there really was something going on, it could lead us to Fran."

She noticed how Dana's eyes were wandering around the living room. As if she were remembering confused messages from the past that could now be seen in a new light.

Tessa's heart beat faster.

Dana pursed her lips and said: "What kind of logic is that? Why, then, would she want to move away from here *with* Hank?"

Tessa didn't answer. But the answer hung there like a bad smell between the two of them. *Because she wants to bury her affair.*

"I understand you, Tessa. We're all very mixed up, even if we don't show it outwardly. In a situation like this, you hang onto every last straw."

Tessa nodded. "Cliff Bight told me about the funeral home director's strange wife. Do you know her?"

"Melanie Pleeke is a quack. That woman should be put away."

"She wanted to bring a soothsayer on the search for Fran."

"She's a fraud. I'll make sure she keeps her fingers off this investigation. That's all we needed!"

They both silently kept eating their soup, each one caught up in her own thoughts.

The dishes made a lot of noise when Dana cleared the table. Tessa took the glasses into the kitchen, which as always looked clean and in order.

Except for two soup bowls on the draining rack. Right next to two wineglasses and two spoons. They were still damp.

"What do the police say about the cat collar?" Dana asked.

"I had the impression that Halprin thinks somebody put it there on purpose in order to get us off track. I had to let them take my fingerprints."

"Really? They think you tried to put them on the wrong track?"

"I'm already in trouble. Especially because of what happened with the pistol."

"What pistol?"

Tessa rubbed her cheeks with both hands. She quickly told her friend about what had happened in Tennigan Park. She didn't mention how Telford Reed hugged her.

"I don't know anymore what I should think. I'm exhausted; all kinds of thoughts continually swirl around in my head. And then there's the constant fear of what might have happened to Fran. The frustration that we're not making progress." Tessa supported her head in her hands.

Dana put her arm around her. "My dear child. I know. I know. It's so hard." Tessa let her head rest on Dana's shoulder until her friend said: "Ron Halprin and his people are still optimistic that they will find Fran."

"Dead or alive?"

"They haven't given up on the possibility that they will find her alive."

"And were they nice enough to reveal to you what the basis is for their optimism?"

"They can't reveal that, Tessa. They can't put all their cards on the table."

"No kidding. That's exactly what is driving me crazy. Our time is running out. And we still don't even know who was out there at the farm with Tsaytis Chelin."

"It doesn't surprise me that Tsaytis won't say a thing."

"I'm surprised that the other person hasn't said anything. That person must have a very important motive for not speaking."

"You have probably spent a lot of time guessing who this person . . ."

At this moment Tessa's cell phone rang. She pressed the answer button without looking at the display.

A woman whose voice she could not identify immediately.

"Who's talking?"

"Noreen Chelin."

When she heard the name, she couldn't believe it. Tsaytis's wife.

Tessa's silence didn't make Noreen uncomfortable. "Tessa, I know that this is really hard for you, but I would like to talk to you. Can we meet up as soon as possible?"

Tessa found her voice again. "What's this about?"

"I can't tell you on the phone."

"Is it about Fran? She's the only one that counts at the moment."

"Yes."

"Time is really of the essence, Noreen. If it is important, tell it to the police."

"I've already told them what I know. But there is something I cannot interpret that you may be able to figure out better."

Tessa thought it over quickly. This would be her chance to fly to Watershed Lodge. With the floatplane, it would be a fast trip.

"When does Kratz fly to the lodge?"

"Around one thirty. He picks up passengers at Whatou Lake."

"Tell Kratz that I'm going to fly with him. I'm coming to the lodge."

There was a moment of hesitation. "Do you really want to do that?" Noreen asked.

"Yes, that's best for me."

"Okay, I'll tell Kratz."

Five minutes later Dana raced away from Whatou Lake like a thief on the run. They had to rush not only because of the flight, but to get away from a reporter who had been standing in front of the house and wouldn't leave. In any case, he didn't follow Dana's car, which Tessa confirmed by looking in the rearview mirror.

"I can't believe Noreen called you up. Are you sure it was Noreen?"

"Yes. I want to go to Watershed Lodge anyway. Maybe I can find some crucial information there."

"Do you have any idea what she wants from you?"

"To tell me something about Fran. She didn't want to talk about it on the phone."

Dana looked at her from the side. "How well do you know her?"

"I met her a few times at the university in Vancouver. Tsaytis had a different girlfriend at the time. Noreen was friendly and open, and we talked about Whatou Lake and Telt-shaa. Later Tsaytis broke it off with his first girlfriend and took up with Noreen."

"And here in Whatou Lake?" Dana asked.

"Here I didn't have much to do with her. For the land claims negotiations, she was only active in the background."

"And now she's the boss at Watershed Lodge."

"That's what I've heard."

"For a time Tsaytis and Noreen went their separate ways. I mean, privately. Tsaytis's parents took care of their children. What that says about their relationship now, I don't exactly know."

"Dana, please. Just because Noreen works at the lodge and is rarely at home doesn't mean that they're no longer a pair." She broke off because it seemed strange to her that she was defending Tsaytis and Noreen's marriage. Although she had actually heard the same rumor.

They were at the fork in the road leading to Tessa's parents' house. Dana slowed down the car as she said: "You know that back then there were rumors that . . . you and Tsaytis were a pair."

Tessa fumbled around with her seat belt. "Why don't you simply just say *an affair*? It was a nasty rumor that made the rounds back then, during the land claims hearings. Typical small-town gossip."

Dana remained unmoved. "I just wanted to make sure you knew about it."

"Tsaytis doesn't hook up with white women, Dana. For him there are no women better than the Sitklat'l. And in any case, what does that have to do with Fran and her dead children?"

"They're the reason you're flying to Watershed Lodge, right? I'm sure you're definitely not going to waste your time on a false alarm."

Dana stopped in front of the house behind the ruby-colored Pathfinder and looked at Tessa with affection. "Your instincts have always been really good, Tessa. I hope that they will lead you to Fran. And to her murderer." Tessa felt the emotional warmth that came from Dana. She could see that her friend was holding back her tears. She hugged her and quickly got out.

"Should I wait?" Dana asked.

"No. Dad can take me to the floatplane. Thank you, Dana. You'll hear from me."

It was only when she opened the door to the house and her friend had already driven away that it hit her like a lightning bolt. *Dana said, her murderer. Dana assumes Fran is dead.*

When she got into the kitchen, the two cats greeted her, meowing and rubbing against her legs. They wore their candy-colored collars and seemed to be hungry. She couldn't see or hear the dogs.

She called hello, but didn't get a response. There was a note on the kitchen table in mother's handwriting: *Savannah and I are in Whatou Lake. Another interrogation by the police. Chicken and mashed potatoes are in the fridge.*

Lost in thought, Tessa fed the cats. She suddenly felt ashamed. She had delivered her mother to the police. She had told Halprin about her remark, that Fran had gone to Whitesand Bay in order to find some ominous proof. What she actually should have been doing was protecting her parents from mistakes they might make when talking to the police and the media. Maybe her mother's remark didn't mean anything. Deep down she knew nevertheless that she had to give everything a try. How often had it happened that seemingly unimportant details were overlooked for years, but eventually solved the crime?

She called for her father. Once again, no response. He didn't answer his cell phone, either. He should have been back from talking to the minister, and his car was in front of the house. Maybe he was out in the neighborhood walking the dogs. She packed her backpack for the lodge because she didn't know if she would fly back on the same day. Then she went outside again. The door to the house had not been locked. Not a good idea. She again tried her father's cell phone, but no luck. After some hesitation, she called Savannah, who for some reason had turned off her phone.

Tessa was getting impatient. She thought it over. If her father didn't turn up soon, she'd have no choice but to take the Pathfinder to the floatplane. She stared at the driveway as she saw a dark-blue pickup drive up, one she didn't recognize. A tall, imposing man opened the driver's door. Harrison Miller.

There was one thing she had to give to him: at age fifty-five, he was still very attractive. His wavy dark hair had only turned a bit gray, and his gait was bouncy. He was known equally for his charm and his untrustworthiness. It was no coincidence that he was the long-standing mayor of Whatou Lake.

"Is Ken there?" he asked without greeting her. Who had time for formalities these days?

"No, his car is here, but he's probably out with the dogs."

"When is he coming back?"

She shrugged. "No idea. He was already gone when I arrived."

Harrison Miller thought a bit and then asked: "I'll come around again on my way back. Tell him that. In about an hour."

He was already opening the car door when Tessa called: "Are you going to Whatou Lake? I have to catch the floatplane."

To her amazement, he didn't hesitate a second. "Sure, I'll drive you there."

The trip in his car would be torture. But she couldn't avoid meeting Hank's father forever, and now she would at least have the chance to talk to him alone.

"I'll be ready in two minutes." She ran back into the house.

In the kitchen she hastily wrote two sentences on the piece of paper: *Important meeting in Watershed Lodge. At the latest I'll be back tomorrow at noon.*

25

During the trip to Whatou Lake, Miller's first question was not why she was flying to Watershed Lodge, but rather "Why won't Ken let me have the dogs?"

This question came so unexpectedly that Tessa was almost at a loss for words.

"But he . . . never said that he didn't want to. He was the one . . . at least that's what he told me . . . who said that you'd get the dogs." When Harrison didn't reply, she added: "What makes you think otherwise?"

"I know exactly why he doesn't want to," the mayor retorted as he turned the car onto the main road. "Because the dogs know who the murderer is. They would never have allowed a stranger onto the property."

Tessa needed a couple of seconds in order to understand the implications of what he had said. "So you think that the killer is one of us?"

"How do the police put it? All options must be considered."

As a lawyer, she had known plenty of people who had suffered so deeply and were so angry that they were open to wild speculation to make what was beyond their grasp comprehensible. She was in familiar territory.

"But Hank was there, Harrison," she replied softly. "He held the dogs back. He always did that when visitors came. He locked them in the storage room."

Harrison ignored her argument. "He was shot dead in cold blood. The dogs know who the murderer is. That's why Ken wants to keep the dogs. Maybe he wants to protect the murderer. Or he wants to make it difficult for the police to carry out their investigation."

"He has absolutely no intention of doing that," Tessa responded, realizing that the discussion was leading to a dead end. She tried to change the topic. "Harrison, I spoke with Telford Reed. He—"

The mayor interrupted her in midsentence and said: "That's another crook they should be investigating carefully. It wouldn't surprise me if he had something to do with the murders. He was interested in getting rid of Hank."

Wow. Previously Harrison Miller had been the slippery local politician who was able to manipulate people with his lacquered charm. He executed the backstabbing secretly. But the world he had ruled with an iron fist as the uncrowned emperor had been turned upside down. The homicide investigators from Vancouver now ruled the roost he was used to controlling without competition. Except from the town doctor, Kenneth Griffins. This Griffins man simply wouldn't leave him in peace. The doctor had even gone so far as to saddle Harrison with a daughter-in-law he didn't approve of, especially not as the wife of his oldest son, Hank. And now Tessa had managed to get herself involved in exactly this mess.

She made another attempt to get the discussion on a different track. "What do you have against Telford? Are you mad because of the outfitter license you wanted to buy for Hank? That in any case wouldn't have been a good investment. Hank and Fran wanted to move away from Whatou Lake to settle down on a farm in Grouse Valley."

Harrison Miller got so mad he jammed on the brakes and the

pickup went into a spin. For a moment Tessa thought she would be thrown out of the car. But he got the vehicle back under control and drove on. Tessa was still shaking in her boots. Luckily she was wearing the seat belt, something the people in Whatou Lake rarely wore. The local police were not in the habit of noticing when someone didn't.

Harrison Miller took a deep breath and roared: "Hank did not want to move away. He didn't want to move at all until the Indians began shooting bears. And Tsaytis Chelin and his band didn't do anything about it! That's terrible for business when Indians kill bears. But I'm sure you don't want to know anything about that."

Tessa sat there, stunned. This confrontation had gone even worse than she feared. *He's lost it. Completely lost it.*

She could see his pulse racing through the veins in his temple. His hands were clamped to the steering wheel. But Harrison was not yet finished.

"Fran is in bed with them," he hissed. "It's fine with her if the economy goes belly-up. For her there is only the environment, environment, environment. What are we supposed to live on? I'm telling you. Hank didn't want to move away; it was only Fran who did, and now both of them are dead."

Tessa was frozen with fear. She held fast to her backpack and didn't say anything, in the hope that Harrison would not get even more furious. They were about five hundred meters from where the floatplane was docked. It was only after she had gotten out of the car that she asked through the open door: "All of them are dead? Fran, too?"

An evil grin spread across his face. "Not necessarily. Why don't you ask your father where he's hidden her so she can't reveal anything?" He put the car into drive. "The police have no doubt already questioned him about it."

With a loud bang, she slammed the door of the pickup.

Harrison Miller drove off with squealing tires.

She stopped where she was and took a deep breath in order to calm her nerves.

"Was that Harrison?" The voice made her turn around.

Kratz Hilder leaned against the wall of the building where he had his office. His firm's logo decorated his baseball cap. *Whatou Wings*. He held a hot dog in one hand and a can of Mountain Dew in the other.

Kratz was a relatively small man, but he was a big-time flyer. As a pilot, there was nobody better than him. Had he heard the end of the conversation between her and Harrison?

The pilot didn't seem to be bothered. "You're coming with us today, Tessa, right?"

"Yes, I just have to run into the office to pay for the ticket."

"We'll be taking off in ten minutes." He cleared his throat. "That's an awful thing that happened with Fran's family. I just can't believe that something like that could happen here."

She was tired of hearing people say this. Kratz probably did feel that way. In his eyes, Whatou Lake was an oasis inhabited by decent, honest people. Earlier, when the land claims hearings were going on, she had often flown with Kratz. She had also helped him to get more money from the government for the care of his disabled daughter.

She shouldered her backpack and turned around once again. "Kratz, in the days before the murders, did you drop anyone off at Whitesand Bay?"

"No, not at Whitesand Bay. But at Beaver Lake."

"Where on the lake?"

"At the north end. "

At Fran's cabin. "Who?"

The pilot looked at his half-eaten hot dog. "Unfortunately I can't tell you, Tessa. The RCMP doesn't want this information to get out."

So Ron Halprin was also in the picture. Didn't have to mean anything. Beaver Lake was very popular with hobby fishermen. But most of them got there on four-wheelers, in pickups, or by

ATV. This time somebody took a plane. Somebody who was in a hurry.

"When was that?"

"On Sunday. No, it's better if I keep my mouth shut."

On Sunday. Two days before the murders. Tessa remained confused. Nothing added up. A flight with Kratz. The murderer wouldn't take such a risk. Maybe it had only been a tourist. She thanked the pilot and went around the corner into the office. Slenka, his wife, was standing behind the counter. She was obviously shocked when she saw Tessa. Most people didn't know how they should react to gruesome events.

Tessa tried to make it easier for her and simply said: "I'm so glad you have room for me so I won't have to lose any valuable time."

Slenka's face didn't relax. "I'm so sorry for you all, Tessa. Hopefully, they'll find Fran soon. This waiting . . . must be terrible."

"Anything that helps to find Fran is worth gold, Slenka. I've been wondering why strangers are flying to the north end of Beaver Lake. Fran and Hank have a cabin there."

Slenka disclosed nothing. She printed Tessa's receipt. "I don't understand the police. They have so many people from Vancouver here. And the only thing they've done is to arrest the park ranger."

Tessa stared at her. "They arrested the park ranger?"

"Yes, I heard that half an hour ago. But nobody knows why. It's really crazy."

Tessa pictured the ranger's car coming toward her very early in the morning at Tennigan Park. She had told Ron Halprin about this. Strange.

She took her receipt and quickly left the office. A white-and-yellow floatplane rocked next to the wooden pier. Two suitcases, some packages, and a backpack waited to be put into the plane's baggage hole. A man filled the gas tank.

The sky was gray, but fortunately Tessa could only feel a light wind. Nothing that could disrupt the flight. She clicked on Halprin's number and was sent right to voicemail. Nothing worked today with the cell phones. She still hadn't heard anything from Savannah or her father. She decided to send Halprin a text message: *I've heard that the ranger has been arrested. Anything to do with Fran? Flying to Watershed Lodge. Hope to find out more about Fran there.*

The man on the pier waved at her; he wanted her backpack on board. An older couple waiting next to her introduced themselves. American tourists from Nevada. They told her they couldn't wait to get some photos of grizzlies. There was also a woman about Tessa's age waiting to depart. She was wearing a gray jacket and her hiking boots looked expensive. Tessa went up to her.

"You're flying to Watershed Lodge?"

The young woman nodded. "You too?"

"Yes. Nice that the weather is cooperating."

"Do you often take floatplanes?"

"Used to. Not anymore. I lived here until five years ago."

"I have to fly a lot because of my job. You get used to it."

Tessa kept digging: "Are you perhaps the new community nurse for the Sitklat'l?"

"No, I'm a wildlife biologist. My name is Lynn Prett. I'm leading a research project about grizzly bears in the watershed area."

A bear expert. Tessa's interest grew.

"Terrific. Are you from Vancouver?"

"Originally I'm from Port Moody. Now I work for the University of Victoria."

"I'm a lawyer in Vancouver. My name is Tessa Griffins."

The researcher's face tensed up. "But you're not . . ."

"Yes, unfortunately."

"Oh, my God!" Lynn Prett's face strained in shock. "It must be terrible for your family."

"Yes, it is."

The propeller began to move.

They climbed into the small single-engine machine. The tourist from Nevada in the front, the three women in the back. Tessa sat next to Lynn. She fastened her seat belt and put on her headphones, which connected all the passengers.

The floatplane taxied out of the bay and took off. It made a loop and rose higher into the air. Its wings almost seemed to touch the flanks of the coastal mountains. The houses of Whatou Lake looked tiny and insignificant from up above, the mountains like stony giants, from which you could only escape via boat.

Suddenly the scenery changed. The land became flat and the coastal forest overran every piece of ground within its reach. It spared only the lakes and the rivers.

From above, the coast of Whatou Lake looked like a human head seen in profile, with its forehead, nose, and lips. Watershed Lodge was located where the chin met the neck. A fjordlike arm of the Pacific Ocean cut into the neck so that the head looked half-decapitated.

When Tessa let her eye wander over the forest below her, it seemed endless, and she asked herself what RCMP helicopter pilots could possibly discover when they were searching for Fran. It would be easier to find a needle in a haystack than a missing person in this wilderness.

It was loud in the interior of the plane. The American couple bombarded Kratz Hilder with questions, which everyone could hear in their headphones, and the pilot willingly replied.

The tourists didn't know who Lynn Prett was, and the pilot only revealed her identity when the Americans asked questions about the bears. Lynn was perfectly happy to give them interesting bear facts: "We are studying the grizzlies for a project at the University of Victoria: their way of life, mating and breeding, food sources, how they move around in their territory, their social relationships. We have observed, for instance, that the mothers often show up with their young at riverbanks, when tourists are there on the viewing platform. The mother bears do that because then the adult male bears stay away. They can pose a danger to the cubs, because they are vying with them for the attention of the female bears."

This is the case not only among grizzlies, Tessa thought sadly. Human adult males are dangerous for children. Fortunately nobody could read her thoughts; the researcher was in her element and continued talking. "I'll explain all this to you on our tour. You won't be disappointed."

"Aren't you afraid of grizzlies?" one of the tourists asked.

"I have a healthy respect for them, but I'm more afraid of aggressive dogs than of grizzlies," Lynn Prett answered.

Up to now the media had not reported anything about the ranger's arrest or the bears that were killed. Their interest had concentrated solely on the murdered people. Tessa figured that would change as soon as the reporters got wind of it. Maybe they would see a connection between the murders and the dead grizzlies. Tessa wondered whether she should question the young bear researcher. Lynn Prett surely must have given some thought to all these events.

Fifteen minutes later another arm of the ocean came into view, and a large red roof, shaped like a rectangular letter C. This was Watershed Lodge, which consisted of a building with three wings that floated on the water of a sheltered bay. The rain forest surrounded it like a protective wall. Tessa counted a half dozen boats docked at the pier. Kratz's little machine came down. The pontoons rattled across the water. Slowly the plane taxied to the lodge. A man ran out on the wooden pier and tied up the pontoons with a rope. The passengers got out of the plane, and Tessa picked up her backpack. Lynn Prett talked with the American couple. Tessa walked to the main entrance, which was flanked by a monumental wooden sculpture. A grizzly, not realistically done but depicted as the Spirit Bear of Sitklat'l mythology.

At the entrance she asked about Noreen Chelin. "She's still out there. She'll be here in ten minutes," the receptionist said, who appeared to be sixteen years old. Tessa went into the almost empty bar, bought a decaf coffee and a muffin, and sat down at one of the large windows. She would have liked to check her cell phone to see if Ron Halprin had answered, but there was no reception for guests.

She saw a boat arrive, and a group of tourists got out. Two guides from the lodge with orange-colored wind breakers took care of them. When they came nearer, Tessa recognized Noreen. Then her sight was blocked by a tall guy who had appeared out of nowhere. He wore a baseball cap and didn't let Noreen go past him. Both of them seemed to be involved in a conversation. Tessa could see the man gesticulating. The tourists caught up with Noreen, and the man had to make way for them on the pier. He turned his head briefly in Tessa's direction and she had to catch her breath.

It was Telford Reed.

26

What was Reed doing here? Was he trying to convince some Sitklat'l that they should buy the outfitter license?

Tessa had the impression that Noreen didn't want to listen to him. She joined her group and left Telford standing on the pier. He followed Noreen and the tourists with his eyes, unsure what to do. Then he went to one of the boats and got on board.

Tessa withstood the temptation to go outside in order to find out about his unexpected appearance. She didn't want to miss Noreen. The tourists streamed into the bar. Loud talking filled the room. Cameras were laid out on the tables and drinks were ordered. A few minutes later Noreen came in. She searched the room. Despite her three children she was still slim. During her university years, Tessa had perceived her as a rival. This black-haired woman with even facial proportions had something to offer that Tsaytis didn't find in Tessa. Something she couldn't possibly give him. Tessa could never figure out what Noreen thought about her, the white doctor's daughter who once had had an undefined relationship with Tsaytis.

She got up and waved. Noreen came over to her. She walked with purpose but there was nothing hectic about it. As if she knew that she would always reach her goal with patience faster.

Time had a different meaning for the Sitklat'l. This was something Tessa had experienced many times. She expected punctuality and speed. But during the exhausting land claims hearings with the government, she learned patience from the Sitklat'l. They were also going through a period of development. They had begun moving around confidently in the business world. Noreen Chelin was one of them. As the manager of a very well-known lodge, she had had to learn how to pay attention to the wishes of her guests, who traveled there from all over the world. Maybe that was the reason why she greeted Tessa with a handshake rather than a hug.

"It is all so terrible," she said. "We simply can't comprehend what happened."

She spoke with the typical accent of the Sitklat'l, a nasal influence that softened the consonants and rounded the tones. She sounds like Tsaytis, Tessa thought.

"Shall we stay in the bar?" She pointed at Tessa's table. "We'll be less disturbed here than at the office."

Tessa had nothing against that. The tourists were out of hearing range and busy among themselves.

"Was that Telford Reed?" she asked.

Noreen wrinkled her brow and looked out the window at the pier. "Yes, I didn't count on him showing up," she answered slowly. "Unfortunately I don't have any time for him. I'm also supposed to be leading some extra tours because Hank isn't here."

Tessa didn't dare ask what Telford Reed might have wanted at the lodge. Instead she jumped right in. "Did Tsaytis tell you what he saw at the farm?"

Noreen waited before she answered. "He only told me that children lay dead in the house and Hank outside in the meadow. The dogs were locked in the storeroom and were going crazy when he was there."

Tessa heard Harrison Miller's voice in her ear. *The dogs know who the murderer is.*

"They are only in the storeroom when people visit who don't

like the dogs or are afraid of them," she replied. "Who was there with Tsaytis? I know that somebody was there with him."

"The police don't want to say."

Tessa didn't give up. "Do you have a suspicion about who was there?"

Noreen didn't say anything.

That's an answer, too, she thought. *She wants to protect someone.* Tessa was too smart to keep pressing. "What is it you want to tell me about Fran?"

Noreen let her eyes sweep around the room. The guests were showing each other their grizzly pictures. "A month ago we had an open house here. For the people from Whatou Lake and the families of our workers, but also for our people from Telt-shaa. We flew in our elders and the students in our cultural program. Fran and her children were also here."

Noreen spoke cautiously without stopping. "Fran came to me and took me aside. She wanted to talk to me alone. I only had a few minutes to spare from everything that I had to do on that day. I wanted to listen to her because Hank sometimes seemed gloomy to me. We went into one of the guest rooms, and she told me that she wanted to move away with Hank and the children. She had to move away for her own protection, she said. I didn't understand why she was so scared. She didn't tell me, either. To be honest I didn't want to lose Hank because he's a very good tour guide. I answered: Hank has a good job and you all have more money. And you have your family, your parents. Fran didn't take my arguments well."

Tessa looked at Noreen expectantly, but nothing more followed. She asked: "So Fran didn't tell you why she wanted to move away?"

"She spoke about having to protect herself and her children. She didn't say what she had to protect them from. She asked me to promise that I wouldn't tell Hank anything about our conversation."

"Did you tell him about it?"

"Yes, and I also didn't promise her anything. Of course I had to discuss the situation with Hank. I'm his boss. He assured me that he wasn't going to move away. That was just one of Fran's bad days, he said. She would get over it. She was having a tough time with chronic pain and was taking strong painkillers for it, which made her moody and unpredictable."

"Chronic pain? None of us knew about that. She certainly would have asked our father for advice . . . or maybe not. In the last few weeks she had been avoiding him."

Noreen shrugged. "Hank was talking about fibromyalgia. That's why Fran went to a doctor, but she apparently couldn't help her."

"Who gave her the painkillers?"

Noreen didn't say anything.

"Did you tell the police?"

"Yes." Noreen hesitated. "I told the police, but I also told them that afterward I didn't know which parents she had been talking about."

"What do you mean by that?"

"Fran wanted to get away from her parents. Maybe she was talking about her biological parents."

"But they don't even live in Whatou Lake. And they have never had the slightest interest in her. Why would Fran want to run away from them?"

Noreen didn't answer for quite a while. "Fran's mother had many children, likely from different men. Fran probably doesn't even know who her biological father is."

Tessa stared at Noreen, whose eyes were constantly searching the boats at the pier. "So you think that Fran's biological father is not the man we believe is her biological father?"

Noreen answered without looking at her: "I think that nobody knows that with certainty."

"Are there rumors about who her real father might be?"

Noreen got up. "I'll get you another cup of coffee. What would you like?"

The truth, Tessa would have liked to exclaim. *I'd like the truth.* But she only answered: "A decaf Americano, please."

Her head began spinning. Nothing made any sense. Up until now it seemed that there was some proof that Fran wanted to put some distance between herself and Martha and Kenneth Griffins. With Martha, she had had some kind of conflict, and she acted dismissively toward Kenneth. Fran's biological parents hadn't played a role in her later life, except that they had left her with deep psychological wounds from her childhood. Fran thought that she had left that behind her. Perhaps she was too optimistic about this. And it was also possible that the Griffins and Fran's psychologist had overestimated the extent to which she had healed.

Tessa saw Noreen standing at the bar and asked herself, even more intrigued, why Tsaytis's wife really wanted to talk to her. She had the feeling that she had not yet stated the real reason. And so it was.

Noreen put the two cups of coffee on the table and slowly sat down, as if she were carrying something heavy, before she continued talking. "On the day of the open house, the park ranger was also present. He wanted to get something off his chest. He complained that Fran had called him up and asked him to kill all the bears he came across. Because she had finally had enough of bears; they prowled around her house, making life difficult for her and the children."

"Not the ranger who was just arrested?"

"Oh yes, that one," Noreen confirmed. She didn't seem to be as relaxed as she had been when they had started talking.

"That's just crazy," Tessa exclaimed. "Fran loves bears. She's dedicated to the environment. That's why she and Hank live in the wilderness. Because she loves nature and the animals. She . . ." Tessa was speechless.

Noreen drank from her coffee and put her cup down. "On the same day, Hank told me that for three weeks they had been having trouble with a female bear roaming around the farm. Fran was worried about the safety of the children."

"That may be, but she wouldn't have asked someone to kill even one bear. Never. Especially not a female bear who might have a cub somewhere or be pregnant." Tessa shook her head, deeply upset. "Noreen, I believe the park ranger made it up. Problem bears are tranquilized and transported elsewhere. Nobody knows that better than Fran!"

"You don't understand what I'm saying, Tessa. I'm getting at something else. It's clear to me that the ranger was spreading rumors. Apparently he wanted to get Fran mixed up in something, to make it look like she had something to do with the poachers."

"Why?" Tessa spat out this word as if it had ten exclamation marks behind it.

Noreen played around with some crumbs on the table that had come from Tessa's muffin. "I can imagine that the ranger was arrested because he was dealing drugs. For a long time there has been talk that—and please don't mention this to anyone—he probably sold drugs to some of our teenagers."

Tessa didn't interrupt her this time, just waited. Noreen kept talking: "We have a drug problem with our kids. We don't know exactly where the drugs come from. They come in regularly and . . . it is a real problem for us."

"That has to be stopped. The quicker the better. But I still have to ask you: What does this all have to do with Fran?"

Noreen took a deep breath. "Take this with a grain of salt, Tessa. I'm simply telling you what I've heard. Maybe it will help to answer some questions. Fran seems to have called the ranger to the farm many times. Officially, because of the bears around her house, but maybe that was just an excuse."

"What do you mean by that?"

"Do I have to spell it out?"

Tessa blinked. "He was bringing her illegal painkillers?"

"Hank thought that was a possibility. But what could he do

without proof? It's not a joke to make such a claim about a ranger. He works for the government."

"Who did Hank talk to about this?"

Noreen didn't say anything.

"Have you told that to the police?"

"Yes."

"What was Tsaytis looking for on the farm? Why was he there?"

"At first Hank told us that somebody was supposed to take over his shift, because he had to stay with the kids a little longer. Fran was supposedly in Whatou Lake because she had so many nosebleeds. But when he didn't show up at work the next day, either, and we couldn't reach him or Fran, Tsaytis and . . ." Noreen stopped herself just in time and continued on with a sigh: "He wanted to go look for himself. He happened to be nearby because he was on the heels of some poachers. The whole thing seemed strange to us. I mean, are nosebleeds an emergency?"

The new pieces of information rolled over Tessa like a rogue wave. She absolutely had to reach Ron Halprin in order to talk to him about it.

"When did the police question you?"

"Last night." Noreen looked at her watch.

Tessa was not yet finished with her questions. "Do you have any idea, any suspicion, where Fran could be?"

"I think the ranger knows more. I also told the police that."

Tessa looked at her. Noreen wanted to keep the drug dealer away from the young Sitklat'l kids. "But you don't really think that the poachers killed Hank and the kids and are responsible for Fran's disappearance?"

"Also seems crazy to me. But the police will certainly look into it."

Noreen got up. Tessa had no choice but to do the same thing.

"Tsaytis and I are really devastated by what happened. We want to do anything to help find Fran."

We. Tsaytis and Noreen. There was still a common bond

between the two of them. A bond that hadn't existed between Tsaytis and Tessa for a long time.

"I've got to go now. We have another tour group going out to the grizzly-viewing platform."

"Is Tsaytis here?" Tessa asked, to her own surprise.

"No, he's looking for Fran." She grabbed Tessa's hand, and her beautiful face looked worried. "In case you need a room for the night, tell them that at the reception. You're very welcome to stay here." She hesitated for a moment, took a look at her guests. "The two of us, you and me, we never had it easy. We always had to fight." After saying this, Noreen walked past the tourists and disappeared through the door.

Tessa felt numb. She couldn't make heads or tails of what Noreen was implying at the end of their talk. If it had been her intention to leave Tessa behind with a question mark, she had been successful. So many unanswered questions haunted her, and she wanted to solve as many as she could as long as she had the opportunity. She put on her windbreaker, went outside, and hurried over to the boat where she had seen Telford Reed disappear.

She called out his name. No movement. She called again.

"Mr. Reed sailed away on a yacht, about ten minutes ago," somebody behind her shouted. Tessa turned around.

Lynn Prett was in a small motorboat, fiddling around with her life jacket. She had a fisherman's hat on her head.

Tessa stood on the pier, unsure of what to do next. "When is Kratz Hilder flying back?"

"In an hour he's returning with three tourists. I'm sure that he could also take you back to Whatou Lake."

The bear researcher put some binoculars around her neck and bent over the boat's motor. Tessa watched her from the pier. Suddenly she had an idea. In front of her was a chance that she didn't want to miss. "Can you take me along?" she asked spontaneously. "I'd like to hear more about your work."

Lynn Prett looked up, surprised. "I don't know whether . . ." Her eyes darted to the lodge.

Tessa knew that now she had to take a risk. "I'm here at Noreen's invitation." She didn't mention that she had only been invited to spend the night.

"In that case, it's not forbidden to take you along," Lynn Prett said. There was a defiant undertone in her voice. "The blue-and-red life jacket should fit you."

Tessa pulled the life vest over her windbreaker and climbed from the pier into the boat. Lynn started up the motor and steered the vessel along the forested coast. Only a small strip of rocks separated the trees from the water. Soft green moss glowed on the dark surface where the ocean fringe met the boulders. She could hear the shrill calls of the bald eagles.

Tessa pulled up the hood of her jacket. Suddenly a narrow fjord opened up in front of them, which looked like an estuary. The water meandered through the bright-green meadows that stood out against the darker background. At the end of the fjord there was a round hill that pushed into the sky and behind it were higher snow-capped mountain peaks that stood like palisades next to each other.

Lynn carefully steered the boat up the fjord, past sandbars. When the waterway became shallower, she shut down the motor. She was constantly looking at the meadows and forests. "About this time, Polly comes here to feed on grass. Somebody killed her youngest cub. It was a seventeen-month-old male. He was very much in danger because Polly had recently chased him off. She wanted to breed again and have new cubs."

Tessa listened carefully. *Somebody killed her cub.* She remembered Harrison Miller's hate-filled tirade in which he claimed that this somebody was a Sitklat'l. That was really an ugly accusation.

"Polly's the name of the mother?"

"Yes, number 23-E in my files, but I call her Polly." The researcher's voice was filled with tenderness. A classic bob surrounded her round face. "These bears are part of my research project." She opened her notebook and typed something in. Then she looked through her binoculars. "There she is . . . good old Polly. Usually around this time, she shows up here. But two male bears have been missing for quite a while now. At least they haven't yet shot our Polly."

Tessa noticed a brown outline in the grass.

"Three dead grizzlies, and the lodge still refuses to let us go public about it," Lynn mumbled, without putting down her binoculars. She stood with her feet wide apart in the rocking boat. "As if we could keep that quiet much longer. They have to catch the guys who did this before they do more damage."

"Lynn, do you think that the murders of Hank and the children have something to do with the dead grizzlies? And with Fran's disappearance?"

Lynn lowered her binoculars and sat down on the bench without taking her eyes off the shore.

"I don't know, but I don't think so. We thought maybe Fran was having a midlife crisis and that she was questioning her whole life. That she was sort of out of control."

"Did Hank tell you that?"

Lynn hesitated. "On the day of the open house, Fran . . . she accused me of wanting to get involved with Hank."

"Do you mean—she thought that Hank and you were having an affair?"

"Yes . . . or no." Lynn struggled for words. "I think she was looking for a reason to convince Hank to move away with her and the children. That was my impression. That she wanted to grind him down."

Tessa decided to risk her next question. "Is that the reason you went with Tsaytis Chelin to Hank's farm? To clear up the matter with Fran?"

Lynn turned her head away. Her eyes were following Polly, who was wandering through the meadow. The longer she didn't say anything, the more convinced Tessa was that her question had hit the mark. She added: "Lynn, what did you see at the farm? I really have to know this."

The bear researcher fooled around with the binoculars. "I'm very sorry," she finally said, "but I can't help you with this matter."

Tessa's voice got sharper. "Maybe your observations would be helpful in finding Fran. We are running out of time."

But Lynn Prett no longer seemed to be listening to Tessa. Instead she called out: "What the hell's going on there?" She put on the zoom lens of her camera and began to film.

Tessa noticed movement at the edge of the forest. She grabbed Lynn's binoculars and stood up so that she could see what was moving out there. Not a grizzly. Before she could say anything, she heard Lynn Prett swearing. "For Christ's sake!"

Then her loud voice ripped through the silence over the delta. It was a war cry that shook Tessa up. The boat began to rock heavily, and they both had to sit down.

The researcher said with a hoarse voice: "Gone, he fled the scene."

Tessa looked through the binoculars. The bear was still there. Lynn wasn't talking about Polly, but about a human figure who had been waiting at the edge of the woods and whom Tessa had also seen with the binoculars.

"Who was that?" she asked, and a suspicion rose in her.

A furious look appeared on the researcher's face. "Whoever it was, I have this person on film." Lynn watched it on her display. "The picture is not very sharp, but I can see that he's carrying a gun. Certainly someone who shouldn't be here." She started up the boat's motor.

Tessa asked again: "What did you see at the farm, Lynn?"

The researcher waved her off, irritated. "I really can't tell you anything about that."

Disappointed, Tessa pressed her lips together. Then she remembered something Lynn had said: *I am more afraid of aggressive dogs than of grizzlies.*

Lynn was telling the truth. She couldn't say anything about the farm murders because she hadn't seen anything at all. Tsaytis had approached the house alone, because Lynn wanted to stay away. She had heard the dogs' hysterical barking and probably asked Tsaytis to take care of locking the dogs up. When Tsaytis saw the first body, he kept Lynn away from the scene of the crime.

At that moment the bear researcher angrily threw a rope to the back of the boat. "Now, you tell me why this guy showed up near Polly with a gun. And why he ran away when he heard me yelling. Hunting is illegal here! I don't know why Noreen won't go public about this." Her eyes glared.

Is it possible that Fran or Hank knew something about the way the poachers worked?

Lynn climbed to the stern. "I've got to get back to warn the others."

"Will you inform Noreen?"

"Yes, I'll show her the film."

"And the police?"

"If I say something to them, I can forget about my project here. Noreen would never forgive me. She has to make the decision about that."

She sat down again, took the memory card from the camera, and put it in the laptop. She worked with great concentration until she had downloaded everything.

Then she tried to hand the memory card to Tessa.

"Give that to the police. I'll tell Noreen that you have seen everything and now she has to do something before it's too late."

Tessa didn't take the memory card. "I just can't do that. It's only a suspicion: he . . . didn't shoot a bear in front of our eyes."

Lynn's face got dark. "What about if it has something to do with Fran's disappearance? It can't just be a coincidence that these . . . things happened at the same time."

The researcher had pushed the right buttons. Tessa put the memory card in the breast pocket of her windbreaker. Lynn got the motor running again, and they glided out from the fjord. Polly was only a brown speck now, and then she disappeared altogether. Tessa had a bad feeling, as if they were sending the bear off to an uncertain fate.

There was another thought that made her uneasy: Maybe the guy with the gun felt threatened. He had noticed the two women in the boat looking in his direction with binoculars and a camera. Could he figure out their identities? If four people had been gotten rid of and Fran had been abducted, what difference did two more deaths make?

Tessa kept her thoughts to herself; Lynn was already worried enough.

When they reached the pier ten minutes later, they didn't see anybody. Lynn tied the boat up, and they gave each other a hand to climb out.

"What are you going to do now?" the researcher asked.

"I want to get back to Whatou Lake as quickly as possible."

27

The flight back in the floatplane seemed really long to Tessa. When she finally put her feet on the ground at the harbor, she looked at the news on her cell phone.

Ron Halprin had written back: *Tell me briefly what this is about.*

Frustrated, she threw back her head. She couldn't possibly put her suspicions in a text message. A man handed her the backpack. She turned around and saw a person at the edge of the parking lot.

"Dad," she called from far away. "How did you know . . . ?"

They hugged, both relieved and distraught at the same time.

"Savannah saw your text message. I called Kratz and hoped you would be flying back with him today."

When they approached the Pathfinder, Tessa noticed the two dogs in the back wagging their tails. Her father hadn't yet given them over to Harrison Miller. As they traveled toward Whatou Lake, she told him about the conversations with Noreen Chelin and Lynn Prett. "Lynn said she thought Fran had gotten out of control," she closed her report. "Didn't you notice that yourself?"

Her father sighed. "We hardly saw her anymore."

But she saw other people, Tessa remembered. *I've gotta talk with Ron Halprin.*

This thought was so important to her that she forgot to tell her father about the car ride with Harrison Miller. And she forgot to ask him where he'd been with the dogs that afternoon when his car was parked in front of the house.

"Can we quickly stop at the police station, Dad?"

Her father nodded.

She regretted her decision right away when she saw a group of reporters and other TV people standing in front of the entrance to the police station. Kenneth Griffins made a quick decision. "I'm going to drive around the corner and wait in a side street."

She pulled up the hood of her windbreaker, put on her sunglasses, and ran as fast as she could up the stairs, past the journalists. Inside she took off her shades.

"I'm Tessa Griffins, Fran Miller's sister," she said to the two officials who were standing behind the counter. "Can I talk to Sergeant Halprin?"

The two men looked her over. A messy-haired woman with dry lips and tired eyes, wearing track pants and a windbreaker.

"Sergeant Halprin isn't here," one of the policemen said. "None of them are here."

"They're still out at the crime scene?" she asked.

The policeman stayed vague. "Probably. But that's closed off to everybody. The best thing for you is to send a text to Sergeant Halprin."

I've already done that, she wanted to say, but she bit her tongue. "Is there a back exit?" she asked. "Because of the media people."

"Sure," the second policeman said, and led her to it.

The Pathfinder was waiting two doors down. Tessa let herself fall into the passenger seat. "It looks like the sergeant is back at the farm."

Kenneth Griffins took a shortcut to the highway. "I'm supposed to give these dogs a run, where nobody will see them."

"There's a grizzly hanging around in Tennigan Park," she warned him. "Along the river maybe?"

"No, it's very likely we would run into somebody there."

"By the lake, then?"

Her father shook his head. "Too exposed." He kept thinking. "Maybe at Bob's?"

Tessa knew who he was talking about. Bob Barker's piece of land was on the west side of the river, hidden in a side valley. Since Bob's house had burned down a couple of years ago, the old man lived with his sister in Whatou Lake. Earlier the land had been for sale. Tessa and her father had gone to look at it. There had been other potential buyers who had been interested. In the end, Bob decided for reasons that weren't quite clear not to sell. A dirt road still led to his abandoned property. There the dogs could run around as much as they wanted.

Kenneth Griffins had already driven by Harrison Miller's pretentious villa. There weren't any more houses off the highway. The riverbed narrowed and the mountains got closer. There certainly weren't going to be any journalists showing up here.

Tessa pushed down her hood and looked at her father. "Where were you this afternoon? The car was there, but you and the dogs weren't."

"I was in your cabin in the woods. I had to get some peace and quiet in order to think things over."

"With the dogs?"

He nodded. "Otherwise, Harrison Miller would have come by and stolen them when nobody was in the house."

"You've got that right." She explained to her father that the mayor had turned up at the Griffins' house because of the dogs. She also described how he had blown his lid during the ride to the floatplane. But she didn't tell him about Miller's worst accusation.

Why don't you ask your father where he's hidden her so she can't reveal anything?

They were silent until they reached the road that went to

Bob's property. Kenneth Griffins drove by a *No Trespassing* sign and parked the Pathfinder on the edge of the dirt road. Tessa reached over the back seat for the dog leashes.

"We can just let them run around here," Kenneth Griffins said.

Tessa didn't agree. "We don't know the dogs very well. We don't know if they'll come back when we call them."

Despite her protests, her father opened the back door. The German shepherd was in no hurry and sniffed around near the car. The husky mix jumped out and ran up the driveway.

"He'll come back," her father said when he saw her worried face. "Hank has trained him really well."

Tessa wasn't so sure. In any case she took the leashes with her and followed the curving path. The German shepherd trotted a couple of steps ahead of them. Suddenly they heard the husky mix barking excitedly.

"Holy shit," Tessa cried out. "It got to be a grizzly."

The German shepherd shot up the path until she was out of sight. Kenneth Griffins wasn't ruffled. "She's probably chased a squirrel up a tree."

How come he wasn't worried? Tessa was irritated. He was a very good doctor, but he didn't know anything about dogs. And this time she didn't have a pistol with her.

The trail took a bend. Two old shacks came into view. The German shepherd sprang onto the door of the shack on the left and scratched it with her claws. The husky mix was still barking wildly.

Kenneth Griffins stopped where he was. "What a strange smell."

Tessa realized what he was talking about. "It smells just like the last time. Is a dead moose lying around here somewhere?"

"The smell is coming from here," her father answered and pointed at the shack in front of them. At the other shack's door, somebody had painted a big *T* inside a circle. After a few more steps, the smell became so unbearable that Tessa instinctively tried to turn away.

"The dogs," her father called as he went over to the husky and put it on a leash. Tessa held her breath and pulled the German shepherd away from the door with the terrible smell.

She handed the leash to her father. "Hold tight to her, I'm going to take a look."

"That's probably not a good idea . . ." Kenneth Griffin's words were drowned out by the wild barking.

She pulled her hood sideways over her nose and mouth and went up to the door. She rattled the rusty lock and stumbled backward when the door immediately gave way. Her eyes had to adjust to the dark. Then she saw something bright in the corner. With a hammering heart, she took a couple of steps over to it.

In a second, she recognized what it was. The body lay on its back, still clad in a sweater and blue jeans.

"Fran!" Tessa screamed, horrified. She kneeled down and tried to find a pulse on Fran's neck, although she already knew that her half sister was dead. The body felt cold and stiff.

Fran's mouth was partly open, also her eyes. Strands of her blond hair covered a part of her face. Tessa pushed them softly away.

She didn't see any blood, and there were no obvious wounds. It was as if Fran had simply gone to rest here.

Her father called from outside. There was panic in his voice. She couldn't understand anything because the dogs were barking so loudly.

She staggered outside and fell to her knees.

28

In the following hours, Tessa felt like she was living in a nightmare. She would have liked to spare her father the sight of the body, but he insisted on it. While Tessa held the dogs' leashes, he confirmed the death of his foster daughter. She reminded him that this was the scene of a crime and that there should be no contamination. In vain. She watched how he stroked Fran's face. Now they would find DNA from her and her father on the body.

In order to get a cell phone connection, they had to drive back to the main road. Tessa could hardly bear leaving Fran back in the shack. But she wouldn't let her father drive off alone. His face was ashen gray and he looked dazed. He also wasn't in any condition to deal with hysterical dogs.

Tessa sat down in the grass, off to the side, while people in white protective suits hurried about. A police photographer came out of the shack with his camera. Ron Halprin was talking with the officer who had visited her mother. Halprin's team had been brought in by helicopter. One of his men had driven away with her father and the dogs in a police van. He wanted to write down Kenneth Griffins's witness statement. Tessa hated all the busyness around her. At least Fran was no longer alone. Nobody could harm her anymore. That was over. Her body was in a safe place. It was a tiny consolation she could hold on to.

"I'm sorry for you and your family." Halprin stood in front of her.

She nodded weakly. The sergeant sat down next to her in the grass. "Do you think you're able to answer some questions?"

She nodded again.

He cleared his throat. "I have to tape this conversation. You have to briefly confirm that you are aware of that. Later they will give the statement for you to sign."

"Yes," she said.

The other officer came over to them. "Corporal Kate Jennings is also listening," he said. He gave Tessa a tiny microphone. "Tell me, to start off: Why did you and your father come here?"

She couldn't recognize her own voice as she answered the sergeant in detail. The dogs. The smell. The discovery.

"Actually somebody should have searched here long ago," she finished off her description. "We should have thought of that right away. The place is remote but not far away from Whatou Lake. And you can reach it with a pickup."

"Why a pickup?"

"Can also be an SUV. Somebody brought her here when she was already dead."

"How do you know that?"

"By the way she was lying there. In the shack I saw some evidence that she had been dragged."

"How do you think that could have happened?"

She looked the sergeant straight in the eyes. "I don't want to suspect anyone who might be innocent. You'll certainly talk to Bob Barker."

"Who knows about this place other than Bob Barker?"

Tessa hugged her knees. "A lot of people in Whatou Lake. A few years ago Barker wanted to sell the property. You could come and look at it. Dad and I also came out here."

Halprin shot a glance at the police officer. "Was there a real estate agent?"

"Yes, Hogan Dole did that. But we just drove out to the property, like we did today, without Hogan Dole, because we didn't want to run into him."

Halprin was already asking the next question: "Have you been out here since then?"

"I haven't."

"And your father?"

"That I don't know." *They will certainly question him about that.*

"Do you think that Fran Miller has ever been here?"

"I . . . I don't know for sure, but I don't think so."

"Did she know Bob Barker?"

"Yes, just like all of us knew him. That means not very well. At least I don't think she ever had anything to do with him personally." With her hand she picked some pieces of grass. "I didn't see any injuries. No wounds. How did Fran actually die?"

"We'll clear that up. Do you have any suspicions?"

Overwhelmed, she shook her head and threw her arms again around her knees. People walked toward the shack. They were carrying a stretcher.

Halprin watched the scene without seeming to be distracted. "Why did you want to talk to me today?"

She discreetly studied his hands, which looked like a farmer's hands. She would have felt better if his hands had been holding her. She would have liked some physical contact, some warm skin. A safe place in this sea of despair that threatened to drown her.

She had to gather her thoughts in order to give him an answer. She took some shallow breaths before she spoke: "Something occurred to me today. Maybe Fran really was at Robert Pleeke's funeral home. Not because of the coffins but because of Melanie Pleeke. That's his wife. Noreen Chelin told me that Fran was at the doctor's because of chronic pain, but the doctor apparently couldn't help her." She loosened her arms around her knees and stretched her legs. The ground felt cool. Despite the light, evening had arrived.

"Melanie Pleeke is probably a quack . . . Cliff Bight told me that she works in black magic. Past-life experiences. Contact with the other side. Stuff like that."

"Cliff Bight?"

"He works for Lionel Miller's firm. Apparently Fran needed help. Maybe she had become more unbalanced than we thought."

Halprin remained silent for a few seconds, then he asked: "When did you talk with Tsaytis Chelin's wife?"

The white-clad health workers carried Fran in a body bag out of the shack and into the ambulance. With her last bit of strength, Tessa told Halprin about her visit to Watershed Lodge. When she started describing the boat trip with Lynn Prett, one of the white-clad people waved to Halprin.

"We'll continue this questioning later," he said and got up.

"Anytime." Tessa handed him the microphone. Halprin reached out when he saw that she had trouble standing up. Her legs felt like rubber.

He held on to her fingers for a very brief time and looked into her eyes. "We've already talked to Melanie Pleeke. She came to us."

When he convinced himself that she could stand by herself, he turned to the RCMP officer. "Corporal, would you take Miss Griffins home?"

Exhausted, Tessa got into the police car. Kate Jennings started the motor and followed the ambulance carrying Fran's body, which was moving along quickly in front of them. Tessa could no longer keep control of her emotions. When they got to the highway, the tears rolled down her cheeks and she was shaken by sobs.

"Should I stop?" the officer asked.

Tessa nodded without saying anything. Everything came out. The shock, the tension, the horror. Only slowly the shaking receded. The RCMP officer handed her a handkerchief and otherwise left her in peace. Tessa was thankful for that.

After several long minutes, she had the feeling that she had herself somewhat under control. She needed strength for what awaited her at her parents' house.

29

Tessa opened the door to the house, but no dogs came running. It was strangely quiet inside. Only one of Fran's cats waited on the stairs.

"Hello?" Tessa called out with a pounding heart and went into the kitchen.

There they all sat, Savannah and her parents, with drained, empty faces. They looked at her with the same red-rimmed eyes that she had seen in herself in the side mirror of the police car. Nobody had yet said anything to her, and the silence felt like a barbed-wire barrier. She would have really liked to hug her parents, and they certainly all would have cried and held each other tight. But now she was afraid to do that.

Finally her mother said: "How did Fran look?"

Tessa glanced at her father, who had turned his face away. He seemed to have stepped out of the picture. Hadn't he told Mom everything?

"She looked as if she had fallen asleep." Tessa was amazed that her voice almost sounded normal, although weak and deeper.

"Had she been murdered?"

"The police haven't said."

"What do *you* think? You actually saw Fran." Her mother

sounded aggressive, but Tessa knew that pain was speaking in her voice.

"I didn't see any wounds, no blood. No sign that she had been strangled or . . . anything. I think somebody brought her there after she was already dead."

"How long do you think she had been dead?"

"I don't know. Maybe a few days." Tessa sat down, depleted. "Dad, say something yourself."

Her father raised his eyes. It was the look of a broken man. "Sorry. It's as if my brain has closed up shop." He looked down again at the tabletop. His words came softly: "I already told your mother. I think it might have been four to five days."

He wasn't a forensic doctor, but he had experience with dead bodies.

"So maybe Fran died on the same day as Hank and the children." Martha Griffins soberly threw this possibility out into the room. "Do you think Bob Barker has something to do with all this?"

Now her husband spoke up. "Darling, Bob Barker has been in the hospital for the last few weeks. He's in pretty bad shape. He couldn't possibly load a body into a pickup and carry it to the shack."

Savannah got up and turned to Tessa. "You look like you could use a shower. Would you like something to eat?" She started working at the stove.

Tessa kept her eyes on her father. "Did you hear anything else from the police? Ron Halprin didn't tell me anything."

Her father shrugged helplessly. "No, they're not revealing anything." The question that she didn't dare to ask was: *What did you reveal to the police when you were being questioned?*

Savannah crossed her arms and leaned on the counter. "I know that they're going to hold a press conference tomorrow afternoon. That's something we have to go to."

"How do you know that?" Tessa said to her. She noticed that her nerves were slowly reaching their limit.

"Just look on the Internet. The police have reserved the sports arena and have asked about the seating arrangements."

Tessa ignored the triumphant look on Savannah's face. She was already somewhere else in her thoughts. "If Fran didn't have any obvious injuries, where did the blood on her jacket, the one Hogan Dole supposedly found at Whitesand Bay, come from?"

"And the cat collar with blood on it?" Savannah added.

Martha Griffins was listening. "What cat collar?"

Savannah put a cup of tea and a plate of warmed-up spaghetti for Tessa on the table. "We found it on the trail to Whitesand Bay. It belonged to the third cat, Rosie. Does anybody else want tea?"

Tessa felt her mother looking at her as she started eating the spaghetti and drank a sip of tea. She had to eat; she had to.

"What did you find out at the lodge?" Martha seemed really interested and less overwhelmed than her husband.

Tessa talked about the ranger's visit to Fran's farm. She also mentioned the illegal painkillers Fran had apparently taken. And she revealed that a bear researcher was the one who had been with Tsaytis Chelin at the farm, but that she probably hadn't seen the bodies.

"Why was this bear researcher at the farm?" a suspicious Martha Griffins asked.

Tessa swallowed the spaghetti before she answered: "I assume that she wanted to convince Fran that . . . that there had been nothing between her and Hank. Apparently Fran had accused her of that on the day of the open house at Watershed Lodge. But Lynn Prett had the impression that Fran was no longer completely stable."

"Maybe it was these strong painkillers that had negatively affected Fran's brain," Kenneth Griffins added. "If I had known about them, I would have warned her. But she . . ." He didn't end the sentence.

Tessa remembered again the conversation she had had with her father. She couldn't suppress it any longer. She knew that she was on thin ice. "I told Dad that Harrison Miller came today to pick up the dogs. I was here briefly to get my backpack, and I had no idea where Dad was. I couldn't find him. And I also couldn't find the dogs. But the Pathfinder was parked in front of the house. Harrison drove me in his car out to the floatplane. While we were driving, he talked a lot of nonsense. He said, for instance, that I should ask Dad where he had hidden Fran so that she couldn't disclose certain things."

Her mother whacked the table so hard that the teacup hopped. "How can you ask your father something like that, Tessa?"

"I just told you what Harrison—"

"Don't you see how much that question upsets your father?"

Kenneth Griffins stroked his wife's hand. "It's okay, darling. It's better that I know what kind of gossip the mayor is spreading around."

Tessa sipped on her tea. "What's the meaning of this rumor, Dad? What was he suggesting?"

"Enough of this!" Martha Griffins stood up as if she was climbing a barricade. "You said yourself that Harrison was spreading a bunch of bullshit. We really don't have to put up with this."

Tessa glanced again at her father. The way he looked told her to wait until they were alone.

Her mother seemed to have the same idea. "I'm going upstairs," she announced. "And you're coming with me, Tessa."

Kenneth disagreed. "Whatever you have to talk about with her, you can deal with it here. We don't have any secrets from each other."

"I don't want to embarrass my daughter in front of everyone, my dear. Apparently I have to remind her of the house rules." She stood behind Tessa's chair and took her hand. "Come, my child." And turning to Savannah, she said: "Can you please feed the cats?"

Tessa avoided the looks of the others and let her mother pull her up the stairs. *Like a sacrificial lamb,* ran through her head. Martha Griffins went toward Tessa's room at the end of the corridor. She shut the door behind them and whispered: "From up here they won't be able to hear anything."

They both sat down on the edge of the bed. Her mother was still holding her hand. "We really have to make sure that this doesn't escalate," she said more patiently, not using the sharp words she had used before. "You don't know everything, dear; that's why you're making some bad mistakes. Now I'm going to explain something to you." With a deep sigh, she continued: "Last February I sat here with Fran in this room. She thought that your dad had used Valium to calm her down when she was a child."

Tessa dropped her mother's hand. "What do you mean 'calm her down'?"

"That he regularly gave her strong sedatives."

"But that's not true, Mom, is it?"

"No, of course not. The pills he gave her work against anxiety and depression. And she only got them once in a while."

"Did you tell Fran that?"

"Yes. The stuff about the tranquilizers is a lot of crap, but Fran continued to believe it. And she complained that these pills were the reason for all her health problems. That your father, against her will or without her knowledge, had given her these strong sedatives."

"How . . . how did she get that idea? She never made even the slightest suggestion of that to me."

"Because it's not true. Somebody talked her into thinking it was."

"Who did that?"

"Melanie Pleeke."

Melanie Pleeke, the wife of the funeral home owner. The woman who had contacted Ron Halprin.

"Apparently Melanie offers some weird therapy," her mother continued. "And Fran fell for this nonsense."

"What kind of therapy?"

"Melanie hypnotizes her clients and takes them back to their childhood. So that they remember and relive various traumatic experiences."

"What? Because of this, Fran thinks she remembers that Dad . . ." She shook her head angrily. "That's crazy, Mom!"

"Yes, it is. But Fran was convinced by it. Because she suddenly found an explanation for all her problems."

"What problems?"

Her mother reached out again for Tessa's hand; her fingers were hot.

"Your father and I . . . we go on the assumption that Fran had a traumatic childhood before she came to us. She grew up in a house with adults who had terrible relationships. We did our best to . . . create a normal life for her. And this is the thanks we get." She swallowed hard and continued, more resigned than bitter: "As a teenager, Fran had suffered from depression and insomnia. Ken gave her medicine to dampen her pain. But Fran claimed in February that he had routinely used tranquilizers on all our foster children."

"How did Dad react to Fran's accusations?"

"He doesn't know anything about them."

Tessa couldn't believe her ears. "You never told him about this?"

Her mother shook her head. "Why should I burden him with this kind of crap?"

"But Mom, he . . . he has to know. He has to be able to defend himself." Tessa tried not to raise her voice, despite her bewilderment.

"Against what?"

"Against this rumor! Against people who could hurt him."

"Only you and I know about this. And Fran told just one other person, and that person warned me."

"This already makes four people. And with Melanie Pleeke, five."

"She won't spill the beans. We made sure of that."

"Who is we?"

"Me, and the person who warned me."

"Who is this person?"

"I can't tell you. Not yet."

Tessa looked at her mother, shocked. "Harrison Miller might also have heard this rumor. That could be why he said that Dad was hiding Fran, so that she couldn't disclose anything."

"Fran definitely never said anything to Harrison. She hadn't even told Hank."

"What makes you think you know that, Mom?" Tessa was losing her patience. All this had happened in the last few months, and her mother had never asked her for advice.

"Fran hid from him that she had gone to Melanie Pleeke. He definitely wouldn't have approved, because he . . . because he thought those kinds of things were crazy."

Tessa got up and paced around the room. After a couple of rounds she stopped and stood in front of her mother. "I know from Sergeant Halprin that Melanie Pleeke asked to talk to the police. What do you think she told them?"

Don't blow your lid now, Tessa. Just don't lose it now.

"Melanie won't talk," her mother repeated stubbornly.

Tessa felt a storm brewing inside her. "And why was Fran supposedly in Whitesand Bay?"

"Fran?"

"Yes, you told me here in this room that she may have gone there to find proof. Proof of what?"

"That I can't tell you, because you would otherwise go and tell the sergeant."

"I had to tell him, Mom, because we were dealing with Fran's life!"

"It hasn't helped very much, as we can see now."

Tessa sat down again. "Did *you* at least tell Ron Halprin why Fran wanted to look for proof in Whitesand Bay?" Her eyes stared fiercely at her mother. She could hardly believe the scene was playing out in front of her.

"I only said to you it was possible that she was there. I don't know for sure. Why should I say anything to the sergeant that I don't know for sure?"

"Aren't you afraid now that I will say something to Halprin about Dad and Fran and her accusations about tranquilizers?"

The dark circles were deep around her mother's eyes; she turned her head away. "No. You would never do something that could harm your father. I know you too well for that."

Tessa sat there, dazed. More and more things were escaping from Pandora's box, and what came out was evil, chaotic, and rotten.

They should be crying in each other's arms, Mom and she, still staggered by Fran's death and the sorrow about so many lost innocent lives. The sorrow had been pushed into the background by new and disturbing discoveries. At some point the soul simply couldn't take it in and mourn anymore. The murderer also has that on his conscience, Tessa thought.

Then another thought came to her. "What did you tell Fran about her accusations against Dad?"

"That I would do everything to protect him. That I wouldn't allow anybody to bring such a miserable lie into public view. I warned Fran that I wouldn't let my husband be thrown to the lions. Never!" Her mother's soft voice had become hard again.

"How did you warn Fran?"

"I asked her to keep her mouth shut. I did so much for her. And now this is the result."

"Did you threaten her?"

Her mother's face froze up. "What kind of nonsense are you saying? She's the one who threatened *us*!"

"But you had to . . ." Tessa heard somebody calling her name. "I'll take a look to see what's going on," she whispered and opened the door.

Her father stood at the top of the stairs. He was holding on tightly to the banister. "Your mother needs some peace and quiet now, and you too, Tessa. We all need a rest."

She gave him a sign and closed the door again. Her mother had collapsed at the edge of the bed. She looked as if she had aged years. Slowly she raised her eyes, got up, walked heavily toward Tessa, and hugged her.

"The most important thing now is to keep your father out of it," she whispered.

30

"The media folks are waiting outside."

Savannah was already working in the kitchen when Tessa came down the next morning. "Please give them a few words. You know best how to get rid of them."

Tessa nodded in agreement. Thanks to a sleeping pill, she had had a few hours of sleep. She quickly took a shower and slipped into a gray blouse and a black suit. Her funeral outfit. She put on makeup, rinsed her mouth, and fixed her hair. Twenty minutes later she stood in front of a group of journalists who had besieged the house. She walked over to the microphones and the cameras and introduced herself.

"After today's press conference in Whatou Lake, I will make a statement from the family," she explained. "Until then, I ask you to be patient and to honor our privacy." The questions poured in. She pushed them away with a hand movement and spontaneously added instead: "We had hoped to the last that our Fran would be found alive. This hope was destroyed last night in a gruesome way. It is a very difficult, sad time for us; we are in deep despair. I understand that you would like some answers, but at the moment we simply don't have any. We have to wait for the results from the police investigation and for the information to be given at the press conference. Please understand this."

Her appeal was actually heard. The journalists left. When she came back into the house, she saw Savannah with a cat in her lap. "Wow, you'll look really great on TV," she exclaimed.

Tessa poured herself a glass of milk. "Sometimes, actually most times, you say the wrong words at the wrong time."

"Unlike you, apparently, as you've just shown. Can you give me a cup of coffee? Otherwise I'll have to scare Lily away." Tessa put a full mug in front of her. She also pushed over a muffin, which smelled as if it had just come out of the oven. No doubt baked by Savannah. Upstairs again in her room, Tessa exchanged her businesslike suit for comfortable yoga pants.

"How did the conversation with Mom go yesterday?" Savannah asked when Tessa returned to the kitchen to eat a muffin.

"If she had wanted you to hear it, she wouldn't have gone upstairs with me."

"I can easily imagine what you wanted to talk about."

"Oh, yeah?"

"One thing is sure: Fran was not the saint that everybody considered her to be."

It was amazing how quickly Savannah used the word *was*, Tessa thought. "Why do you say that?"

"Hank called me up once. Fran had told him that she was meeting me in Whatou Lake. I can tell you one thing: she wasn't meeting me. Not on that day or any other day."

"You told Hank?"

"Sure. I don't lie."

"Hah!" Tessa rolled her eyes. "You always used to snitch on us kids at Mom's."

"Yes, I did. But I wasn't lying."

"And now suddenly you remember that Hank phoned you up. I hope the police know about that."

"Of course."

"If you know so much, who did Fran meet instead?"

"No idea."

"Why not? You were always spying on her."

Savannah choked on her coffee and coughed so hard that the cat jumped off her lap. After she got her breath back, she explained: "I wanted to hang out with both of you. Is that so hard to understand? You and Fran always shut me out of things."

"Your endless tattling didn't exactly make you popular with us. You wanted to get in good with Mom."

"And? In my place, you would've done the same thing. You and Fran, you both had an advantage over me. Mom was your biological mother. And Fran, the goody-goody girl, was always Mom's favorite. Mom would never have admitted that, but that's the way it was. I only wanted. . ." She didn't say the next word.

Even so, Tessa knew what she meant.

Love.

That's what we all wanted: to be loved. Accepted. Part of the group.

Tessa suddenly understood Savannah. It could not have been easy for her to find her place in the big patchwork family. All the children fought in their way to gain Martha and Ken's affection.

But at some point in life, their roles reversed: Savannah became Martha's favorite and Fran the black sheep. And now Fran was dead.

Just as Tessa was thinking about her reply, Savannah whispered: "Once I saw Fran with Harrison Miller. In his pickup."

"What?" All her compassionate thoughts about the troubled Savannah immediately disappeared.

"About three weeks ago." Savannah pushed her cup back and forth on the table. She seemed to have more scruples about passing along this gossip than usual. "In front of the Friendly Piggy. I mean, his pickup was parked across from the gift shop that went bankrupt."

One of the cats meowed, but nobody paid any attention to it. Her parents seemed to still be sleeping. You couldn't hear anything from upstairs. Maybe they were whispering to each other, just as Savannah was doing with Tessa.

"'The Friendly Piggy. Is that the new restaurant? Where the Home Hardware used to be?"

"Yes. I do the cleaning there on Wednesdays when the restaurant is closed. I park my car around the corner, otherwise people think the restaurant is open." Savannah avoided Tessa's look. "At first I thought it was simply that people hadn't seen the *Closed* sign. But nobody got out. So I took a closer look. It was Harrison Miller's pickup. And I could see both of them very clearly. Harrison had his arm around Fran."

"Are you screwing with me? You can't possibly recognize two people in a pickup from where you were standing."

In response, Savannah got up and rummaged around in her purse that was lying on the sideboard. She held up small binoculars.

Tessa dramatically closed her eyes. Savannah the spy. But nevertheless, she couldn't afford to make a scene. There was too much at stake. She wanted to hear the whole story.

"What exactly did you see?"

"I found the situation pretty gripping."

"What? You mean the arm around Fran's shoulder?"

"Harrison's arm was there for a long time. At least five minutes or longer. And their faces were close to each other."

"You can read that the wrong way. Maybe Harrison wanted to console Fran. He probably meant it in a fatherly way."

Savannah's whispering turned into hissing. "You see? Fran's behavior is always excused. She can't do anything wrong in your eyes." Tessa didn't want to admit that she was no longer as sure as she used to be. Savannah didn't wait for a response. "Don't you find it strange? Fran had always hated Harrison Miller, right from the beginning, and she had good reason to. She was afraid of him, aren't I right?"

Yes, Savannah was right. Tessa had to admit that to herself. And Harrison couldn't stand Fran. He'd rejected her as a person and resented that she married his son.

Tessa didn't comment. She needed time to think about everything. Did Harrison blackmail Fran with something? Had he driven her into a corner? Did he want her to leave Hank? One hypothesis after another went through her head. She heard Savannah's voice as if it were far away.

"I think that Fran had him, Harrison, wrapped around her little finger. That's what she did with everybody, right? And she was always successful. She always got what she wanted."

Savannah's words dripped into Tessa's thoughts like water onto dry soil.

She wanted Hank and got him.

She wanted a farm in the wilderness. Hank gave in.

She wanted to have a third child, even though she was really overwhelmed with two kids. She got her child.

She wanted to move away to a farm that might soon be flooded by a dam.

Only this time, Hank didn't go along with it.

Where the hell would she get the money for a farm in Grouse Valley? Certainly not from Harrison Miller. The mayor wanted to buy an outfitter license and then build a lodge. He wanted to have Hank nearby. If Savannah's observations were correct, then there was a question: What did Fran want from her father-in-law? What was so important that she was ready to meet him and let him embrace her?

"I'm wondering what the cops think about this," Savannah interrupted Tessa while she was trying to think.

"When did you tell them about that?"

"Yesterday."

That meant that the police would have confronted the mayor with this. She assumed that Harrison Miller would deny that they had met. That's what ruthless politicians do at first, and then when they are caught, they come up with some half-truths.

She needed some fresh air to clear her head. And a place where she could really sob without someone seeing her. Or hearing her.

"Are the dogs with him?" she asked and stood up.

"With whom?"

"With Harrison Miller."

"Did Dad take them over to him?"

Tessa shook her head. "We'd better find out." She picked up her cell phone and sent Lionel Miller a text message because she wanted to avoid the mayor. *Are Hank's dogs with your father? They're not here."*

Savannah got up and placed her teacup in the dishwasher. "I'm going home briefly. I'll be back soon."

Tessa heard the door slam shut and her car driving off. Aside from the humming of the fridge, it was completely quiet in the house. Even the cats weren't making any sound. Tessa found the quiet to be scary; it felt like the calm before the storm. Curious, a cat sauntered into the kitchen. If only the animal could talk and say what had happened on Fran's farm. Tessa understood why many people considered animals to be messengers from the far side. Messengers of the gods. Like the Sitklat'l. *Send me a message from Fran,* she silently begged the cat. But this cat only rubbed her legs.

There *was* a message, Tessa suddenly realized. The cat collar. If she only knew how it had landed on the path to Whitesand Bay. She put on her sneakers and windbreaker and opened the front door. She took a deep breath of the cool morning air and sucked it into her lungs. The birds were singing. She listened carefully as if on behalf of Fran, Hank, and the children. A gray jay flew from branch to branch. As kids they had let the trusting birds pick breadcrumbs from their hands. Tessa remembered exactly how the birds' claws felt on her fingers. Everything was just as it used to be: the birds, the woods in front of her eyes, the distant screeching of a chain saw. Like before, when Fran and her family were still alive. Tessa trembled. Why couldn't she just wake up from this nightmare?

A sudden noise. She gave a start.

A man was standing at the edge of the forest.

31

As if pulled by invisible strings, she walked over to him.

"You scared me!"

"I want to talk to you," Tsaytis Chelin answered.

"Why didn't you come into the house?" That was an unnecessary question; she already knew the answer. Tsaytis didn't want anybody to hear them.

"I don't want to bother anybody."

"Then let's go to my cabin."

Tsaytis followed her through the woods. It was the first time in two years that Tessa had seen her hideout. Her father took care of it. The key was in its usual hiding place that only he and she knew about.

The inside smelled like cedar. It came from freshly cut kindling her father must have recently stacked up by the stove. Here he found peace and quiet, as she had back in her teenage years. Her books were still lined up on the shelf. Tessa suddenly became aware of the fact that she and Tsaytis were taking a step into their shared past. At the same time, she also knew they were not the same people they were back then.

Tsaytis sat down in the old armchair. He was no longer the shy teenager he had been, but rather a confident, charismatic man who demanded respect. She had done everything she could to separate herself emotionally from him, in order not to stay trapped in the old days. She shivered lightly. The colorful past with Tsaytis stood like an elephant in the room. Tessa sat down on a ripped leather footrest.

Tsaytis looked at her. He spoke first: "You must really be heartbroken. I wish that I could make it easier for you, but nobody can relieve your pain."

She looked through the window at the furrowed trunks of the cedars. "If only it would have an end," she heard herself say. "I feel like a robot. I can't really mourn before they find the murderer."

Tsaytis brushed hair off his face, a gesture she remembered well. "I don't know anybody who isn't shaken to the core. I'm sure that the police know more than they are saying. Maybe I can give you some answers, Tessa. But first, something personal."

She looked at him in anticipation.

His eyes focused on the rustic bookshelf. He had read many of the books on it while staying at the family's house.

"I have a strong suspicion about who killed the grizzlies. It is very probable that two of our young guys did it. I'm on their trail right now." His face darkened. It must be very hard for him to report this, she thought. "Both of them see themselves as warriors. They don't accept the path I've blazed for the Sitklat'l. They don't accept the results of the land treaty we negotiated with the government. They want complete self-government and our own laws on Sitklat'l territory. Not the laws of the white people."

Tessa understood his internal conflict. The arrival of the white settlers had not been good for the indigenous people.

He looked her right in the eyes. A fire burned in his. "But that doesn't explain everything. The young people wouldn't kill grizzlies unless somebody had fired them up. I belong to the Grizzly Clan, and my ancestors honored and respected the grizzly. It belongs to us like the woods and the lakes and the wind and the ocean. The grizzly connects us with the Great Spirit."

Tessa sighed. Where was the Great Spirit hiding? Whatou Lake was plagued by evil spirits. She asked: "Do you have any idea who's behind it all? Is it the ranger?"

Tsaytis got up. "No, I don't think so. Somebody with much darker plans. My feelings tell me that I'm on his heels. You can help me to stay on his track."

She put two and two together. "You want the photo memory card from me, right?"

He looked down at her. "Which memory card?" He didn't seem to know what she was talking about. Hadn't Lynn Prett told him anything about what she had seen? About the video? The bear researcher wanted to confront Noreen Chelin with it. At least, that was what she had said.

Tessa's hand moved quickly to the breast pocket of her windbreaker. She searched through the pocket several times. Her fingers never found anything. She went through all of her jacket pockets. She looked in the inner pockets, too.

Then in the side pockets again. Nothing.

"I've lost the memory card," she mumbled confused. "Didn't Lynn Prett tell you anything?"

He shook his head. "No, I don't know anything about a memory card."

She tried desperately to figure out where it could be. If it was no longer in her hands, it was senseless to tell Tsaytis what had happened. "It's not important," she said quickly. "Why do you think that I can help you? I'm only interested in Fran and Hank and the children, Tsaytis. I want to find *their* murderer. Whoever is pushing the young people to become bear poachers, you'll have to find out yourself."

"Don't you think all of these events are connected?" Tsaytis sat down on the edge of the old chair, his hands clasped. "First somebody kills the bears, and then . . ." Once again he didn't finish his sentence.

She stayed silent. Everything seemed confused and impenetrable to her. Who was telling the truth, who was telling half-truths, and who was dishing out lies? She didn't know anymore. But Tsaytis had never lied to her. He was sometimes so open that it actually hurt. He had driven her into a rage with his honesty. So much that she wanted to leave Whatou Lake.

"You weren't really searching for Fran, right? Not yesterday or when you showed up at Beaver Lake? You were tracking the two guys who killed the bears."

They stared at each other for a few seconds. Then a shadow fell across his face, and the spell broke. "That's not true. I did look for her," he replied. "I wanted to see who was going to show up at her cabin."

"Why?"

"Maybe somebody was looking for something there."

"*I* showed up. Were you waiting for *me*?"

"It was a possibility. But actually I was waiting for someone else."

"So tell me!"

"Telford Reed." He paused. "I had seen him there a week before. Him and Fran."

She looked at him silently while her brain tried to absorb this new surprise.

After she had collected her thoughts, she said: "I think you're on the wrong track, Tsaytis. Fran met Telford because she had heard that Harrison Miller wanted to buy the outfitter license for Hank. She told Telford that Hank wasn't interested in it. That they were going to move to a farm in Grouse Valley. She wanted to convince Telford not to make a deal with Harrison Miller."

Suddenly she realized that something was wrong with the timing. According to Telford, the two of them had met a month earlier. "When did you see them at the cabin?"

"About ten days ago."

"What were they doing?"

"I saw both of them coming out of the cabin. Fran got on her ATV and Telford on his, and they drove off together in the direction of the V4 forestry road."

Tessa thought about it feverishly. Where had the children been on that day? Was Hank taking care of them? Or Dana? She quickly abandoned the thought. Suddenly everybody was claiming that they had seen Fran with other men. First with Harrison Miller in the pickup in Whatou Lake. And now with Telford Reed at the cabin on Beaver Lake.

Fran had not gotten to know many men in her life. Before Hank came along, there had been something going on with a guy from the baseball team. Nothing serious. And then there had been, as far as Tessa knew, just Hank. Hank and once again Hank.

For a few seconds both of them were silent. Then she spoke up again. "Tsaytis, have you . . . discussed this with Telford?"

"No, I'm just giving you this information. Maybe you can get more out of him."

"Did you tell the police about this?"

"They got an anonymous tip. And I hope you don't give me away."

Of course, Tessa thought. Tsaytis didn't want to ruin it with the guy who wanted to sell his outfitter license to the Sitklat'l. According to him, the alleged encounter happened ten days ago. So who was the person Kratz Hilder had flown in the floatplane to Beaver Lake seven days ago, two days before the murders? She simply had to find out more about this.

From out of the blue, she was submerged in a tsunami of despair. A chasm opened up in front of her. She closed her eyes and held on tightly to the cold stove.

"Tessa, what's the matter?" Tsaytis jumped up and stood in front of her. He put his hands on her shoulder and let go of them just as quickly.

She could only speak in fragments: "Is this our punishment . . . for . . . Jenny's death, Tsaytis? Has the Great Spirit abandoned us?"

Tsaytis stood still, like the cedars around the cabin. At some point he went over to the window and looked out. After a long time, he turned to her. "I've often thought about the Doles, about what losing Jenny must have meant to them. The nightmares, which they must have had . . . or might even still have. Imagining what kind of terrible death their daughter must have suffered. " His voice was rough and emotional. "Especially since I now have kids myself." He cleared his throat.

"You and me, we have to live with the memory of her screaming and dying. We were so young back then. What a traumatic event. There was nothing that we could have done, Tessa. People shouldn't feel guilty about things they have no control over. Jenny decided to lie to her parents, take the ATV secretly, and follow us. Every day we make decisions, and sometimes we make mistakes. And if you have bad luck, a mistake can end fatally."

She stared into nothingness. She would gladly have answered him, but her feelings were too complicated to put into words.

"There's no consolation I can offer you," he said softly. "A lot of times there's only pain and despair."

Tessa remained silent. Her throat felt like a knot was tied around it.

Tsaytis suddenly went to the door. "I have to go," he said. "We'll meet again."

A second later the door shut.

She stood there, unable to clear her head. Instantly, she was catapulted back into the past, back to that day, five and a half years ago, when she had sat with Tsaytis in the main office of the Sitklat'l. She had been in a terrific mood; the national broadcast network wanted to send a TV crew to document the successful land claims hearings and to learn about the Sitklat'l's plans for the future. It was all thanks to Tessa, who had used her contacts with a film producer in Toronto. Back then she told Tsaytis euphorically about what a great chance this film offered the Sitklat'l. It would also be great advertisement for Watershed Lodge.

Tsaytis had listened to her patiently, all the way to the end of her exuberant presentation. Then he said soberly: "We are certainly interested, but we want to have control over the film's content."

"These are independent journalists, Tsaytis; you can't control them completely, but I will make sure that you will always be heard."

"We don't want that."

"What is it that you don't want?"

"For you to have your fingers in it as the contact person. We can speak for ourselves."

"Of course you can; I just want to make a contribution by—"

"Tessa, we don't want your help. Just like the journalists, we're independent. We don't want any white heroes in the film playing the role of our saviors."

She looked at him incredulously. "Do you possibly mean me by *white heroes*?"

Unmoved, he returned her gaze. "We hired you as the lawyer for the land claims hearings. You did good work. Very good work. I've let you know that many times. But now a new era is starting up that we want to take charge of."

"What is that supposed to mean?" Deep down she suspected that he was about to say something crucial. Something that would be critical for her. And not in a positive way.

"Our hereditary council has decided we no longer require your services. Some of the members feel that you're pushing yourself too much into the spotlight."

She felt that she had been struck by lightning. For a couple of seconds, she was speechless. Then she looked at him and asked: "And what do *you* think? You don't have to hide behind the elders."

"Times have changed, Tessa. You should understand that better than the others."

Upon hearing this, an anger rose up in her. It was aimed at the man who sat across from her, her former boyfriend, who—as she believed at this moment—didn't want to have anything more to do with her. "Do you know what I think? *You* are behind this. *You* orchestrated the whole thing. Turned everybody against me. And I also know why." She jumped up. "Because every time you see me, you are forced to remember Jenny Dole and Whitesand Bay. Because you don't want to feel guilty about this anymore. Because you"—her voice almost shrieked—"because you feel like a coward for not helping Jenny."

She had gone to the door. "And you know what, today I see that you really are a coward. You're throwing me in the garbage like a piece of worn-out furniture. Just because some of your people want it. Thank you, thank you very much. You did a good job here, Tsaytis Chelin!"

And with these words she had slammed the door shut.

A few months after that, she had moved to Vancouver. She wanted to start a new life in a new place. She didn't want to see Tsaytis Chelin again. And there was another reason: without work from the Sitklat'l, she couldn't survive as a lawyer in Whatou Lake.

Tessa blinked and was once again aware of the trees in front of the cabin. A raven on a branch clucked loudly.

She'd had a childish meltdown back then, a disgraceful scene, but she no longer criticized herself for it. Her anger had actually helped her to cut the ties with Whatou Lake . . . from her hometown, from her parents, and from Tsaytis.

She stopped in front of the cabin and breathed in the smell of damp wood and new buds. She would have gladly walked through the forest for a while just like she used to, with a light step on the soft ground. But there was no time for that.

32

When she returned to the house, Tsaytis was nowhere to be seen. The meeting with him already seemed as vague as a mirage.

Even before she could open the door, her cell phone beeped. She looked at the display. A text from Cindy: *Harrison wants to know what you are telling the press today.*

Immediately her blood was up. Why didn't Harrison contact her directly? Was he too good for that? In any case a normal person could have figured out that she had to wait for the police to give out new information first. And to do that, she had to wait for the press conference. The best thing would be to ignore Cindy's text.

Savannah was preparing a meal in the kitchen. She had returned sooner than Tessa expected. She was wearing a long tight T-shirt under her orange faux-leather jacket and tight leggings. Tessa hoped she wouldn't show up like that at the press conference.

"They're still sleeping," Savannah whispered and pointed to the upper floor.

Tessa also whispered: "Does that seem strange to you?"

"No. Dad probably helped out with a sleeping pill. Where were you?"

"In my cabin."

"It must have been really cold in there."

"Yes, I'm going to put on something warmer." She quietly went up the stairs. One of the cats slipped through the door into the room with her. Her suitcase lay on the floor, only half unpacked. As she sat down on the bed, she heard a fizzing sound. The cat was squatting in the suitcase and the sound came from her.

"Oh no!" She leaped over to the suitcase; the shocked cat fled under the bed. It smelled like piss, and with her fingertips she held up two wet blouses. Good grief! She let the blouses fall back into the suitcase. This was because of her sloppiness. She should have hung up all her clothes. Exasperated, she put on a wool jacket and went downstairs into the kitchen where Savannah was leaning over the stove.

"Lily peed on my blouses in the suitcase," she complained.

"Oh, no." Savannah stopped stirring. "The poor cat must be totally stressed out. Can you wash them?"

"No, I have to take them to the cleaners."

"Guess what, there are no cleaners here within a thousand miles."

"You're not telling me anything new. Maybe I'll wear a white T-shirt under the suit jacket and a scarf over it."

"Cindy sells blouses. Not in my price range, but she has nice things. Today is Saturday. She's probably in the store. Usually it's closed on Monday and Tuesday."

Tessa considered the option and then called Cindy on her cell phone.

Lionel's wife answered immediately.

"I need two new blouses right away," Tessa said. "I can come to your store; then we can also talk about the other thing."

She noticed some hesitation. Then Cindy answered in her slow way, which sounded like melted cheese: "My store is officially closed today because of the press conference. So we can meet there without being disturbed." She didn't hold it against Tessa that she had never been in the store before.

"Do you have dark blouses in my size?"

"Yes, I have a selection to choose from." Cindy seemed to be almost insulted that Tessa was questioning what she had available.

"Good. I can be there in twenty minutes."

"Come in the back door. That way I don't have to shut off the alarm."

Blouses. Colors. Sizes. And five people are dead. Tessa found it absurd. But she had to function no matter what.

Savannah looked disgusted. She couldn't stand Cindy. "Will you be back to eat?"

She dried her hands on the dishtowel.

"I think so. I'll borrow the Pathfinder for an hour." Tessa was already standing in the doorway when Savannah asked: "What should I tell Mom and Dad?"

"That I'm going to meet Cindy because Harrison Miller wants to know what I'm going to say to the press this afternoon."

"He's crazy."

"This time I have to say you're right. Ciao."

On the way toward Whatou Lake, she remembered the dogs. She hadn't had the opportunity to ask her father if they were now with Harrison Miller. And she hadn't heard from Lionel.

Cindy's boutique, which Lionel had renovated, was in the old post office at the edge of Whatou Lake. There was nobody around when Tessa arrived; only Cindy's Mazda Miata stood alone on the parking lot. Cindy's store was the only outlet in Whatou Lake that sold high-priced lady's clothing. Women like Savannah ordered almost everything over the Internet. For instance the orange fake-leather jacket.

The boutique's back door looked almost shabby compared to the front door. She had to push hard to get in. A staircase led to a hallway that had three rooms along it whose doors were closed.

"Hello?" Tessa called.

She heard hurrying steps, and Cindy showed up. She was

wearing a black dress and silver jewelry. You could see by her face that she was under a lot of stress.

"Come with me; I've already picked out a selection I hope you'll like."

Tessa followed her into the well-lit store. At first it took her breath away. The room's modern design would have been at home in Vancouver. There was chrome everywhere, and lots of light-colored wood along with black-and-silver-accented display cases.

"Wow!" Tessa exclaimed spontaneously.

Cindy's face lit up. "You like it?" She kept smiling for a while.

"Very tasteful. Congratulations." Tessa really meant it.

"It's my design. Not everybody can appreciate it."

Her remark surprised Tessa; she had never received a compliment from Cindy before. She walked around the room, looking at all the clothes. A good selection, not everything to Tessa's taste, but the few well-to-do customers in Whatou Lake were guaranteed to find some piece of clothing they liked. Customers like Lola Dole or Glenda Miller, Harrison's wife, and the wives of the mining executives.

Cindy wore elegant clothes, but she was perhaps trying too hard to look wealthy. Her still-athletic figure would have made a better impression in a relaxed, sporty outfit. Tessa remembered Cliff Bight's words. Hadn't he suggested that Lionel's firm wasn't doing so well anymore? Lionel was certainly putting a lot of money into his wife's store. In order to humor Cindy, Tessa supposed.

Women's lingerie hung in one corner. Next to it was a small cosmetics department, and there were wigs, handbags, and jewelry. She looked at the bracelets carefully and recognized the cat collars.

"Did Fran shop here?" she asked Cindy, who had followed her and was carrying three blouses on her arm.

"No. Do you want to try these on?"

Tessa ignored the question. "But she had cat collars like this."

"Your mother probably bought them for the kids." Cindy

moved her hand over the soft material of the blouses. Strong, almost masculine hands. The serious rowing she did in her sporting days had left its mark.

"How's Lionel doing?"

Cindy's pretty face broke down. "Not well. He would like to do so much, but he can't really move around." Her lips trembled slightly. "He should not have picked up the gun. He's really no good with weapons."

"How's his wound?"

"It's not infected, and that's good. But it will take a while until it's healed, the doctor said. He needs peace and quiet. He's really in bad shape." Cindy sighed. "Hank, the children . . . and now Fran." She fell silent and looked at the blouses as if she didn't know anymore why they were there. "What are we going to do, Tessa? I don't know how I can help Lionel."

Move away with him? Away from this place of murder?

"I sent him a text message, but he didn't get back to me."

"He's not available to talk, Tessa. He has withdrawn completely into himself."

"Just let him know that you're there for him," Tessa advised.

"Harrison needs my help now since Lionel can't do anything."

Tessa thought it was strange that Cindy brought her father-in-law back into the picture, although they had been talking about Lionel. But she didn't want to seem negative, as it was very important that the families worked together to find the murderer.

Cindy continued: "Harrison is a good person and has often helped me out. Not like my father, who turned his back on me."

Tessa looked at her, amazed. Hank had told her that Cindy's father had supported her rowing career, both with actions and financially. "Your father was also your coach, wasn't he?"

"It was more about his ego than my career," Cindy answered. "When I couldn't take part in the Olympics because of my injury, he stopped being interested in me. He dropped me like a hot potato. My five sisters openly displayed their schadenfreude. They were always jealous of me and my success—because Dad paid more attention to me than to them."

Tessa had never spoken with Cindy about personal things. Or seen her sensitive side. This was the longest speech she had ever heard from her. It took an unbelievable tragedy, Tessa thought, for Cindy to be so open with me. And for me to listen to her.

Now she understood better why Cindy didn't want to turn her back on Lionel and Whatou Lake. Here she was accepted even without an Olympic medal. Lionel and Cindy shared a terrible disappointment . . . both felt they had been betrayed. Cindy by her father and Lionel by the person who had told the rowing association that he had been using drugs. But was that love?

"The changing room is over there," Cindy said, once again the seasoned saleslady. "Do you know what you're going to say today to the media?"

"I want to remain as vague as possible, no matter what the press conference is about. We don't even know if Fran was murdered or . . ."

Cindy guessed what Tessa didn't say aloud. "Or if it was suicide? I thought of that, too. Because . . . the police said that they didn't see any external wounds." She hung the blouses on the hook in the changing room.

Tessa took notice. "Have you talked to Sergeant Halprin?"

"No, not me. But Harrison did."

Why had the sergeant spread this information around? What was the point?

Cindy lingered in front of the dressing room. "When you realize that the murderer could be right among us . . . it scares me."

"I assume that he's among us. Watch out for yourself . . . and Lionel. Especially now, since his injury is slowing him down so much." Tessa thought about Savannah, who was with her parents. Savannah knew how to defend herself: she was a good bodyguard. She was the only foster child who took care of

Martha and Kenneth Griffins. A sudden rush of thankfulness came over Tessa.

Cindy fingered the shiny chain that hung around her neck. "Now I lock all the windows and doors. And so do others. Lola said . . . ."

"Yes?" Tessa was listening intensely.

Cindy closed the dressing room curtain. "I'm going to get two more blouses."

Tessa quickly tried them all on. She liked four of the five blouses. She decided on a dark-gray high-necked style with a bow and a somewhat sporty light-blue satin blouse with a shirt collar.

Before she left the changing room, she checked her cell phone. Nothing important there, not from Savannah, Tsaytis Chelin, Telford Reed, or Boyd Shenkar. This vacuum stressed her out more than if she had gotten a dozen crucial messages.

She carried the blouses to the counter. "Lola Dole must think about Jenny all the time when she sees me," she mentioned as she put down her credit card.

Cindy concentrated on the financial transaction before she answered. "It doesn't have to do so much with you. It has to do with . . . you know."

Tessa didn't need any more explanation. It had to do with Tsaytis Chelin. Or *against* Tsaytis Chelin. Against the Sitklat'l First Nation. Certain people could not bear the idea that the Sitklat'l had lived in the area around Whatou Lake first, before the arrival of the white settlers. They resented that the indigenous people had been granted treaty rights in this territory. And that, over time, they had succeeded economically.

Tessa considered telling Cindy about her run-in with Lola Dole in Tim Hortons. Of the hatred that she had encountered. She decided not to say anything. She needed Cindy as an ally. As a link of the heavy chain she wanted to see around the murderer.

"You made the right choice with these two blouses, Tessa," Cindy said. Once again she managed a tiny smile.

Cindy knew all the salesladies' tricks: confirm the costumer's excellent taste in order to put her in a good mood. But in Tessa's eyes, given the situation they were in, it was almost grotesque. Maybe Cindy, in face of the terrible events, also clung to daily rituals, just as Tessa did.

She took the shopping bag. "Thanks for personally coming here, Cindy, even though the store is closed today. There must be more urgent things on your plate than selling me clothes."

"That's perfectly okay; it gave me something else to think about. I can't get away in any case."

Away to where? Tessa asked herself. She remembered Cindy and Lionel's weekend cabin in the woods, the one Cliff Bight had told her about. "The renovation of your chalet will probably have to wait now," she said, just to have something to say. As if that was important in the moment.

Cindy rubbed her hands nervously. "Yes, that's not going to happen for a while. I want to support Harrison. And Glenda. She says she would rather be dead."

"I can understand that," Tessa answered mechanically.

Cindy cleaned up and slipped into her jacket. "I put something nice for you in the shopping bag," she said on the way to the back door.

Tessa was almost sad she had always ignored the boutique. She hardly knew Cindy. And, as it turned out, she also hadn't known Fran well, although she thought she had.

"Harrison's coming to the press conference, isn't he?" Tessa asked.

"Absolutely. I will also be there. I don't know about Lionel."

They simultaneously looked at their watches. Still five hours to go.

Tessa got into the Pathfinder. In the rearview mirror, she saw Cindy lock the back door and put something into the flowerpot next to the entrance. It must be the key. Old habits never die, Tessa thought. Cindy locked the windows and doors in her house but apparently felt safe enough to leave the key to the boutique in a flowerpot.

Tessa drove from the parking lot to the main street. She wanted to ask the police about her pistol. Maybe there was a tiny chance they would give her back the gun. She saw Cindy driving away in the opposite direction. Was she going to deliver a personal report to Harrison Miller?

She reached into her jacket pocket . . . and froze. She must have left her cell phone in the dressing room. Damn it. And without it, she couldn't even call Cindy. Coming quickly to a decision, she turned the car around and drove back to the boutique. She parked at the back door, put her hand into the flowerpot, and picked up the key.

Although she didn't see anyone, she looked carefully around, and then she opened the door. Slowly she felt her way down the dark hallway to the brighter sales room, then went past the lingerie to the changing room. Her cell phone lay there. She grabbed it and went back to the exit. But then curiosity got the better of her, and she opened one of the three doors that led off the hallway. A bathroom with a washer and a dryer. Behind the second door, she discovered a room with a wide couch, a modern floor lamp in the corner, a sideboard with a coffee machine, and a microwave. There was a TV mounted to the wall like in a hotel room. Heavy curtains hung in front of the windows.

Everything was very tasteful. Cindy probably spent her lunch and coffee breaks here until the next customer came in. She closed the door again and took a quick look into the third room, a narrow storage room with cleaning equipment. Tessa had no idea who cleaned Cindy's boutique. She was pretty sure Cindy wasn't the kind of woman to vacuum the place herself. Back outside, she turned the key in the lock and found herself in front of the flowerpot.

At that moment, a car pulled into the parking lot.

33

Tessa stood there like a wet poodle. Her discomfort got even worse when she recognized the person getting out of the car.

Glenda Miller.

Hank's mother was only a shadow of her former self. There were deep wrinkles everywhere on her face, and the tone of her skin looked waxen. Even in her fifties, she had been a very good-looking woman. Now the grief about her son and his children's death had destroyed her looks with one blow. And broken her heart.

"What are you doing here?" Hank's mother asked.

Tessa openly admitted to her what had happened. Glenda listened with her hands buried in the pockets of her down jacket, her arms tensed against her body. Then she took the key from Tessa's hand.

"Come, let's sit down in my car, I'm cold."

Tessa didn't see any way of declining. She took a seat next to Glenda, who stared straight ahead.

"My life has been destroyed." Her voice was not shaking, it was full of bitterness. "I don't have any grandchildren anymore. That's the end of that. Lionel can't have children."

Tessa didn't know how she should reply to this revelation. She could feel Glenda's pain and powerlessness right to her core.

Glenda went on: "They were the most important thing in my life, Hank and the children. Now there's nothing left."

What about Lionel and Harrison? Tessa remained silent. She was afraid that a single word could send Glenda into a rage.

"If the perpetrator isn't found soon, I'm going to start shooting people, one after the other."

"Glenda! What are you saying! You can't be serious."

"Oh yes, I really mean that." She was still staring straight ahead. "Somebody knows who it was. Somebody in Whatou Lake. And isn't saying anything. Because it might be the son, or the husband, or a cousin. And it's always been like that here. They don't care about other people. The main thing for them is to protect their own."

To calm Glenda down, Tessa began talking like a lawyer. "Murderers are often family members, but in Whatou Lake there are also poachers, bear killers, and people who want to protect their mining interests."

She had hardly uttered these words when she remembered rumors about Harrison Miller collaborating with mine owners. Dirty business.

Glenda turned toward her. "Harrison sometimes helps Cindy with bookkeeping. But apparently he's not here now."

Tessa felt trapped in somebody else's car. "Glenda, can I help you in any way?"

"Was Harrison here? He wanted to talk about the press conference with you."

"No. It was Cindy who contacted me."

"Aha. She did." Glenda drummed her fingers on the steering wheel. By mistake she hit the horn, and both of them jumped.

"I offered her the possibility of talking it over with you first," Tessa explained. "You shouldn't have any worries about it."

Glenda pushed her hair to the back of her head. It looked messy and uncombed.

"Fran was a good mother," she volunteered. "She gave us wonderful grandchildren, and now there are none left." Tessa had never heard her talk positively about Fran until now that she was dead. "It's terrible, everything is . . . simply awful," she whispered. "Find the murderer, Tessa. Find him fast."

"The police have to do that."

"I know, I know, but you simply can't wait and watch what the police are doing. You can't do that."

No, she couldn't. But she didn't want to admit that to Glenda. She didn't want to raise any expectations she couldn't fulfill.

"The main investigator, Ron Halprin, has a really good reputation . . ."

"If people don't speak up, he can't do anything."

"He'll do everything he can to make people talk. And sometimes they also make mistakes."

"Who? The police or the murderer?"

"I was talking about the murderer."

Glenda pressed her face against the steering wheel. She stayed like that for a while without talking. Tessa smelled something new. She was familiar with it. The smell of fear. Spontaneously she stroked the shoulders of the desperate woman next to her.

Suddenly Glenda sat up. Tessa saw determination in her eyes. "I won't tell Cindy that you were in there alone. And you won't tell anybody I was here."

Tessa thought about it before she asked Glenda: "Can you put the key back into the flowerpot? That's where it belongs."

"As sure as there's Amen at church," Hank's mother replied.

As Tessa headed for the highway, leaving Glenda behind, she thought about their conversation. About the crushed figure behind the steering wheel. It wasn't true that pain unites people, as it is often said. When you're desperate, you're on your own.

Back on the highway to the center of Whatou Lake, she stopped at a dirt road that turned off to the right. During the night she had sent Boyd Shenkar an email about the events of the day. She wanted to hear his opinion. But first she looked in the bag from the boutique in order to see what Cindy had put in it. It was a bottle of essential oil. She opened it and sniffed. The aroma seemed familiar. Where had she smelled it before? She grabbed her cell phone from the passenger seat and called Boyd's number. He picked up right away. And this was on a Saturday.

"So you've found Fran," was the first thing he said. "How are you holding up?" Boyd's voice was as warm as a cozy room at Christmas when you have come in from the cold.

"I'm trying to suppress it all, otherwise I can't think straight. I'm running around like a zombie."

"Then let me help you think, Tessa."

"My father and I touched Fran and left some clues behind. Afterward I was questioned by Ron Halprin, and my father was also taken in for an interrogation. What should I do now? Naturally we are under suspicion."

"Don't sweat it. Cooperate with the investigators. Usually that helps. Tell your father that as well. Drill that into his head."

"Are you trying to say that my father is under suspicion of murder?"

"No, Tessa, I don't want to say anything like that. Apparently you haven't ruled out suicide."

"If it was suicide . . . why would Fran commit suicide . . . maybe even on the same day that the murders happened? And who hid Fran in Bob Barker's shed after her death? I saw drag marks on the ground."

"Did you see tire marks that weren't from your Pathfinder?"

"I didn't notice any. The ground is pretty dry here. In the last couple of days there was some rain but then the wind dried everything up."

In the background, she heard somebody calling Boyd, but he continued talking: "If it wasn't Bob Barker, it was somebody who knew the area around Whatou Lake really well."

"Yes, I agree. It drives me crazy that I'm not making any real progress."

"These are crazy times, Tessa. It would also drive me nuts if it were my family. But as an outsider, I see—"

"Don't try to protect me, Boyd. It can't get any worse for me than it already is."

"It's a big help to the investigators that her body has been found. They don't have to waste their time anymore looking for her. A body speaks volumes . . . DNA, microscopic marks on the body."

"Why can't we find the murderer or the murderers through the gun that shot Hank and the children?"

"Halprin has certainly called in the gun experts. They need time for their investigation. They need time to trace the origin of the gun. Especially if they find out that the gun doesn't have any special features."

"How much time? Weeks? Months?"

He didn't bother answering because he didn't have to give an answer. She knew that as well as anybody. "I can't wait that long, Boyd. Because my parents can't wait that long for an answer."

"Please don't forget: it hasn't even been a week since it happened."

"I know, I know." A feeling of helplessness rose up in Tessa that threatened to smother her. "Today at four the public will be informed. I can hardly wait."

Several cars from Whatou Lake drove by, and Tessa turned her face away from the road. She didn't want to meet any curious eyes.

Boyd dampened her hopes when he gave her one final thing to think about: "My instinct tells me that Halprin is not going to reveal much today. Take that as a good sign. In case they' re close to their goal, they will not want to have the work that they've done so far fall to pieces."

That was not what Tessa wanted to hear. And she also didn't want to hear what Boyd said next: "Please don't try to put a spike in their wheel, Tessa. Don't wake sleeping dogs. They know what they're doing."

She felt exhausted. "I want to see if I can get my pistol back from the police."

This time Boyd was too smart to try to prepare her for another possible disappointment. "Call me at any time. I will be in court on Monday and Tuesday, but I can call you back during the breaks."

"Thanks, Boyd. You're an angel."

"Where there are devils, there are also angels." He ended the conversation abruptly, as if he was already regretting having made a joke.

She closed her eyes and tipped her chair back. *Just give me five minutes before the hunt starts again.* Now and then she heard a car driving by. Her heartbeat slowed down and her breathing relaxed. *Just five minutes.*

A knocking woke her up. She blinked into the light until she saw a face through the glass.

34

"My God, you almost scared me out of my wits," Dana exclaimed. "I saw Ken's car and then I saw you lying in it."

Tessa reacted sleepily. "I was talking with Boyd. Then I just dozed off."

"Oh poor thing, you're so exhausted. Come on over to my place. Then we can talk things over in peace and quiet."

"Okay." Tessa put the seatback up straight and turned on the motor. She felt like a sleepwalker.

Fifteen minutes later she was drinking tea in Dana's living room. Her friend sat in a rocking chair and listened to what she had to say. She was wearing native jewelry. Tessa told her everything, even about her conversation with Tsaytis Chelin, but not about her meeting with Glenda Miller, since she felt obligated not to talk about Hank's mother.

Dana sometimes replied with a *Mm-hmm* or a *Really?* until Tessa started talking about Telford Reed. Then Dana expressed her doubts.

"I don't really understand that guy," she said. "Why isn't he selling the outfitter license to Harrison Miller? Reed seems to need the money. Why is he still trying to make a deal with the

Sitklat'l? Normally businessmen aren't so . . . generous and patient, if you understand what I'm saying."

"Maybe he's convinced that something is more important to him than fast money."

"Yes, sometimes that happens in movies, but in real life . . ."

"He met with Fran at least once in the cabin on Beaver Lake. Somebody saw the two of them."

Dana's eyes opened wide. "When?"

"About ten days ago."

"Really? Tsaytis saw Telford, right?"

Instead of answering the question, Tessa went on: "Telford and Fran came out of the cabin and then drove off on their ATVs in the direction of the V4 logging road."

"You should ask Telford directly about that."

"On Monday, Fran flew to Whatou Lake on the floatplane. She must have arrived there in the late afternoon. Are nosebleeds dangerous?"

"If you can't stop it, it probably is. If she arrived late in Whatou Lake, she must have been in the ER at the hospital and a lot of people would have seen her."

"Maybe she went right to Dr. Kellermann? The doctor's assistant would have known about it," Tessa pointed out.

Dana shook her head. "She's not allowed to talk about such things. She has to be discreet. Otherwise she'll lose her job. The police must certainly know about it."

"And what did Fran do after that? Who did she meet?"

Dana stopped rocking. "Why are you looking at me like that? She didn't come to my place, and I haven't seen her, if that's what you mean."

"Wouldn't she stop at your place on the way? Spend the night here?"

"She used to do that. But not since February. Maybe you should ask Telford Reed about that." Dana stood up. "I'm hungry. You too? Would you like soup and a sandwich? Like the last time?"

"I should at least try to eat. I haven't had much for the last couple of days. I feel groggy."

Soup and a sandwich. Tessa remembered the two plates and the two glasses she had seen in Dana's kitchen after her father had left. *I saw Ken's car,* Dana had said half an hour earlier on the highway. Tessa watched her as she got the food ready.

"Was Dad here yesterday afternoon, before he picked me up at the floatplane dock?" she blurted out.

"Yes, he made a quick visit here." Dana didn't explain further.

Tessa pictured the envelope in Dana's wastebasket that had drawn her attention. She had seen the same envelope in Dad's office. It had a blossoming Pacific dogwood tree stamped on it.

Dana arrived with the sandwiches and handed a plate to her. Their eyes met. She sat down in the rocking chair. "I know what you want to know. I have nothing to hide."

Tessa lowered the sandwich she had just picked up and put it back on the plate. She had the feeling she was about to experience something that would have serious consequences.

"Your father is the love of my life. But it's unrequited love. Nothing has ever happened between us. Ken loves Martha. Period."

Tessa stared at the native jewelry on Dana's black top. Dana laid her hands in her lap. "There's nobody who's his equal. That's why I never married . . . or never lived with another man. For Ken I'm just a good friend, nothing more."

She got up and sat down next to Tessa on the sofa. "Our friendship has lasted over all these years and I'm proud of that. I don't go around talking about it because only a few would understand." She looked right at Tessa.

"Of all people, you're the one who should understand me the best, Tessa."

"Why?"

"Because you once had the same feelings for Tsaytis. But you got rid of them. You went away. I didn't want to leave here.

Whatou Lake needed me. The new social workers could never stand it here for long. And I feel at home here."

Tessa heard the ticking of the old grandfather clock, an heirloom Dana was proud of. In the courtroom and with clients, Tessa always had a reply ready, an argument, an accusation. In her personal life, it wasn't so easy.

"Thank you for your openness, Dana. I . . . simply have to deal with too many other things at the moment."

"Come, eat your sandwich. And your tea is getting cold. That's no big deal. The really big dramas play out somewhere else."

They both ate silently without looking at each other. Tessa understood only too well that her father was a fascinating person to other people. She would have had great difficulty describing her intense bond with him. While her mother was busy giving her attention to the many children, her father's affection had remained unchanged. Their bond also had a genetic manifestation: their feet had six toes. This anomaly that she shared with her father made her feel special.

"Does Mom know about this?" she asked spontaneously.

"Probably not. I never gave her any reason for suspicion. And neither did your father."

"But . . . what about his visits with you?"

"Ken is always visiting people. Women and men." Dana looked at her thoughtfully. "Ken would never leave Martha. Back when he was getting to know her, she pulled him out of a deep hole."

"What deep hole?"

"He was very much in love with a woman who later left him painfully in the lurch. He had serious intentions and big hopes. But then she dropped him and almost immediately after that married another man. Later Ken found out that she had slept with the man while she was still together with him."

Tessa was speechless. She had never heard anything about this story.

"Who was this woman?" she asked when she found her tongue again.

"He never told me that. There's another thing that you don't know about your father. Yesterday . . ." Dana suddenly seemed to realize that she had gone too far. But it was already too late.

"What did you want to say?" Tessa asked.

Dana hesitated, but then she saw that she had to finish her statement. "Yesterday he took the dogs to a woman he knows, where they are going to stay. Her dog had just died, and she wanted new dogs to have around. It's a good home."

"That will make Harrison Miller furious."

"Ken will never give the dogs to Harrison. Never."

"Dad won't get away with it. They were Hank's dogs."

"They were also Fran's dogs."

"And Lionel?"

"Lionel doesn't want them. Cindy has enough to do with her own little dog. The poor animal is sick, diabetes. She has to give it insulin injections every day."

Tessa absent-mindedly chewed on her sandwich. Dana would always defend her dad. Could it be that it was Dana who had warned her mother about Fran accusing Dad of giving her tranquilizers without telling her? She had to put the pressure on.

"Did you, by any chance, pass along information to my mother?"

Dana wiped mayonnaise off her mouth. "What kind of information?"

"Fran accused Dad of having given her strong drugs to calm her down when she was a child. Mom got this information from somebody. Was that *you*?"

Dana's answer was a simple yes. Tessa waited. She had the feeling that her friend was about to spill the beans. Instead she went back into the kitchen and got some napkins. When she sat down, she began to talk again: "Fran came to me after a séance with Melanie Pleeke. She was . . . she was completely out of control. She told me that Melanie had succeeded in taking her back to her childhood. And what she found out was that Ken routinely gave her drugs. Far too many drugs. And because of that, she was now addicted. That's of course complete bullshit, and right away I said that to Fran."

Dana was about to take a sip of tea, but her hands were shaking so much that she had to put the cup down. "I tried to talk her out of that nonsense. I said to her that I would confront Melanie Pleeke and accuse her of slander. Nevertheless, Fran defended Melanie."

Tessa sat there as if she were paralyzed. What had been brewing in Whatou Lake over the last few weeks? And she had had no idea of the looming catastrophe.

Dana continued: "The longer I talked with Fran, the more insistent she became. I could have shaken her in anger. She thought that she had found a scapegoat for her problems." Dana's fury was written on her face. "In the end, she ran outside. She was really upset. She was completely beside herself! I desperately tried to figure out what I could do to stop her from doing something really stupid. I didn't have any idea what she might do with her 'new' information. So I called up the only person I knew who could stop Fran."

"My mother." It sounded like a computer was speaking through Tessa.

Dana nodded. "Martha knows everything about Fran. She would do the right thing to stop her from spreading lies about Ken."

"What do you mean by *stop*? What does Mom know about Fran that we don't know?"

"You have to ask her that yourself."

Dana tried again to drink her tea; she swallowed quickly and almost spilled it.

Tessa was concentrating on what she had heard. On the cross-examination.

"So you and Mom joined forces against Fran?"

"Call it what you want. But in my eyes Fran was a ticking

bomb that was threatening to go off at any time. Not only Ken, but the whole family would have been affected by it."

"Did you confront Melanie Pleeke?"

"Of course."

"How did she react?"

"Like a mouse in a trap. I really scared her. That's the only method that works with such people."

"How did you scare her?"

"As a social worker, I know things about people that others don't know."

"Did you tell the police about this whole matter?"

Dana fell silent. So the answer was no. Tessa pursed her lips and exhaled loudly. She was always amazed at how much people could stick together if necessary. They could be absolutely watertight. People gossiped a lot, and a secret often didn't remain a secret for long. But when it was really important, they kept mum.

Dana opened her palms imploringly. "Why should I spread lies around? You know how it is. There's always something that sticks to you. And Ken doesn't deserve that."

"Nevertheless it would be better to tell Ron Halprin. I know that Melanie Pleeke has made contact with the RCMP."

Suddenly Fran's soft face appeared before her mind's eye. Dead eyes in a sad, pale face. Fran must have felt betrayed by everybody. By Dana. By her foster parents. By Hank, who didn't want to move away. By Harrison Miller, whose oldest son he wanted to win over with an outfitter license that would bind him to himself and Whatou Lake. By Savannah, who was spying on her. By Lynn Prett, the bear researcher, who perhaps wanted Hank more than she was willing to admit. And maybe also by Tessa, who didn't have much time for her. She must have been very confused. Before, Fran never would have had anything to do with a woman like Melanie Pleeke.

Dana turned a worried face to her: "We've got to stick together, Tessa. That's our only chance. We can't afford to let the murderer get away because of a ridiculous thing like this. Fran went through a crisis. She was psychologically unstable. You've got to protect your family."

"If Fran was so unstable, why didn't somebody help her?"

"We didn't know everything. The various pieces of the puzzle are only coming together now."

"So do you think that Fran killed Hank and the children?"

"No, for God's sake, no, I absolutely don't think that is the case. She couldn't have done it; she was here in Whatou Lake."

"We actually don't know where she was on Tuesday morning, as—"

Alarmed, Dana interrupted her. "She didn't have a car, and nobody had taken her out to the farm in the morning. Her body was found here in Whatou Lake. Please stop plaguing yourself with such thoughts."

Tessa nodded weakly. She knew that Dana meant well. She needed her support. Nevertheless the conversation was draining her. She looked at her watch and took one of the blouses out of the shopping bag.

"I've got to change clothes for the press conference."

Slowly she unwrapped the light-blue blouse from the paper tissue. The satin fabric reflected the light that came through the window. She wanted to stand up, but she couldn't. She sat there as if glued to the sofa. She closed her eyes and everything started spinning.

"What's going on? What's wrong with you?" Dana jumped up. Tessa felt her hands on her shoulders. She couldn't react. It was if she had turned to ice.

"Tessa! Tessa! Speak to me!"

A hand nervously rubbed her right cheek. Then the left one. The rubbing became slaps. Slowly, very slowly, Tessa came to.

She blinked. "I can't do this," she blurted out.

"What can't you do?"

"I can't . . . go in front of the cameras . . . all these people . . . I can't talk about Fran and the kids and Hank."

"I know, I know, it's terribly hard." Dana put her arms around her like a mother and drew her closer.

I'd just like to keep sitting here, Tessa thought, and not get up again. "If you had seen the bodies . . . in the morgue . . ." It was as if the terror, the brutality of the murders had only now entered her consciousness. The children's fear as they were hunted down and killed. One after the other. Hank, who perhaps in the last moment realized what would happen to the children. Who maybe realized that he was in the hands of a murderer—and his kids, too. Fran, who was thrown into a shack like a piece of garbage.

Dana's voice got through to her. "Tessa, do it for Fran and the children. You can do that. If anybody can do it, you're the one."

"I don't know . . . I don't know if I can control myself. I . . . What if I start screaming in anger?"

"You won't do that. I know you too well for that, Tessa." Dana patted her on her shoulder.

"What makes you think you know that?"

"You were brought up to function. That's how you're wired. When it really matters, you will work like a machine. Maybe it would have been good for you to scream earlier."

Tessa shivered, and Dana massaged her arms to comfort her. But inside she was still cold.

"I'll leave my pistol with the police," she said. "It's safer there."

Dana gently shook her head. "You have other ways of disarming a murderer, Tessa. You can defend yourself in other ways. You know the whole justice system. The weapons of the law. You are stronger than you think."

Because of that, some people might find me dangerous, Tessa thought.

She was loath to leave Dana's loving embrace. As if in a trance, she went into the bathroom. When she opened the door, she smelled a scent she recognized from Cindy's boutique.

She turned on her heels and went back into the kitchen,

where Dana was putting the dishes away. "Where did you get this essential oil?"

Dana was holding a teaspoon in her hand. "What oil?"

"The fragrance in your bathroom."

"The fragrance . . . oh, the aroma lamp? What about it?"

"Where did you get it?"

Dana looked at her confused. "It must have been a present . . . who gave it to me . . . ?" She put the spoon on the table. "I think it was from Fran."

"Cindy said that Fran had never been in her boutique."

"What does Cindy have to do with it?"

"I got the same essential oil from Cindy this morning as a sample." She showed her the little bottle. "When did Fran give you this lamp?"

Dana crossed her arms.

"That must've been on my birthday. Back then we hadn't fought yet." Her face turned sad. "She also gave me cookies she had baked." She wrinkled her brow. "Fran was certainly in Cindy's boutique at least once. She showed Cindy how to give insulin injections to her dog. Cindy just couldn't get that straight. She didn't want to wait for weeks before the vet flew in again."

Tessa still had the blouse on her arm. "Why in the boutique and not at home?"

"I really can't give you an answer to that. Maybe because it was more convenient? But I can't imagine Fran ever bought anything there for herself. She's really more of a hippie. Why is that so important to you?"

"Because . . . so much just doesn't add up. Savannah told me that three weeks ago on a Wednesday afternoon she saw Fran with Harrison Miller in his pickup. In the parking lot across from the Friendly Piggy restaurant. Harrison had his arm around Fran's shoulder."

"But that's crazy!" Dana said. "I understand why that would upset you. Fran would never let that happen. She hated Harrison. That's another one of Savannah's inventions to make herself seem important." She caressed Tessa's cheek. "I wish that I could keep that all away from you."

Without a word, Tessa pressed Dana's hand and went back into the bathroom. She freshened up, put on the new blouse, and ran a comb through her red-highlighted hair.

It was her last private moment before she drove to the arena where, in an hour, the police would present their information.

35

Tessa made her way through the crowds streaming into the arena, her eyes covered by sunglasses. Dana wanted to hide herself in the back of the hall and let Tessa go alone to the front. The arena had been turned into an auditorium with rows of chairs. There were four tables in the stage area but nobody was sitting there yet. On the side, reporters, technicians, and a number of TV cameras had taken their positions. Tessa saw Savannah's orange faux-leather jacket in the third row next to her mother. Martha looked up as Tessa sat down next to her. The expression on her face didn't look promising. "Where's Dad?" Tessa whispered.

Her mother sounded angry. "He had to go again to a police interrogation."

Tessa was taken by complete surprise. "When?"

"When you went shopping at Cindy's boutique."

Tessa heard the annoyance in her voice. *You weren't there when we needed you.*

"And you also took the car. If Savannah hadn't driven us here . . ."

Tessa didn't listen to her anymore. She was thinking about her father. Ron Halprin must have wanted something from him that was really important, if he had asked for this interview so shortly before the press conference began. From the corner of her eye, she noticed that Savannah was trying to get her attention. She motioned discreetly to the right. Tessa realized that Harrison, Lionel, and Cindy Miller had just sat down. She couldn't see Glenda anywhere. Lionel looked in her direction and greeted her with a short nod. She returned the greeting and noticed the crutches next to him. Cindy looked ahead, motionless; her chestnut-brown hair sparkled in the stage lights. Harrison and Lionel observed the public carefully.

The hall vibrated under the cacophony of voices. The rows filled up. No one went over to Martha Griffins to offer their condolences. The TV cameras seemed to intimidate the people of Whatou Lake. Was Tsaytis Chelin there, too? And what about Telford Reed? Tessa didn't want to turn her head and search the crowd as Harrison and Lionel did; she avoided the stares that came at her from all directions. Journalists sat in the two rows in front of her. They had tape recorders and notebooks ready. Tessa would rather have been standing somewhere in the back, like Dana.

The RCMP officers appeared from out of nowhere. Tessa recognized some of them and of course Ron Halprin, whose face seemed even more serious and tense than usual. They took their seats at the tables in the front. Tessa felt uneasy. Her father had still not shown up.

A local policeman of Whatou Lake gave a short introduction, and then Kate Jennings, the RCMP officer who also acted as media liaison, took over the microphone: "The special forces of the Vancouver Homicide Unit have been asked by the police of Whatou Lake for support in investigating the brutal murders of Hank Miller and his children, Breena, Clyde, and Kayley. Last night the body of Fran Miller, Hank Miller's wife and the mother of the three children, was found on the outskirts of Whatou Lake. We are treating the death of Fran Miller as suspicious. Sergeant Halprin, who is leading the investigation, will comment on the cases now. Later you can ask him questions."

Halprin's voice sounded steady but it wasn't without emotion. "The terrible events of the last days are as shocking to our RCMP officers and me as they are for you. For the last four days we have been working night and day to resolve these crimes. We have excellent experts, and together we are making progress in this investigation. In the meantime we already have gained many important insights, which we are not making public at this time because the investigation is ongoing and so is the coroner's inquest. That's why you will only hear a few details; we don't want to endanger a successful conclusion of the investigation. I hope you understand that." He narrowed his eyes. The bright lights of TV cameras seemed to bother him.

"Passersby found the body of Fran Miller last night on Bob Barker's unoccupied property. The cause of her death is still under investigation. We didn't find any external wounds on the body that would point to a certain cause of death. Bob Barker is not considered a suspect. He has been in the hospital for the last few weeks."

Halprin tried hard to look directly out into the crowd. It had become silent in the arena. "The more help we get from you, the sooner we will get to the bottom of this. There is now a reward of fifty thousand dollars for decisive tips leading to the solving of this crime. Your help is extremely important. The faster we reach our goal of catching the perpetrator, the faster you will feel safe again in your community." He addressed the man next to him. "Constable, I now turn the mic over to you."

Suddenly there was an uproar in the crowd. The noise level made it hard for the constable to begin with his explanations. Tessa couldn't make out whether it was the reward of fifty thousand dollars that had caused the commotion or the fact that Halprin wasn't going to give any details about the investigation.

The constable raised his voice to cut through the noise. "I want to underline the importance of some steps that we have to take. In view of the latest developments, we are advising you to lock your doors. I know that doesn't seem to be necessary here, and that is why we are recommending this strongly. In the same way, you should lock your car doors. Never go out alone if possible. Especially not in the evening or at night. If you really must go out, we advise you to have someone with you. In general make sure you are being careful, and keep a close watch on your children. Pick up the kids from school or from sporting events. Always know where your kids are. Don't leave any guns lying around where people who shouldn't have them could take them. Report to us if a weapon has gone missing. We can be reached at this number on the white board. We are available any hour day and night."

There was a baby screaming somewhere outside. It was now time for questions. A female journalist was quickest. "When did Fran Miller die? Is she a suspect in the murder of her children, or not?"

Tessa couldn't understand why anyone was still thinking that Fran was the murderer when the police had spoken so forcefully to the public about potential dangers. But she also knew that journalists needed direct quotations and therefore had to ask questions like this.

Ron Halprin took over the mic: "We cannot answer your first question at this point because of the ongoing investigation. Your second question: At this point there are no indications that Fran Miller was involved in the murder of her family."

Tessa heard how her mother sighed deeply, but the next question caught her attention. "Do you have any clues that Fran Miller was killed by the same murderer who killed her husband and the children?"

"The exact cause of death of Fran Miller is still under investigation. It's too early to come to any conclusions about it."

Halprin's answer was vague. Tessa didn't expect any more surprises on this afternoon, which simultaneously disappointed and relieved her. It would make her conversations with the media simpler: she could hide behind the silence of the police.

The reporters didn't give up. "You said that Fran Miller didn't have any external injuries. Why, then, is her death suspicious?"

"Because Fran Miller, after the murder of her family, was found dead in very unusual circumstances in an unusual place."

One of the TV reporters jumped in: "Do the killed grizzly bears have something to do with the murder cases? Are poachers perhaps behind it all?"

"We are following all possible clues. We can't exclude anything at this point."

"Could it also be a crime of passion?"

"What do you mean exactly by *a crime of passion*?"

"A disappointed lover or a jealous business associate."

"As we've already noted, we are following all leads. And that's exactly why we need the general public's help."

"So there aren't any clues coming from relatives of the deceased?" It was the reporter from the *Whatou Lake News* who had popped up in the hospital when Tessa and her father had identified the bodies. *Where was Dad?*

Ron Halprin's voice stayed businesslike. "Please understand that we can't divulge such specific information. A police investigation is based on trust and integrity. Both families of the victims have been very cooperative and—"

"So no family members are under suspicion?" the young reporter broke in.

Tessa saw Harrison Miller leap up, his voice could be heard in the arena even without a mic: "This kind of speculation has no place here. Let the police do their work and especially"—he made a dramatic gesture—"the local people should have a chance to ask their own questions."

The RCMP lady tried to calm things down. "Mayor Miller, we understand your concerns and have set aside time just for questions from the local public . . ."

Somebody shouted: "We would like to know why the thugs who are killing our bears have not been caught." A lot of people turned their heads; even Tessa couldn't resist the temptation.

"Somebody is killing the grizzlies and taking away our main source of income. And what do the police do? Nothing!" The man who made this accusation was a member of the Sitklat'l band.

"At the moment we really have bigger problems than a dead bear. We're dealing with the murders of whole families." Tessa couldn't make out whose voice that was.

"Could we please carry out this discussion in an orderly fashion?" the police spokeswoman implored. "We want everybody to—"

A sharp cry cut through the air. More screams followed.

Once again heads turned quickly to the back rows to see what was going on. Tessa had to squint her eyes because she could hardly believe what she saw.

36

Like in a horror movie, a person staggered forward. Blood was splattered both on her face and on her light-colored jacket.

A thin, almost emaciated woman. No longer young, but with a pale childlike face distorted by horror. The woman shook off the hands of people who wanted to grab her. Halprin and his colleagues were already on the move, whereas the members of the local police stared at the woman in disbelief.

Her wild, whimpering voice echoed through the hall: "Where is Rob? Where is my husband?"

Immediately, she was surrounded by the police. Tessa watched how the woman was laid on pillows made from quickly tossed jackets. Quick orders, hectic movements, children crying all around. The RCMP spokeswoman announced: "We are terminating the event now. Please go home in a quiet and orderly fashion."

In the arena it was so loud that Tessa had to scream: "Who is that?"

"Melanie Pleeke." Savannah grabbed Martha by the arm. "It's best that we take Mom out of here."

The walkway between the chairs was swarming with people,

some trying to push forward to see better, and others trying to get to the exit.

Tessa saw a man coming over to her.

Telford Reed.

"Who the hell is this lady?" he asked.

"Melanie Pleeke. The wife of the funeral home owner." Tessa's heart pounded wildly. Where was her father?

White-clad paramedics stormed in, apparently from another entrance in the front of the arena. They laid Melanie Pleeke on a stretcher. There was no sign of her husband.

A shaken Telford Reed looked at Tessa. "Come with me; we'll get out the same way the paramedics and the police came in."

Tessa followed him closely. She ran into Ron Halprin, who at the same moment noticed that Telford was with her.

"Could I talk to you alone for a second?" he asked and pulled her to the side. "I have to show you something. Not now, but this evening. Maybe around seven. I'll send you a text. Okay?"

"But of course," she answered.

She turned around, saw Harrison Miller trying to persuade an RCMP officer of something, but she couldn't hear what. Cindy and Lionel were still in the arena. Cindy was opening a path for her husband through the crowd. With powerful arm movements, she gradually shoved chairs out of the way. Tessa sometimes forgot that beneath Cindy's fashionable clothes and elaborate makeup there was a former athlete. Cindy could have taken part in the Olympics if she hadn't suffered such an unfortunate injury. Lionel sat there patiently, his hands on his crutches. His face had lost the freshness and charm that had once made him the most attractive man in Whatou Lake. He acknowledged Tessa's glance and nodded in her direction.

"They need help," she called over to Telford.

"I'll take care of him," a voice next to her said. Harrison Miller pushed her out of the way. "Your father once again stands out with his absence when he's most needed." Tessa bit her tongue. Harrison had already reached Lionel and Cindy.

"Why is he still acting as mayor, when his son was murdered?" Telford remarked as they found the emergency exit. "He should let his deputy take his place for the time being."

Tessa didn't answer. What could she have said?

Harrison Miller is not a suspect, but maybe my father is.

On impulse, she turned around. Ron Halprin's eyes were still focused on her. This time she didn't look away until a colleague started talking to him.

Telford was already outside. The bright spring light blinded Tessa, although it was already five in the afternoon. She put on her sunglasses again. The parking lot was almost empty, but the ruby-colored Pathfinder was exactly where she had parked it. A few people were still chatting between the cars. A group watched Tessa when a reporter went over to them. Tessa and Telford hid themselves behind a big pickup.

Where had Dana disappeared to?

Telford put his hand on her arm. "Can I drive you somewhere?"

"Thanks a lot, but I came in my parents' car."

"Shall I follow behind you until you're safely home?"

She looked at his worried face. "Do you agree with the police that people in the community are in danger?"

He looked deeply concerned and let go of her arm. "I . . . don't understand it myself. First they said that there was no danger, and now suddenly . . ." He looked back at the people who were still there, now talking to the reporter. "I wonder who attacked the wife of the funeral director."

Suddenly Tessa just wanted to leave. "I have no idea. Forgive me, but I have to go now, my parents are waiting for me. We'll certainly see each other again soon." She said good-bye and got into the car safely. A terrible thought had crossed her mind, but she pushed it away.

Slowly she drove on the main road through the town. Customers were coming out of the supermarket, and a few were leaving the Royal Bank branch, which had an ATM machine. She saw people waiting on benches in the laundromat. She also saw people in little clusters standing on the sidewalk, talking. The residents of Whatou Lake were trying to stay near one another. It had always been like that. Having other people nearby meant that help, support, and protection were at hand. How would they possibly adjust to the idea that they should be afraid of one another, as the constable suggested at the press conference?

Tessa wanted to turn off on a side road that led to Dana's house. But she'd already had her father's car all day. In addition, she wanted to speak with him. She had tried to reach him by cell phone, but nobody had answered. She dialed Dana's number. Got her voicemail. She asked Dana to call back. The last houses of Whatou Lake were now behind her, and she was completely alone on the road. Suddenly she realized she had forgotten to ask Telford Reed about meeting Fran. The blood-covered Melanie Pleeke had captured her complete attention. She looked at her watch. If she wanted to meet Ron Halprin at seven, she didn't have much time left.

She concentrated on the road, driving faster. A fresh green color gleamed against the woods and between the brown patches on the fields. The air felt crystal-clear, and in the late-afternoon glow everything looked unusually detailed and sharp. It seemed to her as if the mountains were ready to fall down into the river valley. She turned onto the long driveway to her parents' house. A coyote dashed in front of the car. She was lucky not to collide with it. An everyday event, but everything seemed different to Tessa. Threatening. Her childhood home still looked the same as it always had, but it was no longer the same house it used to be. It now contained terror and worries, fear and distrust. And secrets.

Her stomach was already in knots before she got to the top of the hill. She parked the car next to Savannah's Ford Fiesta. Through the windshield, she saw her father coming out the door. He gestured. Tessa understood: He wanted to talk to her alone. She greeted him with a hug. At that moment, she loved her father more than ever. She knew she would do everything to protect him from evil rumors. Silently they went to the cabin in the woods. It was only after he had closed the door behind him that he asked, "What happened to Melanie Pleeke?"

"Didn't Mom and Savannah tell you?"

"Yes, but I still want to hear it from you."

"I'll tell you everything, but first I want to know what the police wanted from you today. Do you need a lawyer, Dad?"

He shook his head. "No, that would send the wrong signal. As long as the police handle me decently, I'll remain cooperative."

Tessa sank down into the old stuffed chair. Her father remained standing. She looked in his face, noticed the bags under his eyes, the absent look, his white hair. "What did the RCMP want from you?"

"Sergeant Halprin asked me about Fran's biological father. It seems that she had been looking for him for some weeks."

"Do you know who he is?"

"Apparently she had gotten a new tip. In any case, she was out researching it. She had also sent different DNA specimens to a lab in Vancouver."

"DNA? From whom?"

"I assume from people who could possibly be her relatives."

"And . . . did she get a positive result?"

"The sergeant wouldn't tell me. He wanted me to give him any possible information . . . or theories about who her biological father might be."

"Do you suspect someone?"

"Fran's birth mother slept with many men; it's hard to know them all. Many of them were also married, that's for sure." He looked at the bookshelf on the wall. "Her mother was promiscuous . . . I'm not judging that. People are created differently. They have different needs. She simply loved sleeping with men. But she still should have taken care of her children."

Tessa grimaced. Was it possible that Fran had inherited a strong sex drive from her mother? Were there lovers? Maybe she should tell her father about Fran's meeting with Telford Reed.

Her supposed fling with Harrison Miller. The visits from the park ranger.

Don't wake sleeping dogs. That had been Boyd Shenkar's advice. She was glad to hear her father's voice interrupt her thoughts.

"I helped the sergeant as much as I could. He showed me Fran's drawings." So Halprin had found them.

"What does he hope to get out of them?"

"Maybe he hoped I could add something. A tip, a key—what do I know? But they were only flowers. And two or three landscapes. Watercolors. I really didn't know that she spent so much time drawing and painting." Kenneth moved around in the little hut like a chained dog. "Now that Fran is dead, I realize how little I actually knew her. Although she lived a long time at our house. Although Martha and I brought her up."

Tessa sought neutral territory. "You did the best you could, Dad. I can imagine that bringing up children can be very difficult." She rubbed her fingers together until they got warm. "What else did Halprin want to know?"

Her father shrugged. "Nothing more."

"Then why didn't you come to the arena?"

"I wanted to stop by the hospital. I hoped to find something out about Fran's nosebleeds. Nosebleeds weren't the only thing; it was also because of her light-blue jacket."

"The jacket that was found in Whitesand Bay?"

"Yes. Maybe Fran had left the jacket behind in the hospital. She obviously didn't want to run around with a jacket covered in blood. I found out who was on duty at the reception desk on Monday evening."

"Who?"

"Lola Dole."

Tessa stood up. "Lola Dole could have taken that jacket with her and . . . and Hogan Dole found it at Whitesand Bay. The Doles took the jacket to Whitesand Bay!"

"That's quite possible, but there's no proof."

"Why would they do that? Revenge?"

"Probably. The Doles, in any case, have been stirring things up for a long time. They want to erect a big memorial for Jenny, not just a simple wooden cross. I heard that they have something like a shrine in mind, almost a place of pilgrimage. The Sitklat'l won't have it. Whitesand Bay is a sacred place for them, where many of their ancestors are buried. The Doles can't do anything at all without the Sitklat'l's consent."

Even before Tessa could digest this new piece of information, her father asked: "So what was going on with Melanie Pleeke?"

Tessa had to make a big effort to shift her thoughts from Whitesand Bay to the arena. She described to her father how the ghostly, thin woman looked as she was approaching the police like a ghost. "Her face was covered in blood; it looked like she had been beaten." She hesitated and then she made the big leap. "You told me once that Fran had been looking at coffins in the funeral home. Apparently she had also met with Melanie Pleeke."

"Fran has nothing to do with the attack on Melanie Pleeke."

Attack? What did her father say? So it *was* an attack?

"I didn't mean that, I . . ."

Kenneth was suddenly at the door. "We'd better go back. Martha is taking a bath and will be done soon. Savannah is cooking dinner. We shouldn't make her wait."

"Savannah is really a big help to you, more than I am," Tessa answered.

"You help us in other ways, Squirrel. It's good to have you here; you two are the only ones who have stood by us."

"Didn't any of the others contact you?"

"Oh yeah, a couple of them did. Philip spoke on the phone with Martha. People are busy and can't get away. But Phil wants to come over soon when he can find the time." He said that without any bitterness.

They met Savannah in the kitchen; she was busy cooking. The aroma of the various dishes floated through the house. Savannah, who had put her hair up, was stirring something in a big pan.

"You've come just at the right time. Can somebody convince Mom to get out of the bathtub?"

Kenneth went up the stairs.

Savannah used the opportunity to get something off her chest. "Do you know the latest? The cops visited the high school."

Tessa raised her eyebrows. "Why?"

"No idea. Maybe your boyfriend Ron Halprin can tell you more if you honor him with your nicest smile."

Tessa was about to reply sharply. Then she saw a new tattoo on Savannah's neck.

A big *T* in a circle.

Tessa grabbed Savannah by the arm and pulled her around. Red sauce spilled on the white stove.

"Why do you have this tattoo?"

Savannah looked at her, shocked. "Which tattoo?"

"Here." With her finger, she poked Savannah's neck. "The *T* in the circle. Exactly like the one on the shack where we found Fran's body!"

"Tessa, what's wrong with you?" She heard her father's voice, but she ignored him.

"Why do you have this tattoo?" she repeated.

Savannah put down the dripping spoon. "What, are you crazy or something?"

Tessa got even louder. "This is the exact symbol that somebody painted on the door of Bob Barker's shack!"

"What?" Savannah frowned.

"This *T* in a circle."

"Man, Tessa, that's the logo of the Tennigan Dodgers. Our baseball team, for God's sake."

"Since when have they had this logo?"

"For a bunch of years. You really don't know what's happening here. Now you're really going bonkers." She grabbed the spoon. "Because of a harmless tattoo, Christ."

Kenneth jumped in. "Come on, come on, girls; calm down. We're all under pressure and—"

Savannah interrupted him: "Everybody around here knows it. Bob Barker is huge a fan of the Dodgers. Tessa should chill, and fast."

"Why should Tessa chill?" Martha stood at the doorway in an olive-green bathrobe.

Savannah told her everything.

Tessa remained silent. Her mother looked at her worried. "Sweetie, you should try to get a good night's rest," she said, trying to calm the waters.

Tessa put her arm around Martha's waist. "I've got to go to the police. Ron Halprin wants to see me again at seven."

"You're going to meet the sergeant again? Why?" Her mother's voice was full of mistrust.

"He told me in the arena that he wants to talk to me."

"First your Dad, and now you. Just for a change, he ought to go and talk to the Millers."

"I'm sure he's already doing that," Tessa replied.

Savannah put two bowls on the table. "Now sit down and eat. I don't want to have cooked for nothing."

And then a small miracle happened: They all began to eat, silently and small portions, but it was a sign of their closeness. A sign of their refusal to give in to the hard fate they had been forced to endure.

After the meal, Tessa thanked Savannah for cooking and put the plates in the dishwasher. She was just about to scrub the big pan when a text message from Ron Halprin came in: *Can you come right away?*

37

Twenty minutes later she was sitting across from Ron Halprin. This time there was no other officer present, and the door to the room was closed. It felt almost intimate.

How ironic, she thought, that I meet this interesting man under conditions that make it impossible to get to know him better. She noticed that he was wearing a different shirt than he had worn at the event this afternoon. His hair had a wet shine. Had Halprin taken a shower before talking to her?

He looked her over as he pushed a pile of papers off to one side.

To break the silence, she jumped right in. "Did the incident with Melanie Pleeke have anything to do with the murders, Ron?"

"First, could you please read through this document from yesterday and sign it down here?" He handed her a transcript of the interview they'd done at Bob Barker's property. She took her time reading through everything. Whoever was responsible for this transcript had done good work. She sensed that he was watching her while she went through her answers. She signed, looked up, and didn't lose a second as she came back immediately to her question: "Is there any connection between the attack on Melanie Pleeke and the murders?"

Halprin checked her signature. "Maybe. Did Melanie Pleeke have enemies?"

Tessa leaned back. "I assume that you have investigated her husband. I didn't see him in the arena. Maybe it's a case of domestic violence."

He didn't seem to believe her theory. "Mrs. Pleeke told us that somebody grabbed her neck from behind, as she was standing by her car, and shoved her face against the window."

Tessa closed her eyes briefly. That was even worse than she had feared. "How is she doing?"

"Her nose is broken."

"I guess she didn't see the guy who did that?"

"No. When she came to her senses, there was nobody around. Who could hate Melanie Pleeke so much?"

"You should know that better than I do, Ron. You've already talked to her. What did she have to say when she contacted you?"

"She had recommended a soothsayer to us to help with the investigation."

Tessa was confused. "That was all?"

"No, she had no use for modern medicine in general and psychiatry in particular, and denied that Fran Miller had ever been at one of her séances to make contact with the deceased. They had only talked about the health benefits of fasting and visualization."

"And you believe her?"

He didn't answer the question and continued: "Mrs. Pleeke told us that Fran regularly took pot to alleviate her muscle pain. That this helped her a great deal."

"And where did she get her pot?" Tessa had hardly raised the question before she knew the answer. "From the park ranger."

Halprin nodded and looked at her. "Coffee?" he asked.

She declined. "Fran probably suffered from depression even

when she was young. I didn't know that until my mother told me about it yesterday. My parents . . . apparently didn't want other people to find out about that. Years ago, people didn't openly talk about mental illness. Fran probably didn't want it to be known, either."

"We're looking carefully at Fran's medical history."

Of course. That was something that must be of great interest to the investigators. "So Fran is still a suspect?"

"We are looking at all possibilities."

The tension in her stomach got worse. "What did Fran die of?"

"We're still investigating the cause of death."

Tessa tried to interpret the expression on his face. She was aware that he was examining her face, too. The sergeant sat slanted in his chair, one hand on the edge of the table, the other one holding the chair arm. This time the shirt sleeves were not rolled up.

"I thought you wanted to show me something," she said.

"Did Melanie Pleeke have any enemies?" He could be just as stubborn as she was.

Now she wished that she had a coffee cup in her hand so she could take a sip before answering. She had come to the conclusion that Halprin's questioning strategy was to not let his strategy be identified. That had already occurred to her when she had talked to him previously. He moved around like a hare trying to get his enemies off his trail.

"I don't know Melanie Pleeke personally; I've never talked to her or had anything to do with her."

"That doesn't answer my question."

"If she was going around telling people who was delivering pot to whom, then maybe she had enemies."

Ron Halprin of course didn't fail to understand that she was beating around the bush. But strangely enough, he didn't continue that line of questioning. Was he already focusing on a suspect?

"We have a list of people who were shown Bob Barker's

property. Does anything occur to you when you look at it?" He shoved a piece of paper in front of her.

She bent over and read a dozen names. She knew most of them. People from the town. Her father was on it; Lionel Miller, too. And real estate agent Hogan Dole. There were also some names she didn't know.

"Yes, something does occur to me," she finally said. "All are men. Probably Lola Dole knew this property, too. And my name is missing. I was there with my father."

Halprin nodded. "You already told me that."

She pushed the paper back over to him.

He took a very long sip of coffee, before he asked: "Are you somewhat involved with Telford Reed?"

For a few seconds she was speechless before she found her voice again. "What do you mean exactly by *involved with?*"

"Are you having an affair with him?"

It was clear to her why he was asking. The type of relationship was of interest to the police when it involved a crime. People tended to protect their sex or love partners; they might lie on their behalf or give them a phony alibi or convince them to not talk, or to not reveal something that might be important.

"No, there's nothing going on between me and Telford Reed."

She let this sentence ring out in the room while she thought back. Had somebody been watching them when he held her in Tennigan Park?

In a flash Halprin threw out the next question: "You were with him at Watershed Lodge?"

"No, that is not correct. I flew alone to the lodge in order to meet Noreen Chelin. I saw Telford Reed there by accident, but he didn't see me. Then he disappeared, and I never even talked with him."

Halprin's silence after her answer made her uneasy, much more than if he had managed to squeeze something out of her.

It didn't take her long to figure out why he was so interested in Telford Reed. Tsaytis Chelin had given the police an anonymous tip about Reed's meeting with Fran at the cabin on Beaver Lake. She got the feeling that Halprin's questions could be a warning to her. She decided to pull him out of his corner. "Why are you asking? Does Telford Reed have something to do with Fran's death?"

"Do *you* have such a suspicion?"

"That . . . never crossed my mind."

The sergeant looked at her thoughtfully. Far too long for her taste. She couldn't defend herself against his bright blue eyes. She lowered her gaze to his loosely folded hands, the muscular fingers she didn't usually see on an office worker.

"What did you want to show me, Ron?" she asked to loosen the tension. "Just the list?"

"This here." He pushed a pile of loose sheets of paper over to her.

She flipped through them and was disappointed. They were the same drawings he had shown her father. Watercolors of landscapes and plants. She recognized Beaver Lake and the clearing around Fran's house. More drawings and watercolors of flowers. Many flowers. Wild flowers and cultivated flowers.

She looked at Halprin. "These were Fran's, I guess."

"Have you ever seen them before?"

"No, I'm seeing them now for the first time. I watched Fran making sketches of flowers on a drawing pad when I visited her one time. But she actually didn't show me any sketches, and I had the feeling that she wanted to keep them private."

"Have you had the chance to think about where this sketchbook might be right now?"

She shook her head. "I had the impression it was something like a diary for her."

"We've found some stuff, but nothing like what you've described."

Tessa put the paintings back. "Why are you showing them to me? What do you hope to learn from all this?"

He picked out a couple of sketches and held them up. "Who

gave these flowers to Fran? They look like they were bought in a store."

She looked at them more carefully. Fran had scribbled her name and the day on the right-hand corner.

"There's only one florist shop in Whatou Lake, and it belongs to Melanie Pleeke. You must certainly already know that." She hesitated for a moment. "I . . . I can't imagine that Fran would pay hard cash for expensive cut flowers that have to be flown in."

"Could she maybe have taken photos of the flowers in the store and used them to draw from?" Halprin looked at her questioningly before continuing on with his thought. "Or did she sketch the flowers in a house she happened to be in when she visited Whatou Lake?"

"My father probably told you that Fran has not spent a single night at our place over the last couple of months. And my mother wouldn't buy cut flowers on principle. She prefers the wild ones in her garden."

He put the coffee cup down on the edge of the writing table, out of spilling range of the various documents. His movements were heavy, it seemed to her, as if he was shuffling a huge burden of thoughts around like a loaded pallet.

Was he thinking about the place where Melanie lived, above the funeral home? She couldn't believe for a moment that Fran would have sketched or taken photos there. Fran didn't visit Melanie for drawing lessons. Or was that part of the visualization technique Melanie Pleeke had talked with Halprin about?

Tessa was relieved when he again changed the topic. "We have almost finished the investigation of Hank and Fran Miller's house and the surrounding area. The day after tomorrow, their relatives may go to their property again."

She tensed right up. This was the news that she had been awaiting impatiently. But now that it had arrived, it came as a surprise.

Before she could say anything, Halprin went on: "Do you

want the crime scene to be disinfected first by specially trained professionals?"

Crime scene. Spattered blood. Traces of violence. Traces of the children's brutal death. Breena, Kayley, Clyde slaughtered. She took a deep breath and replied: "No. That's not necessary." She wanted to see where the children were murdered.

Anything was better than uncertainty. Maybe she could even begin to understand what had happened out there. And she didn't want to see any more strangers in Fran's house. "You can't find professional crime scene cleaners around here. We'll take care of that ourselves. Have you informed the Millers of these developments?"

"No. I'll do that tomorrow."

She returned his look. Was he giving her some extra time?

"When exactly will the house be opened up?"

Halprin gathered the papers with Fran's artwork and put them in a folder. "When the crime scene tape comes down along with the seals on the doors."

That was the information she needed. She felt energized. Her hand pointed to the folder. "Will we get the drawings back? These are memories of Fran's my parents would surely like to have."

"I've got to ask you for some patience; I'll let you know." He rolled his chair back. "There's one more thing I wanted to tell you: we discovered a kind of grave with a wooden cross on the farm. It says *Rosie*."

"That's the third cat. . . . I didn't know Rosie had died."

"We took a look at that grave and found a cat. Is that the cat you were looking for?"

"Yes. I . . . I already brought you the cat collar with blood on it and the name Rosie." She rubbed her cheek nervously. "Now I understand even less why we found it on the trail to Whitesand Bay."

He rolled his chair toward the desk again. His hands, which

Tessa could hardly stop looking at, played with a big paper clip. "The cat in the grave was not wearing a collar."

"Did the blood on the collar come from the cat?"

"Let's just speculate for the time being that this is the way it was."

"Maybe the cat was badly injured and died. Maybe she had been attacked by a wild animal. The children might have wanted the collar as a keepsake."

"And then?"

"Somebody took it from the farm and dropped it on purpose on the trail. On the day we were searching for Fran." She looked at him. "It couldn't have been Fran, right? She was already dead."

Ron remained silent. She would have given a lot to read his thoughts. Did he think that *she* had laid the collar on the forest path? But what kind of motive would she have had? "I wish I could read your thoughts," she said out loud. It almost sounded like a sigh.

He stopped for a moment; a look of astonishment lit up his handsome face. Astonishment . . . or was it something else? Tessa tried very hard to recognize what was floating in the room between the two of them. Then the moment was gone. Halprin stood up and held out his hand. "Thanks for coming."

She took his outstretched hand, which felt warm and strong. His spontaneous gesture encouraged her to ask: "How's the case coming along?"

He cleared his throat. "It is difficult, but we've figured out a lot of things. I . . ." And then he broke off.

She kept pressing. "I don't want to . . . sound like I'm giving you a lecture," she said, "but can't you try to encourage the people to make anonymous tips? In a town like Whatou Lake, it's sometimes the only way to make people help the police. They have to be able to keep on living here. Do you know what I mean?"

He lifted his right arm a little and let it sink down again. "I understand you very well, Tessa," he said. "Probably more than you think."

She nodded and quickly went to the door.

"Do you want to take this with you?" she heard him call. She turned around.

Ron Halprin held a plastic bag in his hand. Her pistol.

"Really? I can have it back?"

"Special permission from me. The gun was not used in a crime. But if you lose it again, I'll make sure that your license is taken away."

"I've been losing a lot of things lately. I've also lost a memory card that the young bear researcher at Watershed Lodge gave me to give to the police. Potentially it includes filmed evidence of a poacher."

He pursed his lips. "We found a memory card at Bob Barker's shack."

"That's got to be it!" she said, relieved.

"Well, I hate to disappoint you. There's nothing recognizable on it. Only blurry shadows."

38

Tessa called up Kratz Hilder's office from her car and booked a flight. She was already halfway home when Savannah's Ford Fiesta came toward her. Both of them stopped on the side of the road and got out.

"I'm going to see Melanie in the hospital," Savannah called over to her.

Tessa was surprised. "Do you know her pretty well?"

"We're both on the fundraising committee of the United Church."

My, my. Savannah was a busy fundraiser for the church. Another unexpected discovery. Lola Dole was also a devoted member of the United Church. As was Cindy Miller.

"So you can visit her?"

"Sure, I spoke to her on the phone." Savannah seemed to be proud of it. "Although I could hardly understand her. She has a broken nose."

"How's she doing?"

"Bad, of course. They are giving her strong painkillers."

"Has she said anything?"

"No. As I mentioned, she can hardly talk. Maybe I'll learn more from her in the hospital."

"Who would do something like that to Melanie? Any idea?"

"None at all. She's a bit nutty, tarot cards and stuff. She believes in ghosts. As far as she's concerned, everything is karma."

A shiver went down Tessa's back. "There must have been witnesses."

"Melanie came late. Everybody was already in the arena."

"And Melanie's husband? How did he react?"

"He wants her to stop with this baloney. No more séances and things like that."

"So he thinks that this attack could have something to do with it?"

Savannah pulled the orange fake-leather jacket tighter. "Of course he's shocked. He was always against it. That's why she mostly did it when he was away."

"Where was he when that happened to Melanie?"

"She thought he was in the arena, but he wasn't there."

"Well, where was he, then?"

"He said that he'd been at the airport to pick up the coffins."

The coffins. For Breena, Clyde, and Kayley. For Hank and Fran.

Savannah opened the car door. "I gotta go. Do you want to come along?"

Tessa had mixed feelings. She would have liked to ask Melanie Pleeke some questions. But not if Savannah was there.

"No . . . no, I . . . we can't leave Mom and Dad alone. Tomorrow I'll be away the whole day. Can you look after them again?"

"Where are you going?"

It was easy for her to give the excuse that she had already prepared. "Legal matters. I've got to find out what Fran's estate consists of."

Savannah nodded. "Yes, do that, before the Millers do. I'm sure that they are chomping at the bit to do that. I'll be back early tomorrow morning."

Tessa would have liked to hug her in relief, but there had

never been any hugging between her and Savannah. And this was not the right time to try something new.

The main door was unlocked when Tessa arrived at her parents' house. She locked it from inside and secured it with a bolt.

Her father was on his knees in the two-story living room pushing logs into the wood stove. She took in the unmistakable smell of cedar and crouched down next to him.

"Dad, you've got to keep that door locked. There are violent people running around."

Her father took the poker and pushed the logs farther into the fire. When he put it back on the tiles, she got out of the way.

"Bring them on," he growled. "Then I can take care of them."

He got up, breathing heavily. His face no longer looked so deeply exhausted, Tessa noted with relief. His morning sleep must have done him a lot of good. A moment of calm before another wave of despair would roll over him.

"While you were away, a couple of journalists came by," he said. "Savannah drove them off with a broom."

"Dad, that's no joke. You have to consider Mom, too."

"She's lying in bed and talking on the phone with her relatives."

She's talking to other people, but not with me, Tessa thought. And I'm also not telling her everything.

Her dad blew his nose. They were both fighting with their emotions. "What did Halprin want from you?" he asked.

Tessa gave him a summary when they sat in the kitchen. Then she passed on the important news: "Fran's house is being opened to the relatives the day after tomorrow."

"We've got to get there as fast as possible."

"That's what I'm planning. I've booked a flight with Kratz Hilder. He can get me there tomorrow. We don't have much time before the Millers know about it."

"You want to get there with Kratz? Will he keep quiet?"

"I've talked about it with him. He won't say anything to

anybody. It'll cost me a pretty penny. I'll walk from Beaver Lake to the farm. There I can take Hank's ATV."

"Are you sure that Harrison won't hear anything from Kratz?"

"Pretty sure. When I asked for some information about a client yesterday, Kratz wouldn't tell me anything. Neither would his wife. They don't want to make any trouble for their business."

"Yes, especially right now. He's got to keep his clients coming." Before Tessa could ask what he meant by that, her father went on: "You've got to go there alone, Squirrel. Otherwise people will notice. The fewer people who know about it, the better."

"So you're not going to tell Mom anything?"

"That would just upset her more."

"And you won't say anything to Dana?"

Her father looked at her amazed. "Not Dana, either."

There was a pause. "And the police?" he asked.

"Officially I'm only flying to Beaver Lake. That's not forbidden."

"And if the RCMP are still at the house tomorrow?"

"Then I'll just wait. The sergeant said I can go in as soon as the tape and the seals on the doors are taken down. I don't think they'll be there all day tomorrow."

He rubbed his chin. "Did the police give you back your pistol?"

"Yes."

"Take it with you, Squirrel; you can't run around there without a gun. Take some pepper spray and a flare pistol. Tomorrow you can take the Pathfinder to the pier. I can pick it up there."

Tessa swallowed hard. She suddenly realized that she was on her own. Out there in the wilderness, she wouldn't have any way of connecting to the outside world. And if the murderer was sneaking around? Many killers felt forced to go back to the scene of their crime.

"Does the satellite phone in Fran's house work?"

"I assume so. But if you use it, everybody will know where you are."

"Just for an emergency."

"Don't you want to take Savannah along?"

"No." Her voice sounded sharper than she meant it to sound. "Didn't we just agree that we didn't want other people to know?"

"Okay, okay," her father said. "You've got courage. Take as many photos as you can. I want to know what actually happened there."

He got up and went back to the stove in the living room. She followed him. They heard Martha's weakened voice from upstairs, as the fire crackled and popped in the fireplace. She noticed the two cats on the carpet, sitting so close to each other that she couldn't see any space between them.

"They're waiting to lie down in front of the stove," her father explained.

Tessa felt the heat through the glass door of the fireplace. "I've learned what happened with Rosie, the third cat. She's buried in front of Fran's house. Halprin told me that. Were you aware of this?"

He shook his head. "No. Martha probably doesn't know about it, either, or she would have mentioned it. Strange. The children certainly would have told their grandma. Rosie was Breena's cat, I think. Each child had a cat."

"I found Rosie's collar on the path to Whitesand Bay."

"Yes, Savannah told us about that. With blood on it, she said."

"Yes. I don't have any idea who could have put it there. Or why."

Her father looked at the flames. "Whose blood?"

"Halprin didn't tell me. Surely he knows if it's human or animal blood."

"He leaves us very much in the dark, this sergeant."

"Boyd, my partner in the firm, told me that Halprin is known for that. An unorthodox way of dealing with things, at least at first glance. But Boyd thinks there's a clever strategy behind it."

"The RCMP talked to a lot of people."

They fell silent, lost in their thoughts. Tessa looked into the fire. It threw a flickering light on the floor and walls.

"Harrison must hate you even more," Tessa mumbled, "because you took the two dogs away."

He snorted angrily. "I'm sure Glenda is thanking me for that. She would have much rather taken Fran's chickens if they had survived than Hank's dogs. She sometimes takes care of Cindy's little dog, and that's more than enough for her."

"Why?"

"I'm sure Glenda cannot understand that Cindy spends all that money on a sick dog. Cindy's dog needs an insulin injection every day."

"But we're not talking about Glenda. We're talking about Harrison."

"Harrison's never home. She would have to take care of the dogs. That's really something she doesn't want."

"She was looking for him today. I ran into her at Cindy's boutique."

"Was he there?"

"No, and Cindy had already left."

"Why was Glenda looking for him there?"

"She says that he often helps Cindy with the bookkeeping."

"I suspect he's keeping the store afloat."

"Why would he do that?"

"So that Cindy doesn't run away. Whatou Lake isn't exactly as exciting as Las Vegas."

"Glenda won't have any grandchildren anymore."

She had hardly pronounced these words when she realized she had made a mistake. Breena, Clyde, and Kayley were also her parents' grandchildren. But it looked like her father hadn't really grasped what she had said.

"I wouldn't be so sure of that," he countered. "Harrison must have other children all over the place."

"What do you mean?"

"Because he's that kind of guy, Tessa. A goddamned womanizer."

An idea formed in her head. *Did Fran think Harrison might be her biological father?*

Upstairs her mother called: "Tessa, are you back?"

"Yes, Mom." She went out into the hallway and climbed up the stairs. "I didn't want to bother you." Her mother was standing on the steps, wearing pajamas, her arms crossed. A wave of affection rolled over Tessa, and she gave her mother a loving hug.

"Why don't we sit down together and have a talk, Mom?"

"Gladly, sweetie. But tomorrow would be better. It's already so late. I was on the phone for hours; I need a break. What did the police want from you?"

Yes, what did Halprin really want from her? "He asked me about Melanie Pleeke and whether she had any enemies."

"I don't understand the police. What does that have to do with Fran and Hank and the kids? They should stick to that. Melanie is still alive." They could hear meowing and clatter from the kitchen.

Tessa pushed her mother's hair off her face. "He also showed me some of Fran's drawings and asked some questions about them. I think they're looking at every detail."

"They can't see the forest for the trees, if you ask me."

"Mom, did *you* buy the cat collars? At Cindy's store?"

Her mother looked at her, confused. "What are you talking about?"

"The collars the cats are wearing. I saw them in Cindy's store. Did you buy them there for the kids?"

"No. What gives you that idea?"

"I'm interested in who bought them. Cindy says Fran had never been in her store."

Kenneth called from downstairs: "I'm making tea for us, dear."

"You're an angel," his wife answered. With her fingers she pulled at her fluffy pajama top. "Where's Savannah?"

"She drove into town." Tessa thought it was better not to mention Melanie Pleeke again.

Her mother took her hand: "Come on, some tea would do you good."

"I'm going to quickly change clothes, Mom." She kissed her mother on her left cheek and went into her bedroom.

Outside, dusk was slowly descending on the mountains, valley, and woods. Only dark outlines of the mountaintops could be seen. Tessa turned on the light and closed the curtains.

She hung her new blouses in the closet and changed into comfortable yoga clothes. From downstairs, she heard the door of the wood stove being opened and closed. The cats' meowing got louder and then died down. They must have gotten their food. Tessa picked up her laptop and answered some emails from friends and relatives, saying only: *Thanks for thinking of me. More to follow soon.*

By the light of the bedside lamp, she opened one of the electronic folders on her laptop. Photos of her last visit to Fran's farm. Breena, proudly showing her painted finger nails. Kayley on the ATV with Hank, her small hands on the handlebars, her face delighted. Hank in the kitchen with frozen moose meat he was thawing out for the next day. Clyde next to him, holding a cat. The cat was still without a collar. Fran, who was showing off her herb garden under a grow light. Parsley, basil, mint, and thyme. One photo of her reading *Harry Potter* to the children.

Fran again, this time feeding the chickens. The bears must have been attracted to the house because of them. Hank wasn't happy about it, but as always, he accommodated her. In the next photo, they stood together in front of the house, Hank's arm around Fran's shoulders, and Fran's arm around his waist. Fran looked so young with her hippie-style clothes and her straight blond shoulder-length hair. Fran's pleasant face in the light of the candles on the birthday cake Hank had baked for her. That had been two years ago. When had the shadows begun to fall over their relationship?

Then photos of Clyde's favorite game. He hid something, and the others had to find it while he gave them tips—*hot, warm, and cold*—that would lead them to the hiding place. On that day, he hid Tessa's sunglasses in the chicken coop. Breena found them, thankfully unscratched. She showed her find proudly to the camera, chicken downs in her hair. Tessa couldn't tear herself away from the pictures. They seemed so valuable now, so irreplaceable.

She heard somebody coming up the stairs. Her father appeared in the doorway with a cup. "You busy bee," he said, looking at her laptop. Then he noticed her tearstained face. Shaking, he put the cup on the nightstand and sat down on the edge of the bed.

"Pictures of my last visit with Fran." Her words came out distorted.

Her father took her hand. "That's what I did today, too. Went through the photos. I had to stop because . . . my fury at the murderer was ripping me apart."

He held her tightly, until she stopped crying. Then he gave her the box of tissues that was on the chest of drawers. Tessa could hear voices from below.

Her father sighed. "Martha's girlfriend, Jenita. I've stopped trying to keep rumors away from her."

"Mom is stronger than you think, Dad."

"I hope so, Squirrel; that's what I hope."

He picked up the cat that had followed him; the animal squiggled around and he let it go.

"I'm staying in bed," Tessa sniffled. "I don't want to visit with people downstairs."

Her father nodded. "I hope you can sleep tonight. You have a long day ahead of you tomorrow. Do you need a sleeping pill?"

"Just for tonight," she said. She swallowed what he gave her. He closed the door softly.

She set the alarm on her phone. Then she grabbed her laptop again to close a file. Suddenly she had an idea where she might find Fran's camera.

She had to get to the farm as quickly as possible.

39

"Kratz isn't here yet. He had to make an emergency flight to Flat Top Island. I'm really sorry." The pilot's wife looked contrite.

I'm also an emergency, and I paid a lot of money for this flight, Tessa felt like saying. She calmed down, but only after a great effort.

"When will he be back?"

"Try again around ten."

Two hours. Up until now, everything had been going smoothly. The sleeping pill had worked and the weather was supposed to be good all day. Nobody was sitting in the waiting room, which meant that there wouldn't be any unwelcome witnesses to her plans.

And now this.

"I'll be back at ten. Here's my cell number just in case you need it." She pushed her business card over the counter.

"I'm really sorry," the woman said again.

Yeah, me too, Tessa thought.

She left the floatplane dock, uncertain how she should kill the two hours. Her first choice would have been to go by Dana Eckert's house, but she didn't want to tell even Dana about her plans. She wanted to be on her own at Fran's house for at least a couple of hours and hoped she could still do that despite the floatplane's delay.

She longed for a cup of coffee, but she didn't feel like meeting the eyes of the early risers at Tim Hortons. Before she realized it, the Pathfinder had reached the outskirts of Whatou Lake. Cindy's boutique appeared in front of her. She hadn't planned on driving so far. But the parking lot behind Cindy's store was out of view, and she could answer emails there.

When Tessa turned the corner to the building, she jammed on the brakes. A pickup and a second car were parked at the end of the lot. She was able to make out two people in the pickup. A woman and a man. The woman was a blonde; her long hair reached her shoulders. They were arguing so loudly that their voices reached her even though the motor was running. The door of the pickup opened and a woman hopped out. Furiously she ripped off the long hair and threw it on the ground.

Tessa held her breath. She recognized the woman. Glenda Miller.

Hank's mother ran to her car, sat in the driver's seat, slammed the door, and drove off. Without looking right or left, Glenda roared past her.

Then she heard another door slamming shut. The one belonging to the pickup. Tessa tried to maneuver her car out of the way. Too late. The pickup was already coming right at her. As Harrison Miller drove past, he glanced over to her with a dark and angry look. He didn't stop.

She sat there, completely stunned. Her car was still running. A couple meters away, she saw something bright lying on the ground. Carefully she drove the Pathfinder over to it and got out.

A blond wig. Shoulder-length straight hair. Like Fran's hair.

All of a sudden, she realized what the connections were. Of course it wasn't Fran in Harrison Miller's pickup that Savannah had seen the day she was cleaning at the Friendly Piggy. It was Glenda, and she had been wearing a blond wig.

Only . . . what kind of a scene were the two of them acting

out? Role-playing to keep the sex in their marriage exciting? As a family lawyer, Tessa had heard about so many different sex games that nothing surprised her anymore. She remembered that Cindy sold wigs and hairpieces in her shop. But why did Glenda and Harrison get into a fight—or whatever that was —*here*? Maybe they thought, as Tessa did, that they wouldn't be seen.

If Savannah had made the mistake of thinking that woman in the blond wig was Fran when really it was Glenda, then other people would have made the same mistake, too. They would have thought they'd seen Fran in places she hadn't been.

On impulse Tessa opened her backpack and took out latex gloves and a plastic bag. She didn't want to make the same mistake she had made with the cat collar and leave her fingerprints on items of potential interest to the police. With the tips of her fingers, she dropped the wig into the bag and carefully put everything in her backpack.

At half past nine, she stood again in the office of Whatou Wings. "He should be back soon, but I don't know the exact time," Kratz's wife said apologetically. "These days there's so much going on. The managers at the mines sometimes call on very short notice."

Tessa was running out of patience. "I saw another Beaver down there. Doesn't it also belong to you? You must have a second pilot."

The woman frowned. "He's no longer working for us." She sounded so dismissive that Tessa didn't want to pursue the topic. In addition there was another couple waiting, and Tessa didn't want anyone to hear her conversation. She went outside and turned her face into the weak sun rays that had managed to break through the cloud cover. The Beaver rocked aimlessly at the pier.

Gulls were circling over the cove, and higher up, two bald eagles soared. Somewhere Tessa heard the rumble of a speedboat. A pleasant wind cooled her face, soft as a feather duster. It carried along with it the fishy smell of the water. Everything seemed so peaceful. As if nothing had happened. As if the murders had been only a nightmare from which one could awaken.

A little plane was circling over the harbor and descending until it landed on the water. A DHC-3 Otter putted up to the pier. A man jumped out and tied the plane up to the wooden dock. Kratz Hilder. He waved and she ran over to him. He helped her put the backpack into the storage area and climb into the plane.

"Sorry about the delay," Kratz shouted over the engine noise. Tessa put on her headphones and seatbelt.

"Good flying weather today." She heard the pilot's voice in her headphones. "It looks good for tomorrow as well. We'll be at Beaver Lake very soon."

"What caused the delay?" Tessa asked.

"I can't tell you. Client privilege."

"So nobody's going to know where *I'm* flying, right?"

"No, of course not."

The Otter sped up and climbed. There were numerous fishing boats below them, like tiny islands in the ocean.

"They can already start fishing in June, while everyone else has to wait until July. And that's supposed to be fair." Kratz Hilder sounded mad. Tessa realized right away why he was angry. The Sitklat'l had the right to start fishing earlier than the other fishermen of Whatou Lake as part of the agreement with the government. A treaty Tessa knew to the last detail because she had served as the Sitklat'l's lawyer in the discussions.

"They were here first, Kratz." The sentence just flew out of her, although she knew that it was better to keep her mouth shut.

"The Sitklat'l also came from somewhere. They weren't always here. We're all immigrants, even the Indians."

Tessa had often heard this argument from white settlers. At some point she realized that the arguments didn't matter much. It was really about greed, blindness, domination, racism. She simply had to counter the pilot's statement: "The Sitklat'l have been living here for at least five thousand years; it's their land and their traditional fishing grounds. They've already lost enough because of us. It's about time that they gain something."

She knew that Kratz Hilder was doing a lot of business with the Sitklat'l. The tourist flights from Whatou Lake had to be lucrative for him. On the surface it seemed that Kratz had a terrific relationship with the Sitklat'l. Noreen Chelin's brother used to work for Kratz. Hilder made sure that the young Sitklat'l had enough flying hours to get a pilot's license. What had her father said yesterday, when they were talking about Kratz Hilder? *He's got to keep his clients coming.*

The Otter made a turn away from the ocean and flew over the coastal mountains into the interior. Through the rain forest below them, the rivers meandered like glittering snakes. Tessa would have liked to ask Kratz whether the overwhelming beauty of the snow-covered peaks and coastal rainforests still fascinated him after so many flights over the millions of trees. There was no end to the dark green and light green and olive green and the lakes between them, which glistened like blue jewels. But Kratz flew into a rage.

"It's easy for you to talk, Tessa. You must've earned a lot of money as the lawyer for the Sitklat'l. This entire Indian aid industry is a sham. People like you don't have any idea what kind of damage they're doing. You're robbing many hardworking, honest people of their existence."

Tessa listened, dumbfounded. Apparently in Whatou Lake, a disease called envy and resentment had spread much more than she could have realized. She was relieved when long Beaver Lake appeared on the horizon and the plane descended. The pilot prepared for the landing. Tessa realized it was the wrong end of the lake. A long way from Fran's cabin and even farther from the farm.

"I don't want to land here," she protested. "I want to go to the other end."

"You said Beaver Lake. I'm landing here. I have to deliver something."

Tessa tried not to show just how mad she was. Her anger was mixed with some nervousness. Kratz's behavior shocked her. She was not only dependent on him today; in the evening the pilot was supposed to pick her up. She also didn't understand why he had been so unfriendly. He couldn't afford to insult clients like her.

The Otter set down on the lake and glided slowly toward the pier. The forest came so close to the water, as if the trees wanted to dive into the lake. Kratz climbed out of the machine, balancing himself skillfully on the pontoons. This time nobody rushed to tie up the plane at the pier. Kratz did it himself; he was an experienced pilot. Tessa remained sitting. There was no way she was going to get out here.

He opened the luggage compartment and threw her backpack on the dock. Then he took out several boxes from the plane's belly and piled them on the dock, which began to rock. When he was done, he opened the door. "Please get out." His voice sounded almost mocking.

She tried to show that she was calm, although her pulse was racing. "Come on, Kratz, we can deal with this peacefully. We—"

"That's what you're good at, you lawyers, dickering and manipulating others. But not with me. I've had enough. This is the last straw."

"What are you talking about? Is there something I should know?"

"There's only one thing you should know, lady. This is your last stop."

She shuddered. She was alone here with Kratz. Nobody else for miles. She deliberated feverishly. Only her father knew where she had wanted to go. But even he didn't know that the pilot had flown her here, fourteen kilometers from where she wanted to be. The only clue were the boxes lined up on the pier. Who were they for?

Talking it over was the only way to resolve the situation.

"Does it have something to do with the second pilot?" she asked. "What happened?"

Kratz's face became even more threatening. But now he began to get it off his chest. "I trained him for seven long years. Seven years. And for what? Now he's flying on his own. That's the thanks I get. What an idiot I was! And that's what *you* did to me. All the money that the government threw at the Sitklat'l. They've bought two of their own planes. From now on, they'll do everything on their own. And I can see where I'm going to be stuck. Nobody's going to help me. But you lawyers don't give a shit about that. The main thing is you get your money."

"Kratz, I didn't know that. I had no idea. There must be enough customers for two companies. With the mines and the tourism. Nobody can do that on his own."

He spit on the dock. "That's the way people talk who have no idea. People who don't even live here." With a quick movement he picked up her backpack. "How long should I wait? Do you want me to throw it in the water?"

She had her ID and her credit card on her. An old practice. But her pistol was in the backpack. She had put it in there because she didn't want it to fall out of her jacket pocket again.

Maybe he just wanted more money. "I'll give you another three hundred if you fly me to the other end of the lake."

Kratz turned around suddenly, a surprised look on his face.

She heard a voice, and a man showed up on the dock.

40

"Hello Kratz," Tsaytis Chelin called out. "Have you brought back something nice for me?" At the same moment he noticed Tessa, who was leaning out of the open floatplane door.

"*You're* here?"

He came over to her, held out his hand, and helped her onto the dock. Kratz wouldn't dare to leave her here alone in the wilderness now. She ripped the backpack out of his hand.

"He wanted to kick me off here and leave me stranded," she complained to Tsaytis. "Watch out for him."

"Ah, she didn't understand me right," the pilot replied. "I've got to unload these things, and then I'll fly her on to the other side of the lake."

Tessa grabbed Tsaytis by the arm. "Don't believe him. He's lying."

Tsaytis nodded to her. "I've got it. Who are these boxes for, Kratz?"

"I don't know. My wife drafted the contract. I'm just carrying it out."

Tsaytis bent over the boxes. "They could be for me. But there's nothing written on them. Why don't you go ahead and open up one of them so that I can see what's inside?"

"They're not for you."

"Then I'll just open them anyhow. And you"—he turned to Tessa—"do you have your cell phone with you? Can you film the whole thing?"

She didn't know exactly what Tsaytis was up to, but she reached into her backpack. What her hand touched inside wasn't the cell phone, but her pistol. Her phone was in the pocket of her jacket.

In this moment, Kratz punched Tsaytis in the jaw so hard that he fell onto the dock. With his boots he kicked him in the head and stomach. The dock swung back and forth. Kratz lost his balance and landed on his knees. Tessa quickly pulled out her pistol and pointed it at him.

"Don't move or I'll shoot," she yelled.

Kratz grimaced; the fall must have done more damage than she thought. He tried to get up; one arm dangled at his side. She shot in the air. The sound could certainly be heard all around. Kratz gave a start.

"Don't shoot him," Tsaytis said. He clambered up; his face was covered with blood. "You little shit," he screamed at Kratz.

"He's gone crazy because Noreen's brother quit working for him," Tessa explained, without taking her eyes off of Kratz.

With his hand, Tsaytis wiped the blood off his face. "This is a free market, Kratz. Is it only supposed to work for people like you?"

The pilot contorted his face. "Just keep talking, you goddam idiot; you bedded her to get money from the government."

Tsaytis, unblinking, looked at Kratz, who was cowering on the dock, and then at Tessa. "We really should tie him up." And turning to the pilot, he said: "Don't do anything stupid; the lady here is so angry she could shoot you."

"You'll live to regret this," Kratz snarled. "Somebody will knock you off for this. You can bet on it."

Tessa aimed her pistol at the pilot's head. "Are you

threatening to murder us? The police will really be interested in hearing that."

Tsaytis took a rope from his jacket pocket, something Tessa also always carried around with her in the wilderness.

Kratz tried to kick him, but his injured arm made it impossible to do any damage. His arm and Tessa's gun.

"Leave my arm alone; it's broken," he hissed.

"Maybe it is and maybe it isn't, but we can't let you run around loose," Tsaytis said calmly. He tied the pilot's hands and feet up. Kratz lay on the dock, out of commission and boiling with rage.

With his knife Tsaytis opened the first box.

Two hunting rifles and a lot of ammunition.

In the second box was a bow and a dozen arrows.

Tessa stepped back in shock. "My god. That's meant for the bear poachers."

Tsaytis squatted next to the boxes with a furious look on his face. "That's what I almost expected. Now we have the ringleader." He stood up and looked disgustedly down at Kratz. "So you're in bed with the poachers, you friggin' creep."

"You're nuts. What poachers? I don't have anything to do with them. I don't know what's in these boxes."

"Oh yeah. You're probably also flying drugs around everywhere, asshole."

"You can believe what you want; I'll take you to court for slander until you wish you had never met me."

"Tough luck, Kratz. I have the best witness in the world."

"She's a goddamned whore."

Tessa lunged out with her pistol and would have hit Kratz in the head with it if Tsaytis hadn't grabbed her arm.

"Tessa, Tessa," he warned her. "Put that gun away now; otherwise something worse might happen."

She had trouble controlling herself. Tsaytis kept her away from Kratz. "Put it away, Tessa. The game's up for Kratz Hilder." He picked up the backpack, and she put the locked pistol in it.

Taking her arm gently, he led her away to the end of the dock. They sat down on the shaking boards.

Her heart was beating wildly.

"Did he murder Fran and Hank and the children?"

"I doubt it. But we have to leave that up to the police." He checked his nose. "Doesn't seem to be broken. But it hurts to breathe."

"What are you doing here, Tsaytis?"

"Our people have finally caught two young guys we've been tracking around here for a long time. We thought they were waiting for somebody. Maybe a boat. And who came? Kratz Hilder."

"Have you been suspicious of him for a while?"

"No, not really. But when you warned me about him, it clicked. Suddenly everything fit together. How the poachers could move around so quickly, how they could get to where the dead bears were found later so fast. Kratz flew them around."

They didn't let the pilot out of their sight, in order to make sure he didn't roll into the water.

"What's going on with Noreen's brother? Was Kratz trying to take his revenge?"

"Noreen set up a new flying company with her brother. I think that's a good idea. She's a smart businesswoman." Tsaytis looked out at the lake, which was glittering in the midday sun that had broken through. It was dark on the other side where the tall trees threw shadows onto the water. Only the lapping of the waves and the calling of birds could be heard. "We'll have our own two floatplanes. Before, we always had to take Kratz's plans into consideration. He's less interested in tourism, and more interested in the mining companies and cargo transports."

"I was afraid he was just going to leave me behind here. Did he think he could get away with that?"

Tsaytis looked at her with his dark eyes.

Tessa suddenly remembered a different pair of eyes. Worried, questioning, thoughtful. Ron Halprin's eyes.

I understand you very well, Tessa. Probably better than you think.

"I don't know what Kratz was planning to do with you. After everything that has happened, I'd stay out of his way."

"He's completely out of control. He acted . . . like he was crazy."

"It's not only our new firm. Noreen's brother told us that Kratz's wife wants to leave him. Maybe that was the last straw."

"So you caught two of your young studs red-handed."

"Yes."

She drove off the no-see-ums buzzing around her head with fierce swats. These bloodsuckers didn't seem to bother Tsaytis. He sat there motionless.

"Did they kill another bear?" she asked.

"No, a doe. They probably wanted the cadaver as bait for the bears."

"Did Kratz deliver drugs to these guys?"

"No. He gave them money. That's what they told us. The park ranger was the drug dealer. Kratz wants to destroy our tourist trade. He's completely obsessed with the idea. A hate-filled person."

"What's going to happen with these youngsters?"

Tsaytis took a deep breath. "We're not going to abandon them. We'll try to get them back on the right track. We made mistakes with them and failed to make them a part of the plans we have for the future. They should be proud of our traditions, of what we have accomplished. And also of what we are trying to do now."

She considered it all and counted to three, then spoke: "Tsaytis, I've got to ask you this question, though I find it hard to do. If Kratz can get these young guys to kill bears for money, wouldn't they . . . wouldn't they be ready . . . couldn't they be convinced to do something worse?"

He turned his head. "You mean, to murder people?"

She didn't avoid looking at him directly, but she also didn't answer the question.

Tsaytis shook his head. "On that day they were nowhere near the farm."

"How do you know that?"

"'Cause we've been watching them." Tsaytis threw a glance at Kratz, who was lying there and flinching incessantly, plagued, like Tessa, by the no-see-ums.

"Where are you going to go now?" Tsaytis asked at the same time as she asked him: "What are you going to do now?" For a moment they smiled at each other.

Tsaytis answered first: "I'm waiting for my pals. They should be here soon. We have a satellite phone."

"And then?"

"We're going to call the police and wait here. Then you can confirm what happened."

"No, no, no." She held up her hands. "I don't have any time; I have to get to the other end of the lake as fast as possible."

Tsaytis didn't ask what she wanted to do there. "You can't fly with him." He made a dismissive gesture toward Kratz, whose obscene screaming they could hear very clearly.

"What a disaster." She stood up and impatiently spun around.

Tsaytis remained sitting, looking out over the water. "We have two boats," he said. "You can take mine. A couple of us can fly back with the police helicopter."

She breathed in. "Would you really do that?"

He stood up and stretched. "If you start off right now, you'll be reasonably safe. The wind usually comes up in the early afternoon. I'll give you an extra can of gas. You can make your witness statement later."

He knows for sure that I want to go to the farm, Tessa thought. "Tsaytis, I don't know how I can thank you enough."

He wanted to say something when a man came out of the

woods. A conversation took place between the person and Tsaytis.

Tessa didn't understand every word of the Sitklat'l language. But one word really caught her attention: *bastard*.

41

As she prepared to leave, Tsaytis didn't say much; he had done everything in his power for her. He watched from the shore how she handled the motor. Then she raised her hand to signal that she was ready to sail. There was a silent understanding between them that the murders of Fran and her family didn't involve Kratz, or his young teenage accomplices and the dead bears. That's why Tsaytis didn't insist that she stay until the police arrived.

Carefully she steered the boat across the lake while she watched out for deadheads that could capsize it. It was also possible that the motor could conk out but she pushed the fear in the far back of her mind. From the water she saw nothing but virgin forest. If the motor broke down, she might be able to swim to the shore, but what then? It would be so easy to get injured or lost in the impenetrable forest. A vision that filled her with dread. The wilderness was merciless.

At least the surface of the lake was still calm; there was just a gentle breeze. Beaver Lake could be dangerous even for experienced sailors. She had never steered such a big motorboat before, but its size increased her confidence. In addition, Tsaytis had given her a life jacket. Far and wide, there was no other boat to be seen. The vessel's airflow kept her cool despite the heat of the noonday sun, which stood at its zenith. The journey seemed long to her. At the speed she was going, she would need more than half an hour to reach the other end of the lake. Two bald eagles circled overhead. One of them dove suddenly and came back up with a fish in its yellow talons. The second eagle pursued it. Her eyes scoured the shore; the trees, as straight and sharp as lances, formed a green wall, its reflection dark in the lake. There was movement on the rocks protruding from the water. A wolf or a coyote—at this distance she couldn't tell what it was. When she looked at the lake again, she saw a floating tree trunk straight ahead, just a few meters away. She only missed hitting it by a hair's breadth. Her heart stopped for one beat. Better not to take one's eyes off the water. As she throttled the motor down, she could hear the plaintive cries of the loons.

Finally the other end of the lake came nearer. She could make out the roof of Fran's cabin. Relieved, she steered toward it. When she reached the shore, she tied the bowline to a tree and threw her life jacket into the boat. Almost in a trance, she walked up to the cabin. The door wasn't ajar like last time. Instead she saw the police seal across the entrance. She felt her throat drying up in disappointment. If the seal hadn't been removed from the cabin door, it could mean that it was still on the farmhouse door, too.

She had no choice; she wanted to get there as fast as possible. The shortest route led through the woods, but it was also the most dangerous one. She had only done it once when Hank had led her through the underbrush to the lake to join Fran and the kids. There was no clearly defined trail; she remembered that well. Hank had made his path through the wilderness almost like a sleepwalker. That was too risky for her. She had to take the longer hike on the ATV trail to the logging road.

She looked at her watch. One o'clock.

If Kratz hadn't spilled the beans, she still had enough time before other people showed up at the farm. She fastened the bear spray to the outside of her backpack, drank some water, ate a chocolate bar, and started off. Without a cooling breeze, she began to sweat profusely under her hat with the mosquito netting. The June sun was surprisingly warm. Grizzlies liked to use the ATV trail through the woods; just like humans, they preferred to travel on the most comfortable path instead of crashing their way through the undergrowth. Tessa would have felt better if she had had the four-wheeler instead of being on foot. Continually she looked behind her and into the woods.

She began to talk loudly to herself, in order to give wild animals the chance to notice her and make an escape. She said whatever occurred to her. "I have enemies I didn't know about. Kratz Hilder. Maybe Fran and Hank also had enemies they didn't know about. And that I don't know about. The same goes for my parents. And Dana and Savannah. What have we all overlooked?" Her voice gave out. The pain overcame her like a thousand jellyfish stings. She hiked faster. "I'm going to get you," she repeated like a battle cry. "I swear I'm going to get you."

Intermittently, she took a sip of water. Time and again she stumbled over roots and stumps. Far away she heard a helicopter. The police were following up on Tsaytis Chelin's phone call.

Shortly after two o'clock, she reached the logging road. Her sweaty T-shirt stuck to her back, but the closer she came to her destination, the better she felt. She still had an hour to go. When she heard a truck approaching, she hid in the bushes and let it go by. She'd encountered no other vehicles by the time she saw the driveway to Fran's farm ahead. With a racing pulse she walked up to the house. Other than tire tracks she didn't see any sign that the police was still here. The yellow-and-black plastic tape was gone.

She went around the corner and threw off her mosquito net. There was no seal at the door. She breathed a sigh of relief. Her calculation had paid off, and she had the house all to herself before the Millers showed up the next day.

The door was locked, but she knew where she would find a

hidden key. She picked up a flat stone and found it in a plastic bag underneath it. The people around here didn't put any effort into finding good hiding places. Like Cindy with her flowerpot. Tessa took off her hiking boots and entered the house in her socks. A feeling of cold dread crept up in her. And it wasn't just the cold of the unheated rooms.

She quickly bolted the door behind her.

The afternoon light flowed through three windows into the kitchen. It was the sunniest room and had also been the warmest. It was here that she had sat and talked with Fran over coffee, frequently interrupted by the kids asking questions or wanting to show them something. She remembered how often she and Fran had discussed their shared childhood experiences, school and their teachers, girls and boys they didn't like, tricks that the other foster children had played on them and how they took their revenge. Back then Fran had never mentioned the problems and fears that tortured her. The only thing she did complain openly about was her loneliness.

Tessa noticed old bits of food and crumbs on the big wooden table that Hank had built with his own hands. When Fran wasn't home, Hank hadn't been in any hurry to put the dirty dishes away. Tessa assumed that the police had taken the used dishes and cutlery to check for evidence. She also noticed the many places with white powder on the doors and furniture where the police had clearly searched for fingerprints.

There were colored lines and arrows on the linoleum floors, apparently the paths taken by the killer or the children. Everything else in the house appeared to be completely normal. As if at any moment the children and Fran and Hank would storm in and hug her.

The sweat on her body felt cold. Tessa put on her vest and left her backpack and hat on a kitchen chair. With a dull ache in her stomach, she made her way into the living room, which separated by a sliding door from the kitchen. She had to turn on the light because the room was dark. The colored lines on the floor continued on from here. She took out her cell phone and began to take photographs. This technical procedure gave her some more distance from what she knew was coming.

The first thing that caught her attention in the living room was a lamp that had been knocked over. A children's picture book lay on the sofa, a rumpled wool blanket next to it, a folded map on the side table, Kayley's rocking horse next to the mini piano. Toys for the dogs on the colorful woven rug. The beginning of a knitting project near the window. A string of lights hung over the fireplace ledge.

Tessa had slept on this sofa bed when she had visited. But something was missing. She thought about it, but she couldn't remember what it was. The room smelled of incense, as it always had. She couldn't see any incense sticks, but probably the smell was still in the fabric of the furniture. Fran had laughed when Tessa had teased her about it and said: "Otherwise it always smells like wet dogs in here." The dogs! On the hike to the farm she had come up with a new theory. Maybe Hank had locked them in the storage room on that terrible day because, with their wild barking, they had made a racket when the grizzly showed up. Hank wanted to make sure that the dogs didn't make the bear really mad. And all that noise might have covered up a lot of other noises.

Holding her breath, she went down the hall to the bathroom. The door was partly open, and here she saw dried blood for the first time. Blood everywhere. On the floor, in the bathtub, on the edge of the tub, on the walls. Clyde's blood. He must have tried to get away from the murderer, must have wanted to hide in the bathroom. But he wasn't quick enough to lock the door, which had not been kicked in or shot at. It seemed as if he hadn't been hit right away, but had run around in his prison to try and avoid the bullets whose holes Tessa discovered on the wall and window frame.

She documented everything with her camera, this time as a movie.

Maybe Clyde had tried to get outside through the kitchen door. But somebody had cut off his escape route. Maybe he ran around the sofa into the hallway and then to the bathroom. A six-year-old boy running for his life.

By then, Hank was already dead. He couldn't help Clyde anymore. And Breena, his sister, who was two years older, couldn't help him, either. The attacker must have killed her before the others because he thought that his victims would all be in the children's bedroom. But Kayley and Clyde must have been in the master bedroom, where Fran often let them play. Tessa knew that from her visits there. Breena liked to close the door of the children's bedroom when she wanted peace and quiet.

That was the best explanation Tessa could come up with. She was pretty sure that the children were all on the upstairs floor when the murderer came into the house. It was possible that Hank had sent them upstairs because a grizzly was near the house. Bears were strong enough to knock in house doors. On the upper floor the kids were safer. It was probably a routine event: bear around the house, children go upstairs, close the doors. Fran was in Whatou Lake because of her nosebleeds. The children ignored the shots they heard. Hank always tried to drive off the bears with shots. For some reason he had left the main door unlocked. Maybe the children thought it was their father when they heard steps on the creaking stairs, just like she now heard her own steps.

The children's bedroom was on the right side. Tessa opened the door. She wasn't prepared for the sight of Breena's blood-spotted bed. She closed her eyes for a moment to gather her thoughts and then went closer. The blankets were pushed off to the side. Breena had probably sat down on the bed, propped up by pillows, to read as she liked to do. Blood had soaked into the pillows. Bloodstains were sprinkled all across the wooden wall. Nevertheless it didn't look like there had been a struggle. The murderer had walked in with his gun, pressed it against Breena's temple, and pulled the trigger.

The bunk beds didn't show any signs of violence. There was a book on a stool in the corner: *The Dragon Slayer*. No bloodstains on it. That couldn't have been the book Breena was reading when the killer came in. The police must have taken it with them.

Tessa heard a knocking in the quiet house and listened intently, but it must have been the wind that was beginning to blow. Would Breena have had time to scream? Could she have warned Clyde and Kayley? Maybe not, but both of them must have been able to hear the shot in the children's room.

Hadn't Tsaytis told her father that Kayley had hidden behind the laundry basket?

As if being drawn in by a ghostly magnet, Tessa went to the door of Fran and Hank's bedroom. She had to compose herself before going in. She breathed hard and turned the doorknob. The bed was unmade—not one of Hank's priorities. Tessa let her eyes move around the room. The laundry basket stood in the corner. But she didn't see any blood. Nothing. The parents' bedroom was not where the gruesome deed could have taken place. It was the only room with wall-to-wall carpet, and it had no bloodstains.

But the killer knew he would find Kayley somewhere up here. Tessa suddenly had a hunch where she should search. Just as the murderer had realized where he would hunt down the child. In the narrow corners of the unfinished attic. It was where the cats liked to sleep and where the dogs had their baskets.

The dog baskets. Tessa closed the bedroom door, bent down, and felt her way through a narrow passage into the attic. Here, too, she noticed chalked arrows on the floor. Her nerves were on edge as she turned the corner.

And then she saw it. Dark, dry blood. In front of one of the big dog baskets. And on the cushion in the basket.

Kayley had hidden herself in it. Why hadn't she thought of that before? Fran had once told her that she had been looking for her youngest child when Kayley was two or three years old. Fran only found her after calling her name frantically, again and again: Kayley had been asleep in one of the dog baskets. It was where

Kayley had sought shelter from the murderer. Four years old and so smart.

Tessa stared at the basket and her trachea constricted. She couldn't breathe.

She pushed through the narrow exit of the attic and stumbled down the stairs. Away. She had to get away. From the living room into the kitchen. *Open the door.* Like hunted prey, she unbolted the door and ran outside. She took in deep breaths, over and over.

Her feet felt the grass through her socks. She sat down on a tree stump and looked at the house in the sun that, in better times, she used to find so inviting. An idyllic oasis in the wilderness. Now it was a house of horrors.

The mosquitoes were buzzing around her. Reluctantly she returned to the kitchen, put on her hiking boots, and shouldered her backpack. On her way out, she hid her pistol in her jacket pocket. In front of the house, she crossed the clearing, surveyed the surroundings. A small white cross near the chicken coop caught her eye. The flat heap of soil around it looked fresh. Rosie's grave, which the police had investigated. Somebody had painted cat paws and Rosie's name on the white cross.

Tessa walked to the other side of the house. With her eyes on the ground, she crisscrossed the meadow. She didn't find anything suspicious until she reached the edge of the grassy clearing. A spot that was darker, the grass flattened. Patches of soil, traces of white chalk. That must have been where Hank fell to the ground with deadly bullets in his body that he couldn't have seen coming. The murderer must have been very close. Hank probably talked with him, not suspecting anything evil.

She looked up at the house. Maybe one of the children had appeared under the window when there were voices outside, and the murderer saw the child. And the child saw him. Once again she felt a cold shudder run down her spine. Nearby in the woods she heard a rustling and cracking. A bear? It could be any kind of wild animal. Maybe a deer.

She walked back to the front of the house, where she remembered how Fran had once laughingly told her that she had hidden her camera outside in an old wooden nesting box for birds, because Clyde had tried to take the camera apart to study it. Tessa didn't see any nesting boxes on the wall of the house. A couple of meters from the edge of the forest, she detected a group of three cedars. Quickly she found what she was looking for. The nesting box was low enough on the tree that she was able to open it. Inside lay a compact camera in a plastic bag. The camera she had given Fran as a gift on her last birthday. It had been a present with a message: *Fran, don't dismiss the digital age completely. For the sake of your children. That should also be possible on a farm in the bush.*

She put on her latex gloves and carried the camera out of the shadows into the light of the clearing. To her surprise, she could start up the device with no trouble. She looked at the stored pictures, one after another, while she waved off the bugs. It began with various photos of flowers in a room. After looking at dozens of photos, she knew where Fran had taken the pictures: in the lounge in Cindy's boutique.

It must have always been at night, judging by the light of the lamps. The heavy curtains were pulled shut in all the photos. Now Tessa also understood where Fran had spent the night when she was in Whatou Lake. She must have done it secretly because Cindy had no idea. Fran would never have asked Cindy for permission. She had somehow found out about the key in the flowerpot. Maybe she had seen Cindy by chance when she hid the key.

Just then, a shadow fell across her.

Big and black.

42

Shocked to the core, she spun around.

Cliff Bight.

What in god's name was Lionel's employee doing here?

"Cliff! Have you gone crazy, sneaking up like that? I almost had a heart attack!"

Cliff stopped and shifted his heavy body from one foot to the other. "I'm sorry, Tessa. I didn't know that you—"

"What are you doing here?" Her shock had changed into anger.

The extra-long T-shirt that fluttered around Cliff's massive body was soaked with sweat. He hit himself on the forehead where the no-see-ums were flying around.

"Lionel . . . sent me over here to see . . . whether the police had finished . . ."

"Is Lionel *also* here?"

He shook his head.

Shit. Kratz Hilder had talked. She got angrier. "Why didn't I hear an engine?"

"My pickup is down below. I didn't want to unnecessarily . . . I mean, I didn't know what was going on up here." He looked at the ground and then off to the side. His face folded up like a flower at nightfall.

Suddenly she saw something moving. Cliff had a poker in his right hand. She put her hand in her jacket pocket and took a hold of her pistol. "Cliff, put that poker on the ground and take ten steps back!"

"How? What . . . ?"

"Do exactly what I say," she yelled sharply.

He understood that she was serious. The poker fell on the grass and Cliff stepped some meters away.

She picked it up at once and asked: "Where did you get that?"

"It . . . was lying in the back of my pickup."

"And how did it get here?" She clutched the gun in her pocket.

"No idea." He shuddered nervously.

"Cliff, don't play any games with me. You'll be sorry if you do." She pointed with the poker in his direction.

"I took it with me from the cabin."

"Which cabin?"

"Lionel's cabin. I found it with a load of scrap metal. We're renovating Lionel's cabin. He told me to take all that stuff to the garbage dump. I . . . thought it would really be a shame to throw all of it away."

Tessa tried to figure out what was true and what was a lie. "Don't make this any more difficult than it already is. Why would you bring something like that to the farm?"

His fat arms went up and down. "The bear . . . I saw it wandering across the street. So that's why I brought that thing with me, in case . . ." He stopped and concentrated. "I hear something, isn't that . . ."

"Don't try and change the subject, Cliff. Your hunting rifle, you left it in the pickup?"

"No, at home."

She dropped the poker. Cliff blinked into the sun, confused, but she wasn't finished yet.

"When did you pick up the metal scraps from the cabin?"

"A couple of days ago. On Tuesday."

"On Tuesday?" On the day of the murders. Her heart pounded like a drum.

"Yes."

"And then you unloaded it in the woods, right? That's against the law—you know that."

He shook his head. "I never do that. I always recycle everything according to the law. I went to the scrapyard that day."

Now Tessa, too, heard a sound. Footsteps. She turned around quickly.

Cindy was walking toward them.

Tessa looked at her, aghast. But Cindy only glanced at her quickly before she concentrated on Cliff.

"For god's sake, what are *you* doing here?"

Before Cliff could answer, Tessa said: "Hello, Cindy. I wasn't expecting you here, either." She couldn't keep the sarcasm out of her voice.

It was impossible to interpret Cindy's facial expression because she quickly put on her sunglasses. She was wearing flowery pants and a pink windbreaker. The breeze was messing up her hair. She confronted Cliff again: "What are you doing here?"

"We always take a break on Sunday," Cliff answered, still standing several steps away.

"Did you two come here together?" She aimed this question at Tessa.

"Did *you two* come here together?" Tessa countered. She picked up the poker. "Cliff brought me a present."

Irritated, Cindy stared at the poker.

Right then, Cliff announced: "I'm going back to the pickup, to park it somewhere else." With astounding agility, he ran off.

"You could have told us something," Cindy complained. "We could have come here together. Where is your car?"

"I flew over here with Kratz Hilder, and then I hiked in." And now you have forced me to change my plans, Tessa would have liked to add.

But she was too clever to let her anger and disappointment show. She needed Cindy's help to explain the pictures in the camera, which she had put in the pocket of her vest.

"Have you already been in the house?" Cindy asked.

"In the kitchen," Tessa answered, a half-truth.

"Why are you wearing rubber gloves?"

"I don't want to leave any fingerprints on Fran's possessions." She took out the camera.

Cindy's face looked confused. She took her sunglasses off. "Does that belong to Fran? Where did you find it?"

Tessa ignored the question. "I looked through the pictures, and most of them show the lounge in your boutique. Fran must have spent some time there."

"Let me see them." Cindy stretched her hand out toward the camera, but Tessa was quicker.

"Not without gloves." She put the camera in her backpack. "For instance, she took pictures of the flowers in your lounge."

Cindy turned her head, as if she thought someone was there. But neither Cliff nor the pickup could be seen or heard. "You're mistaken, Tessa. Fran was never at my place, at least not that I know of." She began to wave off the bugs, too. "I've got to go to the bathroom, but going in there . . ." she pointed to the house, "is something I'm not going to do. It's just too . . ." Without completing her sentence she hurried to the edge of the forest.

Tessa took the opportunity and ran into the house. She found the satellite telephone next to the fridge. It worked. She called her parents' number. It seemed like an eternity until Savannah answered the phone.

"Hi, Tessa, what's going on?"

"Quick, give me Dad!"

Savannah lost no time. Tessa heard her father's voice right

away. "Dad, I'm in Fran's house. Cindy is here and Cliff Bight, too. He came with a poker."

"Tessa, what are you saying . . . is everything okay? I heard that Kratz Hilder . . ."

"Dad, I don't have much time. Tell me, how late is the scrapyard open on Tuesdays?"

"Until three. It always closes at three. Why . . . ?"

"I'll explain everything to you later. I've got to hang up now. Don't worry."

She once again looked all around the kitchen. When she opened the front door, she heard a motor and honking and yelling from the back side of the house. Cliff's voice. He sounded alarmed.

She ran outside, in the direction of the noise.

And stopped in her tracks.

Twenty meters away, a grizzly shook its gigantic head back and forth. The animal seemed extremely upset. Its growling and snorting was even louder than the engine of the pickup, where Cliff was sitting behind the wheel. Instinctively she wanted to run back into the house, but an inner voice warned her: *Don't run, don't run!* The grizzly might follow her. The massive animal could run really fast, she knew.

The pickup was not far enough away from the bear, so she couldn't save herself by getting in the vehicle. The honking only seemed to make the grizzly angrier. Tessa took out her gun and shot once into the air.

The grizzly gave a jerk and looked at her with its little eyes. But it didn't run away.

She put the gun back quickly and grabbed the side of her backpack where the flare pistol was. She pulled it out, aimed next to the animal, and pulled the trigger. The ball of fire landed pretty close to the grizzly, who jumped to the side and fled. Cliff drove the pickup up toward her and stopped. He got out, his face still in shock. "She'll come after us," he whispered, as if the animal could hear him. "She's not going to give up."

316

"She's gone," Tessa said, gasping. They both assumed it was a female. She let the backpack sink to the ground and confronted him: "Cliff, the scrapyard closes at three on Tuesdays. You must have left the cabin around or before noon."

He looked at her questioningly before he understood what she meant. His lips began to quiver.

"You've got to tell me the truth, Cliff, for Fran and Hank and the children's sake."

He sucked in his lips, as if he wanted to stop them from talking. His face turned red.

At that moment a voice thundered between them.

"What's going on here?"

Tessa didn't have to turn around to know who it was: Harrison Miller. The mayor of Whatou Lake.

With Cindy in his wake.

Tessa looked at Cliff. "They didn't come with you?"

Cliff shook his head.

"There was a grizzly over there." Tessa pointed to the spot where the animal had angrily shaken its head. "I drove her away with some shots."

"That bear has been haunting the farm for a long time." Harrison looked around nervously. "Hank couldn't get rid of her."

Cindy moved toward Tessa and Cliff. With a quick movement, she tore away Tessa's backpack. In seconds, she had opened it and stuck her hand inside. Harrison looked at her, amazed. Tessa wanted to stop her, but Cindy knocked her to the ground.

"Where's the camera? Where's the camera?" she screamed like a madwoman. Her sunglasses fell down. She threw out the water bottle, the suntan lotion, and Kleenexes. And the blond wig flew out. Cindy's eyes got bigger. "She has that, too? Harrison, *she has that, too!*"

It was obviously getting unpleasant for the mayor. "It doesn't mean anything. Pull yourself together."

Meanwhile Tessa was on her feet again and wanted to get at Cindy. But Harrison came between them and held on to her.

"Stop it, both of you," he ordered. "It's like kindergarten here."

"Don't you see?" Cindy screamed. "She has the pictures from my lounge and also the wig!"

Tessa tried to shake off Harrison. At that point, Cindy was already aiming a pistol at her. "I'm not going to return this backpack to you," she yelled. Tessa froze.

Harrison tried to get a hold of the pistol, but Cindy jumped to the side. Worried, he called out: "What are you doing? Don't do anything stupid."

"She has the wig, Harrison. And the photos. She's going to rat on us."

"Goddammit, shut up."

"Smells like smoke." It was Cliff talking.

Tessa also smelled it. And then she saw it. The smoke was coming from the house.

"Something's burning there," Cliff shouted but didn't move from where he was. "It's burning!"

At that moment, Harrison launched himself at Cindy and knocked the pistol out of her hand.

Tessa turned her eyes to the house again. Flames were licking at the living room window.

"You . . . you've set fire to the house!" she yelled in horror.

A cacophony of voices followed.

"The house is burning!"

"Harrison, she will rat on us!"

"Shut up, damn it!"

"You've set the house on fire!"

"It's burning down!"

Suddenly a loud huffing and snorting came from the edge of the forest.

For god's sake, the grizzly.

Then everything happened very fast. Tessa snatched the

backpack from Cindy, ran over to the pickup, and climbed into the driver's seat. The key was in the ignition. She heard Cliff yelling. With a few large steps, he was at the pickup and jumped in the passenger seat. He could really move quickly for a big man.

In the chaos, she decided that Cliff was less dangerous than Cindy or the fire or the grizzly. She started up the engine and steered the pickup to the driveway. In the rearview mirror she saw the flames spreading. The windows burst with a loud bang.

"We've got to do something, we've got to do something," she said and stopped the pickup at the end of the driveway.

"Keep driving," Cliff roared in panic. "Nobody can do anything in there now. Somebody used a fire accelerant. Get going!"

She stepped on the gas. "What about a forest fire?"

"The trees are far enough away."

"But if the wind blows, the sparks . . ."

"I have a satellite phone. We can stop farther down the road. In the undergrowth. Where they won't see us."

"You mean they're going to follow us?"

"Cindy has completely lost it. She would have made short shrift of you. My god!"

She drove the pickup around the deep potholes. "Why are they burning the house down?"

Cliff didn't answer that.

Harrison or Cindy, or both of them, must have made their way into the house when she was talking to Cliff, and set the house on fire.

She has the wig, Harrison. And the photos. She's going to rat on us.

Goddammit, shut up.

This couldn't be true.

"Do you see the big boulders ahead of us?" Cliff said. "Turn in there just before them."

Tessa slowed down and spotted a way into the underbrush where the pickup couldn't be seen from the road.

319

Cliff took his satellite phone from the back seat. "Do you want to call the police?"

She nodded.

The dispatcher put her through, and an official answered. She briefly described the situation, and also mentioned the grizzly and Cindy's pistol. And her suspicion that a fire accelerant was involved. She gave her GPS position and mentioned Cliff Bight.

"Where are you traveling right now?"

"To Whatou Lake."

"Any weapons in the car?"

"Yes, I have one."

"What is it that you've got?"

"A pistol. I have a license for it."

"And Cliff Bight?"

"No weapon."

"Good. Give us your position again in a half an hour."

"Roger."

She gave the phone back to Cliff and looked at him. "You don't want to talk to the police?"

He looked down. "Not here, not now."

"The quicker you act, the better it'll be for you. That's my advice as a lawyer."

"I've got to tell my wife about it first. What . . . should I expect?"

"You lied to the police. You told the RCMP that you were in Lionel and Cindy's cabin the entire day on Tuesday. And that the two of them were also there the whole day. You all provided alibis for each other. Why?"

"We didn't want . . ." He stopped.

"What didn't you want?"

"Lionel . . . he likes wild game. And so does Cindy. They always give me some of it."

She sighed audibly. Half of Whatou Lake seemed to be poachers. Lionel, too. No wonder that poaching escalated when the ranger was mixed up in drug dealing and didn't care about it.

320

Tessa drummed her fingers on the dashboard. "When did you drive out to the cabin on Tuesday?"

"I got there a little after eleven, and then I loaded the scrap metal."

"Were Lionel and Cindy already there?"

He shook his head.

"When did you drive back to Whatou Lake?"

"Between twelve and twelve thirty."

"You gave both of them a false alibi. That could be seen as an obstruction of justice. Did somebody put some pressure on you?"

"I don't want to lose my job. I have to take care of my family. It's not easy to find work in Whatou Lake. My wife . . . she only works part time as a cashier at the Kmart."

"I don't want to mislead you, Cliff. In the worst case, you could become a murder suspect, if you don't have a watertight alibi." He looked at her anxiously, but she didn't give him a break. "That's why it's so important right now to tell the police the truth about what happened. Do you understand that?"

He shut his eyes for a moment and nodded. After taking a deep breath, he asked: "Can I drive now? I think Cindy and Harrison must have gone to the cabin."

Tessa suspected the same. Otherwise they would have already passed them on the road. The cabin was located in the opposite direction.

Cliff turned the pickup back onto the logging road. For a long time neither of them spoke. It was a depressing silence.

Cliff was the first to break it. "What was all of that about the wig? What did Cindy mean? Why did you have Cindy's wig with you? And why did she pull out a gun because of it?"

It's not Cindy's wig, Tessa wanted to say right away; *she had sold it to Glenda.* But something clicked in her head. Like dominoes that were starting to fall.

What if it *had* really been Cindy's wig? What if Savannah had seen Cindy in Harrison's pickup near the Friendly Piggy, and not

Fran? And not Glenda, either? That would explain Cindy's violent reaction.

She's going to rat on us. Who was *we*?

She has the pictures from my lounge.

A number of scenes appeared in Tessa's mind. The fight between Harrison and Glenda in the parking lot behind Cindy's boutique. Furiously Glenda had thrown the wig on the ground. That morning, she must have followed her husband in the car. Just like yesterday, when she had shown up unexpectedly and come across Tessa, who had the key to the back door of the boutique. Glenda, who had demanded she not tell anybody.

She remembered something else: Harrison, the womanizer. Who was it who had said that? Her father. Yesterday evening. *A goddamned womanizer.* Cliff braked so suddenly that Tessa was stopped short by the seat belt. They were only a couple of meters away from a dark-gray vehicle they hadn't seen before because of a sharp curve. It was parked by the side of the road. Another pickup.

"Fuck," she heard Cliff swear.

That's what she thought, too.

The pickup belonged to Lionel Miller.

43

Cliff turned off the ignition and got out of the pickup. Tessa saw him talking to Lionel through the open window of the driver's door. She couldn't understand what they were saying. As if paralyzed, she just sat there, not knowing what to do.

Tense minutes passed before Cliff came back. He opened the passenger door. "Lionel wants to talk to you."

She didn't want to face that; she looked for an excuse. "I don't have any time now; I've got to get to Whatou Lake."

"It's better that you tell him directly."

"What did *you* tell him?"

"That his father and Cindy are at the farm. That they set the house on fire. And that we drove away because a grizzly showed up."

"Does he have a weapon in the car?"

"I saw a hunting rifle on the back seat."

"Does he know I have a pistol?"

"I didn't tell him about that."

"So what happens if I get out and you just drive away? Then I'm trapped."

"I'll give you the ignition key, okay?"

She thought it over. "When I go over there, I'm going to seize the hunting rifle and give it to you."

He blinked. "And you'll help me find a lawyer?"

"Yeah, okay, I'll help you. I know you're not the murderer."

He handed the key over to her and they both got out. Slowly they approached Lionel's pickup. The window was down. She looked at his nervous face. "Lionel, I thought you couldn't drive."

"I can with my right foot. Get in, I want to talk to you."

"Sure." She glanced over at the back seat as she went around the pickup. Quickly she opened the back door, took out the hunting rifle, and gave it to Cliff.

"What the hell are you doing there?" Lionel yelled.

"Cindy threatened me today with a pistol. I don't want to have that happen again." She opened the passenger door and cautiously left it open a crack.

"Cliff, give me the rifle," Lionel shouted. But his employee didn't respond.

"Cliff, do you hear me, give me the goddamned gun!" Lionel looked like he was going to get out of the car, but then he remembered that his foot was injured and gave up. "So Cindy is at the house?" he asked hoarsely.

"Yes, with your father." She gripped the handgun in her pocket. "Cindy has a pistol with her. What's going on, Lionel? Why is Cindy running around with a pistol and threatening me with it?"

"I have no idea." He avoided looking at her.

"I found Fran's camera. There are pictures of the lounge in Cindy's boutique. Cindy almost went nuts when she heard that. Why?"

Lionel's head dropped onto the steering wheel. He mumbled something.

"What are you saying? I can't hear you."

He slowly pulled himself together. "Because she met up with my dad in the lounge."

"Who? Fran?"

"No, Cindy."

"I know he helped her with the bookkeeping."

He laughed, but awkwardly. "Yes, maybe that as well. But out there at Bob Barker's property, he was screwing her."

His words hit Tessa like a lightning bolt. It took several seconds for her to be able to talk again. "What are you saying? Are you sure?"

"Mom saw them. Mom knows everything. She has . . . she has proof, photos. Hank had already told me that before, but back then I didn't want to believe it."

"Hank? When did you last talk to him?"

"On Tuesday."

Tessa froze. "You called him?" she asked because she didn't want to give up all hope. Hope that it wasn't as bad as it sounded.

"We were there. At the farm. Cindy and me." Lionel didn't look at her.

"Did you tell that to the police?"

He shook his head silently. Pressed his lips together.

She had to force him to talk. "I was in the house, Lionel. It is horrifying. I . . . could picture everything. How it . . . played out. Breena was probably the first. The murderer went into the room as she was reading. I . . . the murderer shot her point-blank in the temple. Like an execution."

Lionel held on tightly to the steering wheel. His hand bones stuck out like the ribs of a starving animal. He was having difficulty breathing.

He has to hear this, Tessa thought. The children's suffering. Now that the house has burned down, no one will ever see it again as she saw it. "Clyde fled from the killer into the bathroom. Blood was everywhere. On the floor. On the walls. It looked like . . ." Words failed her. After a pause she picked up the thread again. "Like in a slaughterhouse. Kayley got the worst of it. She . . . she hid in the dog basket that was up in the attic. Little Kayley. Just imagine, Lionel. She knew that . . . that her life was in danger. But the murderer found her and shot her. It is . . . I can't believe that anybody could do that; I simply don't understand it."

Lionel sat there with his eyes closed. She grabbed his arm and shook him. "How should I understand this, Lionel? Tell me, *how*?"

He took her hand and pressed it without saying anything. Let it go and collapsed in his seat. As if somebody had squeezed every bit of air out of him.

He spoke in a scratchy whisper. "Every day I wish it hadn't happened."

Tessa held her breath. *Now, now it's going to come.* At first he could only stutter, but then Lionel's sentences began to flow faster and faster. "We knew . . . that Fran was in Whatou Lake. Lola Dole . . . she saw her at the hospital and told Cindy about it. I absolutely had to talk with Hank. Your mother . . . Martha had told me that my dad . . . wanted to buy the outfitter license for Hank. I had no idea about that; I was furious when I heard. Why should Hank get everything? Without having done anything to deserve it? He had been unsuccessful in all he did. A farm that didn't bring any money in. A wife who had problems. He wasn't any good as a logger. Hank was a failure. But for Dad he was always number one. Hank, Hank, Hank. Simply because he was the firstborn. And I . . . my firm could go bankrupt, and Dad wouldn't lift a finger!" He hit the dashboard with his fist.

Cliff, who was waiting a few meters away, holding the hunting rifle in both hands, shuddered. Tessa threw all caution to the wind. "Maybe he wouldn't do anything for you, but for Cindy. I've heard that your father gave Cindy some money to keep the boutique afloat."

Lionel tightened his jaw so forcefully that he trembled. "Cindy said that the money came from *her* father. It's probably not the case. I'm sure Dad seduced her with his money. He always gets what he wants."

Lionel is still trying to excuse Cindy's actions, Tessa thought, despite everything that's happened. "How did Hank find out about all this . . . . about Cindy and your dad?"

"No idea. He didn't tell me. Maybe from Mom. Cindy and I drove out to the farm on Tuesday. I went up to the house alone, and Cindy stayed in the pickup, waiting for me. I met Hank in the clearing with a hunting rifle. A grizzly had just been nearby. We started arguing right away. He didn't want to share the outfitter's license with me. He had other plans, he said. You have your own company, Lionel, he said, and I'm going to do something different. I knew exactly what he was planning. He wanted to sell the license to the goddamned Indians. I said that to Dad, but he didn't want to hear anything about it. As usual he believed Hank."

Now he really started confessing. I don't want to hear it, Tessa thought. I don't want to hear it. How could I even stand it? How could I even live with it later?

But Lionel couldn't stop. "I told Hank: It's better if you move away from here. You don't have the slightest idea how Fran spends her time. When the ranger is up at your farm while you're away. What's she always doing in Whatou Lake? I asked him. Does she ever tell you anything? What's she always doing at Rob Pleeke's? Did you explain that to you?"

Lionel began coughing because his voice had become so hoarse.

Tessa didn't say anything. Fran. Hank knew all that from Fran. She told him about Cindy and Harrison. She must have found something in the boutique lounge. Maybe she had watched them having sex. Just like Glenda.

Suddenly they heard a helicopter.

Lionel flinched. "Are they on their way to the farm?"

"Maybe. You can probably see the smoke from far away. Your father's going to have to explain things."

"Tessa. It was *me*. I killed Hank."

"For god's sake, Lionel!" she blurted out.

He looked at her with glassy eyes. "He was outside in the

clearing with the hunting rifle. The dogs and the children were in the house. A bear had once again been in the chicken coop that morning. As I was telling Hank about Fran's affairs, he lost it. He said to me . . . he said: You have no idea who's really screwing around. Ask Cindy. She's going at it with our dad. In the boutique and in the pickup and elsewhere. You have no idea, you idiot. You just close your eyes and pretend that nothing's happening. Just like back then with the doping. Back then, did you really believe that you would have gotten away with it?" Lionel's voice sounded just like Hank's voice when he imitated his brother. "It would have shown up at the Olympics, you know. Then it would have been not only your name, Lionel, that would have been in deep shit, but the whole family's. And all that money from Dad would have been thrown out the window. Simply because you, you idiot, didn't want to see that doping is a dead end."

Lionel looked at her, his face distorted with anger, an anger that he was now reliving. "That's what Hank said. I suddenly understood who had ratted on me back then. It was Hank! He had let the Olympic Committee know. He destroyed my future." Lionel shook his head as if he still couldn't comprehend what Hank had done many years earlier to his sports career. "Then we went at each other . . . and suddenly I had his rifle in my hand and there was a shot and . . . and . . . he was on the ground and not moving."

Tears fell down his face and his voice was like that of a distraught child. "I drop the rifle and run back to Cindy. She's still sitting in the pickup and waiting for me. I say to her: I just shot my brother. I shot Hank dead. Cindy . . . she's shocked. Did anybody see you? she asks. Where are the children? she asks. Where's the gun? Your fingerprints are on it, she says. She jumps out of the pickup, runs up to the house. I wait for her. Then I hear shots. And the dogs barking. A lot more shots. So many shots. And then I know. She's killing the children. I didn't stop her."

Lionel was whimpering like someone being tortured. His whole body was shaking.

Tessa sat silently there. Now that she knew the truth, the real, awful, unbearable truth, she couldn't feel anything more. Her head, her body, her soul refused to digest the words. There was an impenetrable wall that protected her and kept her from breaking down.

Cindy. No, that couldn't be.

Cindy would never kill children. There was nothing she wanted more than to have her own children. She couldn't even kill a dog. She loved dogs.

But then another picture of Cindy appeared in front of her eyes. Cindy with the pistol.

Cindy has completely lost it. She would have made short shrift of you.

Tessa screamed against his whimpering. "Did you tell her . . . Lionel, listen to me! Did you ever tell Cindy that you knew about her and your father?"

"No," he said, depleted. "No, I didn't want to believe it. I thought that Hank just wanted to make a fool of me. Until Mom showed me the photos today. She . . ."

Tessa couldn't understand the rest of what he said because she heard an ear-splitting noise. Shocked, Cliff was waving around his gun and yelling something to them. She tried to understand his gestures and sounds.

It was too late.

A truck loaded with logs appeared out of nowhere and ran into Cliff's pickup, which had half blocked the road.

Tessa fell into a dark well.

44

Later Tessa could remember two things clearly: Ron Halprin, whose hand she held onto as she lay on the stretcher and who had heard her repeatedly naming Lionel and Cindy. "I know," he confirmed, as he pressed her hand gently. And she remembered the noise of the helicopter and how she recalled that only a short time before, Kratz Hilder had been transported by the same helicopter.

She was X-rayed and checked over in the hospital at Whatou Lake. With the help of strong painkillers, she slept until the next morning. She woke up in a room with two beds, but she was the only patient. When she asked, the nurse on duty told her that Lionel and Cliff were in the hospital, too. Cliff because of a broken arm, Lionel had suffered serious, but not life-threatening, injuries. The logging truck driver had already been flown to Vancouver. The nurse didn't have any further details about his condition.

Dr. Rhonda Kellermann, the friendly head doctor, later came in and explained: "It looks as if you got away with bruising and abrasions and a concussion. Thankfully a helicopter was nearby." She asked Tessa whether, after having a nice breakfast and a shower, she felt well enough to undergo questioning by the police.

Tessa nodded, although she felt a little sick. She rubbed her eyes, which hurt because of the bright lights. "Did anybody tell my parents that I'm here?"

"Yes, of course. We won't keep you here for long; we're waiting for the result of one more test. If it is good, we can let you go home. The concussion will cure itself. These days we don't order strict bed rest any longer." The doctor's thoughtful gaze lingered on Tessa. "But you should take a rest whenever you can to help your brain recover."

The brain. Take a rest. Get better.

Tessa didn't have any illusions. The horror was not over by a long shot.

"We also silenced your cell phone," the doctor continued. "It caused too much of a disturbance. If you agree, I can give you a painkiller intravenously that will calm you down but won't make your brain foggy."

Just after ten, Ron Halprin came by, accompanied by a constable. His face looked more determined, his eyes less tired; he seemed full of energy. Tessa understood: he had made a breakthrough in a very difficult case. Halprin pulled his chair up to her bed. She put her hand in his before he began to talk.

"How do you feel?" he asked.

"I don't know, I . . . it was a tremendous shock, and in some ways I still can't believe it." She looked out the window in order to remember better. "So it's true that Lionel and Cindy . . ." She stopped; it sounded so unreal. And so terrible.

"We have Lionel Miller's confession. We had already secretly wiretapped his car. When he was telling you everything, we were also listening in. But we still have a lot of work to do."

"So he was under suspicion the entire time?"

"Members of the family and close relatives are almost always under suspicion. We had checked out who could have a motive." He took his notepad and pen out of his vest pocket and leaned forward. He must have worked all night; he was still wearing his shirt from the day before. "Explain to me again exactly what happened on the farm yesterday."

She told him everything in detail. She was surprised how calmly she could do that. As if she hadn't been part of it at all. They must have given her a very strong sedative. "Where are Harrison and Cindy?" she asked at the end. "What happened to them?"

"They are in custody. Our people were already in the area. We knew that both of them were on the way to the farm."

"Were they being shadowed?"

"Yes."

"Were you also shadowing me?"

"We had been informed that you and Kratz Hilder had flown to Beaver Lake. His wife told us you were going to the south side of the lake, which we found odd. We assumed that you wanted to get to the farm. The south side would have been a strange choice."

"He wanted to drop me off there and not pick me up again because he hates me."

"We'll have to talk about that, but later. Where's Fran's camera now?"

"In my backpack. Take a look in the closet and see if it's there." The other RCMP officer got up and pulled out her backpack. He turned on the camera and looked through the pictures with Halprin.

The sergeant returned to his questioning. "What did you make of the pictures, Tessa?"

"I think that Fran was in Cindy's boutique and slept in the lounge that night. I think she did that several times. She didn't want to sleep at Dana's house or at my parents' house, because . . . she was going through a deep personal crisis. It's pretty easy to get into the boutique since Cindy leaves the key to the back door in the flowerpot. I saw her do that when I bought some blouses from her the day before yesterday. Fran must have also watched Cindy doing it. Or somebody told her about it."

Halprin looked at her, composed. She stared at the wall so that she didn't get distracted. "Cindy denied that Fran had ever been in her boutique, but Fran had done some shopping there. Cat collars. She also had a free sample from Cindy, an essential oil. Or . . ." She stopped talking.

Both policemen looked expectantly at her. "Or Fran stole those things when she was there during the night. That seems more likely to me." She thought it over and then continued: "Fran must have seen or heard Cindy and Harrison in the boutique together. Maybe she hid herself somewhere, until the two of them . . . were done and had left. She had told Hank about it. Or Hank had heard it from his mother. That's also possible. Hank told Lionel about it, since he felt provoked by his brother."

She looked at Halprin, and a new, horrible thought crossed her mind. "You've absolutely got to search through Cindy's boutique, Ron!"

"We already did that yesterday. And we searched Cindy's car, too." He tapped with his pen on his writing pad.

Tessa hid her face in her hands. "Did they also kill Fran? Oh, my God!"

Halprin's voice came through to her as if from far away. "We're still not sure. We still have to clear up a number of matters."

"But somebody dragged her to Bob Barker's shed."

"We found traces in Cindy's car."

"I don't understand . . ."

"We'll have to question Cindy about this to find out more. Please treat this information as confidential. We depend on your discretion."

Tessa nodded and looked at her arm, the bandages and the dressings. "Cindy is . . . I just can't believe that . . . I didn't particularly like her, but she . . . had a heart for children and animals. I know she looked after a kindergarten group at the United Church. And . . . she adopted a dog that somebody wanted to put to sleep. He suffers from diabetes and she has to give it an insulin shot every day. I'm also an animal lover, but I don't know whether I would be willing to take up that responsibility. And the vet must cost a fortune."

Halprin interrupted. "She gives the dog insulin shots?"

"Yes. Daily."

"Since when has she been doing that?"

"It's got to be at least three years. Fran showed her how you do it. Fran was almost a trained nurse."

The officers exchanged a meaningful look. Halprin's colleague left the room while the sergeant took notes.

Tessa was talking more to herself than to him: "Why can't we protect children better? Why didn't I notice what was going on here? What was going to happen?"

Halprin crossed his arms. "I know what you mean, Tessa. I experience that in my profession over and over. We see the tragedies coming at us, but we can't do anything to stop them. We can't arrest somebody beforehand. Not as long as no crime has been committed. Sometimes it's hard to swallow." He glanced briefly at his notebook before he once again looked her in the eye.

"We both have a difficult profession that drives us to the limits, because we see despicable and incomprehensible things. All we can do is to try our best every day and stop worse things from happening. I'm not going to give up—and I don't think you are, either."

She felt that something undefined had just shifted inside her. "I just wonder . . . at what point is it all too much for me?"

Lost in his thoughts, Halprin scribbled on his notepad. Then he looked up. "Sometimes you just have to go off fishing. Geographical distance. That does wonders for me. Go off anywhere, somewhere far away. And sometimes let the colleagues do the work. The key is a good team. Gather good people around you. In your personal life and at work. Give everyone enough room and time to do good."

For a couple of seconds, neither of them spoke.

Tessa felt vulnerable. "Why? At least I want to know why they did it."

"Lionel Miller seems to be cooperating. Cindy and Harrison Miller have gotten lawyers. Both are in jail. Lionel is being treated here in the hospital. At the moment that's all I can tell you." He leaned back and stretched his legs. "The media know about the arrests. We can't stop Harrison Miller from loudly declaring his innocence to the journalists and raging against the police."

"And what about Cliff Bight?"

"Cliff talked to us."

"He gave Cindy and Lionel false alibis. They weren't at the cabin that morning. He already had left the cabin around noon and was at the scrapyard at Whatou Lake just before three."

Halprin nodded. "He admitted that to us."

The constable came back into the room. "Excuse me, sergeant, they're asking for you. We have to go back immediately."

Halpin got right up. "We'll continue this conversation later, Tessa." He nodded at her quickly and they both left.

She was sitting there, alone again, a never-ending train of thoughts pulsing through her head, releasing painful and overwhelming emotions.

In the end, she was simply exhausted.

And then it occurred to her that she hadn't asked Halprin what had happened to the grizzly. The grizzly that had saved her from Cindy's pistol.

45

Tessa couldn't deal with the events alone; she needed help. She needed a sharp analysis in order to get control of the emotional avalanche that was threatening to bury her. She needed Boyd Shenkar. She dragged herself over to the closet and took out her cell phone. A flood of missed calls and emails showed up when she turned it on, but she ignored them all and called Boyd's number in Vancouver.

"Finally. I've been trying to reach you the whole time," her business partner said. His voice was like a life preserver.

"The personnel in the hospital silenced my cell phone because it disturbed them," she answered.

"Where are you now?"

"Still in the hospital in Whatou Lake."

"For god's sake, Tessa, what's going on? Should I come and see you?"

"No, just stay in the office, no need for another person to be away. I have only a few scrapes and a concussion. They're letting me out today."

"Can I do anything for you from here?"

"Are you free for the next hour?"

There was a short pause at the other end. "Good, I'll tell them out front." After a few seconds he was back. "Okay, what's going on?"

She let the words stream out, first haltingly, sometimes with tears, and then getting control again and looking for professional objectivity. Boyd listened to her patiently, concentrated on the flood of information. She could picture him sitting at his desk as he jotted down words on a writing pad, already analyzing them while writing. She had often done the same thing for him when he took on a case. She used to suggest a possible scenario of what might have happened in a particular crime, ponder motives and draw up a psychological profile of the suspect. They had always been a sounding board for each other, played the devil's advocate for each other. She couldn't have imagined a better business partner. Her monologue ended with the words "Now it's *your* turn. What could have possibly driven Lionel and Cindy to commit such a . . . such an unimaginably awful crime?"

She could visualize how Boyd gathered his thoughts while looking at his notes, his elbows resting on the desk, pushing his chin out and then relaxing it. She often had seen him like this before he formulated his conclusions. The conclusions of a defense lawyer who worked on a case and who considered all possible details.

Boyd spoke slowly with only minor corrections. His first sentence bored right through her. "Lionel's violent attack looks a lot like manslaughter. Whether it is voluntary or involuntary manslaughter still needs to be determined. But the attack had been brewing in him for a long time. His father had always preferred Hank. Even to the point of wanting to finance an outfitter license and a tourist lodge. That must have really infuriated Lionel . . . and also hurt him because he was the son who always tried to see his father as a role model. Whereas Hank was, in Lionel's eyes, the son who had always disappointed his father. For instance, with his marriage to Fran or the cattle ranch that failed. The logging job that ended in an accident. And the work in the Sitklat'l lodge. In Lionel's eyes, the proud Miller family didn't have to work for the First Nations people."

Tessa thought about Tsaytis. Where could he be now?

Boyd continued when he didn't hear any reaction from her: "And then Hank claimed that Cindy was sleeping with Harrison Miller. Maybe Lionel had had a dark suspicion, because it was really strange how Harrison took care of Cindy. He probably suppressed that thought with all his might. I think what really broke the camel's back was when Lionel realized that years ago it was Hank who had told the Olympic Committee about him taking drugs. That must have hit him like a knockout punch. In Lionel's eyes, that was the worst kind of betrayal, even worse than Cindy's supposed unfaithfulness."

"I wonder why Hank did that back then. He never said anything bad about Lionel."

"Didn't you mention that Hank always rejected his father's dark machinations? That he didn't want the lodge because Harrison Miller had financed it with dirty money?"

"Bribes from the mining companies, I've heard."

"Maybe Hank wanted to shield his younger brother from worse things. To try to stop him from drifting into fraud like his father. He probably thought that Lionel would be banned from professional rowing for a few months and that would be it. That it would just be a warning. A sensible one. But something worse happened, and Lionel never recovered from that. It was bad timing that the rowing committee officials came down so hard on him; it was because there had just been a doping scandal with the Russians."

"He could have talked with Lionel first."

"Apparently Lionel was very much under the influence of his immoral father. Maybe Hank thought that it wouldn't make any difference. But I'm just speculating here."

Tessa sighed deeply. "His father also betrayed him. His mother, too, because for her it was only Hank and her grandchildren who were worth the time of day."

"Don't forget Cindy's betrayal."

Cindy. Tessa imagined herself in Fran's house, in the bathroom, on the stairs, in Breena's room, in the attic. She began to cry: "How . . . could somebody kill children? How could she possibly do that? I don't understand it. I simply don't understand it."

Boyd waited until she had pulled herself together again. "Maybe we should talk about this another time?" he asked softly.

Tessa blew her nose. "No, no, I want to talk about it. It helps me."

"Cindy panicked when Lionel came back to the pickup where she was waiting for him. She assumed that the children had seen him shoot Hank. She wanted to get rid of these witnesses. And once she shot Breena, she couldn't stop."

"So she wanted to protect Lionel and therefore killed the children?"

"In a certain sense, yes."

"But she had betrayed Lionel with Harrison. Why did she suddenly want to protect him?"

"Not only Lionel, but protect herself, too, Tessa. Her life, her reputation, her social standing. We also shouldn't forget that deep inside she had been angry for several years. Bitter. Her anger about her failed career in sports. One shouldn't underestimate that, not by any means. Her disappointment must have gone very deep; she couldn't shake it. So deep that the day before yesterday she even told you about it."

"But Harrison couldn't save Cindy's career, only the boutique."

"Harrison gave her validation because he was a mayor, a successful but unscrupulous businessman . . . somebody with charisma and a bad boy aura. Some women love bad boys. Cindy was one of six daughters in her family, right? That means that she had to compete with five sisters for her father's affection and attention. For a long time she really was the star. First in the family. And then she had the chance to become an Olympic rowing star for the entire nation. When she was badly injured and could no longer compete at a high level, her father lost interest in her. She complained about that to you in the boutique, didn't she? Her father must have seen her exit from her rowing career as a personal failure. No more national or international fame for his family. Harrison Miller, on the other hand, must have valued her. She came from a good stock, unlike Fran, who was a foster child. And probably she was also a good wife for Lionel. She could have left him when they didn't have any children."

"But she betrayed him, with his own father!"

"It's not all that simple. There are a lot of nuances. People are more complex beings than we think. Cindy fit into Whatou Lake reasonably well; she became popular and was admired, and she was an anchor for Lionel . . . she had status. And as we now can assume, she had taken Lionel's side when they were dealing with the conflict around the outfitter license."

"Yeah, sure. Indirectly she would have profited from that. So in the end it was once again a matter of money, just like it is in most crimes?"

"Indirectly yes, but the way you have presented this situation, it was more a matter of . . ."

"Jealousy."

"Jealousy, rivalry, humiliation, betrayal—in Cindy's case also misguided ambition and snobbism . . . and don't forget that Lionel has a father who apparently is doing illegal things. No great role model."

"Hank was a good person."

"Hank had Fran . . . and he had your family, where he experienced something other than profiteering. He saw idealism. He looked at the divvying up of resources as dubious. His parents apparently showed appreciation to Hank. But not to Lionel. They almost always made it easier for Hank. He didn't have to fight for their affection. Lionel, on the other hand, felt continually overlooked."

"At first they found Fran unacceptable."

"That's right. Until she presented them with the greatly desired grandchildren."

Who were now dead. Killed in cold blood. She closed her eyes and put down the cell phone.

"Tessa, are you still there? Forgive me, I . . . have to tell you the way I see it."

"I know, I know, it's . . . I just simply can't understand it, Boyd. But it's good for me to talk to you. Oh, one second, Boyd."

The nurse had come in again and placed a piece of paper on her bed: *I'm outside. Should I wait? Savannah.*

"Yes, wait," Tessa decided spontaneously. "Not you, Boyd, a visitor."

"Okay. So . . . to get back to Cindy. She probably expected more from the affair with Harrison. For example, that Lionel, and indirectly she herself, would be favored by the father."

"Couldn't she have blackmailed him with this affair?"

Boyd's answer came right back: "How would that have benefitted her? Her marriage would have been kaput. Her reputation ruined. Harrison could have denied everything, and who would people have believed? No, she almost certainly had never thought of this. And her marriage, which for the outside world seemed successful, was obviously something she wanted to hold on to."

"And Fran?" Tessa's heart skipped a beat.

Boyd hesitated for a few seconds, before he answered with a sigh: "Before I know the cause of her death, I can't say anything about that."

Is he trying to go easy on me? Tessa put her head down on the pillow and closed her eyes again. This time Boyd stopped talking.

"And for days we were hopeful," she finally said, "that we would find Fran alive. That she would show up again." Cindy and Lionel had actually played along with this gruesome game. How cruel. She couldn't tell Boyd that the investigators had found evidence in Cindy's car. She had promised Halprin not to say anything about it.

Boyd's voice trailed off, when he said: "Tessa, I've got to go now."

"Just one more thing," she said quickly. "I need a good but inexpensive lawyer for Cliff Bight."

"For the man who gave Cindy and Lionel Miller a false alibi?"

"Like everybody else, Cliff had no idea that his boss was a murderer. It could be that Cliff saved my life."

"I'll see what I can do. Call me again when you need me. I'll always make time for you, whenever I can."

"Thanks, Boyd," was all she could say before she put the phone down.

Instantly, there was silence in the room. From outside not even car engines or cawing ravens could be heard. She turned her head to the window. The mountain peaks were covered in clouds. The treetops swayed in the wind. Eventually, a logging truck passed by. Boy, how lucky she had been. She was alive. Lost in thought, she looked at the door. Savannah. God, she's been waiting for almost an hour in the hall.

Tessa slipped out of the bed and opened the door. Savannah was sitting there with her phone and earphones, listening to music. In her hand, she had a cup of coffee from Tim Hortons. She had replaced her orange jacket with a sweatshirt decorated with faux fur attachments and cheap golden pearls. Her lilac stretch pants matched the color of her bandana. She pulled her earphones out, grabbed her bag, and followed Tessa into the room.

"Finally. That sure took a long time. I almost took root here. You look like a scarecrow. They make patients wear that rag? That's inhuman. Degrading, if you ask me. It's lucky that I brought some clothes along for you. Underwear, too. You must have paid out a fortune for this stuff. Everything silk and lace. Victoria's Secret, right?"

With shaking legs, Tessa turned around and started to cry.

Savannah whispered: "Oh, you poor thing. Don't cry, don't cry." She put her arms around Tessa, and tears rolled down her cheeks, too. They stood there for a while, in the middle of the room, like two lost children.

"Come on, lie down again," Tessa heard Savannah murmur, and she let herself be covered up in blankets. Savannah took out something from her handbag that looked like lip gloss. "Here, here, you look terrible, with the mascara running." She put some transparent gloss under Tessa's eyes and wiped away the black smears. Tessa held still until she was finished and nodded in satisfaction. Afterward Savannah sat in the same chair that Ron Halprin had sat in. "What the hell happened? Harrison and Cindy have been arrested. Do you know what's going on?" She didn't wait for Tessa to reply. "Now there's so much gossiping going round. The journalists and TV people are creeping all over the place like panicking ants. Do the Millers have something to do with the murders?"

Tessa shrugged.

Savannah didn't give up. "I can absolutely believe that about Cindy, if you ask me."

Tessa suddenly was interested. "Why?"

"She hated Fran. She looked down on her completely. For Cindy, Fran simply couldn't be part of the oh-so-upper-class Miller family. I have an instinct for things like this. Many people think that I don't fit in with the Griffins."

Tessa shook her head. "You fit in just fine in our family, but all of us have . . . bruises and injuries."

"You can say that again. The way you look. These logging trucks, they all fly around like bats out of hell. They weren't even allowed to travel at that time of day. Why were you in Lionel's pickup?"

"Actually, initially I was in Cliff Bight's pickup when we left the farm. But then we met Lionel by chance on the logging road, and he wanted to talk to me."

"How come you were with Cliff? What were you doing there? I thought you had to take care of legal matters in Whatou Lake."

"I changed my plans because the police allowed access to the farm."

Savannah had a knowing look. "Doesn't surprise me. You wanted to go before the Millers got there. You could've taken me along."

"If I had, you would also be lying in a hospital bed."

"Now the house is just ashes, I've heard. Totally burned down."

"And the woods?"

"Nothing happened. It's all still there."

"A grizzly was around the house. Did it get away in time?"

"For god's sake, Tessa, of course it would run away whenever a big fire gets out of control. There was no grizzly near the house."

"How do you know that?"

"I'm not going to tell you if you don't tell me something of interest."

"The police don't want me to talk too much before they make the details public. Why didn't Mom and Dad come along?"

"That's my fault. I told them that you needed peace and quiet. You do, don't you?"

Tessa couldn't deny that.

Savannah rubbed her hand. "Mom and Dad will bombard you with questions once you're back in the house. And so will Philip. He suddenly showed up to help. He's going to stay a week, and then one of the former foster kids will show up to take care of Mom and Dad. They want to take turns. Even Patricia made contact; she called Phil up. But she won't come; she's living in Montreal now. That's going to be a lot of fun. All of the Griffins' former foster kids back in Whatou Lake. Others are gone with the wind."

"Who's gone with the wind?"

"Telford Reed." Savannah spit out that name as if it were

chewing gum. "He came by yesterday and asked how you were doing. I texted you, but I didn't hear back from you because you were out there in the bush. He probably also sent you a text. He told us that he had to fly off to Alberta."

Tessa sat up straight and supported herself.

"He owns a company in Alberta. He can't stay in Whatou Lake forever."

Savannah remained unimpressed. "Mind you, he did drop by to ask how you're doing. God knows why."

"Savannah," Tessa said very softly, "you're really getting on my nerves."

She was rewarded with a loving look back.

"And the same to you. Do you need makeup to cover the bruises on your face?"

46

Later she asked herself how she managed to get through the funeral, give a speech about Fran and Hank and the children. When she looked at the two large and three small coffins, she would have liked to run from the church. But she couldn't do that to her parents, or to the deceased. She succeeded in not breaking down in tears as she stood in front of the whole community of Whatou Lake, the mourners who had come in from all over the place, and the journalists and gossipers who had somehow gotten in. She saw Ron Halprin in the crowd, also Tsaytis and Noreen Chelin, her friend Dana, and the police officer Kate Jennings, who had been at her parents' house twice.

She separated herself mentally from her person, as if she were a stranger standing in front of the microphone. This was her way of trying to place the murdered family in the hearts of the people gathered in the church so that they would remember them. Not only as murder victims, but also as people with hopes and dreams and short but remarkable lives. She heard herself talking with a collected voice. She had covered her hair under a soft black hat she had pulled down over her brow. The reddish tone seemed too flashy for a funeral.

With an almost superhuman strength, she held back her fury

and pain for a short time in order to make the dead come back to life again. It was her present to her sister, her brother-in-law and their children, who could no longer speak for themselves. The church was eerily silent; only once in a while someone quietly clearing his throat or coughing could be heard. This changed as the former foster child Philip projected photos of Breena, Kayley, and Clyde, Fran and Hank on a screen. Suddenly, there was sobbing and crying in the church. Her parents kept their eyes shut, as Philip had advised them to, so that they could get through the service intact. At the burial her mother broke down and was taken to the car.

Harrison Miller, who had made bail, and his wife, Glenda, weren't present. The disgraced mayor's lawyer announced that in his opinion neither Harrison nor Lionel nor Cindy could expect a fair trial in Whatou Lake and therefore the trial should take place in Vancouver.

At the doctor's advice, Tessa moved in temporarily with Dana Eckert to recover. In the Griffins' house, visiting relatives and former foster children were comforting to Martha and Kenneth. Tessa experienced those days in a white fog. Dana tried to shield her as much as possible from intrusions. But Tessa found it worse not to be informed than to be kept away from any shocking information.

While Lionel stuck to his confession, Cindy refused to say anything at all and then suddenly changed her strategy: She claimed that Lionel was the ringleader, that he had had the idea to murder Hank and the children, and that he was the one who carried it out. Her lawyer explained to the journalists that Cindy had not come out with this earlier because she feared that he would kill her. She had nothing to do with Fran's death, the lawyer maintained.

It was a fine June day. Tessa sat in the sun in front of Dana's house, always on the lookout for reporters. In the evening, she found out that Lionel, who was about to be let out of the hospital, had killed himself. He had cut his wrists when the nurse left him alone so that he could take a bath. Her thoughts wandered to Glenda. She had now lost everything: two sons and her grandchildren. And also her husband. Harrison didn't care about her, but had started up a campaign against the RCMP because they were supposed to watch his son around the clock but had, in Harrison's words, "failed scandalously."

Initially it looked like a bitter disappointment for the investigation. Then a series of developments. Cindy's facade broke down after Lionel's suicide. A good two weeks after the murders, against her lawyer's advice, she made a confession. Even before this turn of events was made public, Tessa got a call from Ron Halprin. Dana drove her to the police station. When Halprin greeted her, he held her hand with his strong fingers. Tessa found this gesture both calming and exciting.

"I wanted to see you again before we fold up our tents," he began when they sat across from each other.

"Does that mean that the investigation is completed?"

"Yes, we're just about done."

"So you do know what happened to Fran?"

He nodded. "I wanted to tell you that personally. Later we'll tell the relatives and then make it public."

He clasped his hands on the desk. "Cindy Miller told us what happened. What she said matched Lionel's confession as far as the murders on the farm are concerned. And they match our interpretation of the clues in Cindy Miller's car and Bob Barker's shed." He looked at his hands and then once again at Tessa.

"She killed Breena first, then Clyde, then Kayley?" Tessa asked.

Once again he nodded. "She confirmed that with us, but she still held back certain details. It looks like she just doesn't want to admit how gruesome her crimes were."

"What else did Cindy admit?"

"She told us that she and Lionel, after they shot Hank and the children, drove to an abandoned logging road near their cabin to discuss what their situation was and what they should do.

Then they drove to the cabin, but Cliff Bight had already left. Toward the evening they returned to Whatou Lake. Cindy drove alone to her boutique, in order to remove any possible traces of her intimate meeting with Harrison Miller the night before. According to her, she found Fran dead in the storage room."

Tessa shook her head incredulously but didn't say anything.

"She says she has no idea how Fran got there. But it became clear to her that Fran was dead when she tried to talk to her, and then she shook her body. She swore to us that she had nothing to do with Fran's death and she had absolutely no idea how Fran had gotten into her boutique."

"But that's crazy!" Tessa cried out. She felt like leaping to her feet. "Does Cindy think that she can get away with this lie, after everything that's happened?"

It looked like Halprin had expected this reaction from her, since he just continued: "For us policemen, it often sounds crazy, but you know that already. When Cindy made her confession, we already knew why Fran died. We just had to wait for the results of one more blood test because of a piece of information you gave us."

"From me?"

"You told us about Cindy's dog and that Cindy had to give it daily insulin injections. I wanted to clear up whether it was possible that Fran had been killed by an overdose of insulin."

Tessa held her breath. Why hadn't she thought of that herself?

Halprin shook his head as if he had read her thoughts. "It was a false alarm. There was no evidence of medication in Fran's body. And no injection marks. We could completely rule that out. Fran died of a heart attack. It was a natural death."

She looked at Halprin aghast. "No murder?"

"No, and no suicide. It was a natural death."

Tessa looked at him skeptically. Her lips formed words that she couldn't speak.

Halprin raised his right hand as if he wanted to stop her from saying something too quickly. "Let me just explain. Fran must have already been suffering from a weak heart. She didn't correctly understand the symptoms and didn't go to a doctor in time. The guilty party is probably Melanie Pleeke, who didn't believe much in traditional medicine. And experts have told me that women who have heart attacks often are incorrectly diagnosed. Especially young women. Because doctors still diagnose the symptoms based on those of male patients."

Tessa's skin prickled while she listened to him. She swallowed deeply and then asked: "She had a *heart attack?*"

"She actually had two. She had had a mini heart attack sometime in the last year, which wasn't diagnosed as such and was also not treated. Another heart attack finally took her life."

Tessa again shook her head in disbelief. Every time she wanted to ask a question, all she could do was shake her head. She closed her eyes briefly and pulled herself together. "She was only thirty-four! You can't have a heart attack at that age."

"It was probably a genetic defect that came from her biological father. If she had known who her biological father was, she would have known about it."

Tessa crossed her arms and looked out the window at the auto repair shop across the street. "Ron, excuse me, but that all sounds very strange to me. A coincidence like that can't happen. Fran has a heart attack the same evening or the night before her family is murdered. She was seen at the hospital in the late afternoon that day." She didn't want to hide her skepticism from him.

He leaned on his elbows, with his fingers interlaced. "Fran went to the hospital because of her nosebleeds. Dr. Kellermann heard about her symptoms for the first time on Monday. As it turned out, it wasn't just nosebleeds and muscle pain, but also difficulties with breathing, vomiting, sweating, exhaustion. Dr. Kellermann had a suspicion and wanted to check it out the next day. But unfortunately she never had the chance to do that."

"I can imagine all of that is possible," Tessa replied after thinking about it. "But that Fran died so soon before the murders

. . . and Cindy is supposed to have nothing to do with it. I can't believe that."

Halprin straightened his shoulders. "Fran very probably witnessed a sexual encounter between Harrison and Cindy. She had gotten into the boutique with the key from the flowerpot. Suddenly she heard Cindy and Harrison coming in from outside and she hid herself in the storage room. She overheard their intimacy. It must have been a real shock for her. That could have triggered the heart attack."

Tessa tapped her toes, as suddenly something came into her mind. "Hank didn't hear about Cindy and Harrison's affair from Fran. His mother had told him. Glenda. That's the way it must have been. She told Hank about it. But Hank didn't say anything to Fran because she had enough problems. Oh, my god, Fran had no idea until she caught them in flagrante delicto."

Ron Halprin didn't contradict her. "She must have felt so terrible that she didn't even confront them."

"Fran wouldn't have dared to do that without first talking it over with Hank." Tessa did some deep thinking and then asked: "But didn't you find traces of Fran in Cindy's car?"

"Cindy put Fran's body in her car. Not an easy thing to do, but Cindy is strong. She drove to Bob Barker's shed with her. She knew the place because she had been there with Lionel when the property was up for sale. And she had once met Harrison Miller there in secret. For understandable reasons, she didn't want anyone to find Fran's body in her boutique."

"Was Fran at that point already dead?"

"The forensics confirmed that."

Tessa rubbed the side of her neck. "And did Lionel know about it?"

"Cindy denies that. She kept it to herself because she was afraid that Lionel would have a complete breakdown."

That makes sense, Tessa thought. Cindy was strong enough to take care of something like that without Lionel's help. She sat for a few minutes silently, depressed by the revelations. It was crazy.

However, there was no reason to doubt Ron Halprin and his experts. And when one looked at it carefully, there really wasn't any more reason for Cindy to lie. She had confessed to the brutal attacks on the three children; she could have also admitted a fourth murder. It wouldn't have made her situation any worse.

Tessa tried to find some small comfort in the new disclosures. Fran had not simply left her children in the lurch. She hadn't considered committing suicide. She wanted to start a new life with her family. She had fought for that, right to the end. And she never knew anything about the massacre of her children and husband.

With these thoughts in her head, she let herself be driven to her parents' house after the talk with Halprin. During this whole trip she hardly said a word to Dana.

"I can't tell you anything about Fran; I have to talk to my parents first," she said, excusing herself.

"I get it," Dana answered. "Did he say anything about the attack on Melanie Pleeke?"

"No, and I forgot to ask him about it."

Melanie Pleeke's broken nose was not the only thing that had moved to the back burner after the four murders at the farm and Fran's death. Similarly, the media and the general public were only mildly interested in the bear poaching and the floatplane pilot, Kratz Hilder. That was also the case with the young Sitklat'l and the park ranger who turned out to be a drug dealer. Day after day, almost every announcement had to do with the dead Millers.

"The young Sitklat'l poachers are certainly not a simple matter for Tsaytis. Have you talked to him recently?" Dana asked a couple of days later.

"No, and I won't be doing that for the time being," Tessa replied as she was playing solitaire on the laptop, a card game that always calmed her down. "I think we need some distance. It's not right to look for a soulmate in a married man."

"I see," Dana said after a noticeably long pause.

"By the way, I also think that a white woman with my cultural background can never really be right for a Sitklat'l. I let myself imagine that nobody could understand Tsaytis as well as I could. I think that was not only naïve of me, but also . . . presumptuous." With that, she returned to her card game.

Dana was smart enough not to reply. Maybe she'd come back to that a day or two later. But then, there was an unexpected development. Dana was called for questioning at the police station. As she came back, she explained somewhat distractedly that two fourteen-year-old students had seen her in the arena's parking lot. They told the police that on the day of the press conference, Dana had approached Melanie Pleeke's car. Then they had heard a dull thud. "Those are the two potheads who usually skip school," she railed.

"What are you going to do now?" Tessa asked uneasily.

"Nothing." Dana plopped herself down on the sofa. "Nobody will believe them, it's such an unbelievable story. After everything they've done."

"Why did those two kids pick you, out of all the people who live in Whatou Lake?"

"No idea. I was a social worker. There probably isn't a single teen here who doesn't know me."

Tessa frowned. "But you were in the arena when Melanie was attacked. There must have been a bunch of people who saw you there."

"We entered the arena together. So I have an alibi that will clear me."

Tessa stared at the screen, but the cards swam before her eyes. This conversation had taken a turn that she didn't like. "And in any case," she replied cautiously, "how would have somebody done such a thing, with witnesses standing around?"

Dana stretched out her legs and leaned back on the sofa pillows. "Such a dumb idea would never have occurred to me."

I wouldn't just call it a dumb idea, Tessa thought. I'd call it revenge. She didn't say that out loud, all she said was: "You certainly had differences of opinion with Melanie Pleeke . . . about the séances that she had with Fran and about Fran's accusations against Dad . . . Despite that, you certainly couldn't have wanted her to suffer such a fate."

"No, you don't wish something like that on your worst enemy."

"So is Melanie your worst enemy?"

They looked at each other. Dana seemed to be thinking things over and then she said: "That was only a figure of speech."

Tessa dropped the topic like a piece of hot coal. She silently looked out the window.

What was it that Ron Halprin had said? Sometimes it helps to just insert some geographical distance.

It was time to get back to Vancouver.

47

Tessa looked at her face in the mirror. Her eyes searched for the woman she had been just two months ago. Her reddish hair was still there and had become longer and more voluminous. Silver earrings. A lighter color on her lips. She couldn't detect any sharp lines near the corners of her mouth or creases on her forehead.

How could that be possible? The events of the past weeks had to have left some traces behind. Her skin was only a bit darker than it had been at the beginning of June due to the long evening walks, alone, on Jericho Beach or around Stanley Park. It was only the expression in her eyes that was different. More suspicious. More impervious. Spaced out. They were no longer her old eyes.

No longer her old life, either. Although she was still living in the same apartment in the Olympic Village. She looked through her living room window at False Creek and the shimmering dome of the Science World center. On the horizon, the mountaintops of North Vancouver appeared blurred in the haze. She fingered her olive-green pantsuit that was made of a lightweight fabric she liked so much. She wore a white T-shirt under it.

Summer clothes but businesslike, because she didn't know the exact reason why she would be meeting with Ron Halprin. At any rate, she was looking forward to it.

She grabbed her handbag, locked the apartment, and took the elevator down. It was not a sunny day. The air was humid and the sky a transparent gray. She crossed the square dominated by outdoor sculptures of sparrows that were five and a half meters tall, passing mothers with their baby carriages, people walking their dogs, tourists taking photographs, teens with cell phones.

Halprin sat on a concrete bench next to one of the giant Styrofoam birds. There was nothing businesslike in his clothes, she noticed right away: sporty khaki pants, running shoes, a short-sleeved T-shirt that displayed his muscular biceps.

Under other conditions she would have greeted him smilingly, the way Vancouverites do, but these were not normal conditions.

He got up and greeted her: "Hello, Tessa." He was obviously happy to see her. "Maybe we want to go over there and sit on a bench by the water?"

She had a better idea. She wanted to sit across from him.

"Don't laugh, but in the upscale pet shop on the other side, there's a really comfortable corner to sit down where you can talk without being disturbed. I think there's going to be a thunderstorm soon anyhow."

He rolled up something that looked like a windbreaker. "Do you have a pet?"

"No, but the owner lives next to me and I feed his parrots when he's away."

Halprin proved to be uncomplicated. They went into the store, past a sky-blue bathtub for dogs and faux-gold food bowls for cats and sat down on two chairs in a private corner. The store owner's dog came over to say hello and then lay down for a nap.

"A different world than Whatou Lake," Tessa remarked. She was a bit nervous. A new situation with unknown rules. She couldn't help noticing that Halprin's blue eyes were emphasized by his tanned skin. His face looked relaxed.

He came right to the point: "A day doesn't go by when I don't think about Whatou Lake and what happened there. I should know better, but I'm still deeply disturbed by what so-called 'normal' people are capable of. How are you doing?"

"It's a nightmare that doesn't go away. My work helps me. It gives me something else to think about. I call my parents a lot."

"Have you visited them in the meantime?"

"Yes. On a long weekend. I was helping them out with legal matters. My parents still can't understand what happened. They accuse themselves and feel guilty that they didn't notice the slightest sign of danger from Lionel and Cindy. And that's also the way I feel."

"You're not alone in this, Tessa. It's so often the case that after the arrest of a murderer we hear: He was such a nice neighbor. Never seemed unpleasant. Was always so friendly and ready to help. You know the clichés."

She sighed: "I couldn't stop the murders of Breena, Kayley, and Clyde. It keeps me awake at night. Although I know that I'm not responsible." She bent down and patted the dog at her feet. She knew that Halprin was watching her, although she was looking at the dog. She could avoid his eyes but not his voice. She didn't really want to. She wanted him to be close to her. "Murderers are good at going undetected. They manipulate other people and hide who they really are." She looked up and read the compassion in his face.

"People are complex beings, Tessa, just like you and me. Sometimes I feel as powerless as you do."

The dog got up, wagging its tail, and wanted her to pat it some more. She scratched it with both hands behind its ears.

"I heard that Cindy was moved over to the high-security prison in Agassiz?" she asked.

"Yes, she's under constant observation. We don't want to have a second suicide. We're waiting for the court case, but that can take a while. I expect it to be quick since Cindy has confessed. She doesn't want to have a public trial."

"And Harrison?"

"Cindy says that he's the one who set the house on fire. He claims that she did it. But we still don't know where they got the fire accelerant. It's very possible that he gets away unpunished. He will stay in Whatou Lake; his wife didn't throw him out."

"Glenda took him back? Who would have thought . . . after everything."

"That doesn't surprise me. He's the only connection to her dead sons."

Ron Halprin clasped his strong hands like she had often seen him do.

She looked at him. "Did you ever consider me to be a suspect?"

Immediately a smile appeared on his face. Fascinated, Tessa took note of how fast his expression had changed. She felt the magnetism that came from him.

"You mean because of the cat collar?" He shook his head and became serious again. "Our people found traces on it. Tiny fibers. Cindy must have put the collar in her jacket pocket. On Fran's camera, the one you found by the house, there's a photo of Rosie's grave. The collar was hanging on the little cross. Cindy took it from there and put it on the path to Whitesand Bay. Where you found it."

"Why on earth would she do that?"

"She wanted us to concentrate on Whitesand Bay. And she also wanted to cause some confusion."

"But why the cat collar?"

He shrugged his broad shoulders. "It came from her boutique. That may have played a role. There are still some questions in this case that we don't have answers to. And that we may never get. We have done what we could."

"I've never thanked you, Ron." She played with her earrings. "For the hard work you and your team did. I'm really thankful to you."

"I'm glad to hear it." He kept looking at her as if he anticipated that something else would follow.

Three sentences had been kicking around all morning in her head, and now she said them: "You once mentioned to me that it was important to have good people around you. You're a good person, Ron. I would really like to have you near me. I'd really like that."

At first he seemed somewhat confused, like he didn't know what she meant by that.

Her heart was beating like a drum, and she was afraid it would burst, until he replied: "I'd like that, too, to have you close to me, Tessa. But we've got to let some time go by until this case is closed. I don't want to give the impression that there's a conflict of interest. Will you wait for me?"

"Yes, I'll wait. And you, Ron?"

"To tell you the truth, I don't want to wait that long." He smiled again. "But you're worth it to me, Tessa. One hundred percent."

When she looked at the expression on his open face, she felt a warm feeling, a hope that one day her life could become good and safe.

She bent down to the dog again and scratched its ears so that she would not be tempted to take Ron's hand and put it on her cheek.

48

One week later, Tessa sat down in the Terra Breads Café. From here she could see not only the giant sparrows, but also the man she had agreed to meet, who now came striding across the plaza.

Telford Reed stepped into the café and noticed her at once at her window seat.

He steered his way between the tables and sat down across from her.

Without getting a cup of coffee, he began to talk: "I'm so glad that we can finally meet. I really didn't want to leave Whatou Lake so quickly, but there was an emergency in my company and . . . but I've already written that to you."

He looked really different without his cowboy hat and cargo pants, Tessa thought. More citified, but also more at ease. She ran her hand through her hair. "So much has happened since you left, I almost can't keep it all straight."

"I can imagine. How was the funeral? Unfortunately I couldn't make it."

She took a deep breath. Promptly, Telford corrected himself: "Actually I didn't want . . . please excuse me, that was a dumb question."

"No, no, just ask whatever you want. Because I also have some questions for you."

"That's what I figured. Because of Fran, right?"

"Yes, that too. And also because of your talks with the Sitklat'l."

"At least in this case, I can give you some good news. I came to an agreement with the Sitklat'l just a few days ago. They are the new owners of the outfitter license. We agreed on a reasonable price. Both parties think that they were treated fairly, something I'm very happy about. In the end it happened very fast."

Because she was so relieved, she pressed her hand against her heart. This was a victory for the Sitklat'l and also for Tsaytis Chelin. She saw his face before her, the dark eyes, the serious forehead, the determined mouth, and the strong nose. Later, when the time was right, she would congratulate him.

"That's good, that's really good," she exclaimed.

"I'm really happy that we found a solution. We'll announce the news the day after tomorrow." Telford cleared his throat. "I'm sure you want to know why I met Fran at the cabin at Beaver Lake."

Tessa tensed her arms and legs. "You've guessed correctly."

"I thought it would only be a matter of time before you found that out."

She blinked. "Did you want to keep this meeting with Fran a secret, Telford?"

"At the beginning, sure. That was what Fran wanted."

She looked at him questioningly. He stroked his chin. "It's best that I let the cat out of the bag. Fran thought that my father was also her biological father. That means . . . ," he explained quickly, when she couldn't hide her astonishment, "she was in search of her biological father and had heard rumors that it could have been my dad."

Surely that's not true, Tessa thought, but she wanted to first hear the whole story.

"She asked me for a saliva sample for a DNA test. I thought, why not? Then you could cross out that possibility."

"You agreed?" Tessa asked, even more surprised. Her opinion of Telford Reed was changing constantly. Who was this man?

He shrugged. "Why not? I was certain that there was nothing to it, but Fran seemed possessed. If I had been in her place, I might have felt the same." His fingers drummed on the table.

Tessa took a sip from her coffee before she urged him to keep talking. "What happened?"

"The result must have disappointed Fran. The DNA did not confirm her suspicions. My father cannot be her father. I already knew that without the test. I had known for a long time that Eric Reed was not my biological father." He looked at the table and then looked at Tessa, who was concentrating on her coffee cup. Had she heard right?

"One of my aunts told me that my mother, before she got married, was a pretty wild card. That she was sleeping with two different men who didn't know about each other. And that Mom, shortly before her marriage, was unsure which one she should choose. Her parents pressed her to marry the man with the most money. Which she did." Telford pressed his lips together before he continued speaking: "I have a very unusual genetic abnormality. It's a dominant gene, which means that all the children in my family have it. I only found out when I was a young adult."

I know that from my own experience, Tessa wanted to throw in. I have a genetic abnormality, too, that I share with my father. But Telford was quicker.

"Eric Reed didn't have this abnormality. Neither does my mother. My deceased sister also didn't have it. And none of my relatives. Only me."

He sat up and stretched in order to relax. "And my biological father, of course."

Tessa sat as if she were glued to her chair.

"Telford, I . . . I just don't know what to say, I . . ."

He quickly apologized. "I didn't want to put you though this; actually I only came to explain why Fran and I met. It's a terrible shame that during her lifetime she was never able to find out who her biological father was." He rubbed his face, which suddenly seemed flushed, and looked at the counter. "I think I need a big mug of black coffee." He looked at her cup. "Can I bring you another one?"

Tessa didn't answer. She stared at him as if he were a ghost. From a remote part of her brain, a thought broke loose and came to her.

"What is your genetic abnormality, Telford?"

He hesitated, seemingly a bit embarrassed. She asked again, persistent: "Which genetic abnormality did you inherit from your biological father?"

Without saying a word, he pushed the chair back and loosened the Velcro of his running shoes.

Tessa already knew what she was going to see.

A foot with six toes.

EPILOGUE

The grizzly is unsettled. Too many strangers coming into her territory.

So much noise. The terrifying droning in the sky.

Then the droning on the ground.

The animals she would be hunting are fleeing because of the noise.

It makes hunting much more difficult.

Only at night it is quiet.

The bear keeps on walking, down to the lake. She used to find dead fish on the shore. She never forgets a place where she's found something to eat. It's burned into her brain.

On the way to the lake, she goes by the cabin.

Interesting smells reach her nostrils.

She climbs up the wooden stairs. Follows the scent. She scratches and paws at the door with her powerful claws. Presses her two-hundred-kilo body against the obstacle. Pushes until the door gives in.

Suddenly she's inside; here the smell is even stronger.

After that it's easy. She reaches out and grabs hold of a plastic bag. Sweet white sand runs down onto the ground and she licks it up.

Then she bites open a tin and eats the cookies. The can with condensed milk is next. Crisp crackers and peanut butter.

She demolishes everything in the search for tasty snacks.

A successful night.

Toward morning the noise starts up again.

She grabs hold of something that smells like animal skin and drags it into the sheltered forest.

Then she chews on it. It's tough, but it smells really interesting.

Her claws rip open the pages of a sketchbook that has both writing and drawings in it.

Shreds of paper swirl around in the air.

Cover the damp ground.

They contain Fran's words, which nobody will ever read.

ACKNOWLEDGMENTS

My first thanks go to my second homeland, Canada. This wonderful, huge, and, to a great extent, still-wild country keeps on inspiring me and my books.

I love locations that are quintessential Canada for me: wilderness, immense forests, powerful mountain ranges, waterfalls, rivers, swamps and pristine lakes, the Arctic, and rugged coasts—raw, primeval regions where nature puts human intruders in their place, and where one feels equally insignificant and in awe.

Twenty years ago, when I emigrated from Switzerland to Canada, I settled in the province of British Columbia. To this day, I am filled with joy and wonder that Canada welcomed me with open arms.

I would like to thank the indigenous citizens of Canada for the opportunity to live and work in their country, on land that once was occupied only by them. The name of the First Nation in my book, *Sitklat'l*, is fictional, and the community of Whatou Lake and all the other locations in the area exist only in my imagination.

But it is a fact that numerous indigenous communities offer

interesting destinations and adventures for tourists. One can find a trove of information on the website www.indigenoustourism.ca.

Fortunately, the province of British Columbia outlawed grizzly trophy hunting in 2017. Exempt are the First Nations, who are allowed to hunt grizzlies for meat or traditional ceremonies. There are an estimated fifteen thousand grizzlies in British Columbia. Before the hunting ban, every year about 250 grizzlies were killed as trophies. My thanks go to the government of British Columbia, which is now protecting these beautiful animals.

I owe my deepest thanks to my beta readers who examined the German manuscript of *Murderous Morning* thoroughly. Their notes and constructive critique almost always hit the mark and helped me to improve and polish this story. Helen Radu, Christa Mutter, Susanne Keller, Ruth Omlin, Beny Affolter, Peter Stenberg, Gisela and Koni Dalvit, Oswald Abersbach, Irene Zortea, Hans Kurth, Klaus Uhr, and Gerald Chapple—I cannot say loudly enough how much I appreciate your contribution.

I am fortunate to have an editor like Gisa Marehn, who already has worked with me on four books. I admire her precision, eloquence, and aplomb.

I am also grateful for the help of my fellow authors Heike Fröhling, Alec Peche, Kelly Oliver, Anne Cleeland, and my brother Peter.

The English edition of this book would not exist without Rosa and Peter Stenberg, who translated *Murderous Morning* from German into English. It was a monumental task that they accomplished with enormous skill and admirable perseverance. Rosa and Peter are a gift from heaven. Thank you, thank you, thank you.

My American editor Lindsey Alexander, who had already worked on my novel *The Stranger on the Ice*, once again did an excellent job making the language and flow of this story smooth and luminous while guiding me expertly through it all. I am very impressed and equally thankful. Last but not least I would like to thank the proofreaders Constanza Low, Paula Dunn, Cheryl McCarron, Cheryl Shoji and Michele Hodder who took a close look at the novel before it got published and who pointed out mistakes and typos. You cannot imagine how important you are in this entire process! I'd also like to mention all the people who support my work lovingly and unswervingly. Your input motivates me to keep on writing, even after eight books. The next crime scene: Newfoundland and Labrador!

Bernadette Calonego

P.S. Sharing my stories with you, my reader, is such a wonderful experience. I would love to hear from you, either on Facebook, Instagram, or through email (you will find the address on my website: www.bernadettecalonego.com). If you'd also like to leave feedback for your fellow readers (and for me, of course), a review on Amazon, Goodreads, or another platform would be such a treat! It doesn't have to be long. Even one or two sentences will help readers find my book and will encourage me to keep on writing. I'm very much looking forward to seeing and savoring your thoughts and opinions. Thank you!

ABOUT THE AUTHOR

Bernadette Calonego was born in Switzerland and grew up on the shores of Lake Lucerne. She was just eleven years old when she published her first story, in a Swiss newspaper. She went on to earn a teaching degree from the University of Fribourg, which she put to good use in England and Switzerland before switching gears to become a journalist. After several years working with the Reuters news agency and a series of German-language newspapers, she moved to Canada and began writing fiction. *Murderous Morning* is her eighth book and her fifth novel in English. As a foreign correspondent, she has published stories in *Vogue*, *GEO*, and *SZ-Magazin*. She splits her time between Vancouver, British Columbia, and Newfoundland.

For more information, visit www.bernadettecalonego.com.
Facebook: www.facebook.com/BernadetteCalonego.Author
Instagram: @bernadettecalonegoauthor and
@bernadettecalonegobooks

ABOUT THE TRANSLATORS

Peter Stenberg was Head of the Department of Central, Eastern, and Northern European Studies at the University of British Columbia for ten years. His books include *Journey to Oblivion* and *Contemporary Jewish Writing in Sweden*, for which he received yearlong fellowships from the Humboldt Foundation and the Swedish Institute. He has translated many works from German and Swedish, the latest being Edgar Hilsenrath's New York novel, *Fuck America* (2019).

Rosa Stenberg is the wife of Peter Stenberg. She studied German in high school and university, and her knowledge of the language improved greatly as she accompanied Peter on many sabbaticals in Munich. With their son, Josh, a Senior Lecturer in Chinese Studies at the University of Sydney in Australia, she came up with many suggestions for the best wordings of tricky parts of this translation.